OUR
LAST
LETTER

BOOKS BY LIZ TRENOW

The Hidden Thread
The Forgotten Seamstress
The Last Telegram
The Lost Soldier
All the Things We Lost

OUR LAST LETTER

LIZ TRENOW

bookouture

Published by Bookouture in 2020

First published in the UK in 2020 as *Under a Wartime Sky*
by Pan Books, an imprint of PanMacmillan

An imprint of Storyfire Ltd.
Carmelite House
50 Victoria Embankment
London EC4Y 0DZ

www.bookouture.com

ISBN: 978-1-78681-786-0
eBook ISBN: 978-1-78681-653-5

*This book is dedicated to our
great friends Niels and Ann Toettcher,
without whom I would never have come
to know and love Bawdsey Manor.*

'The bomb may have ended the war
but radar won it.'
Louis Brown, *A Radar History of World War II*

PROLOGUE

The town seems to hunch its back against the bitter easterlies; the beach and pleasure gardens are deserted. But the shopping streets are decked in full Christmas plumage and throngs of shoppers flutter like moths towards the glitter of the lights. Children in colourful bobble hats and scarves are gathered around the memorial cross, defiantly shouting out their carols into the biting wind.

He recalls the place in wartime, grey and brown, the streets down at heel and fearful, the beach barricaded with barbed wire, tank traps and pillboxes. In his current mood, he would have preferred it that way. Fleeing from the festivities, he steers his old Volvo to the left, not wanting to risk driving past the station, where he first set eyes on her. His heart recoils. He cannot bring himself even to think her name.

At last, having managed to navigate without mishap the dimly recalled grid of residential streets, he finds himself driving along the familiar undulations of the Ferry Road. It is so misty he can see nothing on either side of the road, although he knows that on a good day he would be able to see the river meandering, snake-like and sparkling, through the marshes to his left, and to his right would be the golf course leading to dunes and beyond to the North Sea.

Half a mile further on, just before the road runs into the river, he pulls up beside the Martello tower and climbs stiffly out of the car, gasping as the chill, sharp wind slices like a scalpel through the loose weave of his old tweed jacket. Curtains of salt spray slap his face. He'd forgotten how wild and unprotected this lonely spit of land could feel; how the weather seems to come at you from all directions.

But he is here for a purpose. He returns to the car, grabs his small case and walks briskly along the rutted road, ignoring the inviting twinkle of Christmas lights in the windows of the Ferry Boat Inn and the tea room. The mouth of the estuary looks as treacherous as ever, a maw of rushing tides meeting the oncoming North Sea in a maelstrom of eddies that have been known to cast even experienced sailors onto the sandbanks.

It is only five minutes to four, but at the landing stage – a new addition; in the old days they had to jump out onto the beach – there is no sign of any boat or ferryman. The ferries used to run all day like clockwork on the hour, until late into the evening, so he waits for a while, watching the water swirling beneath the wooden piling of the jetty, the seaweed writhing in the current like a tangle of mysterious sea creatures.

Then he spies to the side of the landing stage a white-painted paddle wedged against a post, hand-lettered with the words *Call ferry*. Arrangements are clearly more informal in peacetime. He waves it about, feeling self-conscious, stops for a moment then waves it again. *Is Charlie still alive*, he wonders idly, *or perhaps the ferry licence has gone to one of his sons by now?* Either way, no one turns up. He sets the paddle back and wanders towards the harbour master's shed. The door is locked and the lights are off.

How many times has he waited here, in every sort of weather? He even recalls that once or twice, having missed the last ferry, he and Johnnie had crawled beneath the hull of a beached fishing boat for shelter, trying to sleep out the night so that they could catch the first run of the morning and arrive back just in time for the early shift. *Oh Johnnie, how I have missed you all these years.*

The four metal masts, those old familiar friends, are barely visible today through the sea mist, but he knows they are there, on the other side. There too, part hidden behind the pine trees bordering the opposite shore, are the red brick turrets of the manor house itself, that magical, dream-like place, more fairy castle than RAF base, whose secrets were known to only a few. Even now, nearly thirty years later, he feels a flicker of pride.

On the other side of the river he can just make out rusting signs – Ministry of Defence property, strictly private, no entry. So they must still be using the place; although he wonders what on earth for, when the greatest threat these days is a bomb that could wipe out a whole country, even the whole world? However hard he peers through the darkening gloom, he can see no lights in the windows.

Drawn by the sound of the waves crashing on the shore behind him, he turns and struggles across the shingle to the sea. How he has missed this sound, the rhythm of the pounding breakers followed by the shushing of the shingle with the withdrawing wave, repeating itself along the length of the beach: boboom… shhh… shhh… boboom. *No wonder composers like to write about the sea*, he thinks to himself, *for the rhythms are already prescribed*. 'Behold, the sea itself,' he hums, almost happy despite the wet, the cold and his overarching despair, 'Dusky and undulating… and on its limitless heaving breast, the ships.'

At the water's edge he stops, shielding his eyes against the salt spray and scanning the one-hundred-and-eighty-degree expanse for any sign of ships: a tanker, a fishing boat or even a hardy pleasure sailor; but there is not a single vessel in sight. The seascape is empty, melting without pause for any horizon into the grey-blue sky.

He shivers again – he is getting colder and wetter by the moment. There will be no warm welcome at the Manor tonight.

*

That morning, back at home in London – so long ago, it seems almost like another life – Vikram Mackensie walked into the newsagents and exchanged a few words with Bilal, the shop owner, just as he'd done for the past twenty years. He likes Bilal. Although neither of them would ever mention it, both considering themselves to be through and through Englishmen, they have a common heritage. The old country has since been bloodily sliced in two, but they still recognise small signs of a shared culture. Bilal has even been seen to offer a brief and self-conscious *namaste* from time to time.

Bilal is increasingly concerned for Mr Mac, as he refers to him with due deference, since he became a widower. He'd always been so well turned out, clean shaven and unbowed, with that enviably full head of white hair neatly barbered. But lately he seems to have stopped bothering about his appearance. In the past he could be relied upon to wear a jacket and tie even in the hottest of weather; but for the second day in a row, Bilal notices now, the old boy has pulled on trousers and an ancient parka over his pyjamas and thrown his feet into a pair of broken-down moccasins for the short journey down the street.

Of course, it is well known that Mr Mac is a brilliant scientist who did some very important and highly secret work during the war. He'd always had that slightly distracted air of someone whose mind is on higher matters; but these days he is becoming plain eccentric, Bilal opines to his wife. That hair hasn't seen a brush or a barber in weeks, and it's starting to look a bit Albert Einstein.

But Bilal understands that, for Mr Mac as for many other older customers, his brief conversations with them about nothing in particular might be the only human interaction they have in a day.

'Morning, Mr Mac. What can I do you for? December twenty-first already, would you believe? Shortest day. Next thing we know, it'll be 1974, and spring again.' Even though his shop is festooned with festive glitter, he is careful to avoid mention of Christmas. Who knows who celebrates what, these days?

'The usual, please.' Vic cannot imagine springtime – it is enough for him to get through each day without despair – but he is always grateful for the shopkeeper's determined cheerfulness. 'Let's hope 1974 is a better year. No more three-day weeks. No more talk of atomic bombs. And peace in the Middle East. Could you arrange that, please?'

'I'll see what I can do, sir,' the newsagent says, handing over the change with a genial grin.

When he gets back to his flat Vic puts three slices of bread under the grill (the toaster died months ago) and makes a large pot of tea in the old brown Betty. As usual, the toast burns, and as usual he scrapes it vigorously into the sink, scattering charred specks all over the worktop. He carries his plate to the table along with the jar of Tiptree Old Tawny and the butter still in its crumpled, crumb-spotted paper. Even now, all these decades later, it makes him smile to recall how his father, in the heat of India, would arrange special deliveries of 'proper' English marmalade and insist on twirls of butter served in a dish swimming in a pool of melting ice chips.

He pours tea into the mug given to him when he retired from the lab – *Physicists do it with a Big Bang!* – and vigorously stirs in two teaspoons of sugar, an occasional treat that has become a habit since he's lived alone. From the fridge he takes out the milk bottle, sniffs the top: a bit whiffy, but it will do for today.

He takes up his newspaper. His usual routine is, while still standing, to scan quickly through each page to see if anything in particular catches his eye, and then fold the broadsheet into a more manageable size before taking his seat for a long, careful read. He can usually make this last at least a couple of hours, saving the crossword for later, with his afternoon tea. But this time, at the scanning stage, his eye is caught by a headline. He sits down with a thump, his heart hammering in his chest, and reads to the end, disbelieving. Then he sets down the newspaper with a small 'oh' noise, sitting very still.

The world seems to have shifted on its axis. The boss, gone? How is this possible? The man was a force of nature, a bundle of brilliance, of energy and drive and cheerfulness. Dead? And three weeks ago, nearly. Vic's brain struggles to make sense of this new perspective.

He curses himself. How can he have missed the death notice? And now he's gone and missed the ruddy funeral, too. What would the other fellows have thought of him, not even bothering to turn up? Not that he's been in touch with any of them for years now, not since he retired from the company. He wonders with mild curiosity how many of the original team are still alive.

Those were vivid, brilliant years, the best years of his life, but it's all so long ago now. The wake will surely have been a noisy, boozy affair; they'll have made certain the boss got a good send-off. A wave of loss engulfs him. How he wishes he'd been there, sharing stories of the old days and toasting their achievements with fine Scotch whisky. Johnnie would have loved it.

The sound of the doorbell shocks him from his reverie: a neighbour asking whether a parcel has been delivered to Vic's by mistake. Sadly not, Vic replies distractedly. Closing the door, he is suddenly struck with a clear sense of purpose.

It takes him half an hour to locate the car keys, but he eventually finds them under a pile of *New Scientist* magazines on top of the piano. He regards the neglected instrument sadly for a moment: somehow he hasn't been able to bring himself to open it since Ella died. Even the sound of piano music on the radio brings back too many sad memories. Finally, he grabs his best camel coat and dark blue cashmere scarf – her gift on their last Christmas together – picks up the newspaper and lets himself out of the flat.

The car, an ancient Volvo, is kept in a garage down the road and hasn't been out for several weeks. 'Hope the battery's still good,' he mutters, his hand shaking as he tries to insert the key into the ignition. 'Come on, old girl.' After a few turns the engine groans and clatters into life, filling the garage with blue smoke.

'Off we go, then, my friend,' he says out loud, smiling to himself as he reverses out into the road without looking. 'A sentimental journey indeed, Johnnie. What larks.'

He's forgotten how far it is from London to the Suffolk coast. Lately, the furthest he has driven is to visit Ella's cousin, who lives just outside the North Circular. In fact, he muses to himself while sitting in a traffic jam at Chelmsford, even though he has made this journey dozens of times he can barely remember ever doing it by road.

He recalls trains packed with servicemen and women, steamy, smoke-filled carriages, the smell of wet wool and unwashed feet, the air filled with nervous laughter and anxious glances, couples necking in the corridors and lavs, frantically quarrying precious final moments. When you arrived at Felixstowe station, the ancient coach – hastily hand-painted in air force blue – would grind its way down to the ferry where Charlie Brinkley waited, cap pulled down over his left eye and tiller held firmly in the hook that replaced his missing right hand.

That initial view of the Manor, high on its sandy cliffs above the junction of river and sea, was enough to lift the spirits of any weary traveller. What a view: those elegant red turrets, the stone-mullioned windows and balconies overlooking tiers of walled terraces leading down to the enormous green spread of the cricket pitch, said to be even larger than that at Lord's.

As the traffic trickles its way through Colchester, and after what seems like several further hours in another traffic jam trying to circumvent the centre of Ipswich, he begins to fear he might not reach Felixstowe in time to catch the last ferry.

It is punishingly cold here on the pebbles. He dithers, unable to make a decision. Why on earth has he come all this way? Since Ella died, he has found himself increasingly wondering what on earth there is to go on living for. More than once he has thought of ending it. He feels his feet drawn to the water's edge, as though the sea is some kind of magnet. Perhaps this is the solution? A few further steps and the oncoming waves would soon overpower him, sucking him swiftly beneath the surface.

But he is too much of a coward. Years at a minor public school have left him with a fierce dislike of cold water. Besides, the scientist in him knows that however determined the mind, the body does not submit to death without a struggle. There would be splashing and flailing that might even attract the notice of a dog walker, and he cannot bear the thought of anyone else feeling obliged to risk their life trying to rescue him.

The rhythmic chant of the waves seems to mock him, and an especially fierce gust of wind whistles up his sleeves.

No, this simply will not do, Vikram my boy, he hears Johnnie muttering. *Pull yourself together.* With new resolve, he turns away from the sea and begins the trudge back to the car. One thing is for certain: he cannot stay here on this wretched beach.

Safely back in the familiar embrace of the old Volvo, relieved and suddenly warm now that he is out of the wind, he wonders what to do next. He could make the forty-mile drive round via Woodbridge and the long winding lanes out along the peninsula, hoping that whoever might still be in residence at the Manor would take pity on him and offer a bed for the night. Or he could find somewhere to stay in Felixstowe and take the ferry crossing tomorrow morning.

Racking his memory, he dimly recalls a bed and breakfast place on the outskirts, near the golf course. He's never stayed there, of course, but from the outside it always looked rather welcoming. His spirits lift at the thought of a fish-and-chip supper – he can almost smell the fat and the soggy batter – and a comfortable bed.

Rather to his surprise, the guest house is still there, though looking a little down at heel. Times must be hard for the tourist trade in a country bedevilled by labour strikes and power cuts. As he enters, a teenager at reception regards him suspiciously then hitches herself off a stool, hoicks down her miniskirt and smooths her Twiggy bob. 'Yes, we got rooms,' she says, giving him a long glance. He imagines her thoughts: *Don't get many darkies around these parts, wonder where he's from? Probably not a nutter, just a bit eccentric. Speaks posh but looks like he's been dragged through a hedge backwards. A bramble hedge at that. Needs a good haircut. Nice smile, though.*

She offers him a choice of two: the best, with an *en suite* bathroom and a view of the links, is five pounds fifty including breakfast. Cheered by the thought of clean sheets and a hot bath, he eagerly fills out the form in his spidery handwriting and passes it back to her.

'We usually ask for payment in advance,' she says, with a sharp glance. 'Not that we think you'd do a runner, sir, you're not the type,' she adds hurriedly. 'It's just company policy.'

He nods, feeling in his jacket pocket for his wallet, wondering mildly who the 'company' consists of. Her mother and father, probably, who live out the back.

'That'll be five pounds fifty then. Cash is best, if you have it.'

He pats his trouser pockets, first the two at the back, then the two at the front. He cannot remember picking up his wallet this morning. In fact, he cannot even remember what he'd done with it on returning from the newsagents. The dead hand of dread grips his stomach. The wallet is probably still in the pocket of his old parka. He can almost picture it hanging over the back of the armchair where he left it.

He pulls out a handful of change from his trouser pocket: some coppers, two sixpenny pieces he'd never got round to cashing in when everything went decimal – a single twenty pence coin and a crumpled one pound note. One pound thirty-eight pence. Not enough even for the room without breakfast.

'Would you take a cheque?' he stutters, flushing under the young woman's increasingly sceptical gaze. 'I might have a cheque book in the car. Or I could go to the bank in the morning and get cash?'

'If you go and look for your cheque book, sir,' she says coolly, 'I'll go and ask the manager.'

He knows that it is a fool's errand, but he dutifully returns to the car and rifles through old newspapers, empty carrier bags, sweet wrappers, dirty mugs and other detritus on the seats and shelves, in the glove pockets and footwells, even in the boot. He finds a half crown which stopped being legal currency nearly three years ago, a book of Green Shield stamps and some out-of-date Co-op vouchers, but no cheque book. He sits in the driver's seat, rests his elbows on the steering wheel and puts his head in his hands.

He is a mess. *One of life's losers, always have been*, he thinks, dolefully. Other people said he was a genius because he could work with numbers, and abstract concepts came easily. But what's the use of a man who can't even plan the basics of a simple trip, like remembering to bring his wallet and a cheque book?

The consequences of his stupidity are starting to dawn. He has nowhere to stay, and might not even have enough petrol to get back to London. He'd filled up not so long ago, he feels sure, but his memory is not what it was, and the petrol gauge has been stuck on empty for many years, so it is impossible to tell. He has not eaten since breakfast, and is now hungry and thirsty.

Can't even manage to get through the simplest activities in life without making a hash of them, he berates himself, whacking the steering wheel with the heel of his hand. 'Just what is the point?' he shouts out loud, startling himself. 'Just what is the ruddy, bloody point of it all? You're a complete waste of space.' Whatever was he thinking, coming all this way after so many years, out of stupid sentiment? He starts the engine and crunches angrily into first gear, spinning the rear wheels on the gravel.

One pound and thirty-eight pence would buy him a pint and a bag of chips at least, and he could warm up. Perhaps if he has something to eat, his mind will start working properly and he can decide what to do next. He drives back towards the town, parks in a side street and begins to walk towards the centre. There must be a pub around here somewhere.

As he turns a corner, his eye is caught by a cheery window on the opposite side of the street. It looks so inviting: people sitting at tables with red gingham cloths set with pots of tea, and tiered cake stands piled with sandwiches and pastries. A flickering glow on their faces suggests there is a real fire somewhere in the room. He can just make out some fancy italic lettering in an arc across the window: *Kathleen's Kitchen*. His feet stop involuntarily in their tracks.

With a hammering heart, he crosses the road and opens the door, causing the bell to tinkle and the other customers to glance in his direction – obviously trying not to stare at this unusual-looking stranger – before resuming their conversations. But the little room is filled with warmth and firelight and the delicious smell of baking. There's a tiny Christmas tree in the corner and fairy lights strung around the walls. He feels almost tearful with the relief of it and tries not to notice the way they have lowered their voices, as though he is somehow untrustworthy or frightening.

A slightly tubby dark-haired woman, young, perhaps in her thirties, emerges from the kitchen area with a tray and smiles at him. She shows him to a table just to the left of the fire and gives him a menu. Vic sits down and scans it gratefully, noticing that a pot of tea is just ten pence. He might have set his heart on chips, but the cakes nestled beneath their glass domes look so delicious. And then he sees it: 'Carrot Cake – 8p'.

As he waits for his order to arrive, he tries to calm his racing thoughts. Somewhere in the deep recesses of his memory, he seems to remember that she spoke of an auntie, or perhaps it was her mother, who ran a tea room in the town. But that was thirty years ago, even more, and there was nothing to suggest that she would have gone into the business herself, let alone given it her name. It could be anyone's tea room – Kathleen was a common enough name, after all – and the fact that carrot cake was on the menu was hardly surprising. It might have gone out of fashion after the war, but he has read somewhere recently that it's been enjoying a revival among today's whole-earth hippy folks.

When it arrives, the carrot cake looks just like hers: a small block of sponge flecked with orange, auburn as her hair, but this one has a full quarter-inch of soft white topping. Back then, when rationing tightened its grip and there was rarely enough sugar or butter for icing, her cake was usually served plain. With his knife he carefully removes the topping, cuts a small square of the sponge and places it into his mouth. He smiles blissfully. It is hers, he is sure of it.

When the waitress appears again, he beckons her over.

'This cake is delicious,' he says.

'I'm glad you're enjoying it,' she replies, glancing at his plate. 'But is the icing too sweet for your taste?'

'Oh no, it's just that ...' It is too difficult to explain. 'No, it's fine, lovely in fact.' He struggles to find the words to ask what he is burning to know without appearing impolite or intrusive. Then, inspiration: 'In fact, I'd love to have the recipe. Did you bake it yourself?'

She smiles. 'No, sir. I do the scones. They're more my line.'

'Would it be possible to speak to the person who made this cake?'

Her eyebrows rise, ever so slightly. 'I'm sure I could get you the recipe.'

'I would very much like to congratulate them myself, in person,' he says, trying to read the expression that creeps across her face. *Who is this strange bloke, so interested in cake?*

'I'm afraid she's not here at the moment, sir.'

'Is she likely to return this afternoon?'

'It's possible.' Her expression hardens, the little frown lines between her eyebrows deepening with suspicion. 'We close at six, sir.'

He glances up at the clock. It is five-fifteen.

'I will wait then, if you don't mind?'

'Not at all, sir. If she comes back I will tell her you are here. Can I mention a name?'

This takes him aback. If she hears his name, she might decide not to appear. 'She won't know me,' he says defensively at first, then relents. 'Mr Mackensie. Vic. Short for Vikram.'

'Very well, sir,' she says. 'Would you like me to top up the pot, while you are waiting?'

'Er… yes, thank you, miss. And another slice of carrot cake, please.'

He takes out his newspaper. When the waitress returns with hot water to refill his teapot, she notices that his hands are trembling.

PART ONE:

THE MAGIC EYE

CHAPTER 1

JULY 1936

Pa had a friend who worked at the Orwell Hotel and said he could get the smaller lounge for a private function fee of five pounds, so long as they put ten pounds behind the bar for drinks.

'*Drinks?* You're going to let them drink *alcohol* on her sixteenth birthday?' Ma shouted, believing her daughter safely out of range. 'Fifteen pounds? Are you out of your mind?'

Kath, sitting at the top of the stairs, could hear every word and pictured the scene as clearly as though she were there: Pa hiding behind his newspaper, Ma pacing the small rug in front of the old cast-iron Esse fire, unlit of course, it being July and one of the hottest days of the year.

Finally she heard Pa, his voice mild, mollifying. 'It's not every day your only daughter turns sweet sixteen, Maggie. She's a level-headed kid, she won't overdo it. What harm could there be in half a pint on her sixteenth birthday?'

'She might be level-headed, but what about her friends? Especially the boys? They won't be content with just half a pint, you know that. And before long they'll be pickled and getting into fights. Answer me that, Bob.'

He was caving in, as she knew he would.

'And what's wrong with the parish hall, anyway?' her mother's rant continued. 'Mark had a good old do there for his sixteenth. We can do a fruit punch and sausage rolls, put on some of your old records…'

Kath turned back into her bedroom and closed the door. The dreary old parish hall that always smelled of damp, the toilets out the back filled with cobwebs and creepy insects? She didn't want a 'good old do' like her brother Mark's. It was just boring: the boys gathered in one corner, the girls in another, all shouting over the music and ignoring each other.

No, Kath had something more glamorous in mind: fairy lights, a glitter ball, a proper dance floor and a swing band: the world that Hollywood stars like Fred Astaire and Ginger Rogers seemed to inhabit. Okay, perhaps that was stretching it a bit, for Felixstowe. But a fruit punch in the parish hall was not how she'd envisaged celebrating her birthday, the end of her General Certificate exams, the last few weeks of school ever and the start of her life as an adult.

But what was that new life going to look like? She had no idea, and that worried her – not that she was letting on. That Saturday, she and Joan went to the beach and, after a short and numbingly cold dip in the sea, laid their towels on the sand to make a start on their tans.

'This is more like it,' Kath said, stretching out and closing her eyes. 'Summer's here at last. No more exams and soon no more school. Holidays forever.'

'Aren't you going to college?' Joan said, leaning up on one elbow.

'Hadn't really thought.'

'You're going to get a job, then?'

'Not if I can help it. Who wants to work in a shop or serve grumpy tourists in a cafe? On your feet all day?' Kath squinted up at her friend, shielding her eyes with her hand. 'That's not for me.'

In fact, she knew her parents would be expecting her to find a job, at least until she got married. It was inevitable. Kath's mother Maggie had always gone out to work, except when the children were young. Currently she was cook for a private school in Lower Walton, to which she cycled every day come rain or shine. The hours were ideal: she was always there when they got home from school and during the holidays. The extra income meant that the family had been able to buy their own three-bedroomed semi in a tree-lined street not far from the seafront with all mod cons: an electric cooker, a fridge and a vacuum cleaner. They even had a clothes washing machine.

'What're you going to live on, then?' Joan said.

'I'm going to find a rich man,' Kath said. 'Preferably handsome, and good at dancing.'

Joan scoffed. 'Dunno where you're going to find one of them.'

'Mark's got some mates at the station.' She meant the flying boat station down at Landguard, the Marine Aircraft Experimental Establishment or MAEE for short, where he worked as an apprentice carpenter. Unlike Kath, he knew exactly what he wanted to do with his life: he was going to become a pilot. His friends were infinitely more sophisticated than any her own age, and a few were decidedly dishy.

In particular, she had her eye on one called Billy, who came to the house every now and again. He'd sit at the kitchen table rocking back on his chair, chain-smoking and swigging beer direct from the bottle. He wore wide-legged trousers and tight-fitting jumpers, often with stripes, and although Ma disapproved – after he'd gone she would fling doors and windows open wide whatever the weather, muttering about the disgusting smell of tobacco – Kath thought he was the most thrilling boy she'd ever met.

'Surely you don't want to stay in this place forever?' Joan asked. She was one of the clever kids at school, always coming near the top of the class, apparently without having to do any work at all. If she got the grades she was hoping for, she was going to study shorthand and typing at the technical college in Ipswich.

Kath hated it when people complained about the town. As far as she was concerned, it was perfect. It had everything she needed: the beach and the prom, the pleasure park, the tennis club, a good range of shops, dances at the Pier Pavilion or the Town Hall every weekend, the marshes if you needed time to yourself. Why would anyone want to leave? Besides, all her friends were here.

She was one of those girls who seemed to sail through life, having discovered at an early age that a sweet smile could win most arguments and help her get what she wanted. Although not the prettiest in the class and certainly not the most sophisticated, she was one of the most popular; though not the brightest, she was by no means dim; although not good enough at hockey to be the first one the captain picked, she was never the last. She had no idea what her exam results would be, and nor did she really care; she had, until now, given scarcely a thought about what she might do with the rest of her life, except for a vague understanding that she would eventually get married and have children.

The sun disappeared behind a particularly large grey cloud and she shivered, sitting up and pulling her towel around her. 'This is no good. We're never going to get a tan today. Let's get dressed and cycle to the ferry. Pa says there's something happening over on the Bawdsey side.'

Joan demurred for a moment, checking her watch. 'I've got to be back for lunch.'

'It's only half eleven. There's a whole hour before lunchtime,' Kath said, pulling on her jumper. 'So let's get a move on.'

The best part of cycling to the ferry was the long downward slope as you left the town, freewheeling as fast as you dared, bending as low as possible over the handlebars to reduce wind drag – that's what Mark called it – so that you kept going halfway along the flat part. You could compete to see how long you could keep going before having to turn the pedals, or if you were on your own you could judge the distance you had travelled before having to pedal by the little flags marking the greens on the unkempt golf course that lay between the road and the sea.

Cycling was the perfect kind of freedom: the air rushing through your hair, the road speeding by beneath you. Kath hated the winter, when that liberty was often curbed by the weather, but in summertime her bike went with her everywhere.

Some of her wealthier friends rode horses and she'd even sat on one briefly, but Kath could never really see the point of it. 'Why would you want all that bother of feeding them and clearing up their muck when you can get there faster on two wheels?' she'd scoff. 'You just don't get it, do you?' they'd retort, rolling their eyes. 'A horse is a living being. It can love you, and you love it back. You can't have a relationship with a bit of metal.'

They reached the ferry in record time, parked their bikes in front of the Ferry Boat Inn and strolled past the fishermen's shacks. Over on the other side of the estuary, on a small bluff overlooking the junction of the river and the sea, stood the fairy-tale towers and turrets of Bawdsey Manor, an architectural confection built as a holiday home by a Victorian millionaire glorying in the name of Sir William Cuthbert Quilter. Kath's grandfather Poppa had told her that Quilter also owned several hotels in Felixstowe as well as being a Member of Parliament, so there were plenty who'd doff their caps to his memory.

Poppa worked as a gardener at the Manor and had even, on one occasion, been inside the house itself. As a child sitting on his knee, Kath had listened entranced to his descriptions of Sir Cuthbert's study lined in gold-tooled leather, the beautiful wood panelling and heavy oak staircase leading upwards to heaven knew how many salons and bedrooms, the double-height hall with a musicians' gallery above, the mirror-lined ballroom and the wonderful views from the terraces.

'They say there's a hundred rooms,' he said as she tried to imagine what anyone, even someone with a large family, could possibly do with a hundred rooms.

What Poppa coveted most was the billiard room, with racks for the cues and brass sliders on the walls for keeping score. 'I could've spent many a happy hour in there,' he said, the smile crinkling his whole face. 'A glass of port or two, a cue in my hand, and that view across the North Sea with nothing between you and the horizon. What bliss.'

Poppa had taken an especial shine to Lady Mary, Sir Cuthbert's elegant wife, who had designed the gardens herself. 'You should see them, little Kathleen.' He waved his arms expansively, nearly unseating her from his lap, as he described the sequence of separate areas: the Round Garden made from the foundations of a Martello tower, the lily pond in the formal Italian garden, and the kitchen garden the size of a cricket pitch with a beautiful ornate glasshouse they called the lemonry. 'Though whatever you'd want with all those sour old fruits beats me,' he'd muttered.

The most extraordinary feature of the gardens was the way they'd used artificial rocks to build grottoes and tunnels, and even a winding pathway along the very edge of the cliff, with little seats and viewpoints. 'Just like a fairy story,' he said with a wistful sigh. 'Never seen anything like it, not around these parts.'

Everyone had heard tell of glittering nights at the Manor in the old days, when the winding lanes along the peninsula would be clogged with vanload after vanload of food and drink and Lady Mary ordered so many flowers that the ferry had to make three journeys. After dark the place was lit with coloured lights, and orchestras could be heard late into the evening, even from the Felixstowe side.

For her fourteenth birthday Ma had given her a book about an American millionaire who hosted the most glamorous parties in the world, and she'd instantly pictured it set at Bawdsey Manor in that mirrored ballroom and on the terraces from where, Poppa said, you could see the lights of Harwich eight miles away. That the hero failed to find happiness despite his wealth never troubled Kath's visions. She wanted to be the girl he'd fallen in love with and even, for a few weeks, tried to insist that her friends call her Daisy. But it never seemed to stick, and she soon gave up.

Today, as she and Joan stood looking across the river, all the glamour of the place seemed to have evaporated. The fairy-tale castle

looked forlorn, its entrance festooned with officious signs: KEEP OUT.
NO ENTRY TO UNAUTHORISED PERSONS. REPORT TO GUARDHOUSE.
Behind the house stood a tall mast, like the Eiffel Tower, she was
sure had never been there before. All along the wall surrounding the
estate were slung coils of shiny barbed wire. Spanning the gateway
was a new barrier with a uniformed guard standing beside it. As they
watched, vans waited in a queue while he laboriously checked their
papers before allowing them to pass.

'Crikey, look at that. They really don't want anyone in there, do
they? I wonder why?'

'My dad said they'd sold the place to the Air Ministry, and there's
some kind of top secret stuff going on,' Joan said.

'I hope that don't stop us using the beach.' The red-tinted sands
bordering the river, south-facing and sheltered by the low bluff on
which the Manor sat, were a favourite place for picnics. You could
swim at high tide, and if you searched carefully enough you might
find sharks' teeth and other fossils left over from the Ice Age. Crossing
the river by ferry was the only way to get there from Felixstowe if
you wanted to avoid a twenty-mile road journey up to Ipswich and
back, along the winding road from Woodbridge and out along the
northern shore of the River Deben.

Charlie Brinkley, the ferryman, was returning from the other
shore, steering with casual skill against the swirl of an outgoing
tide. That he managed the heavy clinker-built boat single-handed
– literally, for his right hand had been replaced with a hook after a
duck-shooting accident – was never commented upon, so familiar
was the sight. He'd been skipper since the good old days when a steam
boat ran across the river on chains carrying several cars. It was only
very recently the Quilter family had stopped supporting the service,
and the local council said they couldn't afford to pay for it; so the
Brinkleys had acquired two boats and run it as a foot ferry ever since.

'Mornin', girls. Orrite?' Charlie shouted, raising his grubby old
cap in a cheerful salute, a slight smile softening his weather-beaten

features. He was a legend around here; he knew everyone and everything there was to know at this end of town. 'Well, well. You're that Motts girl, am I roight? All grown up these days. Spit of yer mother, if you don't mind me saying.'

'Yes sir, I'm Kathleen Motts,' she said.

'Got those same red curls.' He gave a little sigh. 'Maggie Motts. Quite a looker in her day, believe me.'

'What's going on over there, Mr Brinkley, with that mast and all the barbed wire?'

'They in't tellin',' he said, using his hook to hold the boat against the post while looping the mooring rope with his hand. 'All very hush-hush. Not for the loikes of us ord'nry folks.'

'But who are they? And what are all those lorries bringing in?'

'All them questions, Kathleen Motts. Curiosity killed the cat, in't that what they say?' He tapped his nose with a gnarled finger whitened with salt.

Joan tugged at Kath's sleeve. 'I've got to get back for lunch, remember?'

'I reckon they's getting prepared, after the antics of that Hitler fella,' he suddenly volunteered, as he climbed out of the boat. 'Gearing up for war. Best not to ask too many questions, dearies. Even walls have ears, as they say.' He paused. 'But you could ask your Pa. He'll have seen a few comings and goings up the station.'

'I will, sir, thank you.'

'Best be going along, toime for me lunchtime pint. Look after yourselves, my dears, and send my best to your Ma.'

Later that afternoon Kath made the five-minute walk from home to Town Station. Her father had been a guard on the trains for as long as she could remember, and the family knew the railway timetable by heart. She didn't even have to think twice which service he'd be on for his final shift of the day, when he might be persuaded to buy her a cuppa and a buttered teacake and, away from her mother's sharp ears, she could press him about hiring the Orwell for her birthday.

Waiting on the bench beside the cafe she recalled Charlie Brinkley's words about 'gearing up for war'. Surely they wouldn't allow it, not after last time? She knew from the names on the war memorial that some families had lost two or even, in one case, three members, all much-loved fathers, husbands, brothers or sons.

Pa had spent the last war on the trains transporting the wounded back from France, and although he'd never been in personal danger, the sights and sounds he'd witnessed had certainly left their mark. Ma said he came back changed and even now, when talk of Hitler and Chamberlain came on the wireless, he'd shake his head and mutter, 'they must never let that happen again'. Just thinking of it gave her a sick feeling, like when you've eaten too much ice cream.

At last the train drew in, ten minutes late due to 'cows on the line at Walton', the station master announced. Pa would be grumpy, she knew, having borne the brunt of passengers' grumbles. As the guard, he was always last off the train, but she never minded. Watching the visitors as they arrived was always entertaining. She would try to judge from the look of them, what they were wearing and what kind of luggage they had which hotel or guest house they were headed for, and whether their stay was for business or pleasure.

Sometimes invalids would arrive, frail, wan-faced individuals whose bath chairs needed to be recovered from the guard's carriage so they could be wheeled to the Convalescent Home. Ma had a friend who worked there and said she'd be able to find Kath a job any time, but the thought of sorting soiled laundry, making beds or, worse, emptying bedpans, gave her the shivers. To be a nurse you needed to have a 'vocation', was what Ma's friend said, and Kath was perfectly certain that she didn't have one of those.

Today was 'change-over' day for hotels and guest houses, and she amused herself watching the passengers from first class who were almost certainly destined for the Orwell, the Grand or perhaps some upmarket private 'cottage' at the northern end of town like the one, so it was rumoured, where the King came to visit his mistress. Apparently he wanted to marry her and the newspaper reports were disapproving, but Kath couldn't understand quite why, if they were in love. Was marrying a divorcee such a sin?

Pa's friend who worked at the Orwell said the wealthiest guests were always the worst behaved and gave the smallest tips. But that didn't stop Kath envying their confidence, the way they seemed to assume that they owned the world. As soon as the train drew to a stop, the men leapt out in their pin-striped suits or plaid plus-fours all ready for the golf course, barking impatiently for porters. Their wives followed, adjusting wide-brimmed hats and smoothing crumpled skirts. Some even carried frilly parasols – they'd soon learn that the sea breezes were almost always too brisk for such things to be of any practical use. Close behind came the children, jumping and shrieking with the joy of being freed at last from the confines of the carriage, then being reprimanded and brought to heel by severe-looking uniformed nannies.

So absorbed was she in the scenes before her that Kath failed to notice the gentleman now addressing her: 'I am so sorry to trouble you, miss, but could you advise me, please?'

She leapt to her feet and found herself face to face with a man unlike any she'd ever encountered, so unusual that she instinctively lowered her gaze for fear he might think she was staring. He was dark-skinned and exotic-looking, like those eastern princes pictured in schoolbooks, and yet he did not sound in the slightest bit foreign and in all other respects appeared like any other young Englishman of a certain class.

He was slim, slight and bare-headed with an untamed mop of black hair, his face framed by heavy eyebrows and a pair of thick-rimmed spectacles, the reflections from which obscured his eyes so effectively that she could not tell whether he was actually smiling or whether that expression of slight amusement was just what he'd been born with.

This was clearly not a man who cared much about his appearance. His suit, although well cut and of quality fabric, was terribly old-fashioned and crumpled, as though he had been travelling for days. In one hand he carried a cheap cardboard suitcase, and in the other an ancient brolly fading green with age.

Kath began to babble, apologising for her inattention. 'Oh dear, I'm so sorry. I must have been in a dream. How can I help you?'

'I would like to know the best way of getting to Bawdsey Manor,' he said.

CHAPTER 2

The look of surprise on the girl's face — or was it shock? — scarcely registered with Vic. He was perfectly used to that kind of reaction, and tried not to let himself get annoyed by it. He'd perfected an expression of detached amusement, calculating that if he looked friendly, people were less likely to take offence or feel threatened.

Ever since being dispatched to a British boarding school he'd nearly always been the only brown face in the crowd — the reversal of the situation at his school in India, where he was the palest. His mother explained: 'You are a very special boy, Vikram, because you are part Indian, part British. Some people may call you a lesser person because of it but you can tell them you are actually better, because you have the best of both worlds.'

So Vikram had spent most of his twenty-one years feeling different, always the outsider trying to fit in. The horror of being ripped away from his parents in India at the age of ten had been devastating enough, but then to find himself surrounded by posh white boys in an enormous, cheerless school surrounded by acres of flat countryside in cold, grey England sent him into a miserable self-imposed muteness for several weeks.

After lights out he would curl up under the thin blanket, trying to imagine himself in the comfort of his mother's arms, the tenderness of his ever-present ayah, the heat and colour of Kerala, the freedom of roaming the rolling hills of the tea estate, his friends, the animals, the call of the birds, the sunshine, tiffin on the veranda, the sunsets. He especially missed the food, and found most of the school meals bland and disgusting. But as the weeks went by the memories began to lose their intensity, and had it not been for his mother's letters filled with news of his former life, he might have begun to believe it had existed only in his imagination.

Slowly, with the help of a few kind masters and a friendly matron, he began to settle into the routines of boarding school life. His name was easy enough to anglicise to Vic, and at school he was only ever referred to as Mackensie – Mac for short. The boys seemed blessedly oblivious to the colour of his skin.

Of course, he would never be part of the popular crowd. Although he could catch a cricket ball without flinching, his legs were too short to be any good at running or football, and he was far too slight for rugger. Whoever invented that terrible, brutal game, he wondered, as he froze on the sidelines with the other weedy boys, trying to work out when to cheer and when not to. The rules were unfathomable and seemed to consist of trying to kill your opponents by crashing into them as violently as possible.

By the third term he discovered that music lessons took place at the same time as games, and persuaded his parents to pay for him to learn the piano. He practised hard, delighting his teacher with his interest in what she called 'theory' but he saw as 'patterns': chords, scales, intervals and harmonics. On a wind-up gramophone she played scratched recordings of Chopin and Mozart, as well as tracks by Americans with fantastical names – Fats Waller, Duke Ellington, Jelly Roll Morton. He loved the classics but he loved jazz more, and before long was starting to improvise and compose his own pieces.

He breezed through science and mathematics, having discovered that the logic of numbers could be beautiful, spending hours learning tables and formulae so that he could apply them instantly to solving a problem. He reached the end of the book before the rest of the class was only part way through, and the teacher gave him the advanced version being used by the form above. Classmates would come to him for help with their 'prep', which is what they called homework. In this way he began to find his place.

It was only when his best friend Kenny invited him home for half term that he began to understand how different he appeared to some people, especially adults. As they clambered off the train at Beaconsfield Station, he registered the expressions on the faces of Kenny's mother and father: surprise tinged with a touch of alarm. They all shook hands in the polite English way, and he and Kenny bundled into the rear seat of a comfy leather-smelling Humber for the short journey to their home.

'Where do you hail from, Victor?' Kenny's mother asked.

'My father is Scottish,' he said, to the back of their heads. 'From Edinburgh. He and my mother live in India because he grows tea, but they've sent me over here to have an English education.'

'How very interesting. You must tell us all about it over supper. I imagine you find it rather cold here, dear? We'll bank up the fires when we get home. Do you eat normal food?'

He felt like saying *Just because I'm brown doesn't mean I come from another planet – and by the way, my name is Vikram, not Victor*; but what he actually said was, 'Thank you, Mrs Johnson. I am not a fussy eater.'

Although his mother never ate meat, Vic's father was a true carnivore and had insisted his son should eat everything on his plate. Even so, he'd always preferred the Hindu diet of spicy lentils, vegetables and rice, and had never really got used to the texture of meat. At school he'd found it even more disgusting, always swamped with glutinous gravy and so stringy that it was sometimes impossible to swallow. But, as with all things, he had grown used to it. There really was no alternative.

'Oh, I didn't mean to imply…' she shrilled. 'I only meant…'

'It will be fine,' Mr Johnson said, squeezing his wife's knee as he navigated a sharp corner. Vic wished he would use both hands on the wheel, and anyway his parents would never have contemplated such a public show of intimacy. 'Stop fussing about the boy, my dear, and let's get on with enjoying ourselves. I suppose you like football, Victor? We could invite some friends round for a game.'

Kenny saved him. 'Can we go out on the bikes instead? He can have my old one, 'cos it's too small for me anyway.' Next morning Kenny was keen to show off his tree house, but Vic blanched when he saw the ladder reaching high into the branches of an enormous oak. He'd been frightened of heights ever since he'd broken his arm falling off an elephant – a ride organised as a treat for his sixth birthday.

'Looks great, Kenny. But I thought we were going to try out the bikes,' he said, to distract his friend. 'To get sweets.' Mrs Johnson had pressed sixpences into their hands after breakfast, crooning, 'Buy yourselves a treat, boys.'

'Oh, okay then. Sweets it is.'

They parked the bikes outside a shop with a mouth-watering window display of jars: sherbet lemons, fruit jellies and liquorice allsorts. Inside it smelled deliciously of sugar and vanilla, but after a moment the shopkeeper whispered something to Kenny, and Vic found himself being dragged out of the shop.

'But you said we could buy gobstoppers,' he protested. 'There were some right in front of us.'

'There's a better place down the road.'

Only much later, when they were in bed – Mrs Johnson had made up a mattress on the floor for Vic in Kenny's room – did he find the courage to ask, 'What did that man say to you?'

'What man?'

'You know who I'm talking about. In the first sweetshop we went to. Where they had the gobstoppers.'

'It was nothing.'

'It wasn't nothing,' Vic persevered. ''Cos you dragged me out right away. Was it about my...' He swallowed, hesitating. It was hard to say out loud. 'My skin?'

There was a long pause. Eventually Kenny whispered, 'He said you were dirty.'

This was so plainly absurd that Vic felt like laughing. 'Like I'd fallen in the mud or something? Did he really think that was why my skin is brown? What an idiot.'

'S'pose so,' Kenny mumbled. 'Don't worry about it. We're not going back there. Let's go to sleep.'

Next day, as they stood on the river bank aiming stones at a log in the water, Kenny said: 'Do you mind?'

'Mind what?'

'People calling you dirty?'

The question took Vic aback. Of course he minded. It made him angry and uncomfortable, as though it was his fault or made him a lesser kind of human being, somehow. But his mother and father had explained it was only ignorance that made people rude, and he should take no notice of them. He busied himself searching for another stone.

'Nah,' he said at last, picking up a small rock. 'It doesn't make any difference to what you feel inside. It's only stupid people who don't know that.'

He lobbed the rock and it crashed into the log square on, temporarily submerging it. 'Yeah, direct hit!' he crowed. 'I win.'

After that, Vic decided he would try to ignore any stares or insults directed at him. He spent some hours in front of the mirror perfecting an expression of mild amusement, of looking perfectly friendly while completely detached. The thick spectacles he'd worn since he was twelve certainly helped to complete the impression, he felt, of someone whose mind was on higher matters. He grew his hair as long as the school would allow, in tribute to his hero, Albert Einstein.

When Vic turned sixteen the physics master told him that he would be putting his name down for the Cambridge entrance exams.

'You are easily the brightest boy I've had in my class for many a year, and if you don't pass it with flying colours I'll eat my hat,' he said.

'But sir, if you don't mind me saying, I've never seen you wearing a hat.'

'You're a cheeky sod, Mackensie. Now push off and do your prep,' the man said, giving him a gentle cuff.

Before the end of his final year, Vic's future seemed assured: he would study physics at King's College, starting the coming October. His father made a special journey from India to attend the final school speech day, glowing with pride as Vic was awarded no fewer than three tinny silver-plated cups: best scientist, best attendance record and the joke one for 'greatest sissy at games', earned for his habit of dropping the rugger ball and running away before anyone could tackle him.

After that, father and son took a month-long holiday touring Europe. The only shadow in the seemingly endless sunshine of that summer was the news that his mother, who had originally intended to share it with them, was suffering from some undiagnosed illness that left her weak and unable to travel. There had been no mention of this in her letters, which were still full of delightful and amusing reports about her visitors and observations of the wildlife around the bungalow.

'She'll be right as rain soon,' his father promised. 'Nothing to worry about.'

Cambridge was like a dream, and Vic never quite got over the feeling that he'd somehow landed there by mistake. How could a boy like him end up walking through neatly trimmed gardens bordering the punt-filled river with those gloriously white college towers glimmering in the sunshine on the far bank, or walk into a laboratory filled with all the latest equipment and be invited to work alongside some of the most eminent physicists of the day?

*

Halfway into the Michaelmas term, a telegram arrived:

MOTHER DIED PEACEFULLY IN HER SLEEP YESTERDAY STOP
FUNERAL TODAY STOP FATHER

The shock of it seemed to blind him; he reached for the wall to stop himself falling, and crept his way along it until he reached a chair. He felt physically sick, as though he'd been thumped in the stomach by a flying rugby ball. After an hour or so this receded and he simply felt numb. He just couldn't take it in, and read the terrible words over again and again. Why had Pa not told him how ill his mother was, so that he could have travelled back to see her before she died?

As he sat there, her presence seemed to fill the room: her long black hair, unwound from its usual bun and headscarf, hanging down like a waterfall as she leaned to kiss him in his cot, her soft voice and her dark brown eyes always quietly observing, ready to listen with gentle patience, her slim, elegant fingers stroking his head, soothing him to sleep.

But no, all that was gone; he would never see her again.

He sat there, barely moving, until the light faded and the bedder knocked on the door, asking to turn down the sheets and whether he wanted cocoa before turning in. Much later, shivering in his bed, he determined to book the first available passage to India in the morning.

'This is certainly very distressing news, Mackensie,' his tutor said, pouring minuscule glasses of pale sherry. 'I can understand that you would want to be with your family. But let's think this plan through. How long does it take, the voyage?'

'Three weeks.' Alcohol had never been part of Vic's life, and this was the first he'd taken since the single glass of port at his matriculation dinner. But now the burning of it in his throat felt good and he had to resist the urge to grab the bottle from its silver tray and swig the rest of it.

'Three weeks there, three weeks back, and several weeks in India. You'd miss more than a term's work, old fellow,' his tutor went on. 'I'm afraid we'd probably have to ask you to defer.'

'You mean I'd have to take a year out and start all over again?'

His tutor nodded.

It was an impossible choice. How he yearned for India, for the comforting embrace of his old ayah, the warm nights, the birdsong, the smells of incense mingled with the mouth-watering aroma of spices drifting on the still air from the kitchens. More than at any time since he'd left, nearly a decade ago, he felt adrift, uprooted, alone.

But he had no money to pay for a repeat year.

Vic hardened his heart, and carried on.

As his finals approached, he refused to contemplate what might happen next. Although he still longed for India, he now felt entirely British. He'd lived here for more years than in his home country, after all. His tutor said he 'showed exceptional promise' and hoped he might apply for a doctorate, but Vic couldn't imagine how he might support himself through a further two or three years of study.

He would have to find a job, he supposed, but what could he do? His passion was radio waves. He loved the notion that sounds could fly invisibly through the air, undetectable until they met the human ear or a receiver that could translate them and turn them into beautiful images of waves moving across a screen. Although most people thought radio was just broadcast entertainment, anyone in the know understood the wider potential for wireless telephony between ships and planes. Some had even spoken of interplanetary communications.

The only place he'd heard of doing work in this field was Marconi in Essex, but it was said that jobs there were 'like hens' teeth', from which he vaguely understood they must be very rare indeed. Unlike some of his better-connected colleagues, he had no network of contacts which might ease his passage into one of these prized positions.

He passed his finals with a starred first, and to his astonishment the college offered him a bursary – in effect a scholarship for taking his doctorate, along with ten hours a week of associate lectureship, which would pay for his living expenses. 'We can't afford to lose a brain like yours, Mackensie,' his physics tutor told him, giving him the glad news. 'You have a very bright future ahead of you.'

Vic spent that summer in Tunbridge Wells, where his father had come to live with an unmarried aunt. Since the death of his wife, Mr Mackensie had found life in India increasingly difficult. Gandhi's demonstrations, religious riots and the passing of the Government of India Act had left him convinced that it was only a matter of time before the British were thrown out. His lifetime's investment in the tea plantation could become worthless, he reasoned, so it was better to sell now. It was only once he'd landed on English shores and begun to read the newspapers that he realised there was an even more alarming threat on this side of the world: Hitler and his increasingly aggressive behaviour in Europe.

They were walking his aunt's small yappy dog in the nearby park on the South Downs when Vic's father dropped his bombshell. 'I suppose if we go to war you'll have to join up, lad.'

'To fight, you mean?' Such a notion had honestly never occurred to Vic. 'I'd be a terrible soldier. You know how cowardly I am; the school even gave me a prize for it.'

'Then you'll have to do something with that brain of yours to help us fight the Germans, if it comes to it. What about those radio waves you talk about? Can't you turn them into a death ray or something useful?'

Vic scoffed. 'You've been reading too much science fiction, Father. To kill even a mouse at five yards would require more power than you could possibly concentrate into a radio wave.'

'All right then, clever clogs. Invent something else that'll win us the war.'

*

The conversation set Vic thinking. Of course, that was what he must do. But how? He didn't have to wait long to find out. In the early summer of 1936, as he was nearing the end of his second year, there was a knock at his door. It was the college head porter, bearing his usual cryptic expression. 'The old man wants to see you, now.'

Such a missive could only be bad news. He hastened across the quad to discover that his tutor had company: the head of the physics department, a tall and flamboyantly moustachioed Nobel Prize winner, and another man he didn't recognise.

'Ah, Mackensie. Have a sherry.' He held out a tray with those minuscule glasses. 'Now, let me introduce you. You know Professor Rutherford?'

Vic had barely exchanged a single word with the world-renowned nuclear physicist, but the man stepped forward and shook his hand as warmly as though they'd known each other forever.

'Mackensie,' he boomed. 'I've heard terrific things about your work. You're a clever chap, they tell me. Which is why we've asked you here to meet a fellow Scot of mine…' Vic was so flustered by the unexpected compliments that it took him a moment to register what he said next: 'This is Robert Watson-Watt, from the National Physics Laboratory.'

Friendly eyes twinkled behind round-rimmed spectacles. He was neither tall nor especially distinguished-looking, but you could tell from his bearing that this was a man with the tenacity of a bulldog, a force to be reckoned with.

'So, Mr Mackensie.' The distinctive roll of the R left you in no doubt of his origins. 'Which part of Scotland do you hail from?'

Vic was momentarily thrown. No one had ever assumed he was British, let alone Scottish. 'I'm afraid I've never even been there, sir,' he managed to mutter. 'My father came from the Dundee area, I believe, but he went to India in his twenties and I was brought up there.'

'Ach well then, there's a pity. You'll have to remedy that soon enough.'

His tutor invited them to take seats around the fire. Watson-Watt, apparently not a man accustomed to small talk, weighed in immediately. 'The Professor here tells me you are one of the brightest brains in Cambridge.'

'That is very kind, sir.' *One of the brightest?* Vic felt the back of his neck flushing hotly.

'And that you are interested in radio waves?'

'Yes, sir.'

'Would you care to tell me more about your work?'

Vic began to describe the research he was carrying out for his doctorate and what he hoped to prove. Watson-Watt leaned forward in his chair, nodding encouragingly, interrupting every now and again with searching questions. As the conversation progressed Vic felt his excitement rising: this man knew his subject in such depth and such breadth, so much more than anyone else he'd ever met. But why on earth could he be interested in the research of a mere post-graduate?

At last, Watson-Watt sat back in his chair. 'Mr Mackensie, you have told me enough to convince me that you are the right man for our team.'

His *team?* Vic shook his head, bemused.

'Didn't they tell you? Well, no, probably not, as I didn't tell them either. It's all very hush-hush, you see, and I can't really say what we're up to except that I'm looking for a few extra bods for a government project. Particularly physicists. They talk my language. Would you like to join us?'

'My goodness, I am very flattered, sir,' Vic mumbled, scarcely knowing what he really felt. This was all a bit of a whirlwind, and there were so many unanswered questions.

Most of all he was concerned about his students, and the assistants he'd been working with at the lab.

'But just to reassure me,' Mr Watson-Watt said, 'I'm sorry to be so personal, but I do have to ask. You *are* British, aren't you?'

'Oh yes, sir. My father is Scottish, my mother Indian, but I have been in this country nearly a decade now and have a British passport. Since my mother died, my father has returned and now lives in Tunbridge Wells.'

'That's fine, thank you. Have you got any questions? Not that I'll be able to tell you much, not until you're cleared for security.'

'Could I stay in Cambridge and continue my research?'

'No, you would have to come and work alongside the rest of us, and I'm afraid that would mean putting your doctorate on hold. But Rutherford here assures me that you can always pick it up again when we're done.'

'Where will I be moving to?'

'Sorry, can't say.'

'And how long do you think the project will take?'

Watson-Watt's genial expression slipped for the first time. 'If I knew, laddie, I'd tell you. But no one can predict. It's in the hands of the politicians, heaven help us. Let's just call it "for the duration".'

It finally dawned on Vic what the man was talking about: the project was 'war work'. This was perhaps the most exciting and at the same time most terrifying decision of his life, yet he barely hesitated. 'Then I'm with you, sir. For as long as it takes.'

'Good man, good man.' Watson-Watt pulled from his pocket a small buff envelope. 'Welcome to the team. They'll send you the date for an interview in London, but assuming you aren't a German spy or an invading Martian, we'll see you in a few weeks' time. We'll enlighten you more when you arrive. I hope that gives you enough time to wrap up here?'

'If that is acceptable…' Vic looked at his tutor and the professor for confirmation. Both were grinning from ear to ear.

'Then I look forward to working with you, sir.'

'For goodness' sake, call me Robert, will you? Everyone else does.'

'Yes, sir.'

Vic could hardly wait to reach his room before opening the envelope. When he did so, with heart beating so fast he feared he might faint, he discovered that it held nothing more than a single slip of paper containing an address and rail warrant to a place he'd never heard of: Felixstowe.

CHAPTER 3

No sooner had Kath begun to tell the stranger where to catch the number six bus than another man bustled up. He had a sly look, a bit like a weasel, she thought, with hair curled tight to his head like wire wool. 'Are you Mr Mackensie? Have I got the right person?'

He ignored Kath, even though she was standing right beside him.

'That's right. I'm Vic Mackensie, pleased to meet you,' the stranger said, offering his hand, which Weasel-face failed to reciprocate. *What a rude man*, she thought.

'Frank Wilkinson. Sorry to be late. Bloody ferry had to wait for a bunch of sailing dinghies, of all things! Crazy place. I suppose we'll get used to it, in time. Come with me.'

The stranger turned to Kath with an apologetic smile. 'Looks as though they've sent someone to look after me. Goodbye, miss. And thank you all the same.' He gave a funny little bow and followed Weasel-face, who was already striding out of the station.

At last Pa appeared, rucksack slung over his shoulder. 'Hello, kid,' he said with a weary smile. 'No teacakes this afternoon, I'm afraid. I'm all done in. Let's head home.'

'Good day?'

'Not so bad.'

They began the familiar walk home. 'Did you see your friend today, Pa?'

'Friend?'

'The one who works at the Orwell?'

'Ah yes, Joe. Thinks he can fix it.'

'Fix it? Really and truly?' Kath's mind began to fizz, like sherbet when it hits your tongue. 'Oh Pa, that's ace! I'll have to start making a guest list. How many can I invite? Oh, and I'll have to get Ma to make me a new dress.'

She'd been planning to tell him about the stranger and what Charlie the ferryman had said about comings and goings at the Manor, but all other thoughts were forgotten. The Orwell Hotel was the most prestigious in the town, situated right on the corner of the main roads leading to the sea and the town centre. Although Kath had never been inside, she knew people who had, and they all said it was terribly grand. She couldn't remember having been so excited about anything in months, not even when Billy Bishop had told her she was pretty.

Grand or not, she knew it was going to be a tall order to persuade Ma. Nothing in their household happened without her say-so – and this time she said no, which threw Kath into a two-day sulk. Even Joan couldn't snap her out of it. She should have been revising how to solve quadratic equations, but how could she concentrate when her birthday was going to be a washout? And who needed wretched exams anyway?

In the end, the party at the village hall was a great success. Every-one said so afterwards. Kath had been nearly paralysed with nerves as the evening approached, and the first hour was a bit awkward. But after a while everyone began to dance – boys and girls together – and although some of the lads had hidden a few bottles of cider behind the stage curtains, and some of them were certainly a bit worse for wear, there were no fights.

Billy Bishop actually came – she'd feared he wouldn't because he'd been so casual when she'd handed him the invitation – and danced with Kath on and off during the evening. No matter that he didn't seem to have much conversation except about planes and cars; she'd never felt as proud as she did basking in the attentions of this tall, good-looking eighteen-year-old. She could hardly believe it when he asked her for the last dance. Someone turned down the lights and trained a single spot onto the glitter ball in the centre of the ceiling, transforming the dull little hall into a place of infinite possibilities.

Billy held her so close she could feel the heat of his body and afterwards, when everyone else was clearing up, he pulled her behind the stage curtains and kissed her properly on the lips. She wasn't certain about the tongue thing at first, but after a while it became a bit of a game, like hide and seek, and it made her giggle. That was, until her brother Mark looked behind the curtain and bellowed at them so loudly anyone could hear that if Billy didn't leave his sister alone, right now, he'd get beaten so hard he'd wish he'd never been born.

Kath didn't care. It was her first kiss, and she was definitely in love. She had never felt happier in her life.

Her good humour was only slightly dented when the exam results came in two days later: while Joan passed them all, Kath only got Geography, Domestic Science and Religious Education. She failed four others, including the all-important English and Maths, which was a bit of a blow after all the help Mark and Pa had given her with revision. That evening, her parents suggested they had a 'sit down', which meant a serious chat.

'Now, about these exams,' Ma started.

'Thank heavens they're over and I can get out of that place.'

Pa frowned. 'And what do you plan to do next, missy, with only three passes to your name?'

'Find a rich man and live in luxury forever.'

'This is serious, Kathleen.'

Ma chipped in: 'Of course we hope you will meet the boy of your dreams and live happily ever after, but you're only sixteen. I can't have you hanging around the house all day like a wet blanket. You'd soon be bored out of your mind.'

'Don't worry, I'll get a job.'

'The problem is,' Pa said, 'you're going to need Maths and English certs if you want to do anything more interesting than serving in a shop or washing up in a cafe. And you are perfectly bright enough to get good passes, if you'd only put your mind to it. We think –' he glanced at Ma – 'we think you should consider doing some resits so that you can go to college next year.'

'Go back to *school* ?' she shouted. 'With the form below? You can't mean it?'

'Just for one term, and you could have another go at the history too, perhaps? The school runs special classes for revision. You would resit the exams again in December.'

'Special classes for dunces, you mean? Surely it's not *really* that important? When am I going to need an equilateral triangle ever again?'

'You're no dunce and you know it.' Pa's patience was fraying, she could tell. 'We just think you took your eye off the ball last term. Anyway, have a think about it, that's all we're asking.'

Think about it, she grumbled to herself later, throwing stones into the sea. The beach was always the best place if you were feeling a bit sorry for yourself: that great expanse of ocean, the wind and the waves going on forever. It seemed to even things out in your head a bit, just being there. *They've thought about it, they mean, and that's what they want me to do.*

The trouble was, she knew they were right. She was no dunce. Yes, her teachers had warned that she was in danger of failing unless she pulled her socks up, but they were so easily charmed by a bright smile and her promises to knuckle down. Yes, her understanding of some subjects was a bit shaky, but she'd breezed through till now, confident of being able to pull it off somehow. She knew, inside, that Pa was right. She was perfectly capable of getting better grades. If only she'd concentrated harder in lessons, and done more revision instead of hanging around with Billy Bishop.

'Oh Lord.' She sat down on the shingle and rested her chin in her hands. 'There's nothing for it, Kathleen Motts. You're going back to school.'

But there were still several weeks of the holidays to enjoy. The highlight of the summer was usually the regatta down at the ferry, where she and her mother ran a tea stall to raise funds for the lifeboat. They worked side by side for two days beforehand, baking and brewing home-made lemonade. Ma taught her how to make Victoria sponges, shortbread and carrot cake – this was the one Kath loved the most, transforming those simple vegetables into delicious moist mouthfuls.

The weather was perfect; the sun came out from time to time and there was a gentle breeze to please the sailors. Thank heavens it wasn't raining like last year, when they'd had to take refuge under the porch of the Ferry Boat Inn. As the afternoon drew on the winds became increasingly gusty, and cries of 'ooh' and 'aah' rose from the spectators as dinghies capsized in dozens, sails flattened against the waves like moths floundering in a rain shower.

Bert Stock's Famous Funfair was in operation as usual. Kath loved to watch the little ones enjoying themselves on the rides, indulging in fond childhood memories of going round and round on the top deck of the miniature toy bus. Towards the end of the afternoon there would be a fancy dress parade with children dressed in various degrees of credibility as pirates, ballerinas, wizards or teddy bears. After failing to win a prize two years running, she'd refused to take part ever again.

Of course there was the usual official business, speeches and prize-giving, but perhaps best of all was the culmination of the day's festivities, the pram race. Crowds gathered to enjoy the absurd spectacle of prams precariously overloaded with fully grown men dressed as babies, lining up to be pushed by other men masquerading as grotesque travesties of nannies.

Joan poked her in the ribs. 'Look, there, in the pram. It's Billy.'

'Can't be,' Kath said. 'He wouldn't…' The words died in her mouth. The boy she'd believed to be so sophisticated was sitting in a large pram, naked save for a frilly bonnet and huge towelling nappy, with a baby's dummy in his mouth. His father, complete with skirt, starched cap and apron, stood behind, burly hands clasping the handle.

'How could he?' she whispered. 'How humiliating.' But neither man seemed the slightest bit embarrassed – in fact, they were larking about to amuse their friends, Billy whining like a baby and his father slapping him around the head with a rattle. It occurred to Kath that they and many of the other contestants had been in the pub for most of the afternoon.

It was at that moment she looked up and saw on the other side of the crowd a familiar face: the man she'd met at the station who'd asked directions to Bawdsey, with two others, including Weasel-face. They looked like schoolteachers or office workers, painfully out of place in their jackets and ties, and genuinely bemused by the spectacle before them.

The dark man caught her eye with what she thought was a smile of recognition, although it was hard to tell behind those thick glasses. But just at that moment the starting pistol cracked and a great roar came from the crowd. The course was uneven and it wasn't long before many of the prams were struggling with broken wheels or springs. Some actually collapsed, tipping the 'babies' out onto the ground amid much hilarity. Billy and his father suffered no such mishaps and soon took a commanding lead. Just a few minutes later they passed the finishing post well ahead of the rest.

Kath ran to congratulate them, but found herself pushed aside by a bunch of Billy's friends who hoisted him onto their shoulders, parading and crowing in triumph. He barely acknowledged her, and she headed back to the stall feeling confused and despondent.

Her mother was serving teas to the three men from the Manor.

'Hello there,' Kath said brightly. 'Remember me? I was at the station?'

'Ah yes, thank you. You were most kind. Miss… ?'

'Motts, Kathleen Motts.'

'Do you live in Felixstowe, Miss Motts?' That voice again: gentle, educated, rather posh. There were plenty of that sort at the tennis club every summer holiday, and she usually tried to avoid them. But there was something rather sweet and unsophisticated about this man, his hesitant manner rather endearing.

'We do,' she replied. 'I take it you're not from round here?'

'No indeed. It is a great pleasure to be at the seaside.'

'I suppose after that pram race you must think we're all completely barmy?'

A tentative smile lightened his face. 'You certainly have some curious customs.'

'You found your way to the Manor okay, then?' Kath cocked her head towards the mansion so clearly visible from here, high on its cliff at the other side of the river mouth.

'I see someone's trying to rival the Eiffel Tower. Is it a new tourist attraction?'

The man took the mug of tea, added a careful half teaspoonful of sugar and stirred it thoroughly. 'May I take a piece of carrot cake too, please?'

Kath chose the largest slice and laid it onto a paper plate, along with a napkin. 'That'll be one and six please, sir.'

'Thank you, it has been a pleasure, Miss Motts,' he said, handing her the correct change. 'But now I must join my colleagues. Good day to you both.'

'Whatever were you doing, questioning the man like that?' her mother hissed, when they were out of earshot.

'You know quite well they're not allowed to say anything.'

'How do we know they're not allowed?' Kath countered.

'You've seen the signs over there. Top secret, and the rest. And you asking if it was a tourist attraction, for goodness' sake.' Maggie shook her head. 'It's something they don't want us to ask about and it's best if you keep your mouth shut from now on, my girl, or you'll be getting into trouble. Now help me get this lot packed up; I think we're done for the day.'

CHAPTER 4

'Cripes, what did you make of those yokels! Grown men in nappies – never seen anything like it,' Frank Wilkinson chortled as they clambered off the ferry. It would be some years before a proper landing stage was built on either side, so for the moment embarking and disembarking carried the risk of getting your feet wet, especially in rougher weather.

Vic said nothing. He hadn't really taken to Frank ever since they'd first met at Felixstowe Station. Everyone said he had a brain the size of a planet, but he seemed to have an inflated sense of self-importance to match.

'You go ahead, I'll catch up later,' Vic said. He loved to savour the sights and sounds of the walk up the driveway, the resin smell of the pines as you entered the grounds, the wide green swathe of the cricket pitch. He would usually pause on the humpbacked bridge to listen to the tinkle of the stream they called, for some obscure reason, the River Jordan, watching finches flitting about the bulrushes and keeping an eye out for the kingfisher.

The sight of the Manor coming into view at the top of the slope caught Vic's breath every time. He'd seen plenty of grand English country houses – his boarding school among them – but this place, a fantastical architectural mix of mock-Tudor, Scottish castle and fairy tale, was the most impressive of the lot.

On the right of the courtyard was the Red Tower, built in brick with green copper-topped turrets and ornate stonework balconies shimmering in the sunlight. To the left, a second vast tower in white stone with four further turrets was linked to the first by a grand frontage of stone-mullioned windows that spanned the full height of the building, reminiscent of Cambridge colleges.

At the main entrance, above an imposing porch, was carved the motto of the family who built the place: *Plutot mourir que changer.* Vic, with his schoolboy Latin, translated it as 'rather die than change', which he thought particularly inappropriate for the work they were doing here, these days: creating change which would, they hoped, save lives.

The afternoon he first arrived, just a month before, had felt positively surreal. The long train journey after a night of little sleep and the meeting with that striking young woman with the flame-red curls; the arthritic old bus that transported them from the station, and the ferryman with a hook where his hand should be. And then his first stunning sight of the Manor. He felt as though he'd entered a world of make-believe, like Alice going down the rabbit hole, and he expected at any moment to wake up and discover that it had all been the oddest dream.

His astonishment had only increased as they'd entered the building through the heavy oak door and into the wood-panelled hallway, passed through the lounge with French doors and views over the estuary into a great hall with, he'd been cheered to see, an upright piano. Frank had introduced him to a man called Johnnie – tall, older, rather avuncular – who led him up a wide staircase leading to a maze of corridors and rooms on the first floor.

'This'll be your room, Mr Mackensie. Fifty-four. Not the most luxurious of accommodation but no doubt you'll be used to it after Cambridge. Make yourself at home. Bathroom's thataway. Tea's at four in the Green Lounge. Can you remember how to get there?'

Vic nodded, though he wasn't at all certain. It would be easy to get lost in this place. He unlocked the door and peered into the cell-like room. This must have been part of the servants' quarters, and the lowliest servants at that. It was a curious shape, rather dark, with two narrow windows high in the walls, furnished with a cheap plywood chest of drawers and wardrobe, two chairs and two double-tiered metal bunk beds. There was no sign of other belongings, so he assumed – and hoped – that he might actually have the room to himself.

After making up the bed he lay back and tried to gather his thoughts. It had been a whirlwind few weeks: the interview with a couple of stern fellows in an anonymous Whitehall building seemed to go well, and even though he'd barely understood the purpose of their questions he had tried to answer them as honestly as possible. Then, almost by return, came a letter of acceptance with instructions to use his travel warrant on a certain date and a specific train. He looked up Felixstowe on the map and discovered that it was practically the most easterly point of the British Isles, right on the coast and miles from anywhere. Whatever could Watson-Watt and his team be doing in such a remote place?

Now here he was, but still with only the vaguest notion of what it was all about. No doubt he would get a briefing later today, or perhaps tomorrow, and all would become clear.

The clanging of a distant gong roused him from a deep sleep. Then he remembered: he was at Bawdsey Manor and the sound must be the summons for tea. His mouth began to water: he'd eaten nothing since breakfast in Cambridge that morning. Turning the wrong way out of his room, he quickly became lost in a maze of anonymous corridors lined with closed doors that all looked the same.

At last he found a heavy oak door, different from the rest and slightly ajar. Gingerly pushing it open, he found himself on a balcony overlooking the grand panelled hall with the ornate plastered ceiling. He hadn't noticed the balcony from below, but remembered a similar structure at school, where student string quartets scraped away tunelessly for special events. The musicians' gallery, that was what they'd called it.

Unseen below, he could hear voices and laughter. The sound of cups clinking and the tinkle of teaspoons only served to intensify his hunger and thirst. But how to get down there? He followed a short corridor that led to another door, also ajar, through which he was astonished to discover the most sumptuous billiards room he'd ever seen: oak-panelled and lined with raised benches upholstered in green-buttoned leather. On the walls were racks of cues and scoreboards in brass and gilded lettering, and in the centre of the room was the baize table, over which green glass lampshades hung from the ceiling. It was the sort of place where gentlemen of a certain class would retire after dinner, clutching their glasses of port and expensive cigars; the sort of place that made Vic feel even more acutely like an outsider.

The only other door out of this room opened into a small snug with an oversized stone fireplace, where no doubt the gentlemen would retire when they wearied of the game. Apart from that the only exit was a wide French window leading out onto a few steps and a lawn, beyond which Vic could see nothing but grey sky melting into an equally grey sea.

He'd thought he was on the first-floor level, so this was obviously a raised part of the garden. Sure enough, he discovered a set of steps leading downwards and through a stonework grotto onto a further lawn. At last, he turned a corner onto a terrace with the most spectacular view southwards over the mouth of the river, towards the distant town of Felixstowe. A group of men were sitting at a table in the sunshine, taking tea.

As he approached they looked up with the double-take expressions he'd come to expect from strangers. But at least they all managed to smile.

'Mr Mackensie! Made it at last, old boy. Best view in town, ain't it? Come and join us. We might be able to squeeze the pot,' Johnnie said, leading Vic into an enormous room carpeted and furnished in various gloomy shades of green. On an oval table, several crumb-spotted plates attested to the feast he'd missed. A single piece of fruit cake remained. From the teapot emerged a dribble of molasses-black liquid glistening with scum.

'Sorry about the cake. Shall I call for more hot water?'

'It'll be fine with milk and sugar,' Vic lied. 'I could drink anything right now.'

As they returned outside, Johnnie announced: 'Listen up, chaps: this is Mr Mackensie, who has just joined us from Cambridge University, no less.' A murmur of approval.

They seemed to fall into two types. Some looked like standard academics, dressed in scruffy suits or tweed jackets over shirts and ties, and wearing spectacles. At least he looked the part well enough, he thought. Others were more practical-looking chaps in khaki overalls or jumpers over plain trousers. But no one gave any hint of what they were doing or why they were here, and although he was burning to ask, Vic remembered the fearsome declaration of confidentiality he'd been required to sign, in triplicate. Any breach might result in a prison sentence of up to seven years.

After a flurry of introductions the conversation turned to everyday matters: the weather forecast, the temperature of the sea – he gathered with some alarm that some of them enjoyed immersing themselves in it when the tides were right – and what the cooks were boiling up for supper.

'Saw some veggies and a side of lamb going in the kitchen door this afternoon,' one said.

'Sounds promising.'

'Don't matter what they start with, they'll destroy it. We'll end up with the same bland mush as usual,' Frank muttered.

'Don't listen to Eeyore here. The food's not that bad.'

'I haven't eaten since breakfast,' Vic admitted. 'I'm so hungry I could probably eat a donkey.'

'You might have to.'

'Where do you come from, Mackensie?' Frank asked.

'I've just travelled from Cambridge today.'

'I mean, where do you *really* come from?'

'I was born in India, but my father is British, and I have been here since I was eight.' It was his usual answer, and he steeled himself for what usually came next. Answering would be painful, but at least it usually stopped the interrogation.

'Is your mother Indian, then?'

'Was. She died four years ago.'

There was a murmur of sympathy around the table. 'So sorry to hear that, old chap,' Johnnie said.

He was saved from further questions by the arrival of Robert Watson-Watt. All, to a man, pushed back their chairs and stood in deference. Vic was struck once more by his powerful presence: the genial air, the breezy smile and apparent informality of his bearing clearly concealing a strong sense of purpose. An impatient man, certainly, and nothing about him would happen by chance.

'Sit down, for heaven's sake, there's no need for all that, chaps. Good cake?'

Frank – who seemed to be the leader in most things – offered to go for more.

'Och, don't be bothering them. They brought some to my office earlier,' he said. 'Now, where's my new fellow?' He glanced around. 'Ah, there you are, Mr Mackensie. Found us all right?'

'Yes, I did, sir, with Frank's help.'

'None of this *sir* business, please. I'm Robert, remember?'

'Yes, s...' He found it impossible to envisage ever being comfortable enough to call this man by his first name.

'If you've finished your tea, perhaps you would like to come to my office so that I can fill you in on our work here?'

'Good luck, old boy. See you on the other side,' someone whispered.

*

Robert Watson-Watt's office was perhaps the most opulent Vic had ever seen, thickly carpeted with walls lined in gold-embossed leather above panels of oak carved in an ornate linen-fold pattern. Through stone-mullioned windows was the same astonishing view he'd admired from the terrace. On the table between two leather sofas sat a tray with the remains of tea, including a large slice of fruit cake and a couple of Garibaldi biscuits.

'Take a seat, old chap, and do help yourself. Never could stand the biscuits, not since someone told me the raisins were squashed flies, but I'm told they're perfectly edible. And the cake is pretty good.'

Vic demurred, then weakened. 'It's been a long time since breakfast, s…'

Robert Watson-Watt arranged himself comfortably on the opposite sofa, stretching out his legs and leaning back, hands linked behind his head and elbows akimbo. It was a pose that conveyed ultimate confidence without any need for assertion, and Vic wondered whether he would ever achieve such a state of self-assuredness.

'Go for it, lad. Keep the wolf from the door till supper. Now, I suppose you'll be wanting to know what you've let yourself in for?'

With his mouth full of cake, Vic could only nod.

'Well, it all started when the Air Ministry asked us to develop a death ray. Something that would kill a sheep at a hundred yards, that was their criterion.'

Vic swallowed. 'Surely that would require so much power…?'

'Just so. We managed to persuade them the idea was completely bonkers, because you'd need to cart around a ruddy great power station just to stun the poor animal. But a colleague suggested that radio waves might prove useful in other ways.'

He paused again, peering over his spectacles, his eyebrows raised. Vic was familiar with the expression, the very same that his physics teachers used to adopt.

'For shipping, sir?'

'Of course, of course,' Watson-Watt jumped in with a hint of impatience. *Failed that test, then*, Vic thought to himself. 'They've been doing that to detect icebergs ever since the *Titanic* went down. But what we're doing is different, you see, which is why we have to keep it so ruddy secret. If we can perfect this thing, we'll get Hitler on the back foot.'

He leapt up and began to pace, as though unable to contain his energy.

'This *thing*, sir?' Vic prompted, after a few moments.

'The thing is, Mackensie – is it okay if I call you that?'

'Of course, everyone does.'

Watson-Watt stopped and turned to face him. 'The thing is that it's not just icebergs or shipping we'll need to detect, it's aeroplanes. Of course there will be tanks and artillery on the ground, but any future war will be won or lost in the air. There are already reports of Mr Hitler amassing hundreds of them, and that can only mean one thing: he's planning to drop all kinds of hell – high explosive, incendiaries, poison gas – onto our cities and factories. And our people. It will be an altogether different kind of warfare, more terrifying and just as deadly. We have to find a way to stop them.'

He took his seat again, leaning forward with his legs crossed beneath him like a coiled spring, and lowered his voice confidentially. 'What we're doing here has never been done before anywhere in the world, Mackensie. Imagine a vast spider's web suspended in the sky between us and Europe.' He drew a wide circle with his arms. 'Now, think of that web as being made of pulsating radio waves. It'll be completely invisible, and undetectable – but as soon as anything tries to penetrate it, we will know, in time to send up our own fighters to shoot them down.'

Vic found that he'd been holding his breath. He could see it all too clearly. Over the past few weeks he'd tried again and again to speculate what it was he'd been recruited for, and although he'd assumed it would be something to do with defence, he'd never for a moment imagined it might be anything as astonishing and ambitious as this. And he was going to be part of the team developing it.

'It sounds bloody brilliant, sir,' he breathed. ''Scuse my French.'

'But does it work, you're going to ask?'

Vic nodded.

'The answer is yes, and no. Our first experiment was a near disaster, but we did actually manage to track a plane at around eight miles, which was enough for them to stump up some funding. We started in Orford, which is a desolate strip of sand just north of here; then, thank goodness, this place came up. Here we are, in paradise, I think you'll agree.'

'It certainly is the most beautiful place, s… Mr…'

'Robert. But there are many problems, and that's where you come in.'

For the next hour they exchanged ideas about how to solve the innumerable difficulties in developing such a system. Apart from the practical matters of finding the right places to set up transmitter masts and receiving stations and training staff to use the screens and interpret the blurry blips and squeaks they emitted, there were many knotty scientific problems: how to compress transmitters currently weighing several tons so they could fit inside a plane, how to make the equipment mobile, how to improve low-level coverage, avoiding confusion with church towers and the like – and, perhaps most importantly of all, how to identify aircraft as 'friend or foe'.

'What we have so far is a very basic system. An old horse and cart, if you like,' Watson-Watt said. 'But it is slow and unreliable, and the wheels keep falling off. What you lot are going to do is turn it into a Rolls-Royce fit to win a war. And we don't have long. Political insiders suggest two years, maximum. So I'll see you at tomorrow morning, eight o'clock sharp in the Stable Block.'

'Yes, s…'

His audience with the big man was over.

Watson-Watt stood and opened the door. 'And bring that big brain of yours with you, Mackensie. You're going to need it.'

CHAPTER 5

Summer slipped away, and Kath found herself squeezing into her school uniform once more. It was too small and the buttons of her blouse kept popping open, but Ma said it wasn't worth getting a new one just for a term, and produced a couple of safety pins.

Walking the familiar route to school that first morning she'd pulled her raincoat hood around her face, fearful of being recognised, but within a few days she discovered that her exam resit companions weren't all 'thickos', as she'd so uncharitably called them. Most were kids just like herself who had simply failed to study hard enough. United by a shared sense of the world's injustices, they soon settled into a supportive friendship group.

Which was just as well, because Billy Bishop had dumped her. He was off to engineering college and told her it wouldn't be fair to carry on when he was so far away. Anyway, he said, they were both too young for a serious relationship. Although in her heart she knew he was right, she was hurt and annoyed that it was him, rather than her, who'd ended it.

She'd been relieved to discover they were only expected to revise the previous year's curriculum, so everything felt much more familiar, and without the distractions of Billy and her old classmates it was much easier to get down to homework. A couple of hours each evening began to pay off, and she found herself for the first time actually interested in her subjects.

She re-read *Silas Marner*, the text prescribed for the English syllabus, and even enjoyed it. When the teacher asked 'What is this book about?' she put up her hand. It was about a weaver who was wrongly accused of theft, she said, and became so miserable all he could think of was his hoard of gold. The teacher interrupted. 'That is the *plot* of the story, Kathleen, what happens. But I asked what you think the book is *about?*'

A familiar knot of panic bunched in her stomach. She hadn't a clue what the teacher was getting at.

'After you'd finished it and closed the book, did you think about it at all?' the teacher prompted.

'Yes, miss.'

'Then *what* did you think about it?'

Kath took a deep breath: 'Silas thought money could make him happy, but in the end he realised that it couldn't.'

'Excellent answer. Money can't buy happiness. And what else is it about?'

'We shouldn't judge people just because they have something wrong with them, like his fits?'

'Good answer again. George Eliot was herself a bit of an outsider, because…'

Kath didn't hear the rest of the explanation because she was so startled by the revelation: the author of this book was a woman. Why had she changed her name to a man's?

Rather than display her ignorance in class, Kath went to the library after school and, perhaps for the first time in her life, headed to the section signed *Reference Books*. There, she found a long shelf of heavy tomes called the *Encyclopaedia Britannica*. Taking out a volume bearing the letters E–H, she read the story of a feisty woman called Mary Ann Evans who rebelled against her family, went to London to become a journalist, lived 'in sin' with a married man, flouting the disapproval of Victorian society, and finally achieved success and happiness. But she always wrote under a man's name so that her work would be taken seriously. *What a woman*, Kath thought.

It wasn't only English that began to fire her imagination. In the past, any mention of numbers, of multiplication and division or, worse, algebra and geometry, had seemed to freeze her brain. But their new teacher explained everything very simply, with drawings that helped her to visualise what the numbers really meant. After that, if she ever got stuck on a calculation, she could imagine a tree full of apples, and a great wind that blew some of them onto the ground. Or an orchard full of trees and all the boxes of apples at the side after harvest, and how some boxes went to market or were added to the boxes from another farmer, and some rotted, and so on. Somehow she discovered that numbers weren't so terrifying after all.

Because they were seated in alphabetical order, she found herself sharing a desk with Adam Merriweather, a geeky lad with terrible acne and heavy black-rimmed glasses. *What is a clever boy like him doing in revision classes?* she wondered.

She ignored him at first, before learning from another student that his mother had died just before the summer exams, and he'd failed to turn up for them.

After that she made a special effort to be nice to him, and her friendship was well rewarded: whenever she got stuck with a difficult equation, she would turn to him for help. In class, he would whisper in her ear or write in pencil on the side of her workbook. On a few occasions, she invited him home for tea after school, when Maggie would ply him with tea and cake before they sat down to their homework.

Curiously, the subject she came to enjoy most was the one she'd disliked most before: geometry. Mark, who was obsessed with flying, often talked with Pa about aeroplane design, bandying about terms like 'vector' and 'wind speed'. He would make illustrations with lines and arrows that looked like meaningless doodles, until one day the teacher drew a circle and wrote beside it '360 degrees'. She shaded in half of the circle and wrote '180 degrees', halved that once more and wrote '90', then halved again and wrote '45'. At last Kath understood what an angle was.

The teacher drew shapes and suggested they should imagine them as hedges around a field. From the lengths of the hedges and the angles between them, you could work out the area of grass in the field. If that was too complicated, you could draw in imaginary hedges to divide the field into shapes that were simpler to calculate, then add them up.

By the end of the lesson, Kath understood that geometry was simple if you just applied common sense. Degrees were just a way of measuring angles; lines were just like the boundaries of something. You could even add speed to use them to calculate less tangible things like, as Mark said, wind direction, or the lift applied to an aeroplane's wings. Her teacher returned the essay about *Silas Marner* with a big 'A' written in red at the bottom, alongside the words, 'Excellent work'. And for her maths homework she was frequently awarded eight or even ten out of ten.

'Turns out we were right, Kathleen Motts,' the teacher said.

'Right, miss?'

'You're a bright kid, if only you'd start believing in yourself.'

The only other excitement in the town that autumn was the clandestine visits of King Edward to his mistress, who was reputed to be staying in a grand house on Undercliff Road. It was all supposed to be terribly confidential, although in a place like Felixstowe few secrets passed unnoticed or unremarked upon, even if they were only spoken about in hushed tones.

That October, all became clear. Mrs Wallis Simpson was granted a divorce from Mr Simpson at Ipswich Crown Court, and the press speculated that she and the King were planning to get married, if only they could persuade the authorities to turn a blind eye to the fact that she was a divorcee. For a few brief weeks reporters and photographers crowded the town, and Felixstowe was in the national headlines: CONSTITUTIONAL CRISIS LOOMS AFTER WALLIS DIVORCE, they screamed.

The day before Kath's maths exam resit, she and Joan joined a large crowd at the Town Hall to hear the mayor's announcement that King

Edward had abdicated, and his brother George was to become king instead. She couldn't understand why everyone cheered – it seemed a tragedy that the man had been forced to resign just because he'd fallen in love with someone who had committed the supposedly heinous crime of being a divorcee.

Just before Christmas, Kath learned that she had passed all of her exams. To celebrate, Pa treated the whole family to a meal at the Alexandra Cafe. This was their favourite place for special occasions; the tables were formally laid with starched white cloths and silver cutlery, the service was attentive, the food plain but plentiful and the views over South Beach were spectacular.

'But we have those at home every Friday,' her mother chided when she chose fish and chips.

'But this is proper sit-down fish and chips. On a plate. With a knife and fork.'

'They taste better in newspaper,' Mark muttered.

'That's just silly,' she said, but afterwards thought that he was probably right. Somehow the chips were duller without the smell of newsprint.

'So, my girl, now that you've proved you're a clever clogs after all, how's about going to college next year?' Pa said, after they'd ordered.

'It doesn't start till September, so I've still got time to think, haven't I?'

'And while you're thinking, what are you going to do with yourself?' Ma asked. 'You could earn some money, for example. What about waitressing? In a nice place, mind, somewhere like here, clean with a decent class of clientele who tip well. Let's ask the manager before we leave.'

'No, Ma, please don't. You're so embarrassing.'

*

Two weeks later, Kath found herself kitted out in a black shirt and skirt, with a frilly white pinafore and a stupid little starched white cap pinned precariously to her head, ready for what the manager called a 'trial day' at the Alexandra. 'If you're any good we can offer you a few shifts a week between now and Easter,' he said. 'Once the holiday season kicks in there'll be plenty of work.'

After her first shift she dragged herself home, swearing never to return.

'My feet hurt, my arms hurt, everything hurts,' she groaned, collapsing onto the settee. 'The manager is a grumpy old bastard and the diners are miserable. They complain all the time. I ran myself ragged all day and got just one and six in tips.'

'You'll get used to it,' Ma said. 'Just think of the new clothes you'll be able to afford, come the summer.'

Kath did get used to it. In fact, as she gained experience she even began to enjoy her new skills: how to lay the tables in the right arrangement for breakfast, morning coffee, lunch, afternoon tea or supper, how to carry four filled plates at a time, ranged up each arm, how to serve vegetables with a spoon and fork, always from the left side, or from the right for drinks and ready-plated food, being able to describe each dish on the menu fluently and learning the daily specials off by heart.

She liked the other waitresses too, especially Nancy, who had a wicked sense of humour and kept them all in fits when business was slow, describing her romantic escapades. A couple of years older than Kath, she was one of the most experienced members of the waiting staff, having been at the Alex, as everyone called it, for nearly a year.

Nancy was not exactly pretty, more what they called 'striking' with her unusual height – at least five foot ten, Kath figured – and gold-blonde hair with a natural wave. At work she wore it up, of course, but at the end of a shift when she freed it from numerous kirby grips, her curls cascaded down her shoulders like a Hollywood starlet.

The manager muttered disapprovingly about the bright red lipstick she wore at all times, but Nancy didn't care. She was so cheerful and efficient at her job that the customers loved her, and she always received the best tips of everyone on the shift. Some of the other girls talked behind her back, even suggesting she was 'fast', but Kath assumed they were just jealous. She heard how Nancy spoke to the diners, perfectly polite and deferential but with a teasing tone that made their eyes sparkle, even the women. She saw how the men slipped sly looks as she walked away. Kath wanted to be more like Nancy: bright, confident, funny and eye-catching.

As the days lengthened day-trippers and holidaymakers began to arrive in greater numbers and there were more shifts. Over the Easter weekend the cafe was busier than she'd ever seen it. They were so rushed off their feet she scarcely noticed when a large group of around ten men arrived. The manager bustled about, pulling three tables together by the window.

'Give us a hand, love, would you?' Nancy asked as she stacked a large tray with scones, pots of jam and cream, cakes and buttered teacakes. 'It's just the tea to come, and the hot water, if you wouldn't mind.' Kath busied herself at the urn filling the gleaming silver teapots and water jugs, and it was only as she approached the table with three heavy pots threatening to burn her fingers that she recognised them. They were the men from the Manor.

'Hello, darlin'.' The man with the weasely face smirked suggestively. 'Seen you before, haven't we? At that crazy pram race last summer?'

'Shush, Frank,' said an older man with round glasses. 'You're not here to chat up the waitresses.' Kath put down the pots and enquired whether they would like her to pour. 'Thank you, miss, but I think we'll manage.'

'I'll just bring the hot water then.' As she turned, she caught the dark-haired man watching her, with a shy smile. She smiled back in silent acknowledgement, sensing that he probably didn't like Frank much either.

While serving her own tables nearby she lingered, trying to listen to their conversations, but learned nothing save that the Manor was beastly cold and the food terrible. What a curiously mismatched group they were: a real range of ages, some formally dressed and others in more relaxed garb, none the slightest bit stylish. They were a work team, she thought, rather than friends; people who seemed perfectly familiar with each other and clearly sharing a common purpose, but without much mutual affection.

'I can't see why you seem to find them so fascinating,' Pa said, when she recounted the story later.

'Unless you've got your eye on one of them, you little hussy?' Mark sniggered.

'Not at all,' she bristled. 'They're a plain-looking lot if you must know, and too old for me. I'm just so curious about what they're up to over there. Do you ever hear anything down at the station, Mark?'

'Nah,' he said. 'All we know is they're tight as ticks, which means for certain that whatever they're doing over there is grade one top security.'

It niggled her, not knowing what was happening right on her doorstep. What exactly was so secret about it that they needed a guard on the gate and barbed wire all over the walls? And what on earth was that enormous mast?

Pa was sceptical when she asked if she could borrow his binoculars. 'The marshes are good for migrating birds at this time of year,' she said, repeating something she'd overheard in the cafe. He raised an eyebrow, but agreed to lend them and showed her how to focus each eyepiece. On her next day off, she packed them into a shoulder bag along with a bird book from the library.

On the ferry she chatted to Charlie Brinkley about birds. With his mind on the tide, he paid little attention, but at least he'd make a good alibi should anyone question her. On the Bawdsey side she followed the road around towards the marshes and then slipped off to the right, under cover of the area of scrappy woodland that bordered the Manor's grounds.

Getting within sight of the buildings turned out to be more difficult than she'd expected. Brambles tore at her legs, branches whipped her face and fallen trees caused her to make several diversions, but she pushed on until she encountered a chain-link fence a full six feet high topped with evil-looking coils of barbed wire. Walking along the perimeter, she eventually discovered a point at which she could see through the undergrowth the back of what looked like a stable block, and beyond that, the base of the tall metal mast.

She focused the binoculars as Pa had shown her. At first, the place looked deserted. The mast itself appeared much taller and wider at its base than she had imagined. At the top was a platform, and halfway up – hold on a sec – a tiny speck was moving. She focused again and saw that the speck was a man, climbing down a flimsy-looking ladder.

A heavy hand on her shoulder made her yelp with fright, nearly dropping the binoculars.

'Excuse me, missy. I'm afraid you will have to come with me.' It was a tall, burly man in uniform with a gun holster slung beneath his arm.

'I was looking for birds,' she stuttered.

'And just what kind of birds can you see over there?'

'Ermm, blackbirds, and robins, and…' Her mind went blank.

'I'm afraid you're not exactly convincing me, miss. This is a top secret facility, and we take any breaches of security very seriously. Very seriously indeed. Now hand over those binoculars. You're coming with me.'

When she hesitated, he grabbed them from her.

'Now, do as I say or I'll have to handcuff you.'

His hand was at the small of her back, propelling her forward.

'Am I being arrested for birdwatching?'

'We'll decide whether we think you were spying once we get you back to the guardhouse.'

'Spying? Why on earth would I…?'

'That's exactly what you're going to tell us. And at that point it may be a matter for the police.'

The police? This was serious. Pa and Ma knew most of the coppers based in the town, and would be bound to find out. 'Look, please, just let me go and I'll head over to the marshes, which is where I'd originally intended to go.'

'Just be quiet and walk, miss. You'll have your say once I've got the boss down here.'

At the guardhouse she was taken to a dismal, dimly lit room with metal bars at the window, furnished only with a small table and four hard chairs. As he left, the key turned in the door from the outside. She was actually locked in.

In the silence, she could hear her heart pounding in her chest. How could they possibly think she was a spy?

After what seemed like an hour, the guard returned with another man, tall and moustachioed, wearing a suit and tie. 'Well now, what have we here?' His smooth demeanour and unsettlingly quiet, assured voice was somehow even more terrifying than the threats of the burly man with the gun. 'Now I want you to take a seat and listen to me, miss. Tell me your name, age and address, the names of your parents, if any, what school you go to and where you were born.' As she tried to gather her thoughts and answer calmly, the guard painstakingly recorded everything in a yellow lined notebook, his chubby fingers struggling to manipulate a blunt stub of pencil.

'Honestly, I promise. Hand on heart. I was birdwatching. There's a book in my backpack. Ask Charlie Brinkley.'

The man sighed. 'I'm afraid Jenkins here doesn't believe the birdwatching story on account of the fact that you were clearly looking through your binoculars to observe our mast, which led him to conclude that you were probably spying. You can hardly be unaware that this is a top secret facility, miss?'

She nodded.

'So perhaps you would like to explain precisely what it was you were looking at, and why.'

'I wasn't *spying*. All I wanted was to find out a bit more…'

'What is the difference between "finding out more" and spying, would you say, miss?'

'Look, I know it was stupid, but I wasn't doing it for anyone else, I promise. It was just to satisfy my own curiosity. I'm so sorry. It won't happen again.'

For a few long moments he said nothing. Then, at last, he sat back in his chair. 'Well, Miss Motts, I am inclined to conclude that you are just a silly young girl who is completely unaware of the seriousness of her actions. But I'm afraid we will have to record the details of this incident in our security log and we will also, as a matter of course, pass them to the local constabulary.'

'Do you really have to tell the police? I mean, if you believe I'm not a spy?'

'They won't take any action, not this time. They will just hold it for their own records.'

'You mean, just because…'

He silenced her with an upheld palm. 'Enough, Miss Motts. You have shown a serious lack of judgement and are fortunate that, for now, I have decided not to take it any further. So off you go before I change my mind, and don't let us ever catch you "birdwatching" around here again.'

'Honestly, Kath, what an idiot,' Joan said, when she'd stopped laughing. 'You could have got yourself properly arrested for spying.'

'I *was* properly arrested. They locked me in. Cripes, they really mean business over there.'

Joan didn't seem to be taking her seriously. 'Do you remember what Charlie said?' She mimicked his Suffolk lilt. 'Curiosity killed the cat, in't that what they say?'

'Do you really think they'll tell the police? I could lose my job.'

'Nah, I think they were just trying to scare you,' Joan said. 'Look on the bright side. They didn't shoot you at dawn, or whatever it is they do with spies.'

CHAPTER 6

Vic could hardly believe he'd been at the Research Station for nearly nine months.

His first few weeks had been a blur of information about the various aspects of what they'd been instructed to refer to, even among themselves, as Radio Direction Finding. As the months went by and others arrived, he had begun to feel less like a raw newcomer, growing increasingly confident of his place and often finding himself in demand to help solve the knottiest problems.

Never before had he felt filled with such sense of purpose. No longer was he researching dry academic theory behind laboratory doors, or devising complex theorems inside workbooks. Now, he discovered, his ideas were often pressed into practical application, almost at once. Engineers would beaver away on adjustments to existing equipment or developing additional bits of kit, reporting back within days on whether the trials had been successful or not, and whether more refinements were needed. It was hugely satisfying.

Most mornings, Watson-Watt would drop into their team meetings to check on progress. More often than not they would have to admit they were 'still working on it'. Vic longed to be able to reply, 'Well, yes, we might be onto something.'

Sometimes, after days of wrestling with a particularly complex problem and frustrated by others who would insist on leading their calculations down what he considered to be blind alleys, Vic would take long, solitary walks to clear his mind. Conscious only of his breathing, of taking one step in front of the next, distracted from time to time by the nature around him – a low-flying owl quartering the marshes for prey, or a badger snuffling in the hedgerow – he found tranquillity and clarity. Somehow, although he was never conscious of this happening, it allowed the thoughts in his head to disentangle and reorder themselves.

After supper he would return to his room and start work. He'd unearthed some roll-ends of wallpaper in a cupboard and pinned them back-side outwards to the wardrobe door. Using the thickest of pencils he could beg from the draughtsmen's workshop, he would scribble equations till well past midnight.

The solution would arrive; not on the first evening, perhaps, nor even the second, but usually within the week. The euphoria of discovery was better than any drug, better than wine or whisky, but afterwards sleep was usually impossible.

'I think I've got it, chaps,' he would announce the following morning, rushing to the blackboard to share his results. It was Watson-Watt's management style to take a back seat in such discussions, allowing others to take the lead, but no one could mistake the beam on his face as from the tip of Vic's squeaking chalk would emerge complex equations and diagrams, revealing solutions of elegant simplicity.

Clouds of white powder dusted his shoes as the explanations tumbled from his lips, although he was always careful to claim that they were not 'his' solutions. All he desired was that they might be taken forward as the basis for further refinements of the radio detection equipment, which might in turn help to neutralise any future air attacks, safeguarding the country and its populace. It was an exhilarating feeling.

Not everyone seemed to share this enthusiasm. Glances would be passed, leaving a cold sourness in his stomach. Although at first he thought the nit-picking, churlish and sometimes even childish queries were just trying to catch him out, he began to realise they were really signs of something more sinister: jealousy.

At school he'd become accustomed to being the outsider, the brown boy, the bright boy, lousy at games but good at maths and music, and there were always others like himself to pal up with. At university he'd found companionship with other students working alongside him on their own projects, although never in direct competition. Here, among this small group of brilliant minds closeted away in this beautiful place, none of his old strategies seemed to work. Each of the teams had been personally selected by a man many regarded as a god, but instead of working towards a common purpose they seemed to be competing for his approval.

Vic found refuge in the Manor's gardens, which had been sadly neglected since the Air Ministry took over. The beds in the Round Garden, said to have been the foundations of a long-demolished Martello tower from Napoleonic times, were smothered with couch grass; the roses in the Italian Garden had grown rampant over their pergola, the lily pond was choked with waterweed and the vast walled kitchen garden was cultivating a fine crop of nettles.

What he most loved was the Cliff Walk, a switchback of paths created out of artificial rocks by the former lady of the manor along the sandy crags overhanging the pebbly beach below. Although entirely unprotected from onshore winds, it was often strangely sheltered, even warm. Niches and seating areas created out of the 'rock' provided perfect hideaways. From here there was nothing but the vast vista of the North Sea to interrupt his thoughts.

Unlike the clear blue sea off the coast of Kent, or the wide rivers of opaque green that he remembered from India, the Suffolk seas were usually grey-brown, the colour of milky tea, bulging with the swell or stippled with breaking waves the locals called 'white horses'. But on a few rare occasions, particularly at the height of summer, the sea lay flat as glass, almost pearlescent with blues and whites reflected from sky and cloud, shimmering and shifting like a mirage before your eyes.

It had been such a day during the sudden heatwave that arrived late the previous September – an 'Indian Summer', they called it – when he had been resting in his favourite niche contemplating the latest mathematical conundrum and heard voices below him on the beach, out of sight. Even though they were some twenty yards below him, every sound seemed to be amplified off the sea.

Some of the other chaps were partial to sea bathing. He listened with amusement as they urged each other on, and the howls of shock as they plunged into the water. However calm and beautiful, it was always bitterly cold. The shouts continued – some kind of game: he imagined piggy-back battles, trying to topple each other. A decade in male-only institutions had shown him that if there was no ball to kick around or throw, play-fights always ensued.

The splashing and laughter abated; they must now be out of the water, drying off.

He could identify some voices, including those of Frank Wilkinson and Johnnie Palmer, the older man who'd welcomed him that first day. Although not a fast mind, he had the ability to think deeply and rationally. He might say little during discussions but then, towards the very end, would come out with really sensible, considered suggestions, in a quiet voice that sometimes got lost in the hubbub of competing views. Vic's respect for the man had grown over the months and he was irritated by the way some of the others teased him, mimicking his flat Midlands accent.

'Christ, that was bloody freezing.' That was Johnnie. 'Good, though. Sharpens the mind.'

'Could do with a bit of sharpening, Johnnie-boy, after yesterday,' Frank said.

'What happened yesterday?'

'What the boss said.'

'What did he say?'

'That we don't have much time and we need to hone our problem-solving; to focus more and think tangentially, those were his very words.'

'Sounds like a contradiction in terms.'

Laughter from the others.

'Apparently we need to do both at the same time.'

'Like magicians?'

'Like teacher's pet.'

'Pet? Who's that?'

'Mackensie.'

Vic's stomach knotted painfully.

'Whatever do you mean, *pet*?'

''Cos he always seems to have the answer. Haven't you noticed? The boss adores him.'

'He's a bright lad. Sharp as a knife.'

'Yeah, but can he be trusted?'

Vic found that he was holding his breath.

'Are you saying you don't trust him?'

'Well,' Frank's voice lowered, but was still audible. 'He's not exactly one of us, if you get my gist?'

Beads of sweat broke out on Vic's forehead.

'Because he's got a dark skin? Honestly, Frank, whatever difference does that make?'

'He's only half British,' Frank said. 'So you have to wonder, is he only half-loyal?'

'The boss has picked each of us for different reasons, and if you want to challenge his choices that's up to you, Frank. But me, I'm just happy trying to do my best at the tasks we've been set.' At last, the voice of reason. At least Johnnie was on his side.

Another man, unidentifiable: 'If we don't pull together we'll never get anywhere.'

'Well said.' This was Johnnie again. The pebbles rattled as someone stood up. 'I'm going back. It's nearly time for tea.'

Vic felt unable to move, weighed down by a heavy sense of foreboding. Why was Frank casting seeds of mistrust? Had he done something to annoy him, or was it really just the colour of his skin? Vic wondered. Frank was prickly and rather annoying, but Vic had never imagined that he could be quite so jealous and manipulative. He hoped it wouldn't become a problem.

*

At Christmas they'd been given a week's leave and Vic endured the journey on slow, crowded trains to London, then onwards to Tunbridge Wells. It took nearly a whole day, but the look on his father's face was reward enough.

He broke out a new bottle of Scotch whisky. 'Special occasions and all that, my boy.'

'Just a small one, please?'

His father poured two equal glasses, both large. 'How's it going, lad?'

'Fine, thanks. Fine.'

'You're looking well.'

'Must be all that Suffolk air.'

'And the work? Is it interesting?'

'Very, Father. Very interesting.'

'And…?'

'And that's about all I can tell you, I'm afraid.'

His father reached for the bottle and poured another. 'I can taste the heather in this one, can't you? And the peat. Makes me nostalgic for the old homeland.' His brogue became broader with every gulp.

Is it any wonder I'm confused? Vic thought to himself. Here was his father mithering on (a Suffolk phrase he'd heard Charlie Brinkley using) about his love of Scotland as they sat in a small terraced house in south England surrounded by reminders of what Vic considered *his* homeland. Here was the tri-fold screen with paintings of exotic landscapes, the carved dark-wood settee and the coffee table with its round engraved brass tray, a couple of table lamps with stems of green marble and a mantelpiece crammed with ivory ornaments.

It was strange seeing these relics of his Indian life – so well recalled from the large airy bungalow at the top of the hill in Kerala, with undulating tea bush plantations like puffy green clouds stretching before them in every direction – transplanted into two dark rooms like a set of ill-fitting clothing. Nothing seemed comfortable, or felt at home. *A bit like myself,* he thought wretchedly.

'What exactly is it you're doing there?' his father asked, pouring a third glass.

'It's government communications.' The prescribed wording.

'Wasn't your doctorate on radio waves?'

He nodded.

'Wonderful thing, this new radio of mine.' His father waved in the direction of a mahogany box in the corner with a fretwork sunrise pattern over the speaker. 'Been hooked on the Test Match this past week or so. And the music is like having a symphony orchestra in your own home. A real treat.'

So long as his father believed that he was working on radio broadcasting, Vic was on safe ground. But the relief was only temporary. His father looked up, fixing him with a slightly bloodshot eye. 'So what exactly *are* you doing with radio waves, boy?'

'You know I can't tell you any detail. I've sworn not to.'

'But I'm your *father*. You can trust me.' A shaky finger found his lips. 'Shhh. Won't tell.'

'It's not that I don't trust you. It's just that we can't tell *anyone*. Not even family.'

'Just a hint?'

'Please don't press me. I'd be breaking the law if I told you.'

His father harrumphed, slammed down his glass and pushed himself unsteadily up from the chair.

'Time for bed, boy. You're in the back room.'

Auntie Vera had roasted a chicken for Christmas dinner the following day, and looked crestfallen when Vic asked for a plate of vegetables. 'What's wrong with it?' she asked. 'It's from the farm up the road. Special for Christmas. I suppose this is one of your *mother's* fads?'

She had never approved of her brother 'going native', as he'd once overheard her saying, marrying an Indian woman.

He'd had the same grilling when first arriving at the Manor.

'What, you don't eat bacon, Mac? Is this some crazy religion of yours?' Frank had asked, that first morning.

'I don't eat meat of any kind these days,' Vic had replied. Since leaving school he'd decided to follow his own preferences. He'd even discovered the term for it: vegetarianism. 'And yes, it started because my mother was Hindu, but I still keep the habit even though I'm not religious any more. It's the texture I find difficult, to be honest.' He refrained from adding his usual justification: the Greek philosopher Pythagoras, father of geometry, was reputedly vegetarian.

'Hasn't done the rest of us any harm,' Frank had grumbled. Looking back, it was clear the man had marked him out as different right from the start. But why should that make him any less loyal? Even though he tried not to let it get to him, the suggestion still rankled.

The cooks at the Manor did their best, slathering vegetables with scrambled eggs or glutinous cheese. Although he longed for one of his mother's vegetable curries, coconut rice, sag paneer or a bowl of spicy dhal, Vic forced himself to eat them.

For now, the pulling of crackers and the telling of weak jokes distracted his aunt's attention and it was soon time for Christmas pudding. As usual, this was the only part of the meal he really looked forward to; at the Manor it was stodgy jam or treacle sponges, and even though he knew they were made with beef fat, they were just too delicious to resist, especially served in a pool of custard.

On Boxing Day, his father saw him off at the crowded station.

They shook hands. 'Thank you for everything, Father. And I'll see you again soon?'

'Good luck with that work of yours, boy. I'm proud of you,' his father said. Vic tried to shush him, but it made little difference. 'With those ruddy politicians blithering about, it's good to know that at least someone's trying to figure out how to save us from the Hun.'

It was a relief when the guard blew his whistle.

He'd been unpacking when Johnnie knocked on his door.

'Good Christmas?'

'Pretty dire, actually. Couldn't wait to get away.'

'Sorry to hear it.'

'And you? Family well?'

'Yes, thank you. But I'm afraid I have to tell you there's been a bit of a ruckus while we were away.'

'Ruckus?'

'The boss is stomping around like an enraged bull. The Germans are apparently onto something which could only have come from one of us here at the Manor, and the high-ups in intelligence are saying it must have been a leak.'

'Crikey, that's bad. Have they fingered anyone?'

'No one's said anything, but a couple of chaps have been called in.'

'Do we know who?'

Johnnie lowered his voice. 'Our friend is one.'

'FW? Do you really think?'

'Who knows? But I'm sorry to have to break it to you, old man. The boss wants to see you, too. Pronto.'

A shard of something cold and sharp pierced Vic's chest, making it hard to breathe. 'Should I go now?'

'Reckon,' Johnnie said, clapping him on the shoulder. 'Good luck.'

Robert Watson-Watt seemed to have calmed down. As Vic entered, his expression was almost cheerful. 'Come in, Mackensie. Happy New Year and all that. How was your Christmas?'

For a few uncomfortable moments they exchanged small talk, almost as though the boss was trying to avoid the other issue. Vic could bear the suspense no longer: 'You wanted to see me, sir?'

'Ah yes, this is a shocking business. I want to make it clear from the start that you are not in the frame, Mackensie, not at all. But I'm sorry to tell you that your name has come up in my interviews with others so I am duty bound to question you, for the record.'

'Which others, sir, if I may be so bold?'

'I cannot name them, I'm afraid.'

He didn't need to. The answer was obvious.

The rest of the interview was straightforward, and Vic emerged relieved. Watson-Watt had asked a set of pre-planned questions and took copious notes of Vic's answers. He made it perfectly clear that Vic could not possibly have known the information the Germans seemed to have got hold of. At last, he stood up from his desk, offering a hand. 'Thank you, Mackensie. That will be all.'

'What happens now, sir?'

'Nothing that involves you, I'm pleased to say.'

Vic took a breath. He shouldn't ask this, and he knew there would be no satisfactory answer, but he was going to, all the same. 'Why was I actually named by someone, sir, do you think?'

Watson-Watt shook his head. 'That is for me to deal with, Mackensie. Now, back to work and think no more of it.'

'That Frank Wilkinson is a snake in the grass,' Johnnie opined later, as they dissected the interview. Vic remembered the terror a snake might cause in the village in India, and how his ayah would refuse to allow him out of the house because one of the gardeners had spied a cobra or other venomous creature in the flower beds, or lurking under the veranda.

Then, as now, he felt the ground shifting beneath his feet.

CHAPTER 7

Everyone in Felixstowe was familiar with the sight of the seaplanes based at the station where Mark worked. Each day you would see them lumbering into view, landing on the water and motoring towards one of the long jetties that stuck out like fingers into the sea just beside the Napoleonic fort at Landguard. There seemed to be any number of them coming and going. Some, according to Mark, had been sent here for testing from other stations around the country and even from abroad.

He was obsessed by everything and anything to do with flying, and it had become so all-consuming that it was almost impossible to get him to talk about anything else, like when his friend Billy Bishop might be coming back for the holidays. He spoke about the test pilots so reverently, as though they were gods, his eyes sparkling as he described their skill and courage, how they brought in planes with broken engines or, once, when a propeller had fallen off; how they could analyse precisely what would make a plane fly faster, or higher. They were clever, brave and cool as cucumbers – particularly a certain Captain Burrows, who seemed to feature more frequently than any of the others in Mark's thrilling tales of aerial derring-do.

So it had come as no real surprise when he'd announced, on Easter Sunday, that he was going to apply for pilot training. An uncomfortable silence fell over the table, eventually broken by Pa: 'Well, that's great news, lad. You'll really get to see the world. And the girls will be falling at your feet.' Mark blushed as Ma stood abruptly and began to collect the plates. A few seconds later they heard the loud crash of shattering crockery.

'Go and help your mother, Kathleen,' Pa said quietly. 'And close the door.'

She was standing at the kitchen sink, staring out of the window, shards of china at her feet. 'Why can't he just apply to be an engineer instead? It'd be just as interesting and nothing like to so dangerous. Look what happened to that other chap.' A few years earlier, a plane had simply broken up in the air not far from Felixstowe, falling into the sea and killing the pilot instantly. He had been buried with full military honours, his coffin processed through the town.

Kath pushed her mother gently aside and began to retrieve pieces of broken plate. 'Mark probably won't get accepted anyway. He's only an apprentice carpenter, after all. Don't you have to have all kinds of exams to be a pilot?'

When Mark told them that the seaplane station would be opening its doors to the public for the first time on Empire Day, Kath's first response was irritation. She couldn't get excited about going to look at aeroplanes, and Saturdays were the best shifts for tips. But then Joan declared that she definitely wasn't going to miss the chance of meeting one of those dashing test pilots, so they went out shopping for new summer frocks.

It was a fine day, perhaps the first time the sun had actually given any warmth, and the breeze gentle enough for Kath to wear her hat. 'You look the bee's knees, missy,' Pa said.

Even as they entered the gates she began to sense what it was that held her brother in such thrall. She'd often watched planes landing and taking off, from the windows of the cafe. At a distance they appeared graceful, even beautiful, like swans landing or leaving a lake. And their names, so familiar from Mark's recitations, sounded friendly: Fairey Seafoxes, a Swordfish, Short Cockles, Short Singapores, the Saunders-Roe Princess, the Sara London and the Short Knuckleduster.

Now she could see for the first time how truly enormous these planes were, so powerful and even menacing, with their studded metal bodies and solid-looking engines, the propellers at their snouts and great wings stretching out for yards on either side.

They watched as one of them revved its engines with an ear-splitting roar, motored out to sea and then, gathering speed, skimmed across the waves until it lifted into the sky, circling once or twice as it gained height. A few minutes later the crowd gave a collective gasp as a tiny figure jumped from the plane, falling unchecked for several terrifying seconds until the parachute opened above him like a white flower, jerking him upwards as it caught the wind, and then floating gently down into the sea. Everyone applauded. The plane made another turn and a second man jumped, then a third, as an inflatable dinghy circled below to rescue them.

After the display ended they went in search of Hangar G, where Mark had said he'd be most of the day to staff an exhibition. He was particularly keen to show off a large model aeroplane he'd helped to build and, after giving it sufficient admiration, Kath and Joan wandered around the rest of the exhibits of photographs, uniforms and flags, doing their best to feign interest. It was warm inside the hangar, and Kath's feet were already starting to blister in her new kitten heels.

'I could do with an ice-cream. D'you think they'll have a van somewhere?'

Mark was demonstrating the model to a tall man in naval uniform, and from the way his eyes seemed to follow every gesture and how he laughed immoderately at every comment, it was clear this was someone very important. She'd never seen her brother so apparently entranced.

'Ah, Captain Burrows, meet my little sister Kathleen, and her friend Joan,' he said as they approached.

'My pleasure.' The man gave a formal little bow, and his handshake was warm and firm. He was tall and blond with a small ginger moustache and a smile that crinkled the corners of his eyes.

'Captain Burrows is a test pilot,' Mark said unnecessarily, as though she hadn't already guessed.

'But you're wearing a navy uniform,' she said. 'Shouldn't it be air force, if you're a pilot?'

'What sharp eyes you have, young Kathleen,' the captain responded, with a smile that seemed to light up his face. 'That's because I fly a seaplane. Have you seen her outside?'

'Sorry, seen what?'

'My bird.'

Bird?

'The Swordfish out there on the apron.'

Apron?

'Let me show you. You can sit in the cockpit if you like.' He could be talking Greek, but Kath barely cared. She was already mesmerised. Moments later she and Joan were being led past a queue of people, under a rope barrier and up a set of metal steps beside the plane. From the platform at the top they could see into the cockpit, narrow, bare and uncomfortable-looking.

'That's the navigator's seat,' Captain Burrows said, pointing to a vaguely chair-shaped angle of leather-covered metal, 'and behind him is the rear gunner, which is why he faces backwards. This one in the centre is the pilot. That is, me. Who's going in first, then?'

Joan shook her head. 'Not for me, thanks.' Kath wasn't that keen either, but felt it would be impolite for both of them to refuse.

'Swing one leg over first,' he said, steadying her arm with a firm grip until she found herself uncomfortably straddling the hard edge of the metal fuselage, wishing that she hadn't shortened the hem of her skirt quite so much.

'Now support yourself on your arms and swing the other leg over so you can lower yourself down inside.' She got the distinct impression that he was enjoying her discomposure. With arms shaking from the effort she managed to manoeuvre herself onto the small hard seat, her skirt bunched up to her thighs on either side of the joystick. In front of her was a dizzying array of dials and switches.

'Good show.' The Captain's eyes twinkled, unfeasibly blue. 'I reckon you're the first female ever to have entered my lair. How does it feel?'

'It stinks of oil,' she said.

'Just wait till you're up there,' he pointed to the sky, 'with the wind in your face and all your cares left down below. It's like no other feeling on earth, literally.' He chuckled at his own joke. 'You never really notice the discomfort, though one's bum can get a bit numb after a few hours.'

He gave her a brief run-down of what some of the instruments did.

'Have I whetted your appetite yet?' he said.

'Me, do you mean? What for?'

'Learning to fly.'

'Me, a pilot? Do they take girls?'

'Oh yes.' His expression fell serious for a second. 'Women make great fliers. Look at Amelia Earhart and Amy Johnson. And we're going to need all hands on deck before long.'

'I'd be terrified. It's my brother who wants to be the pilot.'

'So he tells me.'

'But don't you need qualifications?'

'Not if you're prepared to learn fast. Mark's keen as mustard, which is what really counts in the end. Now, let's get you out of there.'

Before she'd had time to object, his hands were beneath her arms and she was being lifted over the edge of the cockpit and lowered until her feet met the wooden platform. Feeling slightly giddy, she held tightly onto the rail as they descended the steps.

'What a dish,' Joan said as they sat on the side of the wharf eating ice creams. 'I nearly fainted with envy when he lifted you up like that.'

'It was just embarrassing,' Kath said, crunching the end of her cone. 'C'mon, let's say goodbye to Mark before we go.'

When they got back to the hangar Mark and the captain were in conversation with a group of others, including a woman in a tight red dress. She'd obviously just said something hilarious, and everyone was laughing extravagantly. It embarrassed Kath to see her brother flirting so blatantly.

'What's the joke?' she asked, as they approached. The woman turned, the smile freezing on her face.

'Nancy? What are you doing here?'

The answer was perfectly plain.

'I might just as well ask the same of you.'

'This is my brother, Mark. And my friend Joan. We met Captain Burrows earlier.'

'If I'd known you had such a handsome brother, Kath, I'd have asked for an introduction earlier.' The wide brim of Nancy's hat emphasised the coquettish tilt of her head.

'Nancy and I work together,' Kath explained, feeling suddenly protective of her brother. She'd break his heart with the flutter of an eyelash.

'The captain is going to show me his joystick,' Nancy giggled. 'How can I possibly resist?'

As they watched the pair walking away, Kath looked at her brother's crestfallen face. *Poor Mark*, she thought, *he's just a kid interested in model aeroplanes.* A girl like Nancy would eat him alive.

CHAPTER 8

Vic was standing at the base of the wooden steps beside the aircraft, awaiting his turn in the queue, when a tall man in naval uniform pushed to the front with a glamorous young woman in a red dress whose face he vaguely recognised.

'What a ruddy nerve,' someone in the crowd muttered. 'We've been here half an hour.'

The girl giggled and simpered, hanging on the pilot's every word. Vic could never imagine any girl, pretty or otherwise, showing him such attention. Not that he'd have any idea how to respond, even if they did. Since the age of seven he'd lived in male-only institutions: prep school, boarding school, Cambridge and now here at the research station. Sometimes, when feeling low or under the weather he would recall his ayah in India, or his mother, and long for the physical comfort of a woman's arms.

Other boys at school and university talked openly about their experiences with girls and although he knew that much of their talk was wishful thinking he understood, too, that he was unlikely ever to reach what they called 'first base', let alone 'go the whole way', at least until he found someone stupid enough to marry him. What would any girl see in him: his thin and weedy frame, his brown skin and thick glasses? No, it was far better to push any thoughts of such encounters to the back of his mind. In bed at night, he found that trying to solve theorems or other mathematical puzzles could be a great distraction.

At last the pilot and his companion descended the steps and disappeared through the crowd.

'Lucky bastard,' someone muttered.

'You wish, you randy old devil.' Everyone laughed.

Vic didn't envy the pilot. On his tenth birthday, his father had taken him up in a glider. He could still remember the terror of the take-off as they bounced along the airstrip, towed behind another plane like a flimsy toy, and the way his stomach churned as they lifted into the air. He'd found himself praying that he wouldn't embarrass himself. Then the tow rope disappeared and as the other plane peeled away everything went quiet, save the whistling of the wind. It was only then Vic realised that the glider had no engine.

'Terrific, isn't it?' his father had shouted, apparently unaware that at any minute they could plummet like a stone to the ground. But through some inexplicable piece of magic the plane stayed up, and they even landed safely, if a bit bumpily. Vic managed to climb out and dash to the side of the field before being violently sick.

He had decided there and then that flying was far too dangerous, and he wasn't going anywhere near an aeroplane ever again. Yet here he was, twelve years later, queuing to sit inside the cockpit of a Fairey Swordfish, because Robert Watson-Watt had given him the enormous honour – that's how Vic saw it, at least – of asking him to join a team working on an extra-secret and vitally important mission, that required familiarising himself with the construction, mechanics and electrics of as many types of aircraft as possible.

At the Manor, developments had moved faster than Vic could have anticipated. Just after Christmas Watson-Watt had announced that the RAF would be using it as the base for the first ever training school for radio direction finding, meaning that the systems they had been working on would be integrated into mainstream government planning for the defence of Britain in case of war. Within a few days new accommodation buildings were being constructed, and before very long the first intake of recruits arrived.

Teams of workers braved all weathers to erect three more masts and below them tons of concrete were mixed and poured, constructing heavily fortified bunkers into which the transmission and receiving equipment would be fitted. Similar installations were being built all around the east and south coast, along with a set of operations rooms at Fighter Command HQ at Stanmore in West London. The aim was for Bawdsey to become the very first 'Chain Home' station to come on line, and that the network would become fully operational by September. All of this activity was being conducted in the utmost secrecy, information being shared on what they called a 'need to know only' basis.

When Vic first arrived, the atmosphere at the Manor had been rather like a dignified gentlemen's club, but now all that had changed. The sense of urgency was palpable. While everyone worked hard, weekends were for letting off steam, and the formerly peaceful air of the place was now shattered by the noise of football games, rowdy bathing parties and picnics. Someone overheard Vic practising ragtime tunes on the out-of-tune upright piano in the hall and he was reluctantly press-ganged into performing for one of the variety shows staged every Sunday evening. Thereafter he sometimes found himself addressed as 'Maestro Mac'.

While non-commissioned RAF men were billeted in temporary huts, their officers were to be given rooms in the Manor, so this meant new sleeping arrangements for the civilian scientists and engineers. They would have to share, chosen by lottery. Vic feared he'd be stuck with Frank or one of the other more tricky customers, so when the list went up he was greatly relieved to find that he'd been paired with Johnnie. They were allocated one of the bedrooms on the first floor of the Red Tower.

'Lucky bastards,' he heard Frank muttering behind him. 'You're on the VIP corridor. Who'd you have to bribe to get that one?'

'What do you mean, VIP?' Johnnie asked.

'They're the largest rooms with the best views, where the family used to live.'

He was right: the room was fully twenty feet square, with two full-length windows overlooking the gardens and the sea. Squinting to the right, you could even glimpse the mouth of the estuary and Felixstowe beyond.

'Whatever did we do to deserve this?' Johnnie asked.

'Search me,' Vic said.

The scale of the room dwarfed its meagre allocation of furniture, which was the same as that in the smaller rooms: two narrow iron-framed beds, military issue, with the thin hard mattresses everyone called 'biscuits', two thin-ply wardrobes incorporating a chest of drawers, two wooden chairs. They discovered hidden behind a screen a large, rust-stained Victorian hand-basin, and the taps even worked. What luxury.

In addition they had apparently inherited from a former occupant two baggy, ragged easy chairs and a coffee table, placed in front of the window. Johnnie sank into one of the chairs before rising again with a yelp. 'Bloody hell, those springs are a bit sharp.' He felt the back of his trousers. 'Hope I haven't torn anything.'

'We'll have to steal cushions from the Green Room,' Vic said. 'But who cares, old chum, when you've got a view like this? I could look at it forever.'

'How long do you think we've got?'

'What, here?'

'Now the RAF's taking over, will they stand us down, do you think?'

'Cripes, do you really think so?' The notion simply hadn't occurred to Vic, and it certainly wasn't welcome. How could he face going back to those dusty old labs at Cambridge after the excitement of Bawdsey?

By now it was clear that they were not going to be stood down any time soon. Even as his original ambitions were being turned into reality, Robert Watson-Watt's restless mind was already moving ahead.

'We're becoming victims of our own success, chaps. The navy is pestering us to develop direction finding for their ships, the RAF want it installed in every one of their planes and the army want us to make the kit portable so they can drive it around to bolster coastal defences. And as I'm sure you're all very aware, there are still many weaknesses in our basic systems. The magic eye is still far from magical. Our masts are not clever at detecting low-flying craft, and we're still picking up signals reflected off tall buildings inland, which is damned unhelpful to say the very least. We're not here to identify East Anglia's many medieval churches, ancient and impressive though they may be. Perhaps most urgent of all, our system still can't distinguish between friendly planes and enemy craft, which will leave us in a right fix when the buggers come a-visiting.

'So if you thought you were going to be able to rest on your laurels now the RAF are here, you'd be very wrong,' he went on, tamping tobacco into his pipe. 'The work is going to be even harder, and more urgent, than before. We're recruiting more specialists and will divide you into new teams, each tasked with a specific set of problems. As ever, you may exchange information between your groups, but you will never, repeat never, discuss it with anyone else – not even the officers or the training lot. Is that clear?' That very afternoon Vic found himself in a room with Johnnie and another scientist called Scott, whom he did not know well, along with a couple of electrical engineers. They were obviously the foundation of a team, but no one had any idea what they would be working on. So it was a little alarming to discover that their leader was none other than Dr A. P. Rowe, a senior scientist with the Air Ministry and close ally to Watson-Watt, as the joint 'fathers' of the venture. If he was heading their work, it must be a very important project indeed.

Dr Rowe had a reputation for being terrifyingly stern, and they all stood nervously to attention as he entered the room. 'Oh for heaven's sake, sit down, chaps. No standing on ceremony here,' he said. 'And before any of you start trying to address me as Doctor anything, the name's Jimmy. And who are you? Tell me your names and what you've been working on so far.'

He turned to Vic with a gaze like powerful headlights. 'Okay, you first. Let's have it.'

'My name's Vikram Mackensie, sir, but everyone here calls me Mac. I was doing a doctorate in radio waves at Cambridge when the boss – I mean, Mr Watson-Watt – recruited me.' As he spoke he felt, for a brief moment, as though he were standing outside himself, observing a stranger. *Is this really me? All these things I'm saying, did we really do all of this?*

The feeling of unreality, of being in a dream, only intensified as the doctor – Vic could no more imagine himself addressing this titan as 'Jimmy' than he could calling the boss 'Robert' – began to describe the work they would be doing: the most important job on the station, he called it. It was a project called 'Identification, Friend or Foe', or IFF, which would involve developing and testing a bit of kit that could reflect or transmit a signal clear enough for the operator to interpret accurately and identify what kind of aircraft they were detecting. It would have to be small enough to fit in any kind of craft, and of course it must be failsafe.

'You will already have ascertained that the success of this country's air defences – indeed the outcome of a war should we, heaven forbid, have to fight one – will absolutely depend on what you six gentlemen come up with,' he concluded. 'The lives of thousands and the future freedom of our country are depending on you.'

CHAPTER 9

'Does your brother see much of that captain?' Nancy asked, a little too casually, next time they were on shift together.

'You mean he hasn't asked for a date yet? I'd assumed it was a dead cert,' Kath said, surprised but also secretly amused. Nancy had never, to her knowledge, been disappointed in love. It was always the men who seemed to suffer.

'Not a dickey bird. Shame, though. A handsome fellow like that needs a girlfriend, don't you think?'

'He might be wedded to his work, you know. Give it time.'

In fact, Kath was about to learn rather more about Captain Raymond Burrows than she would ever let on to Nancy – or anyone else, for that matter. His name seemed to appear in Mark's conversations more and more frequently, and then, one weekend, he came for Sunday lunch.

'He doesn't get home often,' Ma said, by way of explanation. 'Said he missed his mother's cooking. Now lend a hand with these spuds, would you?' She pointed to a colander of potatoes that would surely feed a squadron. 'These young men have big appetites, you know.'

Kath began peeling. 'How do you know so much about the captain, Ma?'

'We had a lovely chat after Mark introduced us at the Empire Day; don't you remember?'

'You invited him to lunch there and then, on the spot?'

'No, silly. Mark suggested it,' Ma said, turning to her. 'Anyway, what's wrong with asking someone to enjoy our meal when they're so far away from their own family?'

Kath couldn't put it into words, somehow. There was something about the man that made her uneasy: his over-friendliness and flirtatious manner, first with herself and Joan and then with Nancy, and the way he'd suggested that just by giving the word he could fix it for Mark to become a pilot.

Despite her misgivings, the lunch was fun. The captain – 'Call me Ray' – was the best of guests, complimenting Pa on the excellence of his carving technique and Ma on the deliciousness of the food, accepting second helpings of everything while talking about flying boats in such a way that even Kath found herself fascinated. Afterwards, they took their customary Sunday afternoon walk to the seafront and when they reached the pier, the captain went to buy them all ice creams.

'Such perfect manners,' Ma remarked.

'He says I've got what it takes to become a pilot,' Mark said.

'I suppose we can't change your mind?'

'It's what I've always wanted, you know that. He'll be putting my name forward for the next intake in September.'

'If they're all as smart as that lad, you'll be in good company,' Pa said, a glow of pride in his voice.

Kath remained unconvinced. Of course Ray was charming, with that self-assurance all posh boys seemed to pick up at their public schools. But there was something slightly overdone about him, something a little too perfect. She couldn't help wondering whether it was all a veneer, as though he was hiding something.

Joan graduated from college, and with the help of a reference from Kath's father she landed a job as an office assistant at the Felixstowe Dock and Railway Company. Kath was jealous at first, but on hearing the paltry salary her friend earned, decided she wasn't going to waste a year in college after all.

Ma was furious. 'Joan has prospects now, with her qualifications. What have you got?'

'About double the weekly pay, if you add the tips,' Kath said. 'I can work the shifts I choose, and it's fun.'

'You could always study something else, if you don't fancy being a secretary.'

'Like childcare? I'll probably get enough of that once I'm married.'

'Or beauty?'

'Really, Ma? I couldn't care less about make-up and hairstyles. Look at me.' She wrinkled her nose and ruffled her curls.

'Or domestic science? You can't go wrong with a career as a chef.'

'Why would I need to spend a year at college? I've got an excellent chef right here to learn from.'

Not long after this conversation, Maggie lost her job. The school where she had worked for the past eight years had announced it would be closing at the end of term, for good.

It was distressing to see her mother so upset. 'You'll find something else soon enough,' Kath said.

'But I like it there, seeing the children every day with their eager little faces.' Maggie wiped her eyes with the corner of her apron. 'And they're so appreciative of my cooking. There's a little lad, Eric his name is, I think, and he often comes over specially to tell me how yummy it was. Once he even said I was the best cook he'd ever known. Oh,' her voice broke once again. 'I'm really going to miss them.'

Pa put an arm around her shoulder. 'It'll work out, love. You never know, what you find next might be even more interesting and satisfying.'

'I'll put out the word at the cafe,' Kath said. 'They might hear something on the grapevine.'

Sure enough, it was only a week later when one of the chefs emerged from the kitchen and approached the waitress station. 'Watch out,' one of the others whispered. 'Grumpy-guts is on the warpath.' He was the one they feared most, a gruff, often bad-tempered man of few words, except when shouting at the waitresses. But today his sour face almost managed a smile as he pulled out a scrap of paper and handed it to Kath.

Temporary cook wanted at Bawdsey Research Station.
Transport provided.
Telephone Felixstowe 2032 or write c/o Bawdsey Manor.

'Great heavens,' she said. 'At the Manor? That top secret place?'
He shrugged. 'They'll probably be okay payers.'
'Wherever did you find it?'
'What you don't know won't hurt you.'
'Thank you so much. I'm sure she'll give it a try.'

Ma returned from the interview bursting with enthusiasm. Kath had never seen her so elated. 'You should see it. It's all turrets and towers outside. Inside, well, it's a bit run down now, but you can just imagine what it was like when the family owned it. Grandpa was right. It's quite a place.'

'Did you get the job?'

'Oh, yes.' She laughed. 'I almost forgot to say. They asked me all kinds of questions about where I'd worked before and such like. Seemed interested that I'm used to catering for up to a hundred at a time, even though I did explain they're only children and they said the culinary tastes of their lot were hardly more sophisticated than kids, anyway. It's institutional cooking, lots of baking, pies and puddings and cakes, the sort of thing I'm really familiar with. They made me wait while they telephoned the school for a reference. The headmaster apparently told them I was very discreet and trustworthy, as well as being a reliable chef.'

'Well done, Ma. When do you start?'

'Two weeks' time. As soon as term ends,' she said. 'Just think, I'll have to take the ferry to work every day.'

'Did they say how long they expected the job to last? Why's it temporary?' Pa asked.

'All they said was, the nature of their work meant they can't offer a full-time contract to anyone.'

'The nature of their work, eh?'

Her mother shrugged. 'Who cares, anyway? I'm just glad they took to me. And I think I'll like it there. The head chef admitted he was struggling with all the new people arriving.'

'Just who are these new people, then?'

'I did try to ask but all I got was this.' She tapped the side of her nose. 'We don't question, and they don't tell, he said. It's all very hush-hush, and you have to sign some kind of secrecy document before you start.'

Kath thought of the horrible grilling she'd received in the guard-house, and sent up a silent prayer that they wouldn't notice Ma had the same surname as their suspected spy.

Nancy's remark caught Kath off guard. 'Your brother's still big buddies with that captain, is he?'

'Yes, I suppose they have become good friends,' she said. 'Ray's helping him apply for pilot training.'

'*Ray*, is it? On first-name terms now, are we?'

'C'mon, girls, chop-chop,' the manager called.

It was only later, as they were clearing the tables after closing time, that Nancy approached her. 'There's something I need to tell you, Kath, only I can't talk about it here. Can I meet you after work?'

'What about a cuppa down at the pier?'

'The pier it is, then.' Nancy picked up the heavy tray and headed back to the kitchen. 'See you there, six o'clock.'

It was only mid-September, but a sudden cold snap was a reminder that autumn was here. Kath wrapped her coat more tightly around her uniform, walking swiftly to keep warm. The seafront always felt forlorn without its adornment of holidaymakers. Deckchairs were stacked at the side of the promenade, their canvas seats flapping in quiet resignation, the empty beach bleak without crowds of children and their sandcastles, and the bandstand silent save for imagined echoes of music from the summer months.

'Any chance of a quick cup?' she called as she approached the tea shack – a converted caravan that would shortly be towed away for winter – where the owner was taking down his signs. His scowl transformed into a smile of recognition.

'Well, I'll be damned. You're Bob Motts's kid, aren't you? You've grown a bit since I last saw you, but I'd know that head of curls from anywhere. How's the old boy getting on, then?'

'My father?'

'We was on the rails together,' the man said. 'Till I retired, that is. Just doing this to eke out me pension. He still there?'

'Oh yes. Says he needs to keep me in the manner to which I've become accustomed.'

The man laughed. 'And that mother of yours? What a catch she was, with that hair. Both keeping well, I hope?'

'They're fine, thanks.'

'Well, give them my regards. Ted Copper. Now, a cuppa, was it? Milk and sugar?'

She'd drunk the tea and Mr Copper had locked up the caravan and departed by the time Nancy appeared.

'Sorry to be so late,' she panted.

'It's freezing out here. Why the cloak and dagger stuff, Nancy?'

Nancy shook her head. 'It's a bit tricky, Kath. I'm not sure how to tell you, to be perfectly honest.'

A chilly gust of wind whistled across the beach. 'Spit it out, then.'

'Me and my fella was under there, you know, having a little snog.' She pointed to the shore end of the pier, where the beach sloped upwards underneath the boardwalk. 'It's quite dark under there so we couldn't be seen and I just happened to look up, taking a breather, and saw two figures approaching. I suppose they thought they couldn't be seen either. It was Captain Burrows I recognised first, and then I saw it was your brother with him.'

'Did you say hello?'

'Gimme a break. We was in the middle of… you know?'

Kath always felt such an innocent in Nancy's company. 'I suppose they'd been for a drink and were taking some air.'

Nancy looked around, and even though the beach and promenade were deserted, she lowered her voice. 'You don't *get* it, do you?'

Kath shook her head.

'They were *properly* together. I mean, like holding hands.'

Nancy's tone was starting to irritate her. 'I can't see what's so wrong with that.'

'And then…' Nancy hesitated.

'And then? Go on.'

'I saw them kissing.'

Kath didn't want to hear any more. It was the same dizzy feeling she had when the teacher put up one of those unfathomable mathematical equations on the blackboard. None of it made any sense. Nancy must be lying. She began to walk away.

'Listen, please.' Nancy trotted alongside her. 'I didn't really want to tell you but I don't want your brother to get into trouble. He needs to stop associating with that man. Do you understand?'

Kath kept on walking.

'If anyone saw them they could be sent to gaol.'

'Gaol?' The word was like a slap in the face. 'Why?'

Nancy took a deep breath.

'Captain Burrows is a homo.'

By the time Kath reached home she'd decided that Nancy was deluded or malicious, or both. Her story seemed so unlikely, and everyone knew, because she'd hardly made a secret of it, that she fancied the pants off Captain Burrows. So when he hadn't asked her for a date – hadn't called, written or anything – she'd obviously got the hump and decided to get back at him by spreading rumours that he was a… Kath found it hard to say the word, even in her head. She had only the barest idea of what it meant, and couldn't imagine that such a thing really existed.

Of course there were plenty of people who lived with friends of the same sex. Her great-aunt Phyllis was one of them. Her boyfriend had been killed in the last war and now she lived with a sweet lady to whom she referred as her 'companion'. And men shared digs together, after all. What was wrong with that? But somehow she'd never imagined anything else going on. And certainly not with men like the Captain, who flirted with anything in a skirt, or Mark, who had so many girls calling for him that Ma had once suggested she'd have to put him under lock and key.

No, it was plainly ridiculous. She wouldn't mention any of it, to anyone. Safer that way.

But as the days went by, she became less certain. What if Nancy decided to spread her nasty rumours more widely? Perhaps she ought to warn her brother, just in case. For a week she vacillated, waiting for the right opportunity.

It was the weekend. Pa was on an extra shift, and Ma was out shopping. Mark was by the back door, rummaging for his Felixstowe Town scarf. He was going to watch the local team play an early-season friendly against their neighbours and fierce rivals, Walton United. There were rumours of a merger between the clubs, so this might be the last match of its kind, he said, and would be sure to draw a good crowd.

'Got a minute?' Kath said.

'Can it wait? I'm meeting the boys for a drink before the match.'

'Not really.' Having steeled herself, she wasn't going to back down now. The longer she waited, the more danger there was that Nancy would start spreading her malice. 'I just want to ask you something.'

'Ask away.' His voice was muffled by coats.

'No, come in the kitchen.'

He sighed. 'It's not that Billy Bishop business again?'

'No, nothing like that. I've been over him for months.'

He sat down, leaning his chair back. 'Okay. Spit it out, kid.'

She'd rehearsed it in her head so many times, but now they were face to face the words refused to come. 'It's just something Nancy said…' She faltered.

'That little minx. Ray says she keeps writing to him, but he's not interested. Too hot to handle, he says.' Mark laughed. 'So what's she been saying, then?'

'She says… she says…'

'Yes? I'm waiting.'

'That he's a…' She swallowed, trying to force her lips into the word. 'A homo.'

He righted the chair with a thud and leaned forwards towards her, his face just a foot from hers.

'She said *what?*'

'Don't make me say it again.'

'Well, whatever she said, it's a load of effing nonsense.' He stood up suddenly and began to pace the small space between the table and the door. 'For heaven's sake. *Ray?* I suppose she's trying to get back at him for ignoring her, the b—' He turned towards her, cheeks streaked angry red. His fists were clenched and for a brief moment she feared he might be about to hit her. 'When did she say this, Kath?'

'A few days ago.'

'Has she told anyone else?'

'Not as far as I know.'

He began pacing again.

'So why's she telling these lies? And why involve you? I suppose it's because he's a friend of mine?'

'That's the thing, Mark.'

'What *thing*?'

She lost courage now. Nancy's claims seemed even more improbable than before. She began to imagine that she might have simply dreamed them. 'Oh, never mind.'

'Tell me, Kath. What other poison has your so-called friend been spreading?'

'She said she saw *you* with him.' She found herself whispering now. 'On the beach. By the pier. Holding hands.'

Mark walked slowly back to the table and sat down, his face a peculiar shade of grey. 'Listen, kid. It's a pack of lies. A pack of *dangerous* lies. You know that, don't you?' His voice was low and menacing.

She nodded.

'I have no idea what her game is, or why she's doing this. Do you?'

'Only as you said, to get back at Ray.'

'Does she know how damaging an allegation like that, however ridiculous, can be for someone in his position? And there's my application to the RAF just going in…' He swore under his breath and sank his face into his hands.

'I'm going to stop this, Mark, before it goes any further. I'm going to confront her and tell her to stop telling lies.'

He looked up sharply. 'No, Kath, don't say anything to her; it might make it worse. Let me talk to Ray, he'll know what to do.' He shook his head, furiously. 'She'd better watch out, though. He'll be hopping mad.'

CHAPTER 10

Vic was having the time of his life. For six weeks that autumn he and Johnnie visited airfields all across the south of England, taking measurements of different aircraft: bombers, fighters, transport and reconnaissance.

He was glad to be away from the febrile hothouse atmosphere of the labs at Bawdsey. One of the men questioned about the leak had disappeared without trace, but it seemed that Frank had been exonerated and nothing more was said. Vic wished he'd had the courage to challenge him, but feared making things worse. Time had now passed, but his resentment had not. He felt constantly wary, fearful the snake might strike again.

The days grew shorter, the mornings misty. Leaves coloured red, orange and brown, then fell from the trees. Time was pressing on, and 'Jimmy' Rowe told each of the two teams he expected 'workable solutions' by Christmas, to be tested in the New Year. Frank crowed that his team's new kit was infinitely superior and nearly ready for use, and they had fully expected to coincide with him at one of their airfield visits, but there was no sign.

'That man's all bluff and bluster,' was Johnnie's diagnosis. 'We don't need to worry about that lot. Just get on with the job in hand.'

The research station lent them a car, a battered old Morris Ten. Johnnie had taught him to drive but Vic usually opted to be navigator, even though his map-reading skills were often tested to the limit; sometimes beyond their limits. Most airfields were quite new and not yet signposted, but getting lost in the lanes of Kent, Sussex or Lincolnshire became part of the fun.

Vic had never seen the English countryside looking so beautiful. The trees still held vestiges of autumn plumage, and bridal veils of white gulls billowed behind the ploughing tractors that turned fields of harvest gold overnight into precise stripes of brown. Johnnie was the best kind of travelling companion: efficient but relaxed, cheerful but not overbearing. He liked a drink, but never to excess. He seemed to enjoy Vic's company, and showed a friendly curiosity about his Indian origins.

'Time for the Brits to get out, isn't it?' he said at breakfast one day, after reading a newspaper report about the progress of one Mahatma Gandhi.

'Of course it is. But people fear what will happen when they lose a common enemy.'

'Why's that?'

'They would fight among themselves instead. Muslims and Hindus both believe they have the right to rule.'

Johnnie, always curious, wanted to know more about the religious differences, but Vic's knowledge was cursory and he struggled to explain. Apart from avoiding meat, he'd barely thought about being a Hindu since his mother died. 'You don't speak the language and seem to know diddly squat about their religions. I don't believe you're Indian at all,' his friend teased.

'So they dropped me in a vat of oil when I was born, I suppose?'

'Don't be a dolt.'

They stayed in RAF barracks and ate in military messes or, if no beds were available, would take bed and breakfast at local inns, for which they'd been given a modest allowance. After the long months of hard graft, with bosses breathing down their necks expecting results and asking for solutions 'by yesterday', the freedom was intoxicating.

Not that they were taking it easy. Their days were busy with visits, taking detailed notes, copying technical drawings and making sketches of their own, the evenings spent writing up their reports and developing potential ways in which the friendliness, or otherwise, of an aircraft could be detected by a radio wave. At night, easing himself into sleep, Vic would recite their names: Blenheim, de Havilland, Handley Page, Avro, Vickers, Fairey, Armstrong. When he finally slept he dreamed of engine sizes, wing lengths and torsion strengths, images of circuit diagrams and the configuration of instrument panels.

One weekend they took a detour to visit Johnnie's home near Petersfield, on the South Downs. When Vic fretted about not having anything smart to wear, Johnnie just laughed. As soon as they arrived, Vic understood why.

They were greeted by his wife Lizzie, a strong, handsome woman digging up potatoes in a small allotment at the front of a semi-detached Victorian farm cottage. She threw down her spade and ran to Johnnie, smothering him with kisses and smearing his face with earth from her hands, but no one seemed bothered. Two adolescent children emerged and jumped on their father, almost knocking him to the ground and then dragging him indoors, leaving Lizzie and Vic to introduce themselves.

'Vikram Mackensie.' He felt awkward, witnessing such effuse expressions of physical affection. 'I'm sorry to intrude.'

'Don't be silly, we love visitors,' she said, wiping her hands on her apron. 'And we've heard so much about you, Mac, or should I call you Vikram?'

'Vic will be fine, but I answer to almost anything. "Here, you" works well.'

Inside, he accepted a mug of tea. The children, a girl and a boy, were talking ten to the dozen to their father, showing off their toys, models and workbooks, leaving Vic time to look around. He'd never seen a room quite so chaotic before: ancient furniture, threadbare carpets, a basket of knitting, a cat nursing kittens in a cardboard box in the corner. Faded watercolours and amateur sketches adorned three walls, and the fourth was covered with books stacked higgledy-piggledy on shelves buckling beneath their weight. Such untidiness usually left him ill at ease, his fingers twitching to restore order, but here he felt immediately comfortable. This was a real home, a place where people cared little about how they looked to outsiders, or about material possessions.

Lizzie produced a delicious supper of cauliflower cheese with kale and new potatoes freshly dug from her vegetable plot. They washed it down with a couple of bottles of beer, and afterwards she served apple crumble and custard. 'Johnnie's favourite,' she said, with an affectionate glance across the table. He responded with the gesture of a kiss, earning him cries of 'Oh, cut out the soppy stuff, Dad, pleeease,' from the children.

Afterwards Johnnie invited Vic to 'play for his supper', clearing a pile of newspapers, clothes and a cat basket to reveal a dusty upright piano. Despite a few stuck keys and a general lack of tuning, he managed to stumble through a few ragtime numbers. Lizzie and the children danced and cheered when he finished, with calls of 'encore, encore,' to which of course he obliged. How could he refuse, when it clearly brought such joy? *This is how family life should be*, Vic thought to himself, not the stilted conversation in the overstuffed drawing room at his aunt's, nor the stifling propriety at the home of his school friend Kenny. His own life seemed so empty, so barren, and his head ached with envy.

When it came time for bed, Johnnie led him upstairs to what was clearly the son's bedroom. 'The boy'll be fine on Beth's floor,' he said when Vic protested. Left alone, he looked around, instantly overwhelmed with nostalgia. Toy trains, lead soldiers, a half-built Meccano crane, piles of comics, and books with titles like *Fun for Boys* transported him immediately back to his bedroom in India. He could even hear the mournful descending scale of the coucal bird and the harsh alarm calls of the parakeets that massed in the trees behind the bungalow, and smell the sandalwood incense his mother burned each day when preparing her puja.

Leaving for England more than a decade ago, little knowing that he would never see the house again, nor hear those sounds, smell those smells, he'd given it scarcely a backward glance. Besides his school uniform and regulation sports kit, the only personal possessions he'd brought with him were a teddy bear and a framed photograph of his mother and father on their honeymoon, riding an elephant.

He took up a tin car and sniffed it. The tang of metal and lead paint brought tears to his eyes. Mourning for his truncated childhood and grieving for the mother he only vaguely remembered, Vic curled up on the bed and finally fell asleep.

Christmas brought another visit to his father in Tunbridge Wells. Aunt Vera seemed to be suffering from some kind of wasting disease, an unspecified illness about which he dared not ask but which seemed to keep her confined to her room most of the time. After the spaciousness of the Manor, the narrow terraced house felt even more stifling than on his previous visit, especially since the weather, which had been snowy and bitter the week before, had turned suddenly wet and unseasonably mild.

There was no roast this year, only a cut of tinned ham for his father, and Smedley's tinned new potatoes and mixed vegetables – soggy and metallic-tasting, even after Vic warmed them up with butter and sprinkled them with grated cheese. In the dead of night, after everyone else had retired, he went downstairs and made toast. His father had become ever slower in his movements and greyer around the eyes, and he felt assailed with guilt for failing to visit more frequently.

But he couldn't wait to get away.

By the spring of 1938, news from the continent was certainly lending an added urgency to work at the Bawdsey research station. In March the German army marched into Austria and the 'Führer' began his triumphal journey to Vienna, where he declared that the country – his birthplace – would become 'the newest bastion of the German Reich'. The prospect of war had suddenly become terrifyingly real.

'By God, Holland and Belgium will be next,' Johnnie sighed over the newspaper.

'Belgium? I thought everyone said he'd expand eastwards?' Vic said.

'Poland'll be in his sights too, I'm sure. They're very vulnerable. But Holland and Belgium have sea ports.'

'Just over there.'

'Too right. Just over there.' Johnnie lifted his gaze, looking out of the window at the North Sea. 'Thank Christ I'm too old to fight again.'

'Again?'

'I turned eighteen in early 1918. Got conscripted the very next day and shipped out to Flanders after training.'

'You fought in Flanders?' Vic was impressed. 'You kept that quiet, John-boy. What was it like?'

'Hell on earth, my friend. Mud, lice, bodies, shells, permanent terror. At least it was only four months. Then I got a bullet in the shoulder and they shipped me home to get mended. The war ended before they could send me back again.'

'Small mercies. I'm glad you made it.'

'After that all I wanted to do was retire to the country, get married and have children, but I still needed to earn a living. Hence electrical engineering and the job with Marconi, which has led me to this little slice of heaven.' He paused, turning his attention back to the newspaper again. 'Thank heavens my boy's too young to get conscripted this time round.'

'D'you think there'll be conscription again?'

'It's a dead cert, I'm afraid. As if they didn't kill off enough of us last time. But don't you worry, Mac, ours will be a protected occupation.'

'Somehow that doesn't feel like much consolation,' Vic said, quietly.

'Our contribution is to build the best possible defences.' Johnnie folded the newspaper and slapped it onto the table. 'So c'mon, we'd better get that big brain of yours back to work. Frank's been boasting about their so-called foolproof system, and we don't want his team winning, do we?'

Frank and his team had chosen an airfield on the south coast for their trial, but Vic suggested that to save time their team could use somewhere much closer to home: the flying boat experimental station he'd visited on Empire Day.

Dr Rowe was dismissive. 'Those old flying boats have seen their day. Lumbering great beasts,' he mumbled. 'Won't be any use in any coming war; they've got no range. And who needs an aircraft that can only take off or land on water, in perfect weather?'

'But we don't need height or range, not for these first tests,' Johnnie persisted.

'And we won't incur any travel costs,' Vic added. They got their permission.

Arriving at the flying boat station, they were greeted by a tall, good-looking man. Vic recognised him immediately.

'Captain Burrows at your service, gentlemen,' he said, shaking hands with a vice-like grip. 'The boss says you've a piece of kit you'd like testing. How can we help?'

Just being in the pilot's presence made Vic feel like a schoolboy once more: in his first term at boarding school, watching the sixth-formers with their long limbs and fine physiques, their careless confidence with the teachers, their effortless grace and skill on the tennis courts or the cricket pitch. He was completely overawed.

Johnnie at least had the advantage of age and experience, as well as nearly matching the man in height. But Vic, almost a foot shorter than both of them, dark-haired to their blond, brown-skinned to their fair, felt even more than usual as though he'd landed on an alien planet.

They repaired to a scruffy office at the back of one of the hangars, and Johnnie explained that because of the secret nature of their work it would not be possible to divulge precisely the purpose of their experiment. 'But we'll need to attach aerial lines – what we call dipoles – from front to aft, probably somewhere on the upper wing to the tail. We don't anticipate they will make any difference whatsoever to the handling or fuel consumption of the plane. All we require is a few passes timed to our own equipment at the Manor. We can choose the day to your convenience. And we'll take your advice on the type of plane you think will be suitable first time around. After that, perhaps we can try a few others.'

The captain listened with an impressive level of attention, asking intelligent questions about the aircraft they might like to use – explaining that he'd been chosen to work with them because he had the widest experience of all types on the station. Within half an hour they found themselves being led out onto a jetty.

From a distance the plane looked like a toy, but as they approached it was clear this was no flimsy biplane like the Swordfish Vic had visited on Empire Day. It had the hull of a destroyer – much of which was submerged below the water line – and two sets of wings spanning what looked like the length of a tennis court. To the underside of the upper set were attached two mighty Rolls Royce engines with propeller blades several yards long.

'Phew,' Johnnie whistled. 'This is a serious piece of kit, Captain Burrows.' Vic smiled to himself. Their recent airfield visits were often eased by his friend's canny ability to say the right thing, and it hadn't taken long to learn that the usual way to a pilot's heart was to flatter him with admiration for his aeroplane.

The wind was blustery and chill out here on the jetty, the sea choppy. 'I can't take you up today. It's too rough,' the captain said. 'But we can go on board if you like?'

The cabin was more cramped than it appeared from the outside, and even Vic had to watch his head. It required a crew of five, the captain explained: pilot and navigator plus three reconnaissance officers, who would operate cameras and if necessary man the guns mounted on the fuselage. 'For self-defence only, of course. Too slow and hard to manoeuvre to be a fighter.' Vic shuddered, sensing how vulnerable the crew might feel, protected only by this thin metal fuselage with large tanks of petrol so close by. He found it claustrophobic, and couldn't wait to get out.

By the end of their visit the plan was agreed – ready for approval by what the captain called his 'big white chief ', and Dr Rowe. Calculations would be finalised as soon as final permissions were given, installation of the dipole wires and instrumentation would follow, and the test flights would be scheduled as soon as the forecasters predicted a spell of more settled weather.

One of the team would need to be on board to direct the path of the flight and take measurements en route, ensuring that the systems on board were in working order. Vic immediately nominated Johnnie, and the rest of the team agreed.

Everything was set for their biggest challenge so far.

CHAPTER 11

Kath tried her best to request shifts so that she did not coincide with Nancy, but it was not always possible, and the other waitresses noticed soon enough.

'Had a tiff, you two?' one asked. 'We thought you was friends, but you seem to be ignoring each other.' Twice, the girls suggested going out after work, and Kath found herself making excuses. By the third time it was starting to become obvious.

'What's up?' they asked. 'Did we say something wrong?'

A few days later she overheard someone referring to her as 'Little Miss Stuck Up'. The situation was becoming intolerable. Although reluctant to raise it again with Mark, she needed to know. 'What's happening about that stuff Nancy told me?' she asked him. 'Did you say anything to Ray?'

He looked cagey, uncomfortable. 'Yes, I told him. He thinks it's best to let sleeping dogs lie.'

'But what if she goes around spreading her lies to other people, Mark? You said yourself it could be damaging to your prospects.'

'Obviously if that happens, he'll act. But for the moment he's in favour of letting it go.' His voice was calm, but his demeanour anything but.

She shrugged. 'Everyone's noticed that I'm avoiding her at the restaurant, and it's making my life a misery. The atmosphere is pretty poisonous.'

'I'm sorry, Kath. But it's his life. I can't tell him what to do.'

'It's *your* life as well, Mark. She was spreading lies about you, too.'

'I agree with Ray. Confronting her would only cause more gossip. It'll blow over.'

But it didn't 'blow over'. One evening after work Nancy ran after her, calling her name. Dusk had already fallen; the pathway along the Seafront Gardens was only partly lit by street lamps, a chill wind whistled in the trees and the sea pounded menacingly onto the beach below. Kath quickened her pace without turning her head, then felt a touch on her arm.

'Kath, please. We have to talk.'

'I have nothing to say to you.' She walked faster and more resolutely this time. Just before they reached the part where the path narrowed, Nancy ran ahead, blocking her way. Stone walls bordering the flowerbeds on either side now hemmed her in.

'Let me by, please.'

'I thought we were friends, Kath. I only told you what I'd seen because I was concerned for your own reputation. And now you seem to be punishing me for it.' Nancy's usually perfect hair was straggling in the wind and her make-up was smeared.

'You expect me to be friends with someone who's been spreading a pack of lies?'

'Lies? You think I made it up?' She looked genuinely shocked.

'You only did it to get back at Captain Burrows because he wasn't returning your letters.'

'Yes, I'll admit that I was upset at first. But it soon became damned obvious why, after I saw him with your brother.'

Kath barged past and did not look back. The next day she handed in her notice at the Alexandra Cafe. The manager was certainly surprised, but he did not question her, and wrote her a glowing 'To Whom It May Concern' reference there and then.

'It's one of the other waitresses. I can't work with her any more,' she explained to Ma.

'Surely you can talk to her, Kath? These things can usually be sorted out with a sensible conversation.'

'No amount of talking will sort out this one. She's such a bitch.'

'Language, Kathleen!'

'I don't care. It's the truth.'

Each time she ventured into the town centre she dreaded seeing Nancy, or one of her gang of close friends. She kept away from the Alexandra Cafe, and after a few weeks she began to relax. The whole unpleasant episode receded in her memory, and neither she nor Mark ever mentioned it until long afterwards.

They'd celebrated New Year's Eve in the White Lion. Captain Burrows, returned from spending Christmas with his own family, brought along some of his pilot mates, who became rather riotous and very nearly drank the place dry. Although she watched like a hawk, she could detect no sign of anything unusual between him and Mark, and after several glasses of port and lemonade she didn't care anyway.

Billy Bishop was there, and they had a cuddle and few kisses behind the toilets. 'For old times' sake,' he whispered in her ear. 'Tha's what Auld Lang Syne means, don't it?' But she knew neither he nor she really had their heart in it. He would be off again before long with scarcely a backward glance.

It was time to find a new job, but they were few and far between. She scoured the local newspapers and post office noticeboards without success, and did a few evenings of babysitting for the posh family at the end of their road. Joan was always either 'too tired' after work, or busy with her boyfriend at weekends. 'I'd come to the cinema with you, honest, but I've promised Sam,' she'd say.

Kath's savings were dwindling fast. 'No job, no money, no boyfriend, no qualifications, nothing to do. I'm so bored,' she groaned, trying to stir herself to go out for the shopping Ma had asked for. 'Something's got to turn up soon.'

It did. Ma announced that one of the kitchen assistants at the Bawdsey Research Station had got herself pregnant – 'stupid girl', she muttered – and left the job. 'Come with me tomorrow, Kath. You can meet the chef and get a feel for the place.'

She hesitated at first. What if the guards recognised her, or if her name was on a list of potential spy suspects? It would all come out in the open then, and what if Ma got the sack because of it? And who wanted to spend their days as a kitchen assistant, anyway?

'What's the problem, kid?' Pa asked. 'Sounds like the job would be perfect.'

'Peeling potatoes and washing up?' she retorted, but he just shook his head.

'Beggars can't be choosers, my girl.'

So when Ma pressed her again, she relented. She'd always wanted to see inside the Manor anyway, and surely it was worth the risk of being recognised? As it turned out, the guards gave Ma a cheery smile and they were waved through the barrier with scarcely a second glance.

She would never forget that first morning. It wasn't raining, but it was blowing a gale and starting to snow. Shivering in the ferry boat despite several jumpers and her warmest coat, she couldn't imagine how anyone would ever want to endure this ordeal just to get to work each day. The make-up she'd so carefully applied was starting to run, her hair was flattened under Mark's woolly football hat and her hands were frozen inside two pairs of gloves.

'I must look a fright,' she said as they jumped down onto the beach, trying not to get their feet wet. She nearly managed it until a sneaky wave caught her, soaking her shoes and socks. Fortunately Ma always took a spare pair, just in case. 'There's a warm cloakroom where we can change into our overalls, and our stuff will dry on the radiators by the time we come home,' she said. 'You'll soon get used to the routine.'

As they trudged up the driveway, a veil of snow parted to reveal the Manor. It was even more impressive than she'd imagined, with the red towers standing out sharply against the white expanse of the cricket lawn below. The filigree carved stonework of the terraces and balconies were picked out in snow and shadow; the turrets of the towers, usually copper green, were capped in white. A glimmer of sun peeped through the cloud, illuminating the scene like an illustration from a fairy-tale book. Only the damp seeping through her boots reminded Kath that this was not some kind of dream.

She'd been hoping they would enter through the grand front porch, and was disappointed when Ma led her towards a gate concealed in the wall beyond. A narrow passageway led to a further door, through which they entered the largest kitchen Kath had ever seen.

Here, a great pine table occupied the centre of the room, piled with serving dishes. An enormous black range took up most of one wall, with shelving to either side hung with gleaming copper saucepans. Through a door to the left Kath could see a scullery with several square sinks in a row, separated by draining boards, with wooden plate racks hanging above them.

'That's where we do the washing up,' her mother said as they passed. 'And this is the prep room.' On the counter sat a mountain of potatoes, carrots and turnips waiting to be peeled.

'Do you do this every day?' she asked the other kitchen maid as they set about their task.

'Most days.'

Mary was a large girl of few words, none of them cheerful. They peeled in silence for half an hour, and the mountain seemed to have shrunk barely at all. If the Manor looked like a fairy-tale castle, Kath thought, this was the story of a poor princess who is captured and forced to do neverending household tasks until she relents and agrees to marry the horrible prince.

Ma popped her head round the door. She was wearing a proper chef's hat; tall, white and starched. 'How are you getting on?'

'Bored out of my brain,' Kath said.

'Consider yourself lucky you're not in the scullery doing the washing up.'

'I expect that'll be later,' Kath muttered miserably.

At last lunchtime rolled around, and she was called to help deliver the food to the dining room. When they reached it, she was so busy gazing in astonishment that she very nearly dropped the heavy pot of mashed potato. This was no ordinary dining room; chandeliers still hung from the ceiling, and all along one wall were full-length gilt mirrors. A beautiful wooden parquet floor gleamed beneath their feet. To the other two sides were long windows leading out onto the gardens and the sea beyond.

'It was the ballroom when the family lived here,' Ma explained as they arranged the plates on a long serving table. Kath wasn't listening. She could hear the orchestra playing and saw herself reflected in the mirror, lit with twinkling chandeliers, gliding about the polished floor wearing a beautiful silk ball gown in the arms of a dashing young aristocrat in white tie and tails, or perhaps an RAF officer in full dress uniform. He would invite her into the garden to watch the moon rising over the sea, and hold her in his arms for warmth before turning his face to hers...

'Come on, girl. We've more pots to bring out,' Ma called.

Lunch was served cafeteria-style, but Kath wasn't trusted to dish up, not on her first day. She needed to understand portion sizes first, Ma said, or she'd dole out too much or too little, and either run out or have too much left over. Either way there would be complaints. Her task was to ensure that the pots and plates of food were always replenished, and 'to watch and learn'.

Ma warned her that anything she might overhear was subject to something called the Official Secrets Act, which meant that she wasn't allowed to breathe a word about it to anyone, not even other members of staff. Of course this only intensified her curiosity, and she listened as best she could from the serving table, trying to glean any hint of what all these men were doing here, cloistered in this extraordinary place, and how they all related to each other.

The RAF officers had slight variations to their uniforms – she made a mental note to ask Mark later what all the insignia meant

– but the civilians were harder to distinguish. The men in overalls were the noisiest, joshing each other and generally having a laugh. The quietest and most reserved were the men in suits, about fifteen of them, definitely the least gregarious and curiously mismatched; a real range of ages and types.

From the way they seated themselves she could sense the level of rivalry, even mistrust, between them. They talked quietly, huddled inward towards each other, so that it was impossible to make out a single word. Which was a pity, Kath thought, because she felt certain that these men were the brains behind the big secret, the masts and the high security.

Then, returning with a fresh pot of stew, she recognised him: small, dark-skinned and slight-framed, with an untidy shock of thick hair as black as she'd ever seen, keeping company with a much taller, broader older man, slightly balding, with an easy smile.

'Hello again,' she said. 'I think we met at the station a while ago? And at the pram race?'

'Ah, yes. Hello.' Once more, she couldn't tell whether that expression of slight amusement was shyness or genuine friendliness. She noticed that he refused the stew, taking only vegetables and a slice of cheese.

'I'm Kath,' she said. 'Just started work here today.'

Her mother's sharp whisper halted the exchange. 'Stop yakking and get another plate of vegetables, please. We're running out.'

As the queue moved forward, the older man nudged his friend in the ribs. 'You're a dark horse, Mac,' she heard him say. 'Pretty girl like that and you never said a word.'

The head chef, Mr Brunetti – a man of Italian heritage with charming manners and a rather short fuse, Ma warned – invited her into his office at the end of the shift.

'Ah, Miss Motts, take a seat,' he said. 'I've heard very good things about your work today.'

'Thank you.' *Clearly he's noted my remarkable potato-peeling skills*, she thought to herself, trying to keep a straight face.

He reached forward, taking up a sheet of lined yellow paper from his desk. 'But I'm afraid there's a bit of a problem.'

She'd seen this type of paper before, and knew at once what he was going to say next. Now that she was about to get the sack, the job suddenly seemed more appealing.

'Now, Miss Motts, you understand this is a top secret establishment and we have to be extremely careful about who we employ?'

She nodded helplessly. How would she ever explain to Ma and Pa why she'd been rejected?

'It says here that you were discovered spying on the Manor and were questioned and cautioned by our head of security? Is that true?'

For a moment, Kath considered reprising her bird-watching story, but decided to be honest. 'It was a stupid thing to do,' she began. 'I've lived on the other side of the river all my life and when they started building masts and putting up fences and barbed wire, and everything was so hush-hush, I was desperate to find out what was going on over here. I was in the woods looking at the Manor through binoculars when they found me. I pretended I was bird-watching, but they didn't buy it.'

Mr Brunetti's smile returned as he picked up the yellow paper once more and began to read from it out loud: 'We concluded that Miss Motts was just a naive local girl whose curiosity got the better of her, and sent her away with a flea in her ear.'

Her whole body seemed to burn with the shame of it. 'But if they didn't think I was any threat, why did you…?'

'I just wanted to reassure myself, Miss Motts. To check whether you would be honest with me. You passed the test.' He crumpled up the piece of paper and aimed it towards an overflowing waste-paper basket in the corner of the room. It missed. 'So now I sincerely hope you will take up my offer of a post.'

Kath sighed with relief. At least she wouldn't have to confess anything to Ma. The job was dull and without tips the money was worse than she had been getting at the cafe, but for the moment she had no other choice. The official secrets document he made her read was terrifying – the penalty for breaking the rules was arrest, or even imprisonment – but she took a deep breath and signed it anyway.

Ma was delighted with her news, and offered to stump up the money for waterproofs and rubber boots so Kath didn't get soaked on the ferry. She soon acclimatised to the rigours of the journey and even began to enjoy it, especially when the milder weather arrived. 'Blows the cobwebs away,' Ma said, and she was right.

Joan said she was mad. 'Going on that boat in all weathers, just to get to work? And slaving away as a kitchen maid,' she said scornfully. 'You're worth more than that.' Kath tended to agree, but for the moment there was little alternative, and she'd promised herself to save for a new summer frock and sandals when the weather improved.

She liked getting to know the 'customers'. The clientele of the Alex had been mostly tourists whom you rarely saw more than once. At the Manor they served the same people every day and although any kind of socialising was strictly discouraged, they would exchange a smile or a few friendly words. She grew to know their preferences; Mac – who also went by the name of Vic – didn't eat any meat or fish, Johnnie was especially fond of ham and bacon, the smiley 'big boss' Mr Watson-Watt liked his portions on the generous side, and serious Dr Rowe never ate desserts, preferring cheese and biscuits.

The magic of arriving by ferry never seemed to fade, and walking between the sighing pines and up the drive as the Manor rose into view always raised her spirits. Although the kitchen and dining room were her usual domain, she was sometimes called to set or clear the table in what they called the Green Room, a large dining room with a fine marble fireplace at one end and French windows opening onto the terrace with views across the river.

Getting there entailed going through the Great Hall, a vast oak-panelled space where they held concerts and dances on Saturday nights. One day towards the end of her shift she overheard someone playing the piano and slipped her head round the door to see who it was. It was the man they called Mac, so completely absorbed in the music that he barely looked up. The tune was a jolly ragtime number, and she found her feet tapping quietly to the jazzy rhythms.

It came to an end all too soon but she stayed hidden, willing him to play some more. The next piece was slow and classical, the kind of music that seemed to grab her heart and root her feet to the ground. The mood built up, louder and louder, until it reached some kind of climax and then slowly, gently, faded to an ending of such soft sadness that, as she crept away, her eyes were prickling with tears.

Slowly, she earned greater responsibilities. Catering for forty or more was a very different matter from cooking at home, and Ma helped her to calculate the right quantities and the best saucepans to use. One day she made the perfect egg custard – never an easy task – which even earned praise from Mr Brunetti: 'I am no great fan of your English puddings,' he said. 'But that was a particularly fine confection.' Another time she baked three large Victoria sponges for teatime and learned later that they'd earned many compliments. She was soon promoted to 'assistant cook', much to the annoyance of Mary, who was left to deal with the mounds of vegetables on her own.

She felt sorry for Mr Mackensie, who didn't eat fish or meat and seemed to survive on vegetables alone, and one day she made him a special cheese and potato pie. It didn't take more than twenty minutes, but with the cheese browned on the top it looked delicious, and when she offered it to Mac his smile was worth every second of the extra effort.

'Really, no meat?' he said. 'What a very kind thought, miss.'

'What makes *you* so special?' Johnnie teased his friend.

'You are welcome to try some, sir,' Kath said, trying to ignore the hotness rising up her neck. Both men returned after their meal to compliment her cooking skills, making her blush all over again. That weekend, she and Ma went to the library to research more vegetarian recipes – vegetable pie, pumpkin soup, stuffed marrows, cheese turnovers – and the presentation of each new dish was rewarded with Mac's sweet, shy smile.

New people arrived – even some women, whom she assumed to be secretaries – and others left, but each day she looked forward to serving her favourites: Mac, Johnnie and a couple of others who always greeted her with cheery smiles. On the other hand, she came to dread the appearance of Frank, the weasel-faced man with ginger hair whose flirty remarks seemed designed to make her blush. 'Morning, gorgeous,' he'd say, or 'What are you doing this weekend, sweetheart?' It was innocuous enough, but it left her feeling uncomfortable. She longed to respond with a sharp remark, but knew that was not her place.

What she disliked even more was the way Frank made disrespectful and sometimes disparaging comments about the others, referring to Robert Watson-Watt, who was portly but by no means overweight and always acted the perfect gentleman, as 'our chubby friend', and to Johnnie as 'the old man' or 'greybeard', even though he wasn't that old and was always clean-shaven.

But his most vicious remarks were saved for Mac, to whom he referred as 'brown boy', 'smarty-pants' and 'too big for his boots', even suggesting he should 'go back where he came from'. Whatever had that mild-mannered man done to deserve such unpleasantness? Kath longed to report Weasel-face, but wasn't sure what for, or to whom. Anyway, it wasn't the place of an 'assistant cook' to comment.

As the weeks went by, she could sense the growing tensions between them. Only Johnnie remained his normal cheerful self. But Vic, normally so sweet and shy, seemed uncharacteristically taciturn and Frank more than usually snappy. Some days, she thought, you could cut the atmosphere in the dining room with a knife.

CHAPTER 12

It was one of those days by the English seaside that arrive like a gift, all the more special for being so rare. The bluest of skies was only softened by the slightest of sea hazes, the sunshine only disturbed by the fluffiest of clouds. The wind that had for months punished the coastline had folded away its flail, and the sea was flat and glassy. For once the Met Office had got it right. It was the perfect day for a test flight.

As he walked the Cliff Path before breakfast, Vic felt sick with apprehension. There was no need, he told himself. Everything was arranged, down to the finest detail. Johnnie would be on board the plane and Vic would be in the receiver room, tuning the RDF frequencies and praying they could prove, once and for all, that their system would reliably identify the plane as a 'friend' and thus not a 'foe'.

Scott would be with him in the receiver room as comms man, liaising on the telephone to his opposite number at the flying boat station. Dr Rowe would be there, too, breathing down their necks. The engineers would act as spotters, one at Bawdsey and the other at the station. Their system would have to be refined in due course. But if this first test failed, they might never get the go-ahead to pursue stage two.

Vic had not slept well, his mind churning over the possible glitches they might encounter, but now all was set. They walked to the ferry with Johnnie, Dr Rowe and the others who would be observing from the seaplane base. As they waited to embark, he found himself pulled into an awkward embrace. 'Good luck, old man,' Johnnie said in his ear. 'It'll be fine. I'm certain we've got this thing right.'

'You're the one who needs the luck, going up in that contraption.'

'It'll be a first for me, going up in a seaplane. Shame you won't be able to wave.'

The ferry powered out into the tide and was then drawn back by the current onto the opposite shore. Johnnie turned with a final wave and thumbs up before climbing onto the navy jeep waiting for them on the Felixstowe side.

Vic waved back, putting on a cheerful smile. They had become so close in the past few months, living and working together, being in each other's company twenty-four hours a day, getting to know each other's ways, even anticipating what the other would say next. They knew each other's bedtime routine, the way they folded their clothes, cleaned their teeth, the little sounds they made in sleep. At work they found themselves having the same thoughts, and would finish the other's sentences. He trusted Johnnie completely and felt they'd become almost two parts of a whole. It was the closest he'd been, as an adult, to having a best friend.

He shook himself. It was hardly a dangerous mission – these planes flew every day. It was just nerves. 'C'mon, Scotty, let's get back to work,' he said, turning back to the gatehouse.

The Radio Receiver Room had been set up temporarily in a wooden hut in the courtyard of the stable block, in the shadow of the receiver mast. It was newly painted, and on that hot day the fumes were fierce enough to give anyone a headache, but they had to keep the door closed to prevent any interference from the transmitting masts just a few hundred yards away. Later, new reinforced concrete bunkers would be camouflaged under great mounds of earth, always damp and musty-smelling.

He seated himself at the desk with its small rectangular screen, next to the tracking table, and turned on the power. The A-Scope slowly came to life, blinking at him with its usual assortment of blurry grey and off-white blobs and lines. Scott stood to his right, next to the brown Bakelite telephone receiver fixed to the wall. Dr Rowe and two others squeezed into the space behind them.

The white-faced clock above their heads ticked loudly into a thick, heavy silence as Vic tinkered with the dials, making the final adjustments. Someone cleared their throat. More silence, more ticking. The clock hand reached the appointed hour. Eleven o'clock. There was no radio connection to the cockpit, so an engineer was tasked with reporting what he could see from the window of an office in one of the hangars. Even though it was expected, the harsh ring of the phone made everyone jump. Scott picked it up.

'They're ready for the off.'

Captain Burrows had calculated with naval precision that it would take seven minutes and thirty-five seconds to taxi out to sea, gather enough power for the lumbering Supermarine Scapa to take off, reach the agreed height and then fly to the starting position to the south, over Harwich. They would pass Bawdsey heading north over the sea precisely three miles from the coast and would then circle and return, repeating the pattern once more so that the system could be tested twice in both directions at three, ten and then twenty miles out.

'Transmitter power on?'

A voice squawked down the phone. 'Roger that.'

Vic visualised the arcs of radio waves fanning out around the coast, floodlighting the air with invisible radio pulse energy, like the three-dimensional spider's web Watson-Watt had described at his very first briefing. Was it a friendly bee or an enemy wasp about to fly into the lair? In the next few minutes, if their calculations were right, they would, for the very first time, be able to tell. If their system worked, it would provide the perfect defence against an enemy: a magic eye, secret, invisible and brilliantly effective.

Slowly, a line emerged, a white squiggle worming its way horizontally across the black screen, left to right. He twiddled the left-hand knob, which identified range, looking for the spike that would indicate the presence of an aircraft or other object reflecting the beams being transmitted from another building half a mile away. Three miles, ten, twenty, thirty… nothing. A good sign. They didn't want other planes in the air confusing their picture, not today.

Forcing himself to work slowly and patiently, he turned the dial the other way, scanning the empty air. The first time he'd been trained to use this screen, back in the first months of his attachment, Vic had found it utterly confusing. How could anyone distinguish anything sensible from the apparently random streaks and quivering smears that appeared and disappeared in an instant? But he'd learned, in time, to understand the subtleties and to interpret them with accuracy. It was like reading sheet music, or Greek, or a child learning language for the very first time.

'They're up,' Scott said, and then, a few moments later. 'At height… turning… approaching now.'

Vic's heart began to thud in his chest. He twiddled the range dial. No sign. Seconds passed, and then, at six miles, he located a deep V cutting through the wriggly line.

'I've got her,' he shouted.

He turned the right-hand dial, the one that would indicate bearing, the direction in which the plane was travelling. Yes, it was heading north, parallel to the coast. He twiddled both knobs now, trying to detect the modified signal.

Then he saw it, and his heart did a double beat. The plane, flying parallel to the coast, was approaching and now, at five miles range, the sharp point of the V shape bisected, forming a double V. This was the signal of interference they'd been praying to see, that they had spent so many months working on, created by the deceptively simple design of dipole wires installed onto the aircraft.

'There it is. Two tails instead of one,' he shouted. 'A friendly aircraft.'

Scott was whooping excitedly into the phone, 'We've got it, two tails. Yes, *two* tails. We've got it.'

'Bloody hell, it works,' Vic said, trying to maintain his focus on the screen. He could hardly wait to share their success with Johnnie. 'Get someone to give them a thumbs up as they pass,' he said to Scott.

'Will do, boss.'

Someone slapped him on the back so powerfully it almost took his breath away. 'Congratulations, Mr Mackensie,' Dr Rowe boomed. 'Your system has proved itself.'

Vic twisted the distance knob, following the signal moving across the screen as the plane approached and then flew past.

'Good man,' Dr Rowe said. 'There'll be drinks on the bar for your team tonight, lad.'

Even at the height of this triumph he knew that he must manage expectations, especially as he had the full attention of the most important man right here in the room, hanging on his every word. 'We still need a reliable way of identifying friendly craft in large groups, or in the midst of enemy planes, sir. That'll need a bit more work.' A lot more work, in fact; requiring a compact powered receiver to emit a much stronger pulse.

'Here she comes again,' Scott announced. 'First south-bound leg approaching.'

The spike grew in length once more, that precious double tail beaming its vital message right into the fuggy room.

In future, when the system was fully operational, the information would be conveyed by telephone to a central operations room at Stanmore being linked up to each new receiving station – two dozen of them, in an arc from Suffolk down to the Kent coast – as they came on line.

Vic still found himself astonished by the immense scale of Watson-Watt's vision, its ambition and audacity. Even though the new masts were now reaching into the skies all around the south of England, very few knew what they were for, or how vital they could be if war was ever declared.

How proud he felt to be part of this great secret project. His eyes swam as he focused on the blip, or tried to, fiddling both knobs, trying to pick up the frequency. The line wriggled across the screen, but he could find no hint of the spike. Where had it gone? He turned the range dial again, one way, and then the bearing dial, then both together, trying to quell the panic rising in his chest. Still no sign. He resisted giving the equipment a kick – it sometimes worked if a wire had come loose.

'Confirm transmission power still on.' He tried to keep his voice firm and confident.

'Roger, power on.'

The instant Scott returned the phone to its base, it rang again.

'Treble R.'

A pause. Squawking down the phone.

'Yes?'

More squawks.

An indrawn breath, followed by a loud expletive.

'Roger that.'

'What is it, Mr Scott?' Dr Rowe asked.

Another pause, then, 'They're saying the plane is down, sir. Into the sea, just off the town. About five miles out.'

'What do you mean, down?' Vic shouted. 'What the hell is he playing at? He was supposed to do another pass.'

The voice at the other end of the phone line chattered for a few more agonising moments.

'She seems to have got into trouble, they're saying. The rescue boat is on its way.'

'In trouble? *Rescue?* What on earth… ?' The words dried in his mouth. *Johnnie.* Johnnie was on board. Suddenly Vic felt violently sick. Pushing past Dr Rowe, he rushed outside into the fresh air. As the nausea began to recede, his chest became gripped with a real physical pain. Doubled up against the wall, he began to moan.

Not Johnnie, please God, keep him safe. If only he'd offered to go up in the plane instead. He had no family to provide for, no responsibilities or children abandoned to grieve their beloved father for the rest of their lives. He thought of that little family in the cottage, of Lizzie, and little Beth and Christopher, the boy with the room of Vic's own childhood, filled with toy planes and books about practical things. *Please, please let him be safe.*

Scott was at his side. 'Chin up, old boy. They've sent two boats out and they're probably pulling them out of the drink as we speak. Don't forget those planes are built to float. I'm sure they'll all be fine. We'll know in a few minutes, anyway. I'll stay by the phone for news. Jimmy's ordered tea – we all need it. Take a couple of sugars.'

The news could not have been worse. No one had any idea why the plane – a solid workhorse with years of good safety records – should have crash-dived into the sea so suddenly, apparently without warning. Captain Burrows, Johnnie and the other crew members were all pulled from the wreckage within minutes, but none had survived. It was the first fatal seaplane crash in more than a decade.

That afternoon, a sombre party led by Dr Rowe went to watch the plane being retrieved. The navy men received them with meticulous courtesy, but Vic could sense the shock and anger simmering close to the surface. Five of their number had lost their lives, including one of their most valued and experienced pilots. The only thing different about this flight had been the equipment installed by Vic's team and the two dipole wires. Although nothing was said, it was clear they strongly suspected this to have been the cause of the crash.

A sturdy fishing boat had been called into service, using its trawler beam to tow the wreckage to shore. It looked nothing like a plane any more, just a mountain of bent metal and tangled wires. The craft would have hit the water with such force that the men must have died instantly.

They were looking at Johnnie's coffin. And it was probably his fault.

His head ran over and over their debates with Captain Burrows about the best way of attaching the dipole wires. Johnnie had favoured a different alignment but, using his old alibi of sophisticated geometrical calculation, Vic had persuaded him round. The fixings had been agreed by the navy men, but were carried out to Vic's plan. So if it was found that the wires had caused the crash he, and he alone, would be to blame.

That evening he walked the Cliff Path in a daze, numbly trying to comprehend what had happened and barely able to contemplate the future, a future in which his friend would not, at any moment, come haring round the corner with his usual cheerful summons, slapping him on the back. 'C'mon, laddie, we've work to do.'

Why did it have to be Johnnie? he asked again and again. The kindest, wisest man he'd ever met, the only man he'd ever considered a true friend; whose adoring wife and children were, perhaps even at this very moment, being visited by police officers down in Hampshire to be told the terrible news? Unwillingly, he found himself picturing the scene; how she would hold herself steady at first, trying to be strong for her children, but then, as the truth finally sank in, would surely collapse. How could anyone stay strong in the face of such unexpected horror?

Johnnie was a scientist, working in an environment they all believed to be relatively risk-free. That was their nature, they were not adventurers.

Now he was gone. Forever.

Vic could not imagine how life could continue. There were a few immediate practicalities to attend to, of course, and he would do his duty, steeling himself to get through them. As soon as the plane could be lifted from the sea it would be inspected by navy engineers, he knew. As part of the formal inquiry process, Vic and the remaining members of the team would be summoned for interview. There would also be memorial services to attend, he supposed. After that, Dr Rowe had insisted, the team should all take a week's leave, to recover.

It would take so much longer than a week; perhaps forever. But Vic dared not think beyond that. Even if they kept him on here at the research station – unlikely, given everything that had happened today – how could he continue, without Johnnie? He would have to resign. But what then? Could he even bear to go on living?

Behind him, to the west, the sun was setting, sending spectacular rays of pink, orange and purple into the sky that somehow reflected off the few fluffy clouds overhead, and onto the water in front of him in constantly moving swirls of colour.

Such heartless beauty, he said to himself, as a groan of despair erupted from his chest. For the first time in his adult life, Vic found himself weeping out loud.

CHAPTER 13

It was a strange, animal sound, like a dog or a fox in distress, Kath thought, coming from the lawn outside the prep room window.

She was in the last quarter-hour of her shift, cleaning up after Mary, who failed to understand the need to leave the sinks spick and span for the following day. But she didn't really mind. The ferry would be running for another two hours at least and it was a perfectly beautiful evening, promising one of those astonishing sunsets that lit up the whole sky and the sea below it. Where else could she work and witness such wonders?

There, once again, was that noise. She couldn't bear to leave an animal in such distress. Letting herself out of the kitchen door, she followed the sound until she found herself at the very edge of the lawn. Beyond here was just the cliff and the beach below, and the great expanse of sea. Where could it be? She listened more closely. Perhaps it was not an animal – it sounded more like a human being, in anguish. She feared that someone had fallen down the cliff and hurt themselves.

But how to reach them? She'd never really explored the gardens before, but instinct took her to the right-hand side of the lawn and down some steps, along a narrow, winding path that cut through the rock across the side of the cliff. Where did all this stone come from, she wondered vaguely as she walked, in sandy Suffolk? The noise became closer until, at last, she found its source.

It was the man they called Mac, the piano player, sitting on a ledge with his head in his hands, shoulders convulsing with sobs. She was about to retrace her steps for fear of embarrassing him when, just at that moment, he looked up.

'I'm sorry,' she said. 'I don't wish to intrude.'

As he turned away again, sinking his head into his hands once more, she dithered. Could she really leave him there, on his own, in such distress? Perhaps he was unwell, or hurt? What if they found him there, cold, the following morning? She sat down on another ledge a little distance away, without saying a word, just to wait and see. After a short while he took a deep breath and then another, then wiped his face.

'Oh, it's you.' His expression reminded her of a startled faun.

'I hope you don't mind. I heard something and just wanted to make sure you were all right.'

He sniffed and managed a weak smile. 'I'll probably live.'

'Perhaps you'd prefer me to leave you?'

A short silence, and then, 'Actually, it sort of helps to have another human being…' He looked out to sea where the setting sun was starting to show off its miracles, and she followed his gaze.

'Amazing, isn't it? It's been a beautiful day.'

'Not for me, it hasn't. It's been a terrible day.'

'I'm so sorry.' She ached to ask more but sensed he might tell her in his own time. They sat in silence, watching the clouds turn from orange to pink to mauve, then to purple and finally, fading into grey.

'It makes you feel very small, doesn't it?' he said, at long last.

'I hadn't thought of it like that, but now you say it…'

'We're just insignificant little specks on a small rock in a universe of millions of other planets, all swirling around among an infinite number of universes.'

The idea made her brain ache. 'I might be a speck, but I don't actually *feel* insignificant. Not inside.'

His smile was like a gift, but it vanished almost as soon as it arrived. 'You're right, of course. But I do wonder why we're all here, struggling away on this planet of ours. No one would miss us if we just disappeared.'

She paused a second, recalling Ma's advice never to ask questions, but then dismissing it. 'But you're one of those important scientists developing clever secret things, aren't you? That's pretty significant.'

'There you are wrong, I'm afraid. Yours is by far the most important work. The human race wouldn't exist without food.'

'Anyone can peel vegetables and cook pies, but what you're doing is...' she stopped herself. Of course she hadn't a clue what he actually did.

'We all make our contributions, and none is more or less important than another,' he said, catching her gaze for a second. *What an odd character*, she thought; unlike anyone else she'd ever met, obviously brainy but so serious, with all this talk of universes and the rest. His face still reminded her of a shy, vulnerable animal, the eyes so dark that they seemed to be concealing something hidden and mysterious, but his expression was kind.

She remembered the pathos of the piece he'd played on the piano, and the question fell from her lips before she could stop it. 'But why are you so fed up?'

'A friend of mine died today.'

The shock of it caught the breath in her throat. 'That's terrible. I'm so sorry.'

'And the worst of it all is...'

She hoped he wouldn't start crying again; it made her feel so helpless. 'You can tell me. It might help to share it.'

'It's probably my fault.'

'How can it possibly be your *fault*? He was your friend.'

He shook his head. Of course he couldn't explain. His work was top secret.

She sat down again on her ledge, feeling the rough stone beneath her fingers. It was odd, not like any rock she'd seen before; not striped or rough, but smoothed into rounded shapes. Now she looked more carefully, she could see that it was speckled with tiny stones and shells, like the sand-castles they used to decorate on the beach when they were children, and she remembered Poppa telling her about it.

The man was watching her. 'It's called Pulhamite,' he said. 'Cement mixed with sand and shells.'

'I thought it was odd for Suffolk.'

'It's completely artificial. It was built by the lady of the manor, way back. She'd seen it used at some grand house or other and decided she needed a rocky cliff here at Bawdsey.'

'How do you know all this stuff, Mr, er, Mac?'

'Please call me Vic. Mac's short for my surname, Mackensie, and it reminds me of being back at school.'

'Vic, then. How do you know about this pull-whatsit?'

'Pulhamite. I can't remember, honestly. Someone told me, or maybe I read it somewhere. Mrs Quilter was a wonderful gardener. Have you seen the rest of the gardens?'

'I don't think we're allowed,' she said.

'It's all a bit overgrown now, of course, but there's a wonderful formal Italian garden, with a pond, and the most enormous walled kitchen garden I've ever seen, with a beautiful lemonry. I'll show you some time, if you like.'

A lemonry? She'd never heard of such a thing. 'That would be lovely, thank you,' she said, politely.

The light had almost completely disappeared from the sky, and a sharp breeze whipped off the sea and up the cliff side. She shivered, pulling her cardigan around her shoulders.

He stood. 'Come on, you're getting cold. We should get back.'

'I'm so sorry about your friend,' she said.

As they retraced their steps an awkward silence fell between them.

'I'd better get myself down to the ferry,' she said at last, starting to walk away.

'Hang on,' his voice came from behind her. 'I'm so sorry. Remind me your name.'

'It's Kath. Kathleen Motts,' she said.

'Thank you for being here, Miss Motts. It's been a comfort.'

*

'Hello? Where is everyone? What's for supper?' Kath called, running through to the kitchen.

Ma turned from the sink, a finger to her lips. 'It's Mark.'

Kath's stomach did a flip. Had Nancy been up to her tricks again? 'What's happened?'

'It's just too awful,' she whispered. 'He won't say much, but Ray Burrows has been in a crash.'

'A car crash? Is he okay?'

'The plane he was piloting for some test flight or other just fell into the sea. Mark's been told no one survived.'

'Christ.'

'Don't swear, sweetheart.'

'Sorry, Ma, but that's just too awful. Where's Mark now?'

'In his room.'

He didn't reply to her knock. When she turned the handle and opened the door a crack, he told her to go away. She decided to ignore him.

'I'm so sorry, Mark,' she said, sitting on the bed beside him. He shrugged her hand off.

'Leave me alone, Kath. There's nothing to be said.'

'It's not actually confirmed, is it?'

'Ma told you?'

'Yup.'

'There hasn't been any official announcement, if that's what you mean. But we all saw what happened. The plane is completely smashed. And they've retrieved six bodies. Five navy, and one of those Bawdsey boffins.'

Her heart seemed to contract. *One of those boffins?* The coincidence was just too great; it must be Vic's friend. In her head she ran through the faces of the men he kept company with at mealtimes: Dr Rowe, Mr Watson-Watt, Scott, Johnnie, Frank? There was no point trying to guess. But whatever was a Bawdsey scientist doing on board a seaplane test flight?

'I just can't believe he's gone.' He wiped his cheeks roughly with his knuckles.

She struggled for words of comfort. 'He was such a great guy, so full of life and energy. We'll all miss him, you know.'

'More than you'll ever know, little sister. More than you'll ever know.' He began to sob again, noisily, interspersed with moans. 'Oh God, oh God, oh God.' And then, 'Go away, Kath. I need to be on my own.' She'd never seen a man cry before today, and now she'd found herself comforting two of them in one evening. The world had turned upside down, and nothing would ever be the same again.

When Mark didn't appear for supper they found him sound asleep on his bed, fully clothed.

'Poor boy,' Ma whispered. 'He was ever so fond of Ray.'

Perhaps a little too fond, Kath thought to herself. 'We all were. He was a great fellow.'

'I just hope it puts him off, Kath.'

'Off what?' For a second, Kath was thrown off balance. Surely Mark hadn't told Ma about their relationship?

'Becoming a pilot.'

Kath doubted very much that it would deter Mark at all. If anything, it would leave him even more determined to emulate his hero.

Around death, just as in life, the secrets of the Manor were carefully hidden. No one spoke of any loss and Kath never repeated to anyone, not even Ma, Mark's unguarded words about 'one of those Bawdsey boffins' having been on board the plane that day. Nevertheless, she sensed the pall of grief hanging over the Manor: in the kitchen everyone was subdued. In the dining room, the men queued for their meals in silence and spoke in hushed whispers at their tables.

When she tried to ask, Mr Brunetti just shook his head. 'It's not for us to know these things, Miss Motts,' he said. But she couldn't help thinking about Vic, hoping that someone was looking after him. She'd seen nothing of him since that evening and assumed that he'd been given leave, until Ma told her that the man called Scott had requested sandwiches, fruit and other snacks that he took to a room in the Red Tower.

The only other person who failed to appear was Vic's friend, the kindly older man, Johnnie Palmer; the one who always had a joke or a compliment as he took his food. Kath reluctantly came to assume that it must have been him who'd been killed in the plane crash, alongside Captain Burrows and the other crew members. She missed his cheery face at the lunch table, and the way he'd showed genuine affection for his friend Vic.

It was the first time that anyone close to her had died – apart from her grandparents – and she felt the loss keenly. She might not have known these two men well, but she'd come to admire both of them for their vitality and wit and the way everyone had held them in such high regard. What a terrible waste it seemed.

Just a fortnight later, Kath and the rest of the family attended a service of remembrance for the five navy men at St John's, the larger of the town's churches. Although in Kath's view it was not a patch on St Peter and St Paul's, the more ancient and atmospheric church in Old Felixstowe, it was just as well they chose this one because it was packed, with standing room only at the back and a full turnout of uniformed men from the seaplane station.

A naval band played sombre numbers that had Kath and Ma in tears before the service even began. She imagined Ray must be sitting in heaven with his ears burning, so fulsome were the words of his commodore, who listed numerous examples of his exemplary and courageous service and the personal attributes that had made him one of the seaplane force's most remarkable pilots.

There were a few familiar faces from the Manor among the crowd, but no sign of Vic Mackensie. Johnnie's name was not even mentioned, which she thought terribly sad.

*

Shortly after this, Mark's RAF acceptance letter arrived saying that he would soon be advised where and when to report for initial training. Ma was distraught, of course, but Kath knew it was the best possible thing. Although her brother had continued to function, refusing to take any time off – 'can't afford to get a poor attendance record now' – getting up each day and going to work, he seemed to be only half in the world.

Friends would call by to invite him out, but he always refused. Kath tried to persuade him, saying it would be a distraction at least; but the one time he followed her advice he returned well after midnight, so drunk that he couldn't even make it upstairs. In the morning they found him asleep on the living room floor, stinking of booze.

One Saturday afternoon Kath heard a voice calling her name and turned to see Nancy, flashy as ever. Anyone would think she was dressed for a big night out in London rather than a little shopping trip to Felixstowe High Street. 'Before you sound off, I just wanted to say how sorry I was to hear about Captain Burrows,' she said.

'Yes, it's a terrible loss,' Kath managed to mumble. *If only looks could kill*, she thought to herself.

'Especially for your brother,' Nancy said. 'I've heard he's not been taking it well.'

Kath turned on her heel and walked away as quickly as she could. Thank goodness Mark would soon be away from it.

Two weeks later it was Mark's leaving party at the seaplane station. He arrived home 'three sheets to the wind', as Pa put it, and promptly fell asleep on the sofa, snoring loudly for the rest of the evening, but no one really minded.

The night before he was due to leave for training, Ma splashed out on a joint of beef roasted with all the trimmings, followed by Mark's favourite, a steamed treacle pudding and custard. He'd been given a bottle of champagne as a leaving gift and they opened it as an aperitif, followed by red wine with the meal. At around eleven, Ma and Pa stumbled unsteadily upstairs to bed, and Kath was about to follow them.

'Keep me company, sis?' Mark waved the bottle of champagne, still half full.

'Haven't we had enough?'

'It's just a little. C'mon. Old time's sake, and all that.'

She took the glass. 'Here's to your success as a pilot. I'll miss you.'

'Me too, little sis.'

'But it'll be good for you to get away, don't you think?'

'Perhaps.' He sighed. 'But I'm still so angry.'

'Angry? With Ray? It wasn't his fault, was it?'

'With those people at the Manor.'

'The Manor?'

He lowered his voice. 'You mustn't tell anyone. Promise?'

She was about say 'Cross my heart and hope to die,' but stopped herself just in time. 'I promise. Whatever is it?'

'That Supermarine has such a good safety record, and it was being flown by our most experienced pilot. The weather was perfect. So what caused the crash?' He lowered his voice further. 'Rumour has it those boffins had put some kind of extra wires onto the wings and tail plane, something to do with the research they're doing.'

'You think their wires actually *caused* the crash?' she gasped, the blood turning to ice in her veins. Could this be what Vic had meant when he'd said his friend's death was probably his fault? No wonder he'd been so devastated that day – no wonder he seemed to have disappeared from view. She hoped he hadn't left the Manor for good.

'There's been an inquiry, but we'll never know the answer. Everything's so bloody hush-hush up there.' The strain was marked on his face. 'If you pick anything up, will you tell me?'

'Of course. It's unlikely I'll hear anything because we're just kitchen staff, and they never seem to talk about work around us.'

'It'd just help clear my mind to know it wasn't anything Ray did.'

'Oh, I'm sure it wasn't anything like that. Not Ray.' But what if those wires *were* found to be the cause? Could Vic and his team be charged with manslaughter, or worse? The implications were so complicated and so terrible, she couldn't really get her head around it.

Mark poured the last of the champagne and they drank in silence. He took a breath, as though about to say something, then fell quiet again. Then he whispered, so quietly that she could hardly hear: 'I miss him so much, Kath.'

'It's only natural. It's a perfectly horrible thing to happen.'

'No, I mean I *really* miss him.'

'We all do, Mark. He was a good friend.'

'He wasn't *just* a friend, though.' A further long silence, and then, on an expiring breath: 'I *loved* him.'

'We all…'

'If only I could make you understand,' he cut in. 'I *really* loved him, Kath, don't you see? It's so difficult… and I can't even talk to anyone about it. I thought I wasn't normal, but then I found him and he's the same as me. *Was* the same as me…' His voice broke and then, to her dismay, his face crumpled and he began to cry.

She went to his side, wrapping her arms around him. He tried to push her away, muttering, 'Oh just leave me…' but she held him tightly until his shoulders stopped shaking and the sobs subsided.

Such loss, such sorrow. She hardly dared ask anything more for fear of upsetting him further, but the truth was slowly dawning: Mark's relationship with Ray *had* been more than simple friendship. But was it *love*, as most people understood it? Like love between a man and a woman? Was this what Nancy had meant by that word, the word Kath still found difficult to say, even in her head?

'Oh Mark,' she whispered, finally. 'You loved him, and I'm sure he loved you back, so you must try to cherish that memory for the rest of your life. And you *do* have someone to talk to. I don't properly understand, but that doesn't matter. I will never breathe a word to anyone else, and I will never judge you. But I will always be here.'

He pulled back and managed a weak smile.

'Thanks, sis.'

CHAPTER 14

All morning Vic had been in his room, fidgeting and unable to settle, gazing out of the window or trying to read. It felt as though he was about to go on trial. He'd written the letter and then noticed a silly spelling mistake, cursed loudly, crumpled the paper into a ball and thrown it across the room before penning it once more. The envelope was now tucked into his inside jacket pocket.

Just be yourself, Johnnie said. At times he sensed his friend as an almost physical presence, but more often it was just a voice. *Tell the truth as far as you can without breaking the law.* He meant the Official Secrets Act, of course. The penalty for breaking it was death, and more than once in the past few days Vic had actually wished himself dead. Living with this terrible guilt was almost unbearable.

At least you'll know, one way or the other, after this.

'Thanks for the reassurance, mate,' he said. Johnnie would have laughed at this point, and Vic would have felt a little better. But now here he was, racked with nerves as he waited with the rest of the team outside the boss's office, like schoolboys steeling themselves for a caning. That would have been painful, but at least it would have been over quickly. He'd have almost preferred it to the grilling they now faced.

Making it worse was the knowledge that there would be no familiar friendly face on the other side of that heavy oak door. Robert Watson-Watt, the man Vic had seen as his mentor, had recently left the Manor, having been promoted to a more senior position in the Air Ministry.

Vic remembered so clearly that very first day, being ushered in to the boss's study: thickly carpeted, with its leather-lined walls and carved woodwork, hard-buttoned leather sofas either side of a grand marble fireplace, and that wonderful view through stone-mullioned windows. What an inspiring vision Watson-Watt had outlined to him that afternoon, filling Vic with an almost religious fervour to use his knowledge for the protection of the country against air attack. The big man's genial, unfailingly positive presence was already much missed by everyone at the Manor.

In a typically impassioned farewell speech, he'd said: 'I cannot adequately put into words my admiration for you all. I brought you together – a motley bunch of brilliant brains here in this beautiful, magical place – but I had no real idea whether we could make this thing work. You have exceeded my expectations, more than I could ever have wished for. So while I leave you with a heavy heart, be assured that in my new role I will be fighting your cause to ensure that this work continues with more funding, more manpower, more recognition. For I firmly believe that our project will become one of the most important defences of our country, our culture and our lives. And without you, it would never have happened.'

Dr Rowe, who'd taken his place, was an altogether tougher kind of chief: more exacting, more controlling, and much less inclined to encourage the kind of wacky ideas that sometimes led to exciting developments.

A trio of stern-faced navy men had arrived earlier that morning, their uniforms glittering with braid, and had been cloistered with the new boss for a full hour. What could they have been talking about all this time? It was such a simple piece of kit, and they'd drilled no more than eight small fixing points in the fuselage. The tensions of the wires had all been checked and approved by navy engineers. How could it possibly have affected the flight so catastrophically?

At last, the heavy oak door opened. 'Come in, gentlemen,' Dr Rowe said.

The dreaded interrogation was, in the end, mercifully brief. They examined the diagrams that had been agreed with the naval engineers, including the fixing points for the dipole wires and the exact size of the holes they were allowed to drill. Vic described the plan for the day: three flights would be made at three, ten and then twenty miles out, passing Bawdsey to the north and then flying southwards towards Harwich. Nothing was said or asked about the purpose of the trials, or where Vic and Scott had been when the plane went down. Nothing was said or asked about Johnnie, almost as though he'd never been there.

'Got off lightly, didn't we?' Scott muttered as they went to find a cup of tea.

'We'll see,' was all Vic would allow. 'I can't understand why they went so easy on us.'

Half an hour later, when he was full of tea and cake and just beginning to wind down, there was a tap on his shoulder. 'Dr Rowe would like to see you in his office at five,' the secretary said.

'All of us?'

'Just you, Mr Mackensie.' His heart plummeted.

'What does the old man want now?' Scott said.

'My guts for garters, probably.'

He'd been expecting this moment, the 'I think it's best if we let you go back to your studies in Cambridge' moment, ever since the crash. As the remaining leader of this disastrous trial, it was only right, and the letter of resignation was in his inside pocket. He was ready for it – had even started to imagine himself back in the lab, cycling to his digs, walking the quads – and perhaps it would be for the best, since there was so much more development to be done to make their system workable, and he could not imagine continuing to lead the team without Johnnie.

He knocked.

'Ah, Mackensie. Come in and sit down. Tea?'

'I've had tea, thank you, sir.'

'Then you won't mind if I indulge?' Dr Rowe began to pour.

'I was going to say...' Vic reached into his pocket for the envelope and placed it on the table.

Rowe looked up sharply. 'What's this? Your resignation? Whatever are you thinking, man?' The tea missed the cup and a brown puddle formed on the table top. 'Dammit, Mackensie. Now you've made me spill the tea.'

He went to the telephone. 'Get someone to come and sort me out, would you, please? I've made such a mess.' Within seconds there was a knock and Kath, the girl from the Cliff Walk, entered with a cloth and began to clear up the puddle.

He'd thought about her quite a bit after that evening: how kind she'd been, how calming he'd found her presence, that sweet freckled face framed by startlingly red curls and the charming little gap between her teeth when she smiled; her soft Suffolk accent, and the astonishment she'd expressed when he told her about the Pulhamite. She was the only girl he'd actually talked to, properly, one to one, for as long as he could remember. What a shame he was going to leave just as he was getting to know her.

'Shall I bring a fresh pot, Dr Rowe?' she asked, avoiding Vic's eye.

'No, that'll be fine, thanks.'

She was gone as quickly as she'd arrived.

'Now, what's this nonsense about resigning?'

'I thought, sir, as I am the leader of the team... and if they find...'

'They won't, man, they won't. There is no way that kit could have caused a crash. Hopefully we'll know for certain when their engineers have finished their inspection of the wreck. But in the meantime, it's business as usual.'

Dr Rowe took a sip of his tea, fixing him with a piercing gaze. 'Though I have to say you're looking rather grey round the gills, Mackensie. Pale, for you I mean.' He took another sip, his chubby little finger curled in a clumsy attempt at daintiness. How Johnnie and Vic would have giggled together about it.

'I'm told you aren't coming down for meals. Is that correct?'

Rowe's unexpected sympathy almost tipped Vic over the edge. He took a deep breath, trying to control his voice. 'I miss Mr Palmer very much, sir.'

'Yes, quite so. Only to be expected. Now listen. I'm going to give you a week's pass. Perhaps go down to Hampshire for the funeral? It's on Friday, two o'clock. I'll organise a travel warrant. Maybe call in to see your father too? He lives south of London, doesn't he? Tunbridge Wells, if my memory serves. Then we'll see you back here next Monday, batteries recharged, and ready to resume your duties.'

'Thank you, sir. That is most generous.'

'And you can put that soggy envelope into the wastepaper basket on your way out, Mackensie.'

On his way back to his room he encountered Frank in the corridor. 'Any news on what caused that crash?' he asked, with a snide smirk.

'I dare say you'll find out soon enough,' Vic said, pushing past. He had no intention of sharing secrets with a snake.

Vic had just vague memories of the only other funeral he'd ever attended, of a great-uncle, long ago in India. It had involved a seemingly endless train journey to another city, then watching long into the night as men sang prayers and poured oil into the flames of an enormous bonfire. The following day they'd climbed onto an overcrowded boat where his mother and all the other women, dressed in dazzling white saris, wailed inconsolably as the ashes fluttered on the wind and settled on the brown river, leaving a long slick in their wake. After that they'd had to stay another two weeks among the crowd of mourning women, waiting for the big feast.

'Naanyi's soul has reached the afterlife,' his mother had said, as though that explained everything.

When, later, she'd stopped crying, he'd plucked up the courage to ask, 'What is the afterlife, Mother?'

'It's where our souls go when we die,' she'd said, tousling his hair in that way he hated.

'Is it nice there?'

'It is wonderful. Better than here on earth.'

The little village church in Petersfield was already filled to bursting. Johnnie must have been much loved. However much Vic wished that his friend was actually enjoying himself surrounded by angels on some blissful cloud, the sight of the coffin borne on the shoulders of six strong men, followed by his weeping wife and children, soon dispelled the vision. Inside that wooden box were the remains of a man who'd meant so much to people here on earth. How could he possibly be happy in heaven, when his passing had caused such sadness?

The words of the service were strange to his ears. As the vicar beseeched, 'O death, where is thy sting? O grave, where is thy victory?' he could hear Johnnie muttering *Search me, mate*, and had to conceal his smile in a handkerchief, which earned him a comforting squeeze on the arm from his neighbour. It felt even more bizarre when they all followed the coffin out into the churchyard – in silence, no wailing women here – and gathered round to watch it being lowered into a deep, straight-sided hole. The vicar began to intone once more: 'Man that is born of a woman hath but a short time to live, and is full of misery. He cometh up, and is cut down, like a flower.'

Not much consolation there, old friend, he thought to himself.

Lizzie and the children were each invited to throw a handful of earth. The process struck him as somehow primitive, and made him shudder. On balance, he preferred his mother's version of death. He slipped discreetly behind a tree, waiting for the right moment to pay his respects to Lizzie before heading back to the train station.

It was the boy who saw him first. In just a few months he'd grown into a young man bearing a disturbing resemblance to his father.

'It's Vikram, isn't it?' he said, holding out a hand. 'Dad's friend from work? I'm Christopher.'

Yes, I am Vikram. The man who may have caused your father's death.
'You've got a good memory, Christopher. When I came to visit, you kindly lent me your bedroom.'

'Come and say hello to Mum. She'll be pleased to see you.'

Lizzie was still surrounded by solicitous women in large hats, but as they approached she looked up with a brave smile, her face pale with strain. 'Mr Mackensie, how kind of you to come all this way.'

'Johnnie was such a good friend to me, Mrs Palmer.'

'You must come back to the house for tea and sandwiches, if you have the time?'

The little cottage was filled with people who all seemed to know each other, talking at the tops of their voices. Vic escaped to the garden with his cup of tea, wondering how soon he could politely slip away, and how he would get back to the station from here. Christopher approached, joining him on the mossy wall.

'Phew. It's quieter out here.'

'You okay?' Vic asked.

'Will be once they've all gone,' the boy said. 'Can't stand all this hugging business.'

'They're doing their best to show they care about you, and about your father.'

'S'pose so.'

They paused, listening to a bird in the tree above them. 'Is that a blackbird?'

'A robin, I think.'

'Your father was good at birds. He taught me the difference between seagulls and terns.'

'He was good at lots of things.'

'That's true. He was a great man, Christopher, very kind and very clever, two virtues that don't usually go together.' The boy's gaze dropped to the ground, and Vic feared he might cry. 'I'm so sorry. I always say the wrong thing.'

'It's all right.' A longer pause. 'He liked you too, you know? He told us you were the cleverest person he'd ever met, and that working with you sort of made up for being away from us for so long, and what you were doing together would make our country safer. He said that your inventions were going to protect us, to make sure me and Beth had a free country to live in, and that was why it was so vital and why we had to forgive him for not being here much.'

'I am very touched, Christopher. Thank you.'

'You will carry on, won't you? Even though he's gone?'

'It'll be much harder without your father, but I'll do my best.'

How could he not carry on, with these expectations behind him? Johnnie's precious boy, who would, please God, never be old enough to fight, was depending on him. This brief conversation had reminded him why the work was so important. Thank heavens Dr Rowe's spilled tea had spoiled his resignation letter.

He didn't want to give up, after all.

When he got back to Bawdsey he learned the inquiry had concluded that the cause of the crash was a catastrophic failure of the airframe. The IFF fixings had been ruled out as a cause. The plane had literally broken up in the air and plunged into the sea. Nothing, not even the skill and experience of Captain Burrows, could have saved them.

He ran to his room and lay on Johnnie's bed, weeping with relief and loneliness. But not for long: there was a knock on the door, and Scott calling: 'Mac, are you in there? Shake a leg. The boss wants a briefing, right now.' Vic washed his face in cold water and dashed down to find seven men already in the office: both the IFF research teams, including Frank Wilkinson.

'Listen up, chaps. We've given up on the Sudetenland, and whatever that joker Chamberlain says, we can be sure our friend Mr Hitler will be rubbing his hands with glee. He won't stop there. It'll be Belgium next, and then he'll be right on our doorstep. There is much to do and so little time to do it. IFF is a key part of our defences, and you fellows here are among the best brains in the country. The system developed by Mr Mackensie and his late partner Mr Palmer proved its credentials at the trial a few weeks ago, but to make it work for larger numbers we need elements of the powered transmitter being trialled by Mr Wilkinson's team' – he nodded towards Frank – 'so I suggest you work together to refine it.'

Scott caught Vic's glance with the slightest of raised eyebrows. Vic shuddered inwardly as he saw Frank's face lit with triumph. It was a look he'd often seen on the face of Tomkins, the bully of the class at school, for whom Vic was the usual target. But one day, it had turned out differently.

Tomkins had wrestled him to the ground. 'Eat the earth, Mackensie. That's all your kind are good for.' The boy was straddling him, pressing down on the back of his head so that his face was mashed into the grass. Another shove. 'Go on, eat it.'

The boy was just too heavy, too strong, trapping him to the ground. But as he struggled, he realised his legs were free. If he kicked his feet backwards, hard enough… He tried it once and failed, earning himself another punch. He tried again, harder, higher, whipping up his heels as fast as he could. They met something soft. Tomkins groaned and fell to the ground, writhing and clutching his crotch.

'You little bastard, Mackensie. I'll get you for this,' he shouted, as Vic ran for it. But he never did. And there was no more bullying.

Working with Frank, there would be two choices: eat dirt, or kick him where it hurt.

*

Numbers of RAF staff at the Manor grew even further. The training school for RDF – radio direction finding – operators was expanding fast. Until now most of the new trainees had been men, but before he left Robert Watson-Watt had recruited three women from the secretarial staff. Although all the men had been sceptical, the women had quickly proved excellent at the task, being both meticulously precise and also patient with the delicate fine-tuning required.

As more women arrived, the atmosphere at the Manor subtly shifted. Sunday evening variety shows were replaced with dances, and Frank, who fancied himself a ladies' man, never missed the opportunity to brag about his conquests each Monday morning. Although, superficially, the two teams had begun to work well together, Vic could sense tensions growing.

It was Scott who mentioned it first. He'd overheard some of the girls complaining about Frank's 'sleazy' ways – the very word they'd used – and had suggested a plan for 'bringing him down a peg or two'. At first Vic flatly refused – the combination of music, dancing and having to make conversation with girls was his idea of hell – but following a bad-tempered team meeting at which Frank was being particularly odious, he reluctantly agreed.

Good on you, Mac. Tame that snake before he bites, Johnnie whispered.

That following Sunday he dressed in his best suit – *great heavens, if you could see me now, Johnnie boy* – and joined Scott in the bar for a couple of stiff whiskies before following the sound of jazz being played at top volume on a wind-up gramophone in the main hall. Vic had never witnessed such a scene before: fully a hundred people, men and women, jiggling about on the dance floor, doing strange things with their arms and legs. It terrified him. The touch of Scott's hand on his back propelled him forward. At the centre was Frank, showing off his best moves, encircled by ten or twelve of the most glamorous girls fawning over him, giggling and dancing suggestively. He was revelling in the attention.

As soon as Vic and Scott appeared those same girls shrieked with apparent delight, abandoning Frank. Vic was led into the centre of the dance floor. Following their instructions, he began awkwardly to move his feet and arms about, taking the hand of one girl then being twirled along to another, while the others called out encouragingly; 'Ooh Vic Mackensie, what a smooth operator,' one proclaimed. 'Doesn't he just make a girl swoon?' another said, and 'Where have you been hiding, handsome?' Plentiful kisses were planted on his cheeks, the whisky warmed his stomach and his feet felt as though they were gliding all by themselves. It was like a crazy dream, and after a few moments he realised that he was actually enjoying himself.

From the corner of his eye, he spied Frank sloping away from the dance floor. When he'd gone, Scott gave the thumbs up.

'You certainly proved a hit with the girls last night,' Frank said in a tone of new respect the following morning. 'You'll have to let the rest of us into your secret.' Vic and Scott exchanged triumphant glances. Never again did Frank brag about his conquests.

But the professional rivalry continued; in fact, it seemed to worsen as the weeks went by. Vic would see Frank at the bar, standing rounds of drinks for the rest of the team, obviously trying to buy their loyalty. And it seemed to work – whenever there was a dispute about the direction in which to take the research next, Vic's opinion was often sidelined. His sole supporter was Scotty.

That was what had happened a couple of weeks previously. Frank and the others had been determined to follow a particular route. Vic had disagreed, but was outvoted. Since then the project had become completely bogged down. Whatever they tried, they could not make the system work.

Then Dr Rowe announced that he would be visiting in two days' time, 'just to see how you fellows are getting on.'

Frank was clearly rattled. 'Right, let's get to it, chaps. We've got to get this effing thing right, or we'll be for the high jump,' he said. But despite long hours of recalculation and recalibrations, they couldn't make the system operate consistently. Vic tried once more to suggest that they try his original proposal, but once again Frank dismissed it. 'It's too late, Mac. No time.'

Later, as he trudged despondently through the gardens, barely noticing the drizzle soaking through his clothes as he struggled to find a way of turning the problem round, Vic heard a familiar voice. *Remember what you told me about the gardener who used to check your bungalow for snakes? Never approach from the front, he said. It'll rear up and strike. The best way of snaring a snake is to take it unawares and grasp it behind the head, where it can't reach you.*

Vic almost wept with relief. Of course. *Thanks, Johnnie.* Now he knew exactly what to do.

Late into the night he worked on the problem. Taking his own starting point, he recalculated the mathematical model and concluded once more that he'd been right. Yes, it would work.

The following evening he confided in Scotty, and the two of them returned to the lab after supper to build a completely new version of the system. As dawn rose they tested it, and it worked. From the outside, the equipment was indistinguishable from the faulty kit, which they hid away in a cupboard, leaving theirs on the bench.

An hour later, Frank and the rest of the team arrived in the lab, accompanied by Dr Rowe. 'Right, chaps. Tell me how far you've got with this little baby.'

Frank looked uncomfortable, his eyes casting around the room for support.

'Well, man? What is it?'

'We've been having a little difficulty...'

Dr Rowe huffed irritably. 'Show me how far you've got, then.'

Frank plugged the system into the mains and began to explain how the test *should* work, the test that had so far failed each time. 'You see, sir...' he began.

'For Christ's sake man, just get on with it,' Rowe snapped.

Sweat broke out on Frank's brow and his hands trembled as he turned the system on. The line on the screen flickered into life. 'Operate friendly craft signal,' he said, flicking another switch. This was the moment when the line should start to show a deep double V that would be clearly visible on the screens installed into other Allied forces' planes nearby.

After a few seconds the line quivered and took a sharp downward dive, and then another. The 'friend or foe' signal was clear for all to see. Frank's mouth gaped open for several seconds before recomposing into a triumphant grin as the room erupted in spontaneous applause.

Dr Rowe was circling the room, shaking hands with everyone. 'Good work, chaps. Soon be ready for testing in the field, then?'

After he'd gone, Frank took out a handkerchief and wiped his brow. 'Bloody hell,' he said. 'That was a stroke of luck.'

'Not luck, Frank,' Vic said, his heart hammering in his chest. This was the moment of confrontation, and he had no idea how Frank would respond. He went to the cupboard, opening the door. 'This is the old kit. The set on the table, the one that works, is ours, reconfigured and recalibrated by Scott and me to the mathematical model that you dismissed when we suggested it two weeks ago.'

He would remember for a very long time afterwards the expression of utter astonishment and shock on Frank's face. The man began to bluster, but it was too late. Everyone ignored him, gathering around Vic as he unfolded several sheets of paper showing his calculations.

'You're an effing genius, Mac,' one said.

Much later that evening, just as he was preparing for bed, there was a knock on Vic's door. It was Frank.

'I've come to thank you, Mac,' he said. 'For saving our bloody bacon. Can I buy you a drink?'

The gall of the man, trying to buy his favour with a drink. 'It's been a long day, so not for me, thank you.'

'No hard feelings?'

This was the moment Vic had been waiting for – his opportunity to tame the snake forever.

'Only on three conditions,' he said, trying to keep the tremor from his voice. 'Firstly, you have to listen to other people's views as well as your own, in future.'

Frank ventured a conciliatory smile. 'Point taken, old man.'

Vic pressed on. 'Second. You never, *ever* dare to question my loyalty to this country.' The smile disappeared.

'And third, if I ever, *ever* hear you suggesting that I was anything to do with that leak…'

A long moment passed. Vic felt his fury rising.

'*Look* at me, man, if you've got the guts. Look me in the eye and swear you will never say anything against me or try to ruin my reputation, ever again.'

Frank took a breath and cleared his throat. 'It's just that…'

'No excuses. I want an apology. Here. *Now.*' Vic's legs were shaking. He'd never been so angry.

Frank began to mutter. 'Everyone knows you're so bloody brilliant, I thought nothing could touch you. I was jealous, I suppose…'

'You're a grown man, Frank. Time to start acting like one.'

At last Frank looked up. Green eyes met brown for a long moment. 'You're right, mate. I'm sorry.'

Vic took a deep breath, blinking away the tears of relief that had unaccountably, embarrassingly, begun to flood his eyes. 'Okay. You give me your word? If you don't, I'll spill the beans to Rowe about that test you so "successfully demonstrated" today.'

Frank nodded and held out his hand.

After a second, Vic reciprocated.

The spirit of co-operation in the team improved beyond all recognition. Within a few months they had developed a new, compact 'powered' system, ready for testing. A trial at RAF Martlesham proved successful. Immediately they began work on Mark II and Mark III versions. 'Identification, Friend or Foe' was ready for installation in all RAF aircraft.

As they read in the newspapers about pogroms against Jewish people and the thousands of shops and synagogues that were smashed, looted and burned, the prospect of war seemed to become even more real. Although the violence was attributed to 'right-wing thugs', no one doubted that it was sanctioned by Hitler. And how could anyone expect such a man to abide by the terms of the so-called 'peace with honour' enshrined in the Munich Agreement?

'Not worth the paper the bloody thing's printed on,' Vic's father muttered over Christmas dinner. Aunt Vera, although still gaunt, had recovered sufficiently from her unspecified disease to cook the festive meal this year. 'I hope you clever chaps get that death ray machine working damned soon, or we'll be in for it.'

'Language, dear,' his aunt tutted mildly.

'Huh. That'll be the least of our worries,' his father retorted. 'We'll all be talking German if they have their way.'

CHAPTER 15

'Look at you,' she shouted, throwing her arms around him. 'Ma, Pa, it's Mark!'

'You don't have to tell the whole ruddy street, sis,' he said, shrugging her off. 'Are you going to let me in?'

Where was the sallow-faced brother who'd left for RAF training just a few months ago? Here, home for Christmas, was a broad-shouldered man, tanned and handsome in his blue-grey uniform, who seemed to have grown at least six inches since she'd last seen him. On his upper lip, as though in compensation for the brutal haircut, grew a moustache, immaculately shaved and shaped just as Ray's used to be.

'Heavens, lad. RAF life seems to be suiting you,' Pa said, slapping his son on the back. 'Come in, come in. Shall we open a beer?'

He was shy at first and curiously formal, shifting in his seat and then padding about like a lion in a cage. Ma sent him upstairs to change out of his uniform. 'You look like someone else in that jacket,' she said, laughing, 'I want my scruffy son back.' Later, after a few beers, he kicked off his shoes and leaned back, putting his feet on the coffee table – no one told him off – and began to talk.

'They never tell you how hard it is at first,' he said. 'All those rules, all that discipline, having to be perfect. Those corporals are mean bastards, too, pulling you up for everything, right from the start, when you haven't even worked out what's up and what is down. I was on the point of quitting several times, as were some of the others. But I suppose it's your pride that keeps you going, and the fear of failing. Anyhow, I stuck it out and passed with good marks.' He sat up, bracing his shoulders, chin high. 'You see before you Aircraftman Motts Number Two Class.'

'Cheers to that,' Pa said. 'Well done, son. We're proud of you.'

'When do you start flying?' Kath asked.

'Cripes, not for ages,' he replied quickly, with a glance at his mother. 'You have to do all sorts of physical tests and written exams, and only the best make it through. But my eyesight is good enough, they say, so that's a start.'

'You're enjoying it, that's the main thing, isn't it?' Maggie said.

'Now I've got used to the discipline, and I'm finding my place,' he said. 'Still hard work, but we play hard too.'

'I hope you are behaving yourself, Mark?'

'We have a good time, Ma. That's all you need to know.' Kath returned his glance with a smile. He seemed to be well on the way to recovery.

They sat up late together, just as they had the night before he left.

'It sounds like hell, the way you talk about it. Freezing barracks, long runs in the rain, horrible food and beastly bosses. Where's the fun in that?'

He laughed, levering the top off another beer bottle. 'It's not *fun*, exactly. It's bloody hard work, most of the time.'

'But from the way you've been talking, you seem to be enjoying it. I'd be running for cover and the comforts of home.'

He took a long swig and gave a deep sigh. 'It's hard to explain, really. You wouldn't understand.'

'Try me.'

'First, it's been good to get away from here and all the sadness, you know, about Ray?'

'That I do understand. You look so much better than when you left.'

'Also, it's very satisfying getting fitter and stronger. I never knew I had all these muscles in my body.' He took another swig. 'Go on, Kath. Have another. Keep me company.'

She opened a bottle to please him, to keep the conversation going.

'But there's another thing, and it's harder to put a finger on… now I feel as though I have a proper purpose.'

'But you had a purpose before. You've always worked hard, Mark.'

'This is real, Kath. It's serious. They won't be needing those trenches they've dug in the Crescent, 'cos we're not going to be invaded from the sea, not any time soon. The next war – and there will be a war, despite what our mealy-mouthed politicians are saying – will be in the air. The Germans have hundreds of bombers and fighters, thousands even, and at the moment we wouldn't stand a gnat's chance. They could bomb us into oblivion. But we're getting ready. We're building planes like there's no tomorrow, and training hundreds of pilots…'

She'd never heard him talk like this before. 'You said it'd be ages before you start flying.'

'That was just to reassure Ma. I start training after Christmas.'

'That's exciting. And terrifying.' Now she wished he hadn't told her.

'I can't wait, Kath. I just can't bloody wait. We're going to show those ruddy Germans.'

'You will be careful, Mark?'

He shook his head. 'It's not a matter of being careful, Kath. You can be the most skilled pilot ever, but much of it is down to luck. Look at what happened to Ray.'

'Did they ever find out what caused that crash?'

'Airframe failure.'

'I don't understand.'

'Nor do I. All they're saying is that for some reason the structure of the plane failed, which is why it broke up and fell into the sea. There was nothing Ray could have done.'

'Whose fault would that have been? Surely the engineers should have picked up the problem?'

'I'm not sure it was anyone's fault. These things aren't always obvious on inspection. Like I said, it was just bad luck.'

From the fact that Vic had reappeared for meals and seemed to be back at work as normal, Kath assumed he had probably been exonerated from any blame. The few times she'd served him at lunch he'd been friendly, although more subdued than normal, quite thin and pale. She'd concocted some extra-special meat-free meals to try to encourage him to eat, and felt satisfied to see that his appetite was slowly returning.

But nothing could alter the fact that both Johnnie and Ray were gone, forever. 'I'm so sorry, Mark,' she said.

'It's fine, honestly, sis. Getting away has been good for me. I'll always love him, but…' He upended the bottle. 'I've made new friends. There are plenty of men like me in the forces and no one questions our choices, so long as we're discreet. Life is good.'

As they clinked glasses he smiled, happier than she'd seen him for ages. She was beginning to understand. Her brother was still the same person she'd always known, now grown into a remarkable, brave and wonderful young man.

As winter drew on and turned into spring, the news became ever more depressing and Kath felt increasingly frustrated. Mark was out there doing something really important, and she was working in a kitchen. She'd been promoted to pastry chef, but catering for so many hungry mouths was a daily slog and everyone had to muck in. The scientists, engineers, RAF officers and administrative teams based at the Manor consumed twenty loaves of bread, six Victoria sponges, five trays of carrot cake – and more than a hundred biscuits every day. She was good at her job and well respected by the other kitchen staff, but every day was much the same as the last.

Yet each day as she stood on the beach waiting for the ferry, she felt grateful to work in such beautiful surroundings. To her left, upriver, yachts and fishing boats rested peacefully on their moorings, switching direction with each turn of the tide. To her right, the calm waters of the river met the sea in a tumble of white horses. And straight ahead were the dark pines through which it was just possible to see, on the bluff rising behind them, the fairy-tale towers of the Manor. However grumpy she might have felt about the thought of another day's slog in the kitchens, the sight nearly always lifted her spirits.

Charlie the ferryman was never short of a cheerful quip, even in the worst of weather: 'Cheer up, girl, it might never happen,' or 'How's the boyfriend?' Or he might whistle the tune of a popular song, 'Red Sails in the Sunset', or 'The Biggest Aspidistra in the World'.

But on this bright, windy April day she struggled to find a smile even for Charlie. She was miserable and confused. Billy Bishop was back in town, his training course completed, waiting for his first posting as an RAF mechanic. They'd met in the pub one evening, and he'd invited her to the cinema. She had nothing better to do, so she agreed. When the lights went down he'd started kissing her and after resisting at first, she thought, *what the hell*, and kissed him back. It was lovely, just like old times. But then it had all gone horribly wrong: he'd wanted more, and kept running his hand up her leg. 'Stop it, Billy. You're not even my boyfriend,' she whispered, pushing him away. But each time they'd gone back to kissing, she'd feel his hand creeping back. 'I said *no*, Billy,' she said again, to which he'd grumpily retorted, 'Stop leading me on, then, you little minx.' He ignored her for the rest of the film, and then left the cinema without a word.

She felt furious with herself for agreeing to go with him in the first place. Why was she drawn back, each time, when she knew it would never lead to anything? He was a snappy dresser, sophisticated, and a show-off. He was a fund of good jokes. But beyond that they had absolutely nothing in common.

She wasn't short of other offers for dates, but they were usually pimply boys of her own age, chain-smoking and desperately trying to look older by attempting to grow ridiculous moustaches. Somehow none of them matched up to Billy Bishop for glamour. Joan was no fun any more; she seemed to spend every evening and weekend with Sam, and many of their other friends had left the town, either for college or for work. Some had even got married and were already producing children.

There must be more to life than this?

The ferry had just cast off from the Felixstowe side when she caught sight of a slight figure running down the shingle, clasping a shopping bag.

'Look out, Charlie,' she said. 'You've got another customer.'

'Ruddy hell,' he muttered, crashing the engine into reverse and swinging the boat around against a fierce tide.

As they crunched back onto the shingle she recognised the figure at once: it was Vic Mackensie.

'Thanks for waiting,' he panted, clambering into the boat. He missed his footing, dropped the bag and almost crashed into Kath before steadying himself with a hand on the gunwale. As he sat down, flustered and apologetic, she saw that he'd misjudged the waves.

'Hello again,' she said. 'Been enjoying the delights of the Felixstowe shops?'

'Oh, just a few little things,' he said, with an embarrassed shrug. 'Sorry to hold you up.' He peered down at his soaking shoes. 'Not sure how I manage it, but I do it every time.'

'Takes great skill,' she said, and was rewarded with a smile.

When they arrived on the other side he climbed off first and offered a hand as she jumped down onto the beach.

'Thanks,' she said, leaping well away from the water's edge. 'Watch your feet,' she called, dragging him away from the tideline.

'I'm already so wet it doesn't matter,' he said, laughing. 'I've just bought myself some more socks anyway.'

They began to walk together, past the guardhouse and through the whispering pines. 'It's got a sort of magic, this place, don't you

think?' she said. 'As though it's hiding secrets?' *Secrets.* What an idiot.
'Oh, I didn't mean…'

'No, I know…'

'I'm sorry…'

'It's nothing.'

They reached the front of the Manor. 'I have to go this way.' She
pointed to the gate leading to the rear entrance.

He paused. 'I wondered…'

She waited.

'Ermm… you know… when we met before?'

She shuffled her feet, conscious that she was already late.

'I mentioned the gardens?'

'Yes, you told me they were rather beautiful.'

'They're not in full flower yet, of course.'

'I'm sure, but look… I've got to get to work.'

'Of course, of course,' he said, face down, shuffling his feet. And
then, 'I could show you later, perhaps?'

'I don't get off till five.'

'Oh well, okay then… silly idea. Sorry.'

'Don't be sorry,' she said. 'It's a nice idea.'

He looked up at her then, his face brightening. 'Really?'

'Meet me at the back door by the dining room?'

'Ah yes, good. Perfect, in fact. Ermm…' He cleared his throat.
'I'll see you there, then.'

Whatever was she doing, agreeing to meet this strange, awkward
fellow? Why on earth would a brainy boffin be the slightest bit
interested in a kitchen girl? Although it was hard to tell, he must
be at least five years older than her, but so diffident that he often
struggled to string a sentence together. Besides, she had no interest
in flowers: she could barely tell a dandelion from a daisy. How on
earth would they be able to hold a conversation about gardens?

She had already decided to make some excuse about having to get
home after all when, at five minutes to five, she caught a glimpse of

him pacing the lawn outside the dining-room windows, and didn't have the heart to turn him down.

Two hours later, as she clambered on to the ferry once more and turned to wave goodbye, she smiled to herself. What a curious couple of hours it had turned out to be; so much more interesting than she'd ever imagined.

It was uncomfortable at first, rather as she'd expected. He was even more tongue-tied than before, and she couldn't think of anything to fill the silences. For a while they'd just walked together without saying anything. He led her through a dark tunnel that emerged into an extraordinary space, a deep, perfectly round dip in the landscape, its sloping sides brilliant with bright yellow daffodils (she knew that much) dazzling in the evening sunshine.

'Wow,' she said. 'That's quite a sight.'

'You know the Martello towers?'

She nodded. She'd always known, somehow, that those strange, windowless round towers dotted along the coastline had been built a century before as defences against Napoleon but had never been put to the test. Now they were neglected and slowly disintegrating, shrubs and grass growing out of roofs and walls.

'There used to be one here too, but they demolished it and built this garden in the foundations.'

The space where the great tower used to stand made a perfect sunken garden, protected from the wind. The paths and flowerbeds were weed-ridden and untidy now, but somehow all the more interesting for that. She remembered, in her childhood, reading a book about children who went through a door and discovered a long-neglected garden which they helped back to life. This place had something of that magic, she felt, as they walked the circular path around the base. She could almost feel her fingers itching to get to work: it would take so little to clear the grass strangling that rose bush, or to pull the weeds out of the gravel beneath her feet.

'It's beautiful,' she said.

'I'm glad you like it.' His smile this time was open and true, not defensive or self-deprecating. 'Hardly anyone else seems to come here.'

'Did you ever read a book called *The Secret Garden*? A children's book?'

He frowned and shook his head. 'I don't recall it.'

As they walked onwards she told him the story and he said he was sure he'd have remembered it had he read it. She offered to get it out of the library next time she was there, and he laughed, saying all the lads would tease him for reading a children's book, and she said he would just have to read it under the covers with a torch like she used to. All their initial awkwardness seemed to disappear.

Another tunnel led into a long rectangular garden, bounded on one side by a tall wall along which had been trained fruit trees. The branches, just coming into blossom, looked as though they were decorated with lace. 'The trees like the warmth of the wall, so they come out early,' he said. 'Those old gardeners knew what they were doing.'

In the centre, either side of a pond, were ranged stone columns supporting a rustic wooden frame covered with a tangle of rose bushes, just coming into leaf. The pond itself was choked with weeds, but even from a distance they could see the surface of the water was disturbed.

'Look,' he cried, peering into the water. 'Tadpoles. And some of them are nearly frogs.'

She approached cautiously, recalling the slimy spawn her brother and his friends used to delight in throwing at each other, and sometimes at her. She remembered, too, trying to memorise a diagram describing the life cycle of the frog for her science exam. As she knelt beside Vic watching the tiny creatures nibbling at the sides of the pond and struggling to climb onto the lily pads, she began to marvel at these strange and rather wonderful little scraps of life.

At the far end of the pond strutted a seagull, one of those large grey ones that always seemed to gather on the fields after ploughing. Every now and again it would stop and tilt its head, peering greedily at the tiny animals struggling at the edges of the pond. No doubt he would make a feast of any that eventually dared to climb out.

He followed her gaze and seemed to read her thoughts: 'Plucky little blighters, aren't they? Only a very few will make it to adulthood. Which is why they have so many in the first place.' He stood and offered his hand to help her up. It was surprisingly warm and soft. 'Come on. There's one last wonder to show you before it gets dark.'

The hinges of the ornate cast-iron gate set in the side of the wall groaned reluctantly as he pushed it wide and they entered a vast walled area with long narrow beds, some filled with weeds but others newly raked and sowed, with labels at each end of the lines. This was more familiar; Kath had helped Pa at his allotment for many years, until she'd grown old enough to refuse. But this space was the size of all the allotments put together, perhaps even more. It was the biggest kitchen garden she'd ever seen.

All along the walls on the opposite side were tumbledown greenhouses, and in the centre stood a tall, ornate wooden structure that had clearly once been painted white, but was now looking sadly in need of attention. Not of scrap of glass remained in its sides or roof.

'That was the lemonry,' Vic said.

'Do they really grow lemons?'

'Not any more, they don't.'

'Do you remember telling me about it when we met on the Cliff Path that day?'

'Did I really? I was in such a state.'

'You were, a bit.'

'Talking to you helped, you know.'

'I'm glad.'

'It's just that...'

'Just that...?'

'You remind me of him a bit. You're so positive, like him.'

'Him?'

'The friend I'd lost that day. My best friend.'

She struggled for something to say that wouldn't make him feel worse, and then remembered Ma talking about visiting a newly widowed friend: 'We spent an hour talking about him and at the end she thanked me, because the worst thing is when people never even mention his name, as though he's been completely forgotten.'

'How do I remind you of him?' she asked now.

He sighed. 'It's just... Oh, I don't know. He was always so optimistic. He loved life and he had such a loving family. Two charming children. I miss him so much.'

'Clever too, I assume?' she coaxed.

'Not only clever, but thoughtful, you know...?' He tailed off, and she waited. 'He'd think around a problem rather than just charging in. We made a good team.' Vic looked up at the sky, as though he could see his friend there.

'I'm so sorry. You must miss him horribly,' she said, moved by his obvious distress.

A long pause, and then, 'Don't think me crazy, but sometimes I think he's still here. He talks to me.'

Kath was momentarily silenced. Was this man some kind of ghost-believing nutter? She tried to formulate a sensible response and came out with the first thing that came into her head. 'Do you believe in souls?'

He laughed, although she couldn't see what was funny. 'Oh yes, Hindus are very keen on the afterlife,' he said. 'It's a kind of bargain. Behave well in this life and you will rise through the ranks in the next one.'

'And if you're bad?'

'You come back to earth as a dog, or a worm.'

Her turn to laugh, now. 'Or a frog? Fancy having to fight with so many others and then getting eaten just as soon as you managed to clamber out of the water.'

'Do *you*?'

'Do I what?'

'Believe in souls?'

'D'you know, I don't think anyone has ever asked me that. I don't believe in ghosts, if that's what you mean. But souls? I suppose in the vague way that we all believe in some kind of God, mostly because it's just too horrible to imagine there isn't some kind of afterlife, that we just go pop like a lightbulb when we die. So yes, I think I do believe in souls, although exactly what it feels like being just a soul without a body is pretty hard to imagine.' It was the longest speech she remembered ever making, and very probably the most curious and fascinating conversation she'd had for a very long time. The clock on the stable block chimed seven. Two hours seemed to have passed in minutes.

'Heavens, is that the time already? I've got to get back for supper. Thank you for showing me the gardens. I've enjoyed it.'

'Me too. Makes such a change from talking shop.' A pause. 'Would you... erm...' He tried again. 'Would you, perhaps... another day...?'

'That'd be lovely,' she said.

Over the coming days they exchanged smiles at mealtimes but he said nothing more, and she began to wonder whether he'd had second thoughts. She wasn't even sure herself. He'd shown no sign of wanting anything other than to walk and talk. Perhaps it was, as he'd said, that he'd enjoyed her company, nothing more. She'd certainly enjoyed the conversation, once they got going. He was so interesting, so well informed and so clever. So different from anyone else she knew. Despite his shyness, she felt relaxed in his company; and that smile, when it came, was enough to melt anyone's heart.

So when, two weeks later, he'd passed her a note at the serving table – *This evening, same time?* – her heart seemed to lift. This time they went to the Cliff Path. The wind was from the west, he said, so it would be sheltered there. He was right. They sat in one of the concrete niches and she produced the carrot cake that she'd wrapped carefully in her shoulder bag.

'My favourite. What a treat,' he said.

'I made it.'

'It's the best carrot cake I've ever tasted. You're a genius.'

'You're the genius, Vic.' Then she remembered. 'And where did you learn to play the piano like that?'

'You heard me?'

'A while ago, yes. I hid behind a door to listen.'

'You sneaky thing.'

She laughed. 'You were playing some jazzy number and I just had to hear it to the end. Then you played something classical, really sad.'

'Chopin, probably. It makes me sad too, but it's cathartic, you know?'

She hadn't a clue what that meant, so said nothing.

'It's so peaceful. I love it here,' he said after a moment.

'I wish it could always be like this.'

'Me too.'

'I envy you, you know, doing something positive to defend our country, having a real purpose,' she said. 'My brother is doing his bit, out there flying his fighter planes. I wish there was more I could do.'

'What you do is important, too.'

She laughed. 'That's what you said before. *The human race wouldn't exist without food.*'

'I said that?'

'You did.'

'How profound.' It wasn't always easy to tell whether he was joking or not, but he was smiling. They watched the clouds tinged with pink from the sunset behind them, just as before.

'Seriously, though, I wish I could do something more...' She struggled for the word. 'Purposeful, important. I don't know. That would make a real difference.'

'You could join the WAAFs,' he said, quite suddenly.

'The waffs? What on earth's that?'

'The Women's Auxiliary Air Force. It's just been announced.'

'You really think they'd have me?'

'As a WAAF, yes. You're clever and have a strong personality. But it'd more likely be support work. Driving trucks, that sort of thing.'

'I can't drive.'

'Doesn't matter, they'd train you.'

'Doesn't really appeal,' she said.

'I suppose you might even get involved in the kind of work I'm doing. The boss, Watson-Watt, says women are better operators than men.'

He had her full attention now. 'Better at what?'

'I can't tell you much, but if it comes to war what we've been developing will help our pilots find their targets more efficiently and save us from air attacks.'

She thought of Mark. 'Will it make it *safer* for them, too?'

'Almost certainly,' he said.

'Then I'd definitely be up for that. But wouldn't I need qualifications?'

'Did you study physics and geometry at school?'

'Up to Leaving Cert.'

'Then sign up, and if they give you the chance to apply for RDF operator, or "special duties", then go for it.'

'I could work here?'

'Not necessarily. You could be posted anywhere all over the country.' This was a blow. She couldn't imagine Ma being very happy about her leaving home, too.

'How old do you have to be?' she asked.

'I expect they'll issue some kind of information soon enough. If I find out, I'll let you know.'

Later, she would wonder what had come over her. Gratitude, perhaps, for believing she was clever enough to get involved in his kind of work; for the notion that she could really do something useful? For loving her carrot cake, and calling her a genius? For his quiet, thoughtful presence? His sweet, shy smile? Whatever it was, she felt a sudden wave of affection, and leaned in to plant a kiss on his cheek.

CHAPTER 16

That night Vic relived the moment over and over, feeling the touch of her lips on his cheek, the flush that had spread hotly up his neck and over his face.

If only he'd had the courage to put his arm around her, perhaps even to kiss her on the lips, but he'd been so confused, consumed with his own discomfiture, that he hadn't had a clue what to do next. How were you supposed to sense whether a girl was interested? It was all such a mystery.

News got round, of course. You can't go walking in the gardens with a girl, twice, without expecting someone to notice. Work secrets might be watertight, but everything else was fair game.

'Got a new girlfriend, have we?' Frank whispered in the lunch queue the following day.

'She's not a…'

'Pretty little thing, nice curls. Bit young for you, perhaps?'

Vic said nothing, moving forward to collect his plate. Best not to fuel the fire.

Work was busier than ever. Now, dotted all around the south and east coasts of England, more than twenty stations operated a twenty-four-hour, seven-day-a-week watch, with their results communicated to a central base at Stanmore. Planes could now be tracked from a hundred and fifty miles, and new wavelengths were being trialled so that even the low-flying craft that had previously proved so elusive could now be detected. Flocks of birds sometimes triggered alarm, but the operators became skilled at recognising the difference between true and false echoes.

Vic's special pride and joy, the IFF Mark II, was already installed in hundreds of planes, allowing them to be distinguished from enemy craft. An improved version, the Mark III, was being tested. There was much more to be done, of course, and Dr Rowe was still driving the boffins to come up with better solutions, but at least they had the satisfaction of knowing that Britain's air defences were no longer dependent on primitive concrete 'dishes' angled at the sky in vain hopes of picking up the sound of an aircraft before you saw it.

At Bawdsey, the transmitter block was in operation and four soaring masts, each nearly half the height of the Eiffel Tower, were in the final stages of testing. The IFF Mark III transmitters had been installed at the top of one of the masts, but still needed fine calibration. The engineers had been up the mast several times, but still the glitches continued.

Dr Rowe was becoming impatient. 'What seems to be the problem?' he asked, at the team meeting.

'The calibration of the transmitting kit, sir,' Frank volunteered. 'On the mast.'

'Then get someone to fix it,' was the terse reply.

'The engineers...'

'I don't want excuses, Wilkinson,' Dr Rowe interrupted. 'I've seen them up there every day, and whatever they're doing isn't working. One of you lot will have to go and have a look. Report back to me once you've done it.'

'Bloody hell,' someone muttered, after he'd gone.

The team shared shocked glances. 'So who's it going to be, then?' another asked.

'Frank? It's your baby.' He was the obvious choice, with his particular sphere of expertise.

'Sorry, folks,' he said, quickly. 'But that stew they served last night has given me a dicky tummy. You wouldn't want to be anywhere below me for the next twenty-four hours,' he added, to much laughter.

Vic's own stomach clenched into painful knots. 'I'm really not good at heights,' he muttered, looking at Scott.

'Me neither,' Scott said.

There was a momentary impasse, until someone suggested: 'Why don't we toss for it?'

For the first time in weeks he heard Johnnie's voice. *Go for it, Vic. Prove yourself to Frank and the rest, once and for all.*

Get lost, old mate, he replied in his head. *Unless you want me joining you sooner than I'd planned.* Then he took a deep breath and said out loud, 'No, don't bother tossing a coin. I'll do it.'

Everyone clapped. 'Good for you, Mac,' Frank whispered, with a new tone of respect.

Told you so, Johnnie said.

There was no time to change his mind; they had to go at once, before the onshore breeze built up. The engineer, who everyone referred to as Sparky, was a gruff, weather-beaten fellow with a rolled-up cigarette permanently attached to his lower lip. When the jeep stopped at the base of one of the masts, Vic looked up in utter terror. The metal structure appeared flimsier than he'd imagined, not much more robust than the Meccano he used to play with, and so tall it seemed to scrape the clouds. Rising through the centre was a spindly metal ladder protected only by widely spaced hoops.

'Blimey,' he breathed. 'Are you sure you really need me up there?'

'Don't worry, laddie. You're young and fit,' Sparky said. 'It's only three hundred and sixty feet.' The numbers meant nothing until they began to climb, reaching the first stage, where two great platforms the size of tennis courts reached out like wings on either side of the mast.

'Sixty feet,' Sparky announced, as Vic struggled for breath. Only *sixty* feet? They were still just one sixth of the way there. At the next stop, two hundred feet, he began to feel seriously wobbly. His lungs were hurting and his fingers cramped from gripping the narrow metal rungs of the ladder. The wind that had been barely detectable down on the ground now buffeted them like a gale. He clasped an upright spar with both hands as though his life depended on it.

'Don't look down, mate. Just enjoy the view.'

It was certainly a magnificent sight, enough to distract him for a few moments. To the south, the River Deben glittered before them; the town of Felixstowe was bounded in the distance by the silver band of the River Orwell, and the docks of Harwich on its further side. It was the sight a German bomber might see, if it managed to penetrate their air defences.

They reached the top at last. Vic's lungs were hurting as he gasped for air – was it thinner up here? – and his heart thumped so fast he feared he might collapse.

'It's just your mind playing tricks, laddie. The fear. But it's no more dangerous up here than at sixty feet. If you fell, the result'd be the same.'

'Thanks for the encouragement.'

Battling against the wind, they inspected the transmission kit together. At first they could find nothing wrong, until Vic noticed that the calibration of the meter was slightly out, which then required a slight adjustment to the direction of the aerial.

'Hope that works,' he shouted.

'If it don't, we'll be up here again tomorrow,' Sparky retorted with a wry smile.

The downward climb was, if anything, even more terrifying, because he had to look at his feet to make sure they were securely on the next rung of the ladder, which made his head spin with vertigo. When at last they reached the ground, his legs were so wobbly that Sparky had to support him to the jeep.

'Get that down you, and you'll soon feel better,' he said, pouring from a flask of sugary tea. He swigged his own, then lit a cigarette.

'Didn't think you had it in you, laddie. Some first-timers don't make it with clean underpants, if you get my gist. You done well.'

Their hard work was rewarded with a visit from none other than Winston Churchill, the MP and former chancellor who, according to Watson-Watt, was a staunch supporter of their work. Even from the back benches he'd been warning of German rearmament, and he was a fierce critic of the Prime Minister's policy of appeasement.

'Best foot forward, chaps,' Dr Rowe said. 'He's on our side, this fellow, so we need to make a damned good impression.'

Vic was aware that Churchill had been vociferously opposed to the idea of Indian independence, claiming it would bring disaster for the British economy, and had called for Gandhi to be allowed to die if he went on his threatened hunger strike. How would he react to meeting an Indian man at the heart of one of the government's top secret defence establishments?

The reaction was the very opposite of what he'd feared. After the RAF top brass had taken him on a tour of the masts, transmitter and receiver blocks, Churchill returned with Dr Rowe to the Manor to meet the non-military staff, the scientists and engineers.

As they waited in the Green Room, Vic found himself watching Kath as she laid out the table, marvelling at her quiet efficiency and economy of movement, the twist of her body as she leaned across the great oval table to place the cups and saucers, plates, knives and napkins in perfect order. She caught his glance and he gave a discreet thumbs-up, rewarded with that sweet gap-toothed smile that made his heart leap like a fish on a line. She returned several times with platters of sandwiches, scones with pots of jam and thick cream and six cakes of different varieties, including – he was pleased to see – carrot cake.

The great man arrived and began to work the room like any seasoned politician, bestowing smiles of appreciation during the introductions and then listening, apparently rapt, to each individual he spoke to, exuding the energy of a much younger man. Close up, he was shorter than Vic had imagined: about the same height as himself, but powerfully built, with a strong chin and skewer-sharp eyes of the palest blue.

Vic was just taking a bite of cake when the heads of his companions swivelled. Churchill was approaching, holding out his hand. 'Just had to come and say hello to this fellow.' That voice, so sonorous and commanding, seemed to penetrate the general hubbub, and Vic felt his ears burning as everyone turned to watch.

He swallowed fast, nearly choking himself. 'Vikram Mackensie, sir.' The handshake was strong and firm. He hoped Mr Churchill wouldn't notice his sticky fingers.

'What part of India are you from, young man?'

'I was born in Kerala, sir. My father was a tea planter.'

'Know it well, know it well,' Churchill said. 'I spent several years in India in my younger days, you know. Spent a few months on the North West Frontier, although most of my time was in Bombay and Bangalore. Bloody love that country, and especially your people; though I fear for their future, should the Gandhis of this world get their way. D'you play polo, by any chance?' His mind seemed to move so quickly that it was a struggle to keep up.

'I'm afraid I haven't been back since I was ten years old, sir,' Vic replied, deciding not to mention his fear of riding horses. Like elephants, they were just too high above the ground.

'Never mind, never mind. You have other talents. I'm told you're one of the brightest fellows here.'

'Oh, I don't think so, there are lots of...'

'The work you are all doing here is splendid, splendid. Warms my heart. Feels as though I've been shouting into a void all these years, warning about German aggression, but at last I'm among people who're doing something about it. With the help of your radio waves, I'm confident that we'll have a fighting chance of beating the bastards.'

'Thank you, sir.'

'Keep up the good work. You've made me a happier man today.'

The audience was over. Churchill moved on.

'What was he saying to you?' Kath asked later, as they sat on the beach below the Cliff Walk.

'He asked if I played polo.'

'I don't even know what that is.'

'It's a kind of hockey, played on horseback.'

She laughed. 'Sounds crazy. And do you play?'

'What do *you* think?'

'I think chess is probably more your kind of game.'

'You think right.'

'D'you mind if I paddle? Standing in the kitchen all day makes my feet ache.' He watched her wading into the water in her bare feet regardless of the pebbles, marvelling at her boldness and confidence.

'Come on in. It's lovely,' she called.

'I bet it's cold.'

'On a day like this? You're just a sissy.'

'How did you guess?' All the same, he found himself taking off his shoes and wading in beside her. She held out her hand, and he took it. The pebbles hurt his feet and the water was shockingly cold, but somehow he didn't seem to notice. A larger than usual wave caught them by surprise, soaking her skirt and his trouser legs, but they both just laughed. He'd never felt more alive.

'My feet are going blue,' he said, after a while. He held out a foot to show her, and nearly fell. She held out an arm to steady him, and they found themselves in a near-embrace. 'This is nice,' he whispered, although afterwards he couldn't remember whether he'd actually said it out loud. All too soon she pulled away, leading him out of the water.

Afterwards they sat on the beach, drying off. She wiggled her toes, he wiggled his in response. 'I've just noticed you've got pink soles,' she said. 'Like your pink palms.'

He loved her guileless honesty, the way she said exactly what she was thinking. 'That's because the brown rubs off, you know.'

She gaped at him for a second, and then, 'Don't tease. How am I supposed to know?' She exaggerated her accent, 'When oi'm just a silly Suffolk lass?'

'You're so much more than that, Kath.'

And then, out of the blue, she said, 'I got that leaflet about the WAAF. From the post office.'

His heart seemed to contract. 'And?'

'I'm torn. I want to do something useful, but I don't want to end up working in catering again, or driving lorries, and it seems you don't really get a choice. Plus, I'm not sure about leaving home. My brother's already gone. He joined the RAF, you know?'

'You mentioned it.'

'He's training to be a pilot. Ma's worried enough about him. If I went too, she'd be devastated.'

'I'd miss you too.' It was the truth, although he'd never imagined himself admitting it.

'You're such a sweet man, Vic. As your reward…' She looked into her bag and produced two slices of chocolate sponge. 'Sorry it's not your favourite. There wasn't any carrot cake left over.'

He took a bite. 'Mmm. Delicious.'

She smiled. 'You only love me for my cake.'

'Not true,' he said. 'I love you for…'

'Go on.' She nudged him with an elbow.

'Everything about you,' he managed.

She snuggled her arm into his, resting her head on his collarbone. Their bodies seemed to fit perfectly. Surely this was the sign he'd been waiting for?

'Kath...?' The words stuck in his throat.

She waited, quietly.

'Would you mind if I kissed you?'

'I thought you'd never ask.' She turned her face to his, and he bent down to hers so that their lips touched, oh so briefly, before a loud holler from the Cliff Walk above made them both jump.

'Go, Romeo, go!'

'Kiss, kiss, kiss.'

'Woo-hoo!'

'Christ, it's those bloody engineers. I'm so sorry.'

But Kath didn't seem fazed in the slightest. She laughed and stood up, shouting at them: 'Go away, you idiots, we're busy.' Then she sat down again, took his face in her hands and kissed him on the lips for a long minute. There were more whistles and catcalls, but Vic didn't care.

When they'd finished, his head was spinning. It was just a pressing of closed lips, the most innocent kind of kiss imaginable, and yet the feel of that gentle imprint would stay with him for a very long time.

CHAPTER 17

On the first of September 1939, Mr Brunetti called the kitchen staff to a meeting at the end of the day. His usually animated face was grave.

'You may not have heard the news, but I have to tell you that the Germans have invaded Poland.'

'This is it,' someone behind Kath whispered. *This is what?* she wondered.

'If they don't withdraw, then Chamberlain says we will declare war.'

She didn't understand. Why would Britain go to war over Poland? There had been plenty of speculation but somehow no one really believed it would come to this. Brunetti was still speaking.

'This is grave news, of course. But there is an added implication for us in this room.'

He seemed to pause, as though for dramatic effect, although afterwards Kath realised that he must have been struggling to contain his emotions. 'Dr Rowe has told me that should we go to war, all of the non-military personnel at the Manor will be evacuated.'

Oh hell.

'What will happen to us?' she heard Ma asking.

'Catering will be provided by the RAF.'

'Even for officers?'

'Even for officers.'

'What will happen to us?' Ma repeated.

'I'm afraid –' he paused again, his chin working – 'we are all being made redundant. Me included. With immediate effect.'

Double hell.

An audible 'oooh' seemed to suck all the air out of the room, and Kath found it hard to breathe. She turned to her mother, dizzy and disorientated. 'Whatever shall we do?'

'We'll get by, I suppose,' her mother whispered, pulling her close. 'Being out of work is going to be the least of our worries, sweetheart.'

It was only once they'd left the building, walking in silence with the rest of the kitchen staff down the driveway, that she looked back at the Manor and remembered the other thing Mr Brunetti had said. *All non-military personnel will be evacuated.* Would that include the scientists? Would it include Vic?

Despite her earlier misgivings, she'd come to look forward to their walks. She loved his company, his interesting conversation, his knowledge about so many things. He was funny, often making her laugh, and so refreshingly different from most other boys, who seemed to feel the need to brag about their achievements. Vic was modest to a fault. Their kisses were sweet but chaste; he didn't appear to want anything more and, she had to confess, neither did she. There was none of that stomach-turning swoony recklessness she'd felt when kissing Billy.

She did not consider herself to be in love, although she sensed the possibility of it. But now, there would be no chance. She felt suddenly bereft. It was Friday afternoon and she was not due back at work until Monday, the day after the so-called ultimatum expired, and the country would officially be at war.

No one had the appetite for Sunday lunch, not after that terrible announcement and the almost immediate sounding of air-raid sirens that had brought everyone out into the streets, anxiously scanning the skies. Pa had built a shelter in the garden, but nobody wanted to sit in its damp darkness. Ma was putting on a brave face, but every now and again would break down in tears.

'Whatever will become of us?' she wailed. 'And Mark, out there in his plane? Oh, I wish he'd just come home and get a safe, ordinary job.'

'He may not have the choice, dearest,' Pa said. 'They'll be calling all of us up before long.'

'Not you, too? You're too old, surely?'

'Depends how desperate they are.'

And so the conversation went, round and round, until the doorbell rang and Pa went to answer it. Probably Joan, Kath thought.

'There's a man on the doorstep asking for Kath,' he called.

'Hello there.' She looked down at Vic's suitcase. 'Are you moving in?'

Confusion flooded his face. 'Mr Brunetti gave me your address. I hope you don't mind,' he said, shuffling his feet. 'We're all being evacuated. I couldn't leave without saying goodbye.'

'Sorry, I was just being silly,' she said, blushing. 'We've all been laid off, too. It's lovely of you to find me. Will you come in?'

He checked his watch. 'Sorry, my train goes at three. I'm not sure there's time.'

'Then I'll walk to the station with you.' It was all so sudden. 'Let me get my jacket.'

They walked in silence at first. What was there to say? They were not officially girlfriend and boyfriend, and they would probably never see each other again. They rounded the corner, and the station came in sight.

'Do you know…' she said, and at the same time he started: 'I hope you…'

'You first,' she said, laughing.

He paused, then, 'I don't want to leave you, now we've just met.'

'Me neither, but we can write, can't we?'

His face brightened. 'You'd like to? That'd mean a lot.'

'Do you know where you're going?'

'Not yet, but I've got your address now, so I'll write just as soon as I know.'

The train was steaming up, and the clock above the platform read nearly three o'clock. 'You'd better get on board.'

He took her hand, lifting it to his lips like an old-fashioned gentleman.

'I'll miss you, Kath.'

'Me too,' she said. 'Here, take this.' She pressed into his hand a small paper bag containing two pieces of the carrot cake she'd baked over the weekend.

'Is this what I think it is?' She nodded.

His face, so serious until now, melted into the sweetest smile. At the other end of the platform, she could see the stationmaster lifting the whistle to his lips.

Vic climbed on board and leaned out of the window, waving until the train went around the curve and out of sight. It was only then that Kath realised that she was standing in precisely the same place where she'd first met him. She hoped it wouldn't be the last time.

October 1939

Dear Kath,

I hope you are well and pray you and your family are all safe. Please write soon and reassure me.

I've just written 'pray' although of course I don't ever really do that in the formal sense. Apart from anything else, my mixed background leaves me confused about who to pray to: the single Christian god, or the several dozen of the Hindu type, each of which has several forms? My favourite is the elephant god, Ganesh, who is famous for removing obstacles. Elephants are immensely strong and used for heavy lifting, so that makes sense. He's also the patron saint of letters, which is slightly odder, since although they are fabled to be wise and have very long memories I've never met an elephant who could wield a pen in his trunk, but I shall dedicate this one to him all the same.

Work is fine but we don't get out much up here, and anyway there's not much to get out to. Just the pub inhabited by ancient hobgoblins who speak in an incomprehensible tongue and drink beer so watered down that the description 'pale ale' has never been more appropriate. I've taken to whisky, following my father's example.

In these remote, pale-skinned parts they've never seen anyone like me before. The children dare each other to run up and touch me, to see if I'm real, and then dash away giggling. They must think I'm some evil wizard or something. For a while I took to telling them my dark skin gives me special powers and I could make their wishes come true. But that backfired when a little lad made me promise to bring his daddy home safe.

My special powers are now producing sweets from behind my ears. It's safer that way, and just as popular. I pity any other brown people arriving here in future – I'm a hard act to follow.

We are well away from the fray, which leaves me with a conflict of feelings: guilt that I am not doing something more active to fight the Hun, and relief that I don't have to endure the misery of barracks life, parade grounds and the rest. Can you imagine me, trying to march, when I can barely tell my right from my left? I'd be a disaster as a soldier.

My only real discomfort in this war is the food here, which is worse than awful. My goodness, how I miss your carrot cake. But more than that, Kath, I miss you, and our conversations. Getting to know you has helped me recover from losing Johnnie, and I'm quite miserable now we've been parted.

Please write back, c/o the post office number at the top of this letter.

Your friend, Vic

*

November 1939

Dear Vic,

Thank you for your letter. Don't worry, we are perfectly safe, although the war came pretty close to home when a ship got hit by a mine in Harwich Harbour and more than fifty poor sailors died. Apart from that, nothing exciting is happening here, except for people digging up the parks to plant vegetables. The beaches are off limits, covered with barbed wire and mined, apparently. Pill boxes seem to spring up like mushrooms. They've even blown up part of my beloved pier. It's horrible. I hate this war already.

We have a young Cockney woman with her two-month-old baby billeted with us after being evacuated from London. She's perfectly nice but the baby cries all night which is making everyone tired and tetchy! She's sad, of course, because she misses her family and her husband is away in France. Yesterday when we read the news of the latest defeat she said, 'I wonder what kind of world I'm bringing this lad into.' At least we only have ourselves to worry about.

Ma and I have been job hunting but there's nothing around so we do our best, cooking for the Women's Royal Voluntary Service. They've even tried to teach me how to knit socks and woollies for 'our boys' but I'm hopeless and keep having to unravel everything and start again. Perhaps crochet is the best thing for me, although the very word makes me feel like an ancient maiden aunt.

Your letter made me laugh. I can just imagine the 'hobgoblins' in the pub. The encyclopaedia I looked up in at the library says they're 'a mischievous and ugly fairy, sometimes portrayed as small, hairy little men'. Come to think of it, there are plenty of those in the pubs around here, too.

Fondest regards,
Kath

Ever since they'd started corresponding, she had struggled to find the right words for her sign-off. 'With regards' was too cool. 'With love' was too warm. 'Best wishes' was too distant, and sounded like a birthday card. He had cleverly chosen 'Your friend, Vic', which seemed to strike exactly the right note. She plumped for 'Fondest regards', which also seemed to work well.

Apart from that day on the Cliff Walk, neither of them had ever mentioned love, not in any serious way; but she missed him more than she'd ever imagined.

PART TWO:

WAR

CHAPTER 18

MAY 1940

It was Dunkirk that really brought home to Kath that they were properly at war.

Although the wireless news reported on the progress – or lack of it – of the Expeditionary Force, and the number of casualties seemed to be mounting, somehow it all felt very far away. As far as she knew, none of her friends were over there.

Dunkirk was different. Fishermen left Felixstowe and Harwich in their little boats and returned as heroes, but two of the crews never made it home. They were the first local civilian casualties of the war, and the Ferry Boat Inn flew its flag at half-mast. No matter how the politicians tried to play it, everyone knew it had been a disaster.

Lately she'd begun to recognise the faces of lads she'd known at school returning to the town, war-weary and aged beyond their years. Ma's nursing friend said the convalescent hospital was full of them, and some were so badly injured – with missing limbs or facial disfigurements – you knew that their lives would never be the same. It was shocking to see them hanging around in the park, clasping bottles of booze concealed in brown paper bags. Some even resorted to begging, a pitiful sight. At midday, just before opening time, they could be found queuing outside the pubs, eager to spend the proceeds of the townsfolk's generosity on drinking their memories into oblivion.

One day, when walking home through the park, she spied a face she recognised, although the thick-rimmed spectacles she remembered had been replaced with sunglasses.

'Adam Merriweather? Is it you?' As he turned, she saw the terrible red, distorted skin on the other side of his face and the bald patch over half of his skull. Burn scars.

'It's me – Kath Motts. From those revision classes, remember?' It was only as she approached that she noticed the thin white stick in his hand. Burned and blinded, too.

'Of course I remember.' Adam gave a lopsided smile. 'Sorry, everything's a bit of a blur these days.'

'Heavens, Adam, whatever happened?' She sat beside him on the bench.

'I joined up. Conscripted. No choice.'

'Surely you were too young?'

'I was nineteen,' he said, simply. 'And anyway, I wanted to do something useful. My brother was out there already, and there's nothing much left for me at home, so it seemed the logical thing to do.'

'How did you get these...?' She gestured to the scars before remembering he couldn't see her hands.

'Bomb. On the beach at Dunkirk. We were trying to shelter in an old fishing boat, but they bombed it and it caught fire. Still, I'm lucky to be alive. Most of the others didn't survive.'

'How on earth did you get home?'

He gave a half laugh, a sort of snort. 'Bloody irony is that if I hadn't been burned, I probably wouldn't have made it out of there at all. They were taking the injured first, so they hauled me across the sand and plonked me on the deck of a trawler. I was howling, of course, but they carried on dousing me in sea water the whole way home and that's probably what kept me alive, the docs said.'

Kath chewed a nail, wondering how you could possibly return to normal life after an experience like that, and so terribly maimed. 'Is there anything I can do, Adam?'

'Not a lot,' he said. 'Just don't feel pity for me. It hurts too much. I'm trying to learn Braille so I can carry on with my studies. There's a lovely lady in the library who's helping me.'

'Would you like to come back for a cup of tea? I think there's cake.'

That crooked smile again. 'That would be lovely, Kath. Thank you.'

She called at his house a week later to be greeted by a bleary-eyed man – his father, she assumed – who was plainly drunk.

'Could I speak to Adam?' she asked, reeling from his breath.

'Gone,' the man slurred. 'Rehabili-whatsit.'

'Rehabilitation?'

'Tha's the one.'

'When do you expect him home?'

The man shrugged. 'Who knows? Maybe never, poor old lad.'

'Please tell him I called, could you, when you see him next?'

'Will do, missy.'

She never saw Adam again.

Londoners who had been evacuated to the town just after the declaration of war were told they should go home, now that the threat of an imminent German invasion meant Felixstowe was no longer a 'safe area'. The young woman and her baby billeted in Mark's old room went with them. Although they didn't miss the baby's night-time crying, everyone was sorry to see her go.

Then on one fine June morning, as if to reinforce the point, a German plane broke through the air defences and flew over Bawdsey, dropping high-explosive bombs. Fortunately their aim was poor and the bombs fell harmlessly onto farmland. No one was hurt either in the village or at the Manor, which was still fully operational as an RAF base. But, Kath thought, what if she and Ma had been at work in the kitchens, and the bombers' aim had been more accurate? They weren't surprised to learn soon afterwards that all female staff, including the WAAFs, had been evacuated.

Mark hadn't been given leave for months now, and they knew he would be flying almost every day. What Churchill called the Battle of Britain was raging over the south coast, and the nightly bombing of London and other big cities followed. He declared that 'never in the field of human conflict was so much owed by so many to so few'. Mark was one of 'the few', Kath knew – and she also knew that the casualty rate was high. His occasional letters were brief but determinedly cheerful. Each day the family steeled themselves, fearing the arrival of the postman or the telegram boy and scouring the newspaper lists of casualties. 'No news is good news' became their morning mantra.

Felixstowe began to feel like a ghost town. Notices were posted at the Town Hall declaring that all children and their mothers, as well as the 'aged and infirm', should leave the town for safer areas inland. Schools were closed, and by August just a few thousand residents were left. But the railways were vital for bringing in troops and supplies, so Pa was deemed an 'essential worker' and Ma simply refused to leave without him.

'Whatever will we do if the Germans invade?' Kath asked.

'We'll go to stay with Auntie Phyllis.'

'I'm sure she'd welcome us with open arms.'

'Don't be so cheeky, young woman,' Pa said.

Kath recalled their last visit to her great-aunt's dark little flat in Stowmarket, crowded with over-large furniture and dusty pot plants, and the way that Phyllis had fussed around them, adjusting the lace antimacassars that seemed designed to slip from the backs of the chairs. When the adults weren't looking, Kath had taken a peek into the other rooms: the tiny old-fashioned kitchen, a bathroom with a rust-stained bath, a bedroom dominated by a large double bed and a further room she'd expected to be for Phyllis's lady companion, but which seemed to be in use as a study.

*

The WAAF leaflet sat on Kath's bedside table. As her twentieth birthday approached, she raised the topic. It was a mistake. Ma went pale and slumped into a chair. 'How could you even think of it, Kath?'

'I need to do *something*.'

'But I can't lose both of my children.'

'You haven't lost one yet.'

'You know the odds, for heaven's sake.'

Later Kath heard her weeping upstairs, being comforted by Pa. So for the moment she kept herself busy, volunteering for the Home Guard, issuing gas masks, helping with the evacuations, helping with civil defence tasks, evacuations and 'digging for victory' by turning the back garden into an allotment.

With only one income, there was much drawing in of belts. There was little to spend their money on anyway, since many of the shops and all the seaside attractions had closed 'for the duration'. There were even, it was rumoured, mines buried beneath the fabled golden sands where, just the previous year, children had made castles and tried to dig to Australia. Somehow it was this, above all else, that gave Kath sleepless nights. *What has my beloved town come to*, she asked herself?

When Mark finally managed to come home for a few days he was clearly exhausted, but after sleeping for twelve hours he reappeared in a buoyant mood. Ma had been saving ration coupons for weeks, and laid on a feast.

'We've got the bastards on the run,' Mark declared, loading his plate. 'We were massively outnumbered, but we've got them scared. A thousand German planes shot down in just a month, they're saying.'

'What's your personal tally, son?' Pa asked.

Mark frowned and tapped his nose. 'Not allowed to say, sorry.'

'But if we were so outnumbered, how did we manage to see them off so successfully?' Kath asked. 'Are our planes that much better?'

'C'mon, sis. It's the skill of the pilots, of course.'

'Another piece of pie, anyone? More carrots? They say they help to make your eyesight sharper,' Ma said.

'Puh,' Mark snorted, holding out his plate. 'That's just propaganda, Ma.'

'Carrots?' Kath said, confused. 'What on earth…?'

'So the Germans don't suspect the real reason for our success,' he finished cheerfully. 'It's all a game of bluff and counter-bluff, this war.'

'Some kind of game, when people are getting killed in their hundreds.' Just as soon as she'd uttered the words she regretted them, lowering her gaze to avoid her mother's furious glare.

'What's all this talk about some kind of magic eye in the planes?' Pa asked. 'Do you know anything about it?'

'You don't have to tell us, Mark,' Ma said. 'If it's secret.'

Mark leaned back in his chair, his cheeks flushing. 'Is that what they're saying? Well, Ma's right, I can't tell you anything, sorry. But just to reassure you, we do have some very clever bits of kit that the Germans don't have. Or at least, theirs is not as clever as ours. Not yet, anyway.'

Kath's twentieth birthday was a low-key affair celebrated with fish and chips from the shop, wrapped in newspaper, followed by a few pints in the local with Joan and her boyfriend Sam as well as a couple of girls from school. All the talk was of the people they knew who were away fighting: Mark, Billy Bishop and all the boys from school who had already been conscripted. Kath told them about her meeting with Adam Merriweather and everyone agreed he'd had a tough life, with his mother's death and then getting so horribly burned and losing his sight.

'And all for what, you wonder?' Kath said.

'To stop the Germans?' someone said, sarcastically.

'I know that,' she snapped back. 'I meant, why are the Germans doing it?'

"Cos of the way they were treated after the last war, perhaps?'

'They started that one too. Whatever can they expect?'

The conversation rumbled on. Sam was the only boy in the group, and Kath wondered how he'd managed to avoid conscription. He was a tall lad, blond-haired, gangly and often hopelessly clumsy, as though his limbs had somehow outgrown the ability of his brain to control them. As a schoolboy he'd been painfully shy and never 'one of the gang'. Quite what Joan saw in him Kath had never quite understood, until that evening.

He seemed more at ease in his body these days. He spoke quietly but amusingly about his work at a large bakery in Ipswich, and he was generous with his money, buying two rounds of drinks in a row and refusing to let anyone else chip in.

Talk turned to what they would do if the government, as was widely expected, extended the call-up to women. One girl wanted to work on farms, and the other was already training to be a nurse. Joan fancied being a driver – perhaps even an ambulance driver, even though it probably meant joining the ATS, enduring hours of square-bashing and having to wear unflattering khaki.

'Isn't it terribly dangerous, driving ambulances?' Kath asked now.

'Isn't everything dangerous in war?'

'What about you, Kath?' one of the girls asked.

'The WAAFs, of course. My brother's in the RAF,' she said. 'Besides, that's where all the good-looking men are.'

'But they don't take women pilots, do they?' someone asked.

'There are a few, Mark says, but there are plenty of other jobs women can do, like communications work.'

'Communications? What's that?'

'How do you think all those planes know what to do, when to scramble, which direction to fly in?' She stopped. *Careless Talk Costs Lives*, the posters shouted. Even mentioning in the most general terms what Mark had talked about could get him – and her – into trouble.

'What about you, Sam?' she asked, to change the subject. 'Which service do you fancy?'

Joan jumped in, a little defensively: 'He's exempted because he works in a bakery.'

'There's more to it than that,' he said quietly, pausing to study his nearly empty glass.

'Go on, Sam. You're with friends,' someone prompted.

'My parents are Quakers,' he began at last. 'And one of the most basic requirements of their – well, my – faith is to promote peace and oppose war. We believe there are other ways of settling disputes between people, and even countries.'

'Didn't Chamberlain and everyone try that already?' Kath asked. 'Do you really think we could persuade that madman to back off, just by having a cup of tea and a little talk?'

Sam flushed. 'I'm only telling you what we believe. So in the last war, my father registered as a conscientious objector, even though he knew he would be court-martialled and sent to prison. He ended up spending three years in gaol.'

Kath held her tongue. Surely even gaol was better than dying in the trenches.

'They were treated terribly, not allowed to speak to any of the other prisoners and given the worst rations. He nearly died,' Joan added.

'Even then, he always claimed he was fortunate because some of them were sent over to France and told that if they disobeyed orders they would be shot as deserters,' Sam added.

'You're lucky, though, with your exemption,' one of the other girls said.

'I'm not so sure, to be honest. It just doesn't seem right when all the other boys are out there, but my parents would probably disown me if I joined up. When I mentioned it, my father hit the roof and wouldn't talk to me for days. Mum said he considered it disrespectful to the sacrifice he made for his faith.'

'Poor Sam,' Kath said, as she and Joan walked home together. 'I had no idea. What do you think he'll decide?'

Joan said nothing, and when Kath looked up she realised her friend was close to tears.

'Oh, cripes, I'm sorry I said anything,' she said, feeling in her pockets for a clean handkerchief.

'It's all right,' Joan sniffed, wiping her eyes. 'We have to face it one way or another. He feels very strongly that he ought to fight because, as you said, talking was never going to stop Hitler. But they're such a close family. It would break his heart if they really did carry out their threat to disown him.'

'And what do you want him to do?'

'I want…' Joan stopped walking, and her words were swallowed up by another wave of tears. 'Oh, sorry. I'm such a ninny.'

'Take your time. I'm here to listen,' Kath said.

'It's just that… I've never loved anyone but Sam, you know?'

'I know.' She put her arm around her friend, waiting for the sobs to subside.

'Oh Lord, I hate myself for being so selfish, Kath. But what I really hope is that he'll choose to stay as a baker rather than dying on some blessed battlefield. Is that so wrong?'

'Of course not,' Kath reassured her, thinking of Adam. But was it wrong? She couldn't decide.

They heard the planes just as they reached Joan's house. There were no sirens, so they assumed they were friendly. But just as they were wishing each other goodnight, a series of enormous explosions seemed to shake the ground beneath their feet and within seconds the sky to the north lit up with a ghastly reddish-yellow glow.

'Bombs!' Kath shouted. 'Bloody hell, it's the Manor.'

Another huge explosion.

'Shouldn't we go to the shelter?' Joan gasped, as a couple of RAF fighters screamed overhead.

Kath imagined her brother in his cockpit, racing to shoot down the enemy planes. It was unbearable not knowing what was happening. 'I'm going to the ferry,' she said impulsively. 'Will you come with me?'

'Are you crazy?' Joan cried, just as her father appeared on the doorstep.

'Whatever are you doing out here, girls? It's a raid, for God's sake! Come to the shelter.'

'We're going to see…' Kath said.

'You're not going anywhere, miss,' Joan's father said. 'Not you either, young Kathleen.'

For a second she hesitated. 'I think I'll get off home, thanks.'

'Run, then,' he said.

The streets were filled with pale, fearful faces peering up into the sky, but by now the planes had gone and the night was silent once more. Kath grabbed her bike and cycled as fast as she could down towards the glow lighting the sky to the north.

Drinkers from the Ferry Boat Inn had already gathered to gawp at the conflagration on the other side. Even though she knew no one who worked at the Manor any more, Kath felt a powerful attachment to the place and would have been devastated had it been hit. She could see now that the fires seemed to be well away from the main building, and the masts still seemed to be reaching into the sky. But what about the other buildings, and the people working there? And all the workshops in the stable block, and the vital pieces of equipment Vic and his fellow scientists had worked on so hard? This could be a major disaster.

Charlie and several others climbed into the ferry and set off across the swirling river.

'Where's they off to, then?' someone said.

'To bring back any casualties, God bless 'em.' Soon afterwards an ambulance arrived at the ferry, with its lights flashing and bell clanging, and Kath realised that bringing the injured across the river would be far quicker than taking them to hospital via the long winding road to Woodbridge. As if to prove the point, it was a further ten minutes till the fire engines arrived on the Bawdsey side.

Before long the glow of the fires began to diminish. Charlie, arriving back on the ferry boat, announced that there had been no casualties and little serious damage. 'Damn fool Krauts couldn't hit a barn door,' he said. 'All them bombs just fell in the grass.'

When Kath finally reached home it was well past midnight, but the lights were still on in the house. Her mother ran to her, clasping her in a tight embrace.

'Thank God you're safe,' she said. 'We went to Joan's and she said you'd gone to the ferry.'

'I had to see what was going on at the Manor. They said no one was hurt, thank heavens.'

'But you gave us a real fright. Never, ever, do that again,' Pa raged. 'Why do you think we took all that trouble to build the shelter? To keep us safe.' He was nearly shouting now. 'Pray heaven it never happens again, but you must promise that if it does, you will come straight home.'

Everyone was on edge after that. They were fearful, gloomy times. King George visited to inspect the troops at Landguard Fort, apparently to rally morale, but it did little to cheer the townsfolk.

Kath volunteered as an air-raid warden, spending most nights in cold, damp shelters peering into the sky with binoculars or brewing endless cups of tea on an old camp stove in an attempt to keep warm. It was scary and boring all at the same time – she even began to long for a bit of excitement. In her first week she went down with a cold, which seemed to linger for weeks. She never felt properly well.

Even though Ma kept herself busy catering for the WRVS, at home she was often tearful, especially when they heard the drone of bombers flying towards Europe. With binoculars it was possible to see distant dog-fights taking place over the North Sea. The worst shock came later in August, when German planes dropped sixteen bombs onto the town centre, destroying houses and the signal box near the station. The train Pa was working on had just left for Ipswich. Although no one died, several people were injured. It was another very close shave.

She wrote to Vic:

Just to reassure you that although we've had a couple of air raids, and some damage to the town, we are all still safe here. I still long to join up as a WAAF and feel that I'm actually doing something useful but for the moment my parents won't even consider the idea, so I'll just have to wait till there's a call-up and they won't have any choice but to let me go.

At Christmas, Mark was given a couple of days' leave. He gave little away, saying only that his work was exciting and of course he would stay safe. But later, when he and Kath stayed up late, she asked him. 'I suppose you were just flannelling the parents earlier?'

'Can't have them worrying even more than they have to,' he said, cracking open another bottle of beer.

'Aren't you terrified, most of the time?'

'Just for a few moments, when the call comes, yes, I'm bloody petrified. But when we're flying there's never time to think about it, and when we're back on the ground we're either partying or asleep. That's my life.'

'Have any of your friends been killed?'

'Of course; some of them close friends.' He lit another cigarette, and blew an expert smoke ring towards the ceiling. 'But you can't dwell on it. You just have to get on with it and do your job as best you can. There is no other choice. The idea of Germany taking over our country is unthinkable, so if I die, it will have been in the best possible cause. The strange thing is that even though we face death almost every day, I've never felt more alive.'

Kath envied him so much: his sense of purpose, his certainty that the Germans would soon be sent packing, his faith in British aircraft and technical ingenuity. She longed to follow his example, to do something useful, to experience that heightened sense of being alive. All her closest friends were having adventures, and her own life seemed to be on hold.

Later that spring, the call-up for women began. Kath overheard one of the other air-raid wardens saying that if you volunteered, rather than waiting to be conscripted, you would be more likely to get the service you chose. Next day, she went to the Town Hall and signed up.

CHAPTER 19

She didn't break the news until after tea, when both of her parents were at home.

'I've got something to tell you,' she began, heart in mouth.

'I already know what it is,' Ma said, putting down her knitting. 'Norma saw you leaving the Town Hall this morning. Made a special point of singling me out after our shift. "Your girl gone to sign up at last, has she?" The sanctimonious witch…'

'Shush, Maggie,' Pa murmured. 'You know her son was badly injured a few months ago?'

'That doesn't give her the right…' Ma turned to Kath. 'So, *have* you?'

'I was going to be called up anyway, and I wanted to be able to choose. They've got vacancies in the WAAFs, they said.'

Ma gave a little gasp, but said nothing.

'Perhaps you'll be posted somewhere nearby?' Pa volunteered.

'You know I'll have to go where they send me.'

'You might even bump into Mark.'

Ma seemed to be studying her knitting with particular care.

'We'll miss you, sweetheart,' Pa said, filling the silence. 'But we're very proud of you; aren't we, Mags?'

Ma came over to Kath's chair, putting her arms around her and kissing the top of her head. 'Just so long as you're safe, my darling,' she said, quietly.

Three months later, after a thoroughly embarrassing medical examination declared her to be A-1, Kath's call-up papers arrived. She was to report to an RAF base north of London, and a rail warrant was included, along with a precise timetable. Waiting for the connection at King's Cross she met another recruit, smartly dressed and well made up, her auburn hair resting in perfect curls onto her shoulders.

'Marcia Bonham; pleased to meet you.' The handshake was firm and confident, her vowels posh, so it was quite a surprise when she told Kath that she'd been working in a factory, 'making bits for bombs'.

Kath struggled to imagine this educated, fashionable woman wearing factory overalls. 'Why did you give it up?'

Marcia smiled. 'Not sure, really. Suppose I just wanted to be more in the thick of it.'

If only I had an ounce of her confidence, Kath thought. 'I hope you get what you want. I'm told it's the luck of the draw.'

'If I learned nothing else in the factory, it is that you have to be bold or you'll never get anywhere. Men are successful because they decide what they want and go all out to get it. Women have been taught to hold back and think they're not good enough, so we're always lagging behind. We need to think and act more like men.'

Kath laughed. 'I hadn't really thought of it that way.'

'And if all else fails, we still have our special persuasive powers.' Marcia cocked her head, gave a false smile and fluttered her eyelashes. 'Works every time.'

Kath's first few days in the WAAF were a series of horrible shocks. Each time, she felt it could not get any worse.

She'd been warned that they'd have to bunk up, but hadn't expected to find nearly fifty others sharing a flimsy corrugated iron hut set in a field. The iron bedsteads were equipped with three two-foot squares of hard wadding (known to all as 'biscuits') that you had to jam together to make a mattress, a pillow stuffed with prickly straw and a single woollen blanket so heavy it felt like sleeping under lead weights. Everything was damp, the rain battered on the roof like gunfire and she barely slept a wink.

On their first morning they were set an initial intelligence test. She found it nerve-racking, not knowing what importance they would place on the results when deciding your fate. At first the questions were easy, lulling her into a sense of false security, till she came across this one: *Mary, who is sixteen years old, is four times as old as her brother. How old will Mary be when she is twice as old as her brother?*

Her brain froze as the seconds ticked by. She made a stab in the dark, discovered that it was wrong. *Get a grip, Kath, just use logic.* She wrote out Mary's birthdays until she reached twenty-four. Yes, that was right. Phew. She hurried on.

Which number logically follows the series? That was easy enough to calculate, using plus, minus, multiplication and division signs. *Which of the following animals is the odd one out?* Again, fairly obvious; a snake doesn't have four legs. Except that the elephant is the only one with a trunk. She dithered before opting for the snake.

How many of the smaller shapes can you use to fill the largest shape? Kath panicked, looking up over so many heads bent intently over their papers. Then she pulled herself together. *The field with the hedges*, she told herself, *how to calculate surface area.* She visualised Adam whispering, 'Don't panic, it's simple if you just…' Across the room she saw Marcia, also looking up. She smiled back. *Think like a man*, she said to herself.

The rest of their induction went by in a whirl of instruction, marching, physical jerks and yet more form-filling. Kath ate well and slept more soundly than she had in months.

One afternoon she accompanied a friend to the only public telephone in the camp. They joined the queue of recruits and watched as each girl entered the box, lifted the receiver, inserted her two pennies, waited and pressed button 'A', her lips just managing to form the words 'Hello Mum' before dissolving into tears. However much she longed to hear her mother's voice, Kath was, for once, relieved that they did not have a telephone at home. Instead she wrote a letter:

> *To be honest it's hard going right now, but nothing worse than I expected* [this was a lie]*, and we live in hope. I miss you, and home comforts, but I feel certain things will get easier as I get used to WAAF ways. We don't yet know which 'trade' we'll be given, but I'll let you know just as soon as I get a more permanent address.*

There was just one final test to survive, the most important of all. The 'trades allocation' interviews would seal their fates for the rest of the war – and who knew how long that might be? Possibly years. There were three choices: becoming a Motor Transport (MT) driver; a batwoman, which, she gathered, involved being just an officer's personal servant; or an RDF operator, which, following Vic's advice, she'd set her heart on. But this was deemed a 'Grade Two' trade requiring a good educational standard and a sound knowledge of geometry, and she was by no means confident that she would make the grade.

The alternatives just didn't appeal. Her family had never owned a car and she'd never had any inclination to drive, so she reckoned that would count her out as an MT driver. But the thought of spending the rest of the war as a batwoman, making tea and shining senior bosses' shoes, filled her with horror. Oh, the humiliation, and sheer boredom.

Next day, crammed onto hard benches in a stuffy hut with nearly a hundred other girls, her head ached and somehow the big breakfast she'd consumed wasn't settling. As she waited she took out her old schoolbook, glancing through the notes she'd made for her school cert exams, looking for nuggets of knowledge that might help her persuade them of her desirability as an RDF operator: how to calculate the surface area, arc length and areas of squares, polygons, circles and cones, the main theories of trigonometry and how vectors worked. The numbers seemed to swim before her eyes.

In the interview room was a table with a single chair on one side and, on the other, a man and a woman who barely acknowledged her presence save for a curt, 'Miss Motts? Sit, please.'

She settled herself and waited.

'So why do you want to be an RDF operator?'

'Until the outbreak of war I was working at Bawdsey Manor.' She saw their eyes widen, as she knew they would. It was a bold gambit and might backfire, but she'd decided to spin it anyway. Work at the Manor was always top secret, but Mark had told her that the name, along with that of Robert Watson-Watt, had become legendary.

'I know almost nothing about what RDF is or does,' she added quickly. 'But I saw the interesting people involved in the work there, and that's what inspired me to apply.' She certainly had their attention. They shared a glance, and were now regarding her with the curiosity a biologist might give to a rare specimen.

'Do you mind telling us a bit about what you were doing there, if it's not confidential?' the woman asked.

There was no point in lying; she'd soon be found out. 'I was working in the kitchens.'

'So you're a *cook*?'

Kath's heart sank, certain that her gambit had failed. 'It was just an interim job, sir, after leaving school. But I have always been interested in science, especially physics and geometry.'

He gave her a withering look. 'I admire your confidence, Miss Motts. Let's have a little talk about what you actually *do* know.'

His first three questions were basic and she responded with ease. The fourth and fifth were harder, and she struggled before hazarding answers she felt by no means certain were correct. The final question foxed her completely.

'Take your time,' the woman said more kindly, pushing a notepad and pencil towards her. 'Use this, if you like.'

She took a breath, drew a rough diagram and added the numbers. They simply didn't make sense. Then she realised: it was a trick question. 'I think you have me there,' she said, turning towards the man with a slight tilt of her head and a single, oh-so-subtle flicker of her eyelashes. 'Because unless Pythagoras was mistaken, the hypotenuse should have been three point four, not three point eight – which would mean that the vector is…'

He held up his hand to stop her.

'Very good,' he said. 'Very good indeed, Miss Motts. I am sorry to have challenged you in this way – but you did so well in the intelligence tests that we just wanted to find out what else you could do.' He glanced at his colleague, who nodded.

'So I think I can say we are both fully persuaded that you are most suitable for RDF training. Congratulations.'

CHAPTER 20

For Vic, the demands of work seemed to become ever greater and more urgent.

During 1941 he had moved three times: first to Dundee, then to Dorset and now to just outside London. He was currently managing three teams working on extending detection ranges, refinements to 'friend or foe' systems and AI – air interception equipment that could be carried on the planes themselves, so they could detect the whereabouts of enemy aircraft without the need for sending signals back to land for interpretation. It was exciting, challenging and satisfying.

And yet – he had to admit it – when not at work he felt lonely and dispirited, cast adrift in a world that seemed intent on tearing itself to pieces. Cambridge days felt like a lifetime ago; all his previous research into the potential of radio waves for his doctorate was now completely outdated. War had provided the unexpected bonus of driving scientific invention at a rate that could never have been imagined in peacetime. If he ever went back into academia, it would have to be from an entirely different starting point.

His colleagues were a cheerful bunch in the main, but none of them came near to replacing the deep understanding of friendship he'd found with Johnnie, nor the surprising joy of human closeness he'd discovered with Kath. Although they were still writing to each other, he knew that the fragile links that had just begun to form between them would weaken still further with every month apart.

His father had written to tell him that Auntie Vera had finally succumbed to her mysterious illness: 'a blessing, really, an end to

her suffering'. They'd 'given her a good send-off ', but Vic was not
to worry about him being lonely, because he had met 'a lovely lady
called Diane' at the bowls club.

It was this last nugget of news that filled Vic with the greatest
unease. What did it mean? A delightful companion who would
relieve his filial responsibilities, or a gold-digger after the old man's
fast-diminishing savings? He felt an urgent need to find out for
himself, to reassure himself that his father, the only family he had
left on this side of the world, was well and happy.

When he went to Tunbridge Wells for Christmas, his worst fears
were realised. His father introduced her as 'my lovely new wife,
Diane': a short, rather tubby sixty-something, with restless energy
and an innate ability to say the wrong thing.

'Let me have a proper look at you.' She clasped his shoulders and
gaped at him. 'Heavens above, your father did warn me, but I never
realised you'd be so dark.'

It transpired that they'd married at the registry office just two
weeks before and Diane was now securely installed in his father's
house, and had already embarked on what she termed 'brightening
up the old place'. Both downstairs rooms were transformed: his
father's heavy furniture had been replaced with pale plywood cabinets,
uncomfortable chairs and curtains in garish yellows and pinks that
gave Vic an instant headache and the urge to run away.

Where was the painted screen, and the coffee table with its brass
tray engraved with elephants? The Indian ivory ornaments on the
mantelpiece had been replaced by a parade of porcelain figurines:
frolicking shepherdesses, kittens with red ribbons, even a ghastly,
grinning Toby jug. Not a single reminder of Vic's homeland, his
childhood or his beloved mother remained.

'Why didn't you tell me you'd got married?' he whispered when
Diane went off to the kitchen to make tea.

His father flushed. 'She wanted to make it a quiet affair. We didn't
want to bother you, son. You and your important work.'

'What have you done with your own things, the stuff from India?'

'Oh, we sold it as a job lot,' his father replied breezily. 'Didn't want any of that old-fashioned stuff, did you?'

Vic bit his tongue. What else was there to say? It upset him to think of his father spending the rest of his days under the thumb of his new wife; but at the same time he felt mildly relieved that someone else would be there to look after the old boy. And whatever would he have done with that furniture anyway, without a home of his own?

Diane emerged, bearing a tray with a flowery tea set and a plate of little shop-made cakes iced in pastel pink and yellow, matching the floral curtains. His father watched adoringly as she placed the tray onto the oval occasional table that now dominated the centre of the small room.

'Isn't she just the ticket? I'm a very lucky man, don't you think?' his father said, patting her on the bottom in a disturbingly over-familiar way.

She giggled and gave him a noisy, sloppy kiss on the cheek. 'Isn't he such a dearie?' she said. 'It's me who's the lucky one.' As she continued to coo and fuss Vic felt his stomach turning, and after tea he excused himself, claiming the need for fresh air.

Dusk was already falling as he walked the streets of Tunbridge Wells. It was twilight, not yet time for the blackout. Through every window he could see glowing fires, Christmas trees twinkling with coloured lights and families with glasses in hand, trying to put from their minds for just a day or so the dismal realities of a country at war and in perilous danger of invasion.

It began to drizzle and then to rain more heavily, but he hardly cared. In the town centre he encountered a beggar sheltering in the doorway of a closed shop, holding out a sign that read: *Spare a penny for a veteran.*

Automatically, he reached into his pocket and took out half a crown. 'What happened to you, old friend?'

The man was plainly drunk and his speech slurred, but Vic understood him well enough. 'Family gone, no home, no job. Thanks for the money, mate.'

'Is there anything else I can do to help?'

'Lost me blanket,' the man muttered.

It was such a simple item, but where could Vic get such a thing at this time of day? On an impulse, he took off his overcoat. It was a fine navy wool and cashmere his father had bought for him at Joshua Taylor's when he first went up to Cambridge. 'You'll want something to wrap up in on these blasted fens,' he'd said. It was old now, but still perfectly serviceable.

'Here you go,' Vic said. 'This'll keep you warm.'

The beggar fingered the fabric approvingly before pulling on the coat in a hurry, as though fearful that Vic might change his mind. Then he resumed his position on a pad of flattened cardboard, reached into a canvas bag and pulled out a bottle.

'Care to join me?'

'Keep it for yourself, my friend.'

'You're a true gent, sir,' the man said. 'Merry Christmas.'

By the time he got back to his father's house Vic was soaking wet and shivering with the cold, yet somehow happier. The following day he felt worse, but Diane had been slaving away in the kitchen since early in the morning, so he felt duty bound to appear for Christmas dinner.

When he explained that he didn't eat meat, she muttered about 'strange habits' and how his father could at least have warned her, adding that she wouldn't have spent all that money on a chicken if she'd known. The only moment of relief from her constant chatter was when his father turned on his radiogram – one item that had not been banished – for the royal Christmas message.

The King seemed to be grasping at straws:

Never did heroism shine more brightly than it does now, nor fortitude, nor sacrifice, nor sympathy, nor neighbourly kindness, and with them – brightest of all stars – is our faith in God. These stars will we follow with His help until the light shall shine and the darkness shall collapse.

Ha ha, Johnnie whispered. *Leaving it all up to God now, are we? Run out of options? But who is God going to choose, when our little pal Hitler also believes that he's on their side?*

Vic escaped on the first Boxing Day train, claiming that he was expected back at work. This was a lie; he'd been given a full week's leave, but he couldn't bear to stay a moment longer in Tunbridge Wells. Although it had never really felt like home, at least he'd once felt as though it was a place of shared memories – but now even that had changed. To make things worse, there were no seats on his train. As he stood in the corridor some Tommies pushed roughly past him, muttering about 'bloody foreigners'.

He had never felt so miserable.

Whatever are we going to do with you, old boy? No coat, no home, no Kath, and not expected back at base for four more days?

At Charing Cross, Johnnie's question appeared to answer itself. As the destinations flickered round on the departures board, Vic's eye settled on a familiar place-name. He blinked and looked again. Surely the last time he'd been there, for Johnnie's funeral, he'd travelled from Waterloo? But yes, the train was certainly stopping at Petersfield, leaving in just seven minutes. Fired with new energy, he ran for the ticket office and leapt on board just as the guard blew his whistle.

There were no seats on this train either. It was packed with navy lads returning to Portsmouth after the Christmas leave. By the time the train arrived at Petersfield Vic was feeling distinctly unwell, aching and shivery, regretting his impetuous decision. The walk from the station seemed longer than ever, and by the time he reached the cottage he was light-headed, almost delirious.

Lizzie stared at him as though she had seen a ghost. 'Vic? Is it you? Is something wrong? Come in, come in. Quickly, out of the cold.'

'I'm so sorry…' he managed, before collapsing in the doorway.
'Chris, Beth – come and help me!'

He became vaguely aware of being supported by many hands into a room bright with candles and firelight. He felt the soft comfort of an armchair, heard Lizzie's murmurs of concern, offers of tea and biscuits. Then, nothing.

*

Vic is asleep in his bed in India. The night is dark, but he can hear the chatter of his parents and their visitors on the veranda, the clink of glasses, the creak of the floorboards as the servants go about their tasks, the snuffling of nocturnal animals in the forest and the occasional hoot of a bird. He is comfortable and happy to be home at last, so blissful that he feels almost like crying. He hears a whimper, and realises that it comes from his own mouth. He feels the ayah's cool hand resting on his forehead. 'Hush, now,' she whispers. 'Everything is all right.' Then he sinks once more beneath the deep, warm blanket of sleep.

*

Next time he woke, it was daytime. As he opened his eyes he saw his familiar toy train on the table, a pile of comics beside it. But something was not quite right. The air was surprisingly cold, the sunlight beaming through the window creating sharp-edged shadows. Wherever could he be? Slowly the memories returned: the train, the walk, being helped up the steep stairs; the blackness and the dreams. He was not in India but at Johnnie's house, and this was Christopher's bedroom, not his own.

There was a knock at the door, and he half-expected Johnnie to walk in until, with that sinking feeling of loss, he remembered.

'Ah, you're awake at last,' Lizzie said, pushing aside the comics and putting down a tray. 'We've made some vegetable soup, just in case you're hungry.'

'How long have I been here?'

'A couple of days,' she said, sitting on the edge of the bed. 'We were worried about you. How are you feeling now?'

He considered for a moment, checking himself out. His head had stopped thumping, his breathing felt easier, his body was calm, no longer shivering. 'A lot better, thank you,' he concluded. 'I'm so sorry to dump myself on you like this.'

'Don't be silly. We're always pleased to see you. I'm glad you seem to be on the mend.' The soup was delicious. She sat smiling beside him as he finished the whole bowl and then lay back on the pillow, exhausted. A few hours later she returned with a tea tray, and passed him a plate with a hot buttered crumpet.

'Johnnie always said you were an angel, and now I know what he meant,' he said, tucking in. He was so busy trying not to get butter on the sheets that he failed, for a moment, to notice how her smile had disappeared. 'Oh, I'm so sorry.'

'It's all right,' she said, rearranging her features with a slight sigh. 'And it's sweet of you to tell me what he said. About being an angel. I'll cherish that.'

'He was a good man, Lizzie. The best.'

'We do miss him so, but life has to carry on. We don't really have any choice, do we?'

The next day was New Year's Eve. Vic felt strong enough to come downstairs for supper, and after the children had gone out to see friends, Lizzie coaxed the fire into flame with a new log and took out a bottle of port and two glasses.

'How's about it?'

'Don't mind if I do.'

'Builds you up, Johnnie always used to say.'

'To Johnnie,' he said, holding up his glass.

She clinked her glass to his. 'To Johnnie - and a happy New Year, Vic.'

'Heaven knows what 1942 will throw at us.'

'Let's not think about that tonight,' she said.

'Quite right. Enjoy the moment. But I'll have to be on my way tomorrow, alas.'

'Are you really well enough for work?'

'I'm afraid so, though honest to God, I'm reluctant to leave. I don't know how I'll ever repay you.'

'It's been a pleasure,' she said, refilling his glass. 'But you can grant me one thing in return.'

'And what is that?'

'Satisfying my curiosity. What brought you here in the first place? Are you okay?'

'I don't want to burden you with my woes.'

'I'm a good listener. It might help,' she said, her sweet face attentive in the firelight.

He took a breath and then, tentatively at first, began to describe what had happened over Christmas with his father and Diane; how he felt guilty complaining when that poor tramp had so little, but how he now felt so adrift, not attached to anywhere, no longer knowing who he was. There were no footholds, no places of safety, comfort or solace. He didn't even have anywhere he could call home any more. 'I've even given away my coat.'

She jumped up. 'I can solve that.' A moment later, she returned with a fine camel coat. 'It was Johnnie's. It'll be too big for you, but you're welcome to it if you would like it.'

'No, I couldn't.'

'I'll only give it away otherwise.'

Vic tried it on. It swamped his shoulders and hung down to his calves, but it was warm and smelled of Johnnie's shaving soap. It felt like a hug from his old friend.

'Are you certain?' he said, placing it over the back of a chair with more care than he'd ever accorded his own coat.

'I've never been more certain. And, look, you are always welcome here any time, you know that, Vic?'

'Actually, I feel more at home here than anywhere else. Perhaps that's why I jumped on the train. I'm not usually that impulsive.'

'But there's something else, isn't there? I know you can't tell me any details; but it is work? Or a girl, perhaps?' She looked him in the eye, challenging him to be honest.

He lowered his gaze.

'Sorry, that's a bit nosey of me. If you'd rather not…?'

He looked up now. 'No, you are right. There is a girl, someone I met at Bawdsey. She's a few years younger, and we're really very different sorts of people, but I've grown very fond of her.' He paused, trying to find the words. 'The thing is, you see, I am so inexperienced at this sort of thing, I don't even know if she's interested in me. We've been writing to each other, but because of this bloody war it could be years till our paths ever cross again. I'm afraid it'll all come to nothing in the end.'

She placed a hand on his. 'It'll only come to nothing if you let it, Vic.'

'What do you mean?'

'Sometimes you have to fight for what you want in affairs of the heart, just like in the rest of life.' She sat back, taking another sip of port. 'I had to fight for Johnnie.'

He could hardly believe what he was hearing. 'You mean he didn't jump at the chance?'

'We were so young. He was ambitious, and felt he couldn't get on with his career with a wife and family to worry about.'

'What a dolt. He came round, obviously?'

'I just persevered,' she said. 'Taking every opportunity. I wrote often, made long journeys to wherever he was and generally made myself indispensable. He caved in eventually.'

'So that's what you'd advise me to do?'

'Exactly.'

Talking seemed to crystallise his feelings. At a time of deep despair, Kath had helped him rediscover his sense of purpose – even a level of optimism that, although his best friend was dead, it was possible to laugh and enjoy life once more.

'I don't want to pester. What if she doesn't want to see me?' he said.

'My guess is she will. You just have to keep in touch, however you can. Write, visit, send Christmas cards, small birthday gifts.'

'Heavens, I don't even know when her birthday is.'

'Then it's time you found out, my boy.' Lizzie leaned over and planted a kiss on his cheek. 'You're so handsome and clever, Vic. She'd be mad to turn you down. But keep me posted on your progress, won't you?'

Kath's letter was waiting for him at his lodgings.

Dear Vic,

The next time you write, please address me as Aircraft Woman Level Two Motts!

Yes, I've made it and, better still, you'll be proud to hear that I passed the interviews. Do you remember what you told me, one day on the Cliff Walk? Of course I still haven't a clue what the work really entails, but if it turns out to be rubbish I will hold you fully accountable.

We're currently completing our initial training in a seaside resort and it feels distinctly strange. We are billeted in holiday boarding houses and even though it rains most of the time we feel we should be gathering our towels, deckchairs and windbreaks and heading for the beach each morning, but alas instead it's 'spit and polish', drill and PE, lectures, gas drills, more lectures and endless marching.

At least it's better than the dreadful camp where we spent our induction. Our landlady is an excellent cook, the food is plentiful and we're allowed some time for rest and recuperation. We're all girls of course, and our weekly £10/6d (!) doesn't go far as you can imagine, but we manage to have fun anyway. Ma sent me half a crown which meant we could go to the Winter Gardens last night and pretend to be posh. It was lovely to have a bit of glamour after all that trudging about in mud and sleeping in damp huts. The band played 'Oh, I Do Like to Be Beside the Seaside'. We bellowed out the words and made them play it again!

One of our number claims to be a relative of Lupino Lane and after a few drinks she actually stood up and sang 'Doing the Lambeth Walk' with the orchestra. She made a pretty good fist of it, too, doing all his actions, even though it looked pretty incongruous in her ill-fitting WAAF uniform!

Soon we leave for our technical training somewhere we haven't yet been told, but you probably know where these things happen. I'll send you an address as soon as I know. I wonder where you are, and whether it is anywhere near?

If this reaches you in time, have a wonderful, peaceful Christmas. I miss our chats, and hope you are well?

Fondest regards,
Kath

As he read to the end of the letter, his head began to spin. She remembered their conversation on the Cliff Walk. She missed their chats. She was learning all about his inventions. He lay back on his bed, holding the envelope to his chest and smiling to himself.

Yet even as his heart rejoiced, he felt a pang of envy, even fear. They might be 'all girls' on the initial training, but the technical training would almost certainly be at RAF Cranwell. He'd spent several weeks there himself, and knew all too well the social whirlwind in which Kath would find herself. Hundreds of recruits, male and female, were trained there, as aircrew and in all kinds of wireless operation. The place was enormous and the facilities excellent. There were several

Navy, Army and Air Force Institutes, the NAAFIs, serving good food as well as supplying basic necessities such as toiletries, dancehalls, cinemas and entertainment of all kinds. There would be any number of single men, handsome in their uniforms, ready to steal the heart of a beautiful young woman like Kath.

And then, after that, she could be posted anywhere in the country to any one of the RDF stations now operating as far down south as Devon, and as far north as Grimsby. The chances of them being able to meet up 'for the duration' were slimmer than ever.

This was the moment, as Lizzie had said, to be bold.

Dear ACW2 Motts,

I was thrilled to get your letter. What great news. Congratulations!

Of course I remember our conversations on the Cliff Walk. It was difficult because of the secrecy surrounding our work, but by now you will have a general understanding of what I've spent the last six years working on. I hope it hasn't disappointed. For my part, I feel very proud of our inventions, especially since they are being put to such good use right now. Your work will be challenging and exciting, and make an enormous contribution.

If your technical training is based where I think it is, I am not far away. I've checked the trains and buses and it is quite doable for a visit. Perhaps we could meet in the city which is only a half-hour bus ride away from your base? I'm told it's an interesting place, and the cathedral is a 'must'. We could have lunch? My treat, of course. If you like the idea, please send me your leave dates and we can try to co-ordinate.

I do hope the training is going well. I'm sure they will be working you very hard. But I do hope you will be able to find time to see me.

Your friend,

Vic

CHAPTER 21

Everyone said Cranwell would be a blast, and after weeks of square-bashing, living in miserable tents, surviving on tasteless rations and revising hard for exams, Kath was more than ready for some fun.

She also felt confident that, with all the hundreds of personnel arriving and leaving the training base at Cranwell, there would be at least a few familiar faces. Sure enough, in the queue for supper in the mess hall that very evening she heard behind her the unmistakably posh tones of Marcia Bonham.

'Marcia! It's you.'

'I knew you'd get here some time, darling,' Marcia said smoothly, as though she'd been expecting her. Before long, Kath had been led to a table and introduced to so many other girls that her head was spinning with names.

'You coming to the dance in the NAAFI tomorrow evening?' one said.

'I'm in,' Marcia said.

Kath dithered. It was all a bit soon. 'How much does it cost?'

'It's free, you ninny. Except for the drinks.'

'I haven't anything to wear.'

'Come back to the barracks at six-ish tomorrow and we'll find you something,' Marcia said.

They weren't really allowed any mufti, but as usual Marcia had ignored the rules, and the next day, when Kath went to her barracks, she produced a large leather case containing a complete fashion wardrobe.

'Try this one.' She held out a silky blouse in glorious blue, like the sky on the clearest of days. It was too big around the bust but they hauled it in at the back, tucking it into waistband of Kath's uniform skirt. 'Perfect. Looks great with the auburn hair. Now, what are we going to do with that?'

Twenty minutes later, both were splendidly coiffed. Marcia produced from her washbag a range of lipsticks, eyeshadows, mascara and face powders, which she chose with care and proceeded to apply to Kath's face with the expertise of a qualified beautician.

'My mother was a great society beauty,' she explained. 'I used to sit at her dressing table watching her every move, learning it by heart.'

'That's a lovely memory.'

'Actually it isn't, not really.'

'Why not?'

'I was always on edge, because I thought that if I was perfectly behaved and didn't say a word, Mother would want to stay at home with me. But it never worked. She would put on her latest satin number, twirl in front of the mirror and ask me to tell her she was beautiful before leaving me with Nanny. For days, sometimes weeks on end. I haven't been able to bear the smell of Chanel No. 5 ever since.'

Kath felt suddenly grateful. She'd thought her own upbringing dull and unadventurous, her family boring. They would never be able to afford great luxuries; Ma would never wear silk dresses or posh perfumes. Her parents had gone out to work, but there had always been other family members nearby to look after the children. In her memory, everyone was kind to one another.

'It got better once I was sent off to boarding school,' Marcia said.

'Weren't you terribly homesick?'

'At first, but then, everyone is. After a while you make friends and it's a good laugh.'

'I never spent a single night away from home, not until I signed up,' Kath said. She recalled Vic's astonishment when she'd told him.

'You're very fortunate,' he'd said wistfully. 'I've never really known what home is, or where it is. I've lived here longer than I ever lived in India, and my home there was sold when my mother died. My father calls England home, but Tunbridge Wells will never feel anything like home to me.'

Marcia put away her make-up, zipped the bag and stashed it away in her trunk.

'Isn't it time for a tipple? I'm going to introduce you to the joys of Martini, and then we're going to dance the night away.'

'It's a seven o'clock call in the morning.'

'Who cares?'

'I'm Donald,' he shouted over the band. 'Would you do me the honour?'

It was perfectly thrilling, being whirled around the dance floor by a handsome blond-haired officer. He might not be very tall – about the same height as Kath – but he was a terrific dancer, and he held her so expertly that it hardly seemed to matter that she didn't know the difference between a waltz and a quickstep. Two large Martinis had left her feeling more carefree than she had in months. This was more like it.

As the dance ended, she felt a tap on her shoulder.

'Kath Motts?'

As she turned and recognised the face, her stomach sank. 'Nancy? What on earth?'

'I could ask the same.'

'But… it's odd, meeting you so far from home.'

'Indeed.' Nancy leaned forward and whispered in her ear. 'Which is why we should bury the hatchet, don't you think?'

'Is this young woman bothering you?' Donald interjected.

'Er… no, it's fine. But thank you,' Kath said, as the band struck up another number. 'She's an acquaintance from home. Can I come and find you in a few minutes?'

In the bar Nancy took out a silver cigarette case, offered one to Kath, who refused, then lit her own with a matching silver lighter. Trophies from some poor besotted officer, Kath thought bitterly. Nancy looked different in uniform, and without her usual heavy make-up; her hair had darkened and lost its sheen, and grey shadows ringed her eyes.

She took a long drag and exhaled, batting away the cloud of smoke. 'Can I buy you a drink?'

Kath hesitated, thinking of Donald, and then decided that he'd wait. 'I've just been introduced to Martini.'

'Two Martinis it is, then.'

They took their drinks to a corner table and spent a few moments in small talk. Nancy lit a second cigarette and expertly exhaled a procession of smoke rings.

'Look, Kath, what I said was inexcusable. Both times. You and your brother didn't deserve it.'

'Let's forget it.' It all seemed such a long time ago; it barely mattered any more.

'I was feeling very sorry for myself and hitting out at everyone.'

'That soldier?'

'Oh, him. That was nothing.' Nancy paused. 'No, it was life at home. My parents, or rather my father. He was going off the rails.'

Kath waited.

'He'd been laid off because of his drinking, so he decided the remedy was to drink some more.'

'I'm so sorry, Nancy.'

'Which is why I'm here. I just had to get away. The first couple of months were ruddy awful, but this is a bit better, isn't it?' She glanced around at the bar, filled with men in uniform. 'Just my cup of tea.'

They laughed.

'Your brother is a brave man,' Nancy said, draining her glass. 'They all are, those pilots. We owe them our lives.'

'We cross our fingers every day. No news is good news.'

Neither spoke of Captain Burrows. It was probably best that way, Kath thought, as they finished their drinks and wandered back into the dancehall. Across the floor of whirling couples she could see Donald dancing with a rather glamorous woman several inches taller than himself, auburn hair swinging to her shoulders.

She looked again. It was Marcia, but she didn't honestly care – at that moment the world seemed a gilded place, her footsteps gliding along the path back to the barracks. But when she lay down, the room was spinning dangerously. She drank a glass of water and swallowed down an aspirin for the headache, which would soon turn into the worst hangover of her life.

The eighteen girls of Course 82, undergoing intensive training in the theory and practice of radio direction finding, were constantly reminded that although they were allowed to let their hair down from time to time, their main task was to work hard and pass their exams.

If you failed you would be declared FT – which meant that further training was needed – or, the greatest ignominy of all, CT, meaning 'cease training', in which case you would be sent off to become a driver or a batwoman instead. There was another incentive to pass: on completing the training they would be given a whole week's leave before being posted, which could be anywhere around the country.

At first, Kath feared that the other girls would all be cleverer than her. But the science was so far beyond anything taught in school that they were all, in effect, complete beginners, and she soon discovered that she could grasp the principles quite quickly. Even so, she was careful to revise each lesson at the end of the day to make sure she fully understood before they moved on to a new topic.

Only now was she beginning to appreciate the scale and ambition of the operation in which they were to play a small part, with its vast network of transmitting and receiving masts that linked all along the south coast of England, and up the east coast as far as Hull. She

was awed by the thought of the legions of men and women working
to track the movements and co-ordinating the responses of fleets of
ships and squadrons of fighter and bomber planes in the seas and
airspace between the British Isles and the continent.

Although the operators were mostly hidden away inside concrete
bunkers in remote locations, watching signals on fuzzy screens and
communicating their information down crackly telephone lines,
Kath now felt very much 'in the thick of it'. She began to understand
properly, perhaps for the first time, some of the terrifying realities
of war: how alone Britain was, with the Germans nipping at their
heels from just across the Channel and thousands of men and women
risking their lives each day to fight them off.

The more she learned, the greater her respect grew for the inventions of Vic and his fellow boffins. She never tired of watching the
radar echo from an aircraft when it first appeared as a tiny blip in
the noise on the cathode ray tube, and then grew slowly into a big
deflection as the aircraft came nearer. This strange new ability to 'see'
things at great distances, through clouds or darkness, seemed like a
very special power – a magical extension of the usual human senses.

But this 'special power' also brought with it heavy responsibility.
Failing to decipher the dots and squiggles on the tube correctly
could cost lives; not only the lives of British airmen, but also those
civilians whose homes and factories lay beneath the path of the
German bombers.

The need for complete secrecy was impressed upon them at every
turn. RDF developments were a 'cat and mouse game', they were
told; the smallest leak of information would hand the advantage back
to the enemy, with disastrous consequences. No one, however near
or dear, was to be given any information about the stations or their
operations – not by word of mouth and especially not in writing.

Enemy agents were all around, they were told: in person, tapping
telephones and intercepting letters. She shuddered to recall how naive
she had been that day, snooping on the Manor with her binoculars.

Little wonder they had treated her with such severity. Even whispers could cost lives. They were told that rumours had been designed and circulated, just as Mark had hinted, to lead the general public into believing RDF masts were actually transmitting some sort of 'magic eye' or death ray, and that the success of British attacks was due to the superiority of their planes and the skills of the pilots. Someone asked about carrots improving the eyesight of flyers. That, too, was propaganda, the instructor confirmed.

Two days after the dance, Kath received a note from Donald:

> *There's a quiz night at the NAAFI this evening. We could do with some more brains on our team (as well as beauty)! Can you join us?*

She showed the letter to Marcia. 'Has he invited you, too?'
'Donald? Who's he?'
'The fellow you danced with the other night.'
'Which fellow?'
'Blond, good dancer. Shortish.'
'Oh, him. Made me feel like a giant. No, I don't think he was interested in me. Anyway, I'm such a dimbo at that sort of thing. You go, have fun.'

To her surprise, Kath enjoyed the competitiveness of the quiz. She contributed correct answers to several questions that stumped the others and helped the team take second place, winning a free round of drinks from the bar.

Donald invited her to the dance the following weekend. Dancing with him was like flying, she decided. Her footwork was improving, and she loved the exhilaration and freedom of allowing the music to transport her away from harsh reality. This time, as they walked home, he leaned in for a kiss, and she soon discovered that he was something of an expert at that too. Like Billy Bishop, his hands seemed to roam everywhere at the same time. It was flattering and thrilling to be the object of such passion, and she felt her own desire for him growing.

One evening, after they had drunk more cocktails than usual, Donald said he had something special to tell her, in private. For a fleeting moment she wondered if he might produce a ring.

In the shadows at the back of the NAAFI, he pulled her to him and kissed her. 'You are the most delicious girl…' he said, pressing the length of his body against her. 'I wish we had more time to get to know each other.'

'More time?' Desire scrambled her brain.

'I'm due to be posted next week,' he said, nuzzling her ear. 'Who knows when we'll see each other again?'

'Oh, Donald.' This was a blow, she had to admit it. 'Do you know where?'

'This could be our last chance,' he whispered. As he kissed her again, even more passionately, she felt herself weakening. 'I've got the key to an empty hut. Come and spend the night with me.'

She didn't exactly say yes, but allowed herself to be steered along the darkened paths, past her own hut and on into the night. *This is it*, she said to herself, heart pounding. *The big moment.*

They reached the empty hut, and Donald tried to turn the key in the lock.

'Ruddy thing, I think it's rusted,' he said, shoving the door with his shoulder. He struggled some more with the key, took out his handkerchief for a better grip and, with two hands, gave it a strong wrench. The key broke, hitting the ground with a small clink. He cursed loudly and fell to his knees, scrabbling in the dark.

By the time he looked up, Kath was already walking away. Sobered by the chill in the air, she had realised that what she felt for Donald was not love, nor anything like it.

*

The following day, she replied to Vic's letter. She'd been putting it off, wondering whether there was really any future in their friendship. She recalled their conversations with fondness, but it all felt so long ago. Their backgrounds could not be more different. He was older, more serious, shy and socially awkward. But was any of that an excuse not to meet him?

Dear Vic,

You guessed right, of course, about where I'm based.

Four weeks into technical training, my head is crammed full of facts and figures but I'm enjoying the learning and managing to have fun too. The more I learn and understand, the more I respect what you and your colleagues have been so busy working on. My biggest fear now is that I won't be up to it and will end up failing and having to resign myself to slogging away at some menial task for the duration – not what I signed up for!

You are right about the buses, too. They go every two hours. It'd be lovely to explore the city with you. I get leave every other Sunday.

Fondest regards,

Kath

Dear Kath,

Great news. I'm so pleased we can meet. I can manage the Sunday after next (20th) if that works for you?

We could meet for coffee at the White Hart, say around eleven o'clock, and then spend the day exploring the city. I'd like to buy you lunch and if your bus runs late enough we could end with high tea. What a wonderful English institution that is. For a long time I thought the 'high' meant it was for posh people, or perhaps only served in places like a roof terrace. It took me a while to work out that besides the cuppa you also get the full spread of sandwiches and cakes!

Do let me know whether this is possible and I will make my arrangements around that. I am so looking forward to seeing you again. I miss our chats. I'm sure that the study won't be as difficult as you fear and you'll pass first time round.

Your friend, Vic

CHAPTER 22

As the bus approached and the three towers of Lincoln Cathedral came into view, white stone lit by the sunshine like sentinels against the flat countryside, Kath's stomach fluttered with nerves.

It had been nearly three years since they'd last seen each other on the day after war broke out, and so much had happened since then. She felt like a completely different person, had travelled the breadth of the country, befriended – or at least found ways to get along with – people from all walks of life, learned so much about the war and the way it was being fought. She'd grown physically strong and mentally confident. Somehow, her uniform actually fitted properly these days and she even felt quite smart in it. The studies were going well.

Despite persistent questioning from Marcia, she'd admitted only to meeting 'an old friend'; nevertheless, that morning Kath had been forced to submit to the full beauty treatment. Her hair had been rolled, dried and styled, her skin exfoliated and moisturised before the application of foundation, powder and eye make-up. She'd tried on three silk blouses before choosing the pale green – 'matches your eyes' – and she was wearing a pair of silk stockings and several dabs of Vol de Nuit perfume.

'Well, look at you now, Kath, all grown up,' she'd whispered to herself in the mirror. 'I wonder if he'll still like this new me?' Then another, less welcome thought: three years had passed for Vic as well, three years of working with different people in different parts of the country. *If I'm different, surely he'll have changed too?*

She need not have worried. As she entered the hotel lobby, she knew him instantly by the set of his shoulders and the shock of black hair. He turned, as though he'd known she was there even before she'd said a word, and smiled. It was awkward at first, and absurdly formal. They shook hands.

'Kathleen Motts! Is it really you? You look wonderful.'

She laughed. 'Did I look so awful before?'

Embarrassment clouded his face. 'I'm sorry, I always seem to put my foot in it. It was meant as a compliment.'

'I was only teasing,' she said quickly. 'Thank you for the compliment. I've got a friend who's a whizz with hair and make-up.'

'Then it's my turn to be flattered. Now, what shall we have? Tea or coffee? Teacakes or biscuits?'

After that, conversation flowed so readily that it was easy to forget they'd ever been parted. When they'd finished tea, Vic suggested they go for a walk. Away from prying ears, they could talk more freely. She amused him with stories of her initial training and the postings in Whitstable and then Devon, and he described, in guarded language, the developments his new team had been making, initially in Dundee and then in Stanmore, expanding and refining the applications of radio direction finding. It felt so good to learn more about his research at last, now that she was part of the RDF 'club' and could actually understand the language. Well, some of it.

'I don't want to embarrass you,' she said, 'but now that I know a bit more about what you and your colleagues were getting up to at Bawdsey, I just want to say that I think you have achieved the most extraordinary thing ever. If anything can protect us, your inventions will.'

'That's sweet of you, Kath. Although it's Watson-Watt who should get the credit.'

'But it's personal for me. My brother's been flying for nearly four years now, and although he rarely talks about it, he says what he calls

the "magic eye" has saved him more than once. And that is thanks
to you and your team, Vic.'

He tried to speak, but she held up her hand. 'No, let me finish.
What I wanted to say is…' The words came out in a rush. 'I am so
proud of you.' She looked into his eyes, disconcerted to see them
welling with tears, and reached out to take his hand. 'I really mean
it. I don't think any of us would still be here without you.'

'It wasn't only me.'

'But what you achieved, you and your team…'

He went quiet, and she feared she'd said too much.

'Vic?'

'Oh, sorry. I was in a dream.'

'A good one?'

'Good and bad. I was remembering my friend Johnnie. The one
who died in the flying boat accident. You met me on the Cliff Walk
that terrible day.'

'I remember. You were in quite a state.'

Vic sighed. 'We'd worked so well together, and I almost gave up
after that. Couldn't see the point. But at the funeral I talked to his
son, a lovely young lad, who said his father had told him we were
doing our best to make the world safe for the next generation, and
that I must carry on, even without him.'

'What wise words. I'm so very glad you did.'

He squeezed her fingers and they walked on in silence, hand in
hand.

Vic had booked lunch in the hotel dining room, and a table in the
window. Dear Vic – nothing left to chance. The room, comfortably
old-fashioned with faded furnishings and carpets that had seen better
days, reminded them both of Bawdsey Manor.

They ate well – surprisingly well, considering the restrictions on
supplies: omelette and chips for him, roast chicken for her. They

even ordered glasses of wine. Vic seemed to know which colour went best with which food, and ordered a different, sweeter version to go with their dessert of apple crumble with custard. It was fun being with someone so confident around such sophisticated matters. She began to relax and enjoy herself properly. She'd almost forgotten: this was what normal life was like.

Kath was entirely unprepared for the astonishing size of the Cathedral. From the outside it was impressive enough, but the interior, with its vast columns reaching upwards supporting a ceiling criss-crossed with what Vic called vaulting, took her breath away.

'Quite something, isn't it?' he whispered into the silence.

'I've never been very religious, but I can see how a place like this could make you believe in God,' she whispered.

'Hindu temples are so different,' he said. 'Dark and smoky from all the incense and candles, and noisy with people chattering and children playing.' He pointed to a carving at the top of a column. 'That's more the sort of thing you'd see in an Indian temple.'

She could see the carved face of a grinning imp, oddly out of place in the otherwise respectful piety of the place.

'He's quite famous,' Vic said. 'Apparently he was causing so much trouble, the other angels decided to make an example of him and turned him into stone.'

'What a mean lot.'

A little further on, Vic went to speak to one of the clerics, and returned looking disappointed.

'What's wrong, Vic?'

'Ruddy war spoils everything,' he muttered. 'I wanted to show you the copy of the Magna Carta, but he says it's been removed for safekeeping along with all their other valuables.'

'Why's it so important?'

'It's one of only two known copies in the country, and it's seven hundred years old. All our laws are based on it: the rights of individuals, the right to justice and the right to a fair trial. It's one of the best things the English brought to India. That and trains.'

'Crikey. I never knew all of that.'

'And it's those freedoms we're fighting to protect,' he said, with a small sigh.

'We'll just have to come back after the war to see it.'

'Together, I hope. Now, are you feeling strong?'

'Strong?'

'Three hundred steps kind of strong?'

'After all that square-bashing I could climb a mountain.'

Once they'd gathered their breath at the top of the tower, they could see for miles in every direction. The sun's rays sliced between gaps in the gathering clouds, illuminating the patchwork of flat fenland fields below.

'It reminds me of those religious paintings,' Kath said. 'When they're trying to paint God's divine light.'

'I don't think God's got much to do with it,' he said. 'I'm afraid it's just science: the rain falls, the sun comes out and evaporates it, clouds form and grow so they can't hold the moisture any more, so it rains. And that lot over there,' he said, pointing to the tallest clouds of all, lined up to the horizon like a fleet of ships, 'are the ones our flyers fear the most.'

'Why's that?'

'They bring thunderstorms.' Even now, they could see stripes of rain falling from the dark underbelly of the clouds to the earth below. At that moment, they both noticed a rumbling noise. A deep vibration at first, and then louder.

'Is that thunder?'

'Doesn't sound right.'

The sound was constant and growing.

'Look.' A shadow beneath the clouds grew larger until they could see that it was actually made out of dozens of individual dots. They were planes, squadron upon squadron of them, too far away to identify at first.

'It's our boys,' Vic said. 'Bombers setting off on a raid.'

As they watched the deadly machinery of war gathering in the sky, the magic of that golden afternoon evaporated. In four hours it would be night-time over Germany, and the planes would unleash their cargo of high explosives onto enemy factories, army bases and airfields. Dozens, perhaps even hundreds or thousands of civilians, including women and children, would die, and some of those crews would not come home.

What if Mark was piloting one of those planes, even now disappearing into the haze? Kath shivered. Vic took off his jacket and placed it round her shoulders. She snuggled into it, enjoying its weight and warmth, the smell of him.

'Come on, let's go and have a cup of tea,' he said.

'Thank you for a lovely day, Vic,' she said, as they walked back to the bus station. Holding hands somehow seemed to have become natural now. She'd noticed some of the townspeople giving second glances, and wondered why. It was only much later she realised that it would have been unusual to see a brown man hand in hand with a white girl. But what did she care? It was none of their business.

'Would you like to do it again?'

'Depends where I'm posted. I'll know in two weeks.'

'Any idea?'

'Could be anywhere. But I hope there's a bit of life to the place, at least.'

'I suppose you've been enjoying Cranwell? Their dances are the stuff of RAF legend.'

'I thought you hated dancing.'

'I do, but I just can't bear the thought of you having fun without me.'

'Shall I lock myself into a nunnery, then?'

He laughed. 'Yes, please. If you don't mind.'

'But I have my work to do.'

'You can watch a diode screen in a habit and veil, surely?'

As they reached the bus station the bus rumbled into view, pulling to a halt with a sharp squeal of its brakes and a cloud of oily smoke.

He turned to her, putting a warm hand to her cheek. 'It's been wonderful to see you, Kath,' he said. 'You really are the best thing that's happened to me in a very, very long time, you know. I hope we can meet again soon.'

'I'll write when I know where,' she said. Other passengers were already getting on board.

This time it was a real kiss, combined sweetness and sorrow almost frightening in its intensity. This might be their last chance for a very long time.

As she climbed onto the bus she felt the loss of him already. Marcia crept along the gangway and took a seat next to her.

'What are you doing here? I didn't know you were coming to Lincoln today?'

'Buying these.' Marcia pulled from a carrier bag a smart woollen scarf and leather gloves. 'Ready for winter. How was your date, by the way?'

'Date?'

'Spies are everywhere, don't you know? You didn't let on that your beau was an Indian prince. How terribly exotic.'

'He's not a prince, idiot. He's just got an Indian mother, that's all,' Kath whispered. 'He's English as they come otherwise. And he's not my beau. He's just a friend.'

'Sorry, doesn't wash, sweetie. You were definitely kissing.'

'A peck, that was all.'

It wasn't really all, though, as she was beginning to admit to herself. She was beginning to fall for him.

It was the last week of their course, consumed by frantic revision, practical tests and written examinations. There were papers on the theory of radio direction finding and the practice of its operation, with simulated exercises to test their nerves in 'real-life' situations, which were of course entirely silly and made Kath and Marcia giggle.

All too soon they found themselves sitting in the anteroom to the officers' quarters, once more awaiting results that would decide their fate for the foreseeable future. Although she'd acquitted herself reasonably well in the practical tests, Kath was still nervous and not entirely certain of her performance in the theory papers. So when she learned that she had passed with flying colours, it was all she could do to stop herself whooping out loud.

She stood and saluted, before shaking hands with each of the officers.

'Well done, ACW2 Motts,' they said. 'And good luck. You will take a week's leave from next Monday. This envelope contains details of where and when you are to report on Monday week, and a travel warrant as necessary.'

Back in the barracks, Marcia had already opened hers.

'So...?'

'Just my ruddy luck,' she said. 'I'm being shunted to the back of beyond. Never heard of the place.'

'Where?'

'They call it RAF Bawdsey.' She pronounced it 'bowdsey'.

'Heavens! Bawdsey Manor? In Suffolk? They must be letting the WAAFs back. I live near there. I actually worked there, before the war.'

'Worked? What as?'

'Assistant chef. Oh goodness, Marcia. I'm so jealous. I so want to be posted there, to be close to my family, see my friends. There's not a lot of social life. But it's such a beautiful place.'

'Where are you going, then?'

'Here, you do it.' As she passed the envelope over, Kath's hands were shaking.

Marcia ripped it open and looked up with a smile. 'Someone up there's looking after you, you lucky blighter.'

The words slowly came into focus. 'Where the hell is RAF Bentley Priory?'

'It's Stanmore, you ninny. Headquarters of Fighter Command.'

'You're joking?'

'Dowding wants you as his batwoman.' Air Chief Marshal Sir Hugh Dowding was a legend, the feared and respected Commander-in-Chief of RAF Fighter Command, the man who had co-ordinated the Battle of Britain. He had also been one of the earliest exponents of RDF, making sure that Robert Watson-Watt got the funding for the first experimental work.

'No, seriously, whatever would they want with a rookie operator?'

'I guess you'll just have to find out.'

Bomber Command was housed in a stately home that must once have been rather grand, but was now covered in ghastly green and brown camouflage paint. The WAAFs were accommodated in forty-bed wooden huts and the shift system meant the place was never free of comings and goings, day and night.

Kath and five other WAAF newcomers were told they were here 'to observe and learn', although what this was in preparation for was never made clear. On their first day they were led in pouring rain to a newly constructed concrete bunker called the Operations Block. Entry was through several doors in blast-proof metal and down a rough concrete stairway to a long underground corridor that smelled oppressively of stale sweat and cigarette smoke.

The map in the huge Filter Room was unlike any other Kath had seen. The North Sea, the Channel and areas of Holland, Belgium and France were filled with a spider's web of wide arcs in a rainbow of colours, showing the coverage of RDF stations and the location of planes and ships, friendly and hostile. Here, WAAFs received reports by telephone from dozens of stations around the coast ready to be 'filtered' and verified against other reports before forwarding them to the Operations Rooms down the corridor. There, senior officers decided on RAF and US air force deployments, air-raid warnings, states of readiness at ack-ack gun sites, Observer Corps and barrage balloon stations.

After a couple of hours there was a change of shift, and one of the operators was asked if she could spare a few moments to speak to the new recruits.

'Any questions?' she asked.

'Do you enjoy your work?'

'Frankly, we're too tired to think about it much. I've been on shift eleven hours and it's been non-stop. Sometimes we're following fifty tracks every minute. But I suppose it's satisfying, knowing we've done our bit to help.' She was very young, possibly only nineteen, Kath estimated, and her face was grey with exhaustion, her hair falling lankly from its bun.

'*Fifty* tracks?'

'There are hundreds, sometimes thousands, of planes and ships out there, as you've seen.'

'Why aren't there any men doing the plotting?'

She grinned. 'They're not quick enough. So we've been told.'

'What do you do when you're off shift?'

That mirthless laugh again. 'Eat, wash, try to sleep.'

'Try?'

'Often we're so wound up it's almost impossible to sleep, wondering what's happening to the planes we've been tracking. Especially when we know people who're out there.' Kath's thoughts turned to Mark. Perhaps that was why he never told them when he was going to be 'out there'.

'What's the social life like?'

'No such thing,' she said, shaking her head.

After ten days of 'observation', the new recruits were becoming restless.

'Have I missed something? I'm still confused about why we're here,' one asked, after lights out.

'Training to be filter room operators?' someone suggested.

'Then when does our training actually start?'

'Does anyone actually *want* to work here?' A general murmur, with some voices of dissent.

'Who's going to ask her?'

'Ask what?'

'Why we're here. Kath, you're good at asking questions.'

'And get my head chopped off?' Their leader was an older WAAF with impeccable uniform and hair stiff as a wig, who never seemed to smile.

A chorus of voices: 'Go on, Kath. We're depending on you.'

In the end, there was no need for Kath to put her head on the block. After breakfast the following Monday they were invited to a meeting with a new officer who seemed altogether friendlier.

'Well, my friends. You are halfway through your familiarisation visit. I hope you are finding it useful?'

'Very interesting,' Kath ventured. 'Although it would have been helpful if we'd been told why we were here in the first place.'

The officer looked surprised. 'I'm sorry if that wasn't made clear. The six of you were chosen because you showed exceptional promise in your RDF examinations, and we expect you to rise quickly through the ranks,' she said.

'Can you explain how that works, please, ma'am?'

'In return for your time here, we are now charging you with the responsibility to spread that knowledge. We want you to take what you have learned back to your new postings and explain to your colleagues how their reports are used and why their work is so vitally important. Will you do that for us?'

Someone else had a hand up.

'Yes?'

'How do you recruit filter room operators, please?'

'Is it something you would like to apply for?'

'Yes, ma'am. I'd be interested.'

'May I enquire how old you are?'

'Twenty-two, ma'am.'

'Then I'm sorry, but you are too old. They only recruit girls under twenty, who're believed to have faster brains and greater stamina.'

A gasp of astonishment. Someone said, 'We're over the hill, ladies,' which was met with a burst of giggles.

'Anyway, it's been a pleasure meeting you all, over the hill or not,' the officer said. She took up a sheaf of buff envelopes and began handing them out. 'Here are your new posting details. The bus will be waiting for you on Friday at eleven hours, sharp.'

This time Kath did not hesitate. She ripped open her envelope and gave a little whoop of joy.

'Bawdsey! At last!'

CHAPTER 23

It was raining that first day, a chill sleety rain coming in off the sea, but Kath didn't care. She'd had a wonderfully relaxing few days on leave, eating home-cooked food and going for long walks with Joan, who had also managed to get a forty-eight-hour pass.

They hadn't seen each other for more than two years and had much to catch up on. Joan was now married to Sam, who had eventually decided to sign up but had soon been injured – his hand badly shattered – and shipped home. He was recovering in a convalescent home in south London, just two bus rides from her own billet, so that Joan could visit him quite easily on her days off.

'At least he's safe there,' she said. 'I just hope he doesn't recover too quickly and they send him back again.'

Without going into specifics, Kath talked about the highs and lows of her WAAF training, about Donald, and how she'd met up with Vic in Lincoln and thought it might be growing into something.

'Whatever would your parents think, you dating an Indian?' Joan asked.

'He's only half Indian,' Kath retorted, more sharply than she'd intended. 'Anyway, I don't care what anyone thinks.' *But he's such a long way away*, she thought to herself now as she clambered off the ferry, remembering how he never managed to avoid getting his feet wet. The last time she'd been here at Bawdsey, he'd been here too.

The weight of her kit bag made fast walking impossible, but she deliberately took her time up the long driveway from the ferry, allowing the Manor to emerge slowly as she rounded the bend.

Pausing at the bridge over the River Jordan, she took a few breaths to calm her nerves before lifting the pack once more.

At the front porch she paused again. This would be the first time she had ever entered the building through this doorway. She was no longer a servant. She belonged here, had a right to enter. A *duty* to enter.

She knocked once, twice and then tried the handle, a ring of heavy iron which turned surprisingly easily. The wooden door gave way, and she was inside. The cavernous hallway was deserted. She put down her pack. To her left was the great wide staircase. Ahead of her, double doors stood open, leading into the great hall with its panelled walls and balcony above. The old out-of-tune piano was still there – she wondered whether Vic was able to practise wherever he was these days. Beyond that, she knew, was the Green Lounge, where she'd served tea for Winston Churchill.

It felt good, like coming home.

After a short exploration she found herself in the open doorway of a large room panelled in oak and lined with leather, and knocked. 'Come in, come in,' came a female voice.

'ACW2 Motts 526843, reporting for duty, ma'am.' She saluted and clicked her heels as crisply as the thick carpeting would allow.

'At ease,' the woman said, moving forward to shake her hand. 'Section Leader Bartlett. Good morning, Motts. Bit nippy on the ferry today, I expect?' She tipped her head towards the window and the panoramic view of the estuary.

'I live round here, ma'am, so I'm used to the weather.'

'Very good, very good. You have been at Stanmore, I understand? Interesting?'

'Very interesting, ma'am.'

'I expect you to tell the other recruits all about it, when you can.' She turned back to her desk, running her finger down a list of names. 'Now let me check. I believe you are... yes, here we are. Room fifty-four, White Tower.'

'Yes, ma'am. And thank you, ma'am.'

'I suppose you're aware that it's only in the past couple of weeks that WAAFs have been brought back since we were evacuated at the start of hostilities?'

'Indeed, ma'am. I am delighted to be back here again.'

'When were you here before, Motts?'

'I was an assistant cook here, before the war, ma'am. I was brought up in Felixstowe and my parents still live there.'

'Excellent. Then you'll know your way around already.'

'I'm afraid we never strayed far from the kitchens.'

'Mess facilities in the Manor are only for officers these days, I'm afraid. You'll be eating in the cookhouse across the way, in the old stable block. It's plain fare, but there's plenty of it. I suggest you find your room, make yourself comfortable and then head over for lunch, twelve-thirty. Afternoon briefing is in the hall here, two p.m. sharp. Then you'll get your detail, and you won't have a moment to think. It's all go out there.'

Kath wandered through several corridors, up and down short flights of stairs, encountering a couple of dead ends and having to retrace her steps several times before finding number fifty-four.

For some reason she'd imagined that all the rooms in the Manor would be of baronial proportions, and was sorely disappointed to discover that she was in what must have been part of the servants' quarters: a whitewashed cell with high, narrow windows like arrow slits into which five double bunk beds, five cheap plywood chests of drawers and a single wardrobe had been awkwardly squeezed, given the cramped dimensions of the room. Only one of the beds, a lower bunk closest to the door, remained unmade. Standing on tiptoe to peer through the window, she could see the courtyard below. Now she understood. The room was in one of the towers, which accounted for its odd hexagonal shape.

At least it's not a corrugated iron hut, she thought to herself; and the bathroom was just along the corridor, not across a damp field.

She made up the bed, covering the thin, hard mattress with one of the blankets under the bottom sheet – a trick she'd learned from the early days of her induction. She unpacked her kit into the only drawer that remained empty, took off her jacket, kicked off her shoes and lay down, trying to calm her nerves.

The weeks at Stanmore had been an eye-opener, bringing home even more forcefully the critical importance of accuracy in reading and reporting what hundreds of WAAFs around the country were trying to interpret on their fuzzy screens and sometimes temperamental equipment. The success of Allied raids and the lives of hundreds of flyers were entirely dependent on it.

Would she come up to the mark under pressure? Would she manage to keep calm, to analyse carefully, to stand her ground, to trust her instincts? Apart from a short experience in Devon and the mock scenarios in examinations, she had never been properly tested. She might have been, as the officer at Stanmore said, one of the best at the theory tests, but now she would have to prove she could do it in practice.

She'd hoped to meet Marcia at lunch, but her friend was nowhere to be seen. When she enquired, one of the other WAAFs explained: 'She's probably on duty, or asleep. We're all on different sites and watches.'

'Do you ever get a chance to socialise?' Kath asked. Oh yes, you got thirty-six hours off every four days, they said. And there were dances in the hall every Sunday evening.

'Plus, if you get the chance to go to one of the USAF dos, go for it,' one girl said. The others laughed knowingly. 'The drink and grub they lay on is incredible,' she added.

'The music is cracking – real bands, you know, jazz and stuff,' said another.

'Need to be good at fending off wandering hands, though,' warned a third. 'There aren't any women on USAF bases, so those fellas are pretty hungry.'

That afternoon the eight 'new girls' received their briefing instructions before being given a tour of the site. Bawdsey, having been the centre of research from the very beginning, had more types of equipment than any other, all for different purposes and all known by confusing acronyms such as CHL (which could detect aircraft inland as well as out at sea) and K (for low-flying planes and shipping).

The watch system started with a night shift beginning at eleven and ending at eight in the morning, after which you got the day off and started again in the evening at six. Next day you covered the afternoon from one o'clock till early evening, and the day after that you were on the morning shift till lunchtime. Once again, they were reminded, there was to be no work talk off shift or outside your own site, not even with friends.

At the end of the tour and briefing, Kath was invited to give a brief description of her time at Stanmore, sensing from their questions the admiration and even envy of her fellow recruits. At the end, everyone clapped. 'Thank you, ACW2 Motts, that was most interesting,' the leader said. 'You are very fortunate to have experienced the most vital part of our operation, first-hand.'

She started her first shift that very evening, at the CHL site.

By midnight she had already been on duty for an hour, and her eyes were telling her that she should have taken a proper nap that afternoon. Three large RAF raids had been to Germany earlier in the evening and while many had returned, there were now a number of stragglers on their screens. Some were obviously in difficulty; judging by their heights some were already dangerously low and liable to ditch into the sea. She plotted them continuously, praying that they would make it to the coastline and ready to alert the air-sea rescue instantly should they disappear.

At one-twenty she saw the start of a new track, a faint blip at 115 miles. She found the bearing and pressed the button for the grid reference. It was just off the Dutch coast, she calculated. She switched to the height aerials, pressed more buttons. Height twenty thousand feet. She studied the blip again, estimating forty-plus aircraft, and passed the information through to the plotters, who would send it on to Stanmore. Soon afterwards it was confirmed: identification HOSTILE Track 153. Stomach churning, she took more plots. The range was now a hundred miles, height unchanged, and she could see there were more than sixty of them.

Most of the RAF planes were now in, but one had disappeared from her screen twenty miles from the coast. Sending the urgent alert, she visualised the air crew scrambling out of their sinking plane, perhaps looking around for the others, praying that they all managed to get into their dinghy and that air-sea rescue was able to find them.

She turned back to the hostile blip, now estimating seventy-five-plus aircraft, apparently heading straight towards Suffolk. *How vulnerable we are*, Kath thought, *so visible and right on the edge of the coast*. The plotter at the table at the other end of the room said grimly, 'Been nice knowing you, girls.' But there was no time for being scared. She took two more plots. The blip was fading, indicating that they had veered south-east, probably heading for London. The information went through to Stanmore.

Soon enough, RAF fighter crews would be scrambling from their beds, running across darkened fields and into their planes; ack-ack teams would be getting their range, and Londoners would be wearily making their way into air-raid shelters and underground stations, facing yet another disturbed night ahead.

Turning quickly back to the 'tube' screen, Kath detected a new blip at three miles heading away from land: two aircraft, or possibly three. The double V showed they were friendly. At eighteen and twenty miles out they began stooging around, back and forth, round and round. Must be the air-sea rescue looking for the ditched crew.

Her eyes were burning. Two hours was quite long enough to focus on that fuzzy screen, and it was time to swap places. She moved across to work at the plotting table and then, at the next swap, to take her turn as 'teller', passing information through to Stanmore on the telephone. She imagined the frantic WAAFs at Stanmore, rushing between phone and table, the hubbub of shouted instructions, the serious faces of the top brass observing from the balcony above as the raid headed for London, and prayed that Mark was not already in the fray.

And so the night went on. At first light their screens burst into life, filled with large blips all moving towards Belgium and Holland. 'It's the Yanks,' someone said: the USAF taking off from their new airstrips, en route for Germany's war installations. The screen was soon a solid mass of blips from zero to thirty miles.

'That'll be a sight for sore eyes,' the shift supervisor said. 'Take it in turns to take a quick dekko.'

It was the noise that struck them first, the persistent roar of low-flying heavy aircraft. But the sky was empty. Then, from the west, came hundreds of them in great ordered flocks, filling the sky as far as the eye could see, some low, some higher up; and now, as they watched, starting to pass over the coastline and heading out towards the continent. It was an impressive sight, enough to make your heart race. Was Mark up there, heading out on what would undoubtedly be a dangerous mission? Was he looking down on his home town and wondering when, or whether, he would ever get back here? Kath's eyes filled with tears, her thoughts in a turmoil of pride and terror.

Someone beside her whispered, 'Go get 'em, boys.'

'Second that,' she said.

At the end of the shift they headed for the cookhouse, but the dried-up toast and grey-looking scrambled egg made from powder looked unappetising, and Kath felt too tired to eat. The excitement of witnessing the extraordinary might of the combined RAF and US air forces had kept her going on adrenalin for the last hour, but now all she wanted was to get to bed and sleep.

'Kathleen Motts, as I live and breathe. You're here at last! How come? I thought you'd be running the war by now.' It was Marcia, glamorous as ever, heading back from the cookhouse with a gang of three others, as Kath made her way towards it. 'We're just coming off shift, sweetie, and heading out for a drink or several across the water. Want to come?'

'Sorry, I need to grab a bite before my shift,' Kath said.

'Shame. We'll have to catch up later. What room are you in?'

'Fifty-four.'

'Great – not too far from me. I'm in eighty-two,' Marcia shouted as she dashed away down the corridor. 'See you soon.'

After coming off shift again in the early hours of the morning, Kath crept into her room. In the light from the corridor, she saw that four of the bunks were occupied with sleeping figures. On her own, there was a note.

Hello sweetie. I'm so delighted you're here, after all. Why aren't you running the world from HQ any more? Did they sack you? Can't wait to catch up but it looks like we're on clashing shift patterns right now. Next Saturday evening we've been invited to Martlesham – the US base. Absolutely NOT TO BE MISSED! Write it in blood in your diary and bribe someone to swap shifts if necessary. Kisses, M.

CHAPTER 24

The work of Vic and his team had been turned upside down by the arrival of the US air force.

He and another British research engineer were paired with a couple of American scientists and sent all over the country visiting newly built USAF bases. Their job entailed making sure that 'friend or foe' transmitters and receivers were properly installed into hundreds of newly arrived Flying Fortress bombers and other aircraft, and that AI, the air interception equipment that allowed aircrews to follow the flights of other nearby aircraft directly from their cockpits, was working correctly.

The work was pressured and exhausting, demanding all of Vic's powers of diplomacy, but the living conditions and meals were more luxurious than anything he'd ever experienced. Once they'd accepted that he wouldn't eat their delicious-smelling crispy bacon, hamburgers and hot dogs, they came up with plenty more to satisfy his taste: proper eggs cooked all ways, pancakes with maple syrup and, for lunch or dinner, plenty of fresh vegetables along with the crispiest chips – or 'fries', as they insisted on calling them. Their ice cream was simply out of this world.

American scientists and engineers were assigned to each development team, and they had only weeks to make sure that all of their systems were co-ordinated. He didn't take to them at all, at first. They were so loud, and so bossy, so certain their way was right. For a start, it seemed inevitable that they would have to adopt the new American term RADAR – for Radio Detection and Ranging – even though it just seemed like an overblown version of their own acronym.

The Yankee dollars were very welcome and their research budgets quadrupled overnight, but it took time to get used to each other's way of working. The best way of dealing with them was as he'd done with other overly confident characters like Frank: let them have their big bluster first, getting it out of the way, after which he would quietly but insistently point out the flaws of their argument. It didn't make him especially popular, that he knew from experience; but it earned him respect and, more importantly, it saved time.

The other trial, of course, was dealing with their questions about his origins. One of his teammates, Randy (short for Randolph, but Vic couldn't trust himself to say it out loud for fear of sniggering like a schoolboy) said quite bluntly that he'd been surprised to find Vic working alongside 'white folks'.

'Back home, the blacks are segregated, even in the military.'

'Segregated? You mean, kept apart by law?' Vic was aghast.

Randy explained it was only in some states where seating on buses, schools, swimming pools and working areas in factories were divided into 'black' and 'other'.

'But why?' Vic gasped.

'Gee, it's so normal I don't really know why, and never asked. That's the way it's always been, so I guess folks feel more comfortable that way.'

'*White* people feel more comfortable, you mean?'

His friend clapped him on the shoulder. 'Aw, don't take it amiss, Mac. It don't make a bitty bit of difference between you an' me, eh? It's great working with you, chum.'

But for all the constant company, Vic was lonely.

Most of all, he missed Kath. That day in Lincoln glowed in his memory; his hand could still feel the imprint of hers as they'd walked together, and he could still taste the astonishing sensation of her lips meeting his as they'd waited for her bus. His heart seemed to ache in his chest when he thought of her, and he felt sure this must be what they called 'falling in love'. But did she feel the same about him? He longed to see her again, to reassure himself.

By now, he felt sure, she would have had her post-training week's leave in Felixstowe. With Lizzie's words about persistence ringing in his ears, he had written several times to Kath's home address. He'd received nothing from her apart from a brief note thanking him for the lovely day in Lincoln.

He told himself to be patient. In these troubled days everyone was on the move, sometimes with only a few hours' notice. No one could be sure of where they might be posted next.

Another week went by. Surely by now she would be at her first real posting? His requests for leave had thus far been refused 'due to operational priorities', but he was certainly due some time off, and hoped to use it to visit Kath. But where was she?

And then, on the very same day, two envelopes arrived in his pigeonhole. The first was addressed in Kath's rounded, generous hand.

Dear Vic,

Thank you for the two letters, which I picked up from home when I came back on leave a week ago. I'm sorry for the long silence and hope this reaches you now that you are doing so much travelling. Still I am sure your work is interesting, as ever, and you are achieving yet more great things!

You won't believe it but I'm back here, where we first met. The place is full of memories and reminders of the times we had here. Not that I've had much time to think, trying to get used to the crazy shift patterns and feeling dog tired most of the time. Also, the weather is so miserable I haven't been able to get out into the gardens. Our favourite walk is out of bounds anyway, covered with barbed wire and the rest, as you can probably imagine.

I had a very exciting week at HQ before this, seeing what they do with what we tell them. I half wondered whether I might see you

there, but no luck. Being there brought it home to me, all over again,
how critical your work has been, and still is. Hats off to you all!
  I'm still a novice, but learning fast. It's terrifying and exhilarat-
ing and exhausting all at once. I've got no idea when I'll get leave,
but will let you know. In the meantime, if you're ever up this way
it'd be so lovely to see you. Write again soon.
  Fondest regards,
  Kath

The news was better than he could have possibly hoped. That they were allowing women back to Bawdsey was surely a sign of the Allies' growing confidence that the dangers of enemy invasion or air attack were receding. The world suddenly seemed less bleak, and he was so thrilled by the warmth of her words that he lost himself in a brief reverie and almost forgot to open the second envelope. It was the official buff variety marked confidential, top secret and *Not to be opened by any unauthorised person*. It contained a rail warrant with the usual cryptic instruction: *Report to USAF Martlesham 1400 hours Friday*. That was in just two days' time.

He ran to the lab and pulled down a map. USAF Martlesham was, by a quick reckoning, just a dozen or so miles from Bawdsey. 'Thank you, gods,' he gasped, barely able to believe his good fortune.

He allowed the reverie to return, imagining Kath on board the ferry, in one of the rooms in the Red Tower or the White Tower, or with her head bent over a screen in one of the bunkers along with her fellow WAAFs. The image now began to include himself, walking those paths hand in hand with her, the gardens filled with spring flowers, the sun in her hair, her laughter, the feel of her lips…

Vic and his English teammate Monty had been at USAF Martlesham for just three days when Randy told them about the dance planned for the coming Saturday in the new mess hall.

'They're flying in a swing band from Austin. It'll be a knockout. You have to be there, kiddo.'

Vic had become accustomed to being called 'kiddo', and assumed it was because he was so much smaller than most of them. They were all giants, dwarfing even Monty's five foot ten, though their faces were so youthful they looked as though they'd only just learned to shave. And although they spoke the same language, he often failed to understand them. A swing band? And where on earth was Austin? It didn't matter anyway, because he didn't plan to go, knockout or not. Monty was keen, but Vic rolled out his usual excuses: can't dance, nothing to wear, bit of a headache. But Randy was nothing if not persistent.

'Look,' he said, lighting up a Lucky Strike and lounging back on Vic's bunk as though he owned it. 'I hear what you're saying, Mac, you don't feel comfortable at dances. And I get it. There's your colour an' all, and those uptight English ballroom affairs are enough to make anyone uncomfortable. But have you ever been to an American dance, with a *jazz* band? It's *black* music, man. There're no fancy doo-dah steps to learn, you just do what feels right. I guarantee you won't be able to resist tapping your toes, and before long you'll be on the floor, 'specially with a couple of daiquiris inside you.'

'Thank you, but I really don't think so...' What on earth was a daiquiri, anyway?

Randy's voice took on a confidential tone. 'I shouldn't be sayin' this, but it really ain't the done thing to refuse. The brass hats might think you ungrateful.'

Vic recognised at once that he'd been checkmated. These Yanks might act stupid some of the time, but they were clever devils underneath.

'Okay then, I'll come for a short while, just to be polite,' he conceded.

'Good man. See you in the bar, seven sharp.'

*

A daiquiri, Vic discovered, was a drink of rum mixed with ice and lime juice that slipped down so easily that it was only quarter of an hour later you realised how strong it was. After drinking two of them, he belatedly recalled being warned that American measures were double or even, sometimes, treble those served in English pubs.

As Randy led them from the bar across the stretch of tarmac to a nearby hangar, the fresh air helped to clear Vic's head and he felt ready for anything. Even so, the sheer noise of the band, the size of the dance floor and the numbers of dancers, at least a couple of hundred, was daunting. Randy and Monty disappeared, leaving him clinging to the wall like a gooseberry. He soon discovered that his feet were actually tapping, all by themselves, to the irresistible rhythms of the music. No one seemed to be taking any notice of him. Dancers whirled past, flinging themselves from side to side without any semblance of formal steps, and he was so transfixed that he failed to notice the young woman sidling up beside him.

'You look lonely,' she shouted over the din. 'You're not from round here, are you?' Her Suffolk inflections reminded him of Kath. Must be one of the girls they bussed in from nearby villages for these affairs.

'No,' he said. 'I'm from Tunbridge Wells.'

One eyebrow raised in a sceptical arc. 'Pull the other one, fella.'

'Honestly,' he said. 'I'm half English, half Indian.'

'I've never met anyone even partly Indian.'

'We're perfectly harmless, as you see. Don't bite, or whisper evil spells.'

She laughed. 'Would you like to dance?' How bold girls were becoming, these days. Must be the war. He rather liked it, this turning of the tables.

'Not really,' he said.

'You don't have to know any steps.'

Too drunk to resist, he allowed her to take his hand and lead him into the melee. They danced – or rather, he moved his feet around and after a while, cautiously, his arms – until he was quite out of breath.

'Can I buy you a drink?' he said, pulling out a handkerchief to mop his brow.

'That'd be nice,' she said. 'My name's Carol. What's yours?'

'Vic.'

'Short for Victor?'

'Short for Vikram.'

'That's more like it,' she said, threading her arm through his. 'Now, where's the bar?'

Just as they were crossing the tarmac the boom of music from the hangar stopped for a second, and in the unaccustomed silence they heard a giggle, then another.

'Someone's having fun,' Carol said. 'C'mon, I'm dying for a drink.'

Peering into the darkness, Vic could just about make out two figures in the shadows, at the corner of the building. Another giggle. A male voice, American: 'You're a sweet kid, d'ya know that? D'ya wanna see my Thunderbolt?'

The girl spoke, and his heart seemed to stop beating. Even though he couldn't hear the words, it sounded just like Kath's voice.

'Gimme another kiss, and I'll show ya.' The man gathered the girl into his arms again, smooching her so intimately, so intensely, that it made Vic's stomach turn upside down. The kiss seemed to go on forever. She didn't seem to be resisting; in fact, she seemed to be enjoying it.

'Ooh, you are naughty,' the girl said, with a giggle that sealed his certainty. It *was* Kath. What on earth was she doing here? The answer was perfectly plain.

He felt Carol's hand trying to take his, pulling him along. 'You coming, or what?'

But his feet were rooted to the ground, watching helplessly as the couple pulled apart from their clinch and disappeared behind the building. His head was spinning, he felt nauseous and desperate to lie down.

'Sorry, I'm not feeling very well,' he shouted to Carol and turned away, stumbling in the direction of his barracks. Once there, he dragged himself along the corridor to the bathroom, where he was violently sick. Back in his bunk he succumbed to misery, silently weeping for the girl he'd missed so much, on whom he'd pinned such ridiculous hopes.

The girl he'd believed himself to be falling in love with.

The girl he'd allowed himself to imagine might, just might, have been starting to feel the same.

CHAPTER 25

'Kath? Where the hell have you been? It's going any minute now.'

Marcia grabbed her hand and dragged her towards the row of buses rumbling impatiently in a cloud of exhaust by the gatehouse. There hadn't even been time for a goodnight kiss. Shame, he was such a good kisser, that Harry; or was it Larry? She turned to wave at him, but he'd already disappeared.

They stumbled up the steps onto the bus and took the only empty seats, at the back.

'Goodness, that was so much fun.' Kath's head was swimming. 'Those cocktails certainly pack a punch.'

'I couldn't find you anywhere. The driver was threatening to leave you behind.'

'Larry took me to see his Thunderbolt,' Kath said rather too loudly, her words falling into a sudden lull in the general hubbub. The bus erupted with hysterical laughter.

'Was it a big one, his Thunderbolt, Motts?'

'Your first Thunderbolt, was it?'

'Not fair. I want to see his Thunderbolt too.'

The teasing went on for at least ten minutes before the girls tired of it and fell asleep, the silence punctuated only by curses from the driver as he navigated narrow winding lanes illuminated only by 'blackout slit' headlights. Kath climbed into bed with a throbbing head and set her alarm clock. There were just four hours till the start of her next shift.

*

At breakfast, the teasing began again. By now the whole station seemed to know, and even perfect strangers came up to her asking about the Thunderbolt. After her shift she sought refuge in Marcia's room.

'Go away,' her friend groaned, pulling the blanket over her head.

'Time to wake up. I'll get water for tea, shall I?' Despite strict rules banning food and drink in their quarters, Marcia's roommate Frances had 'borrowed' an electric element from the workshop where her boyfriend worked, which they suspended into a large metal teapot, adding tea leaves when the water began to boil. A sprinkle of dried milk and a spoonful of sugar made a very acceptable cuppa. By the time it was ready Marcia had unearthed a packet of only slightly stale 'squashed fly' biscuits from a drawer.

'I gather you rather enjoyed yourself last night?'

'Don't you start. I had enough of that at breakfast. What about you?'

'The band was brilliant, wasn't it? So refreshing after all those boring old waltzes and quicksteps, and a nice change to find partners actually taller than me.' Marcia took a bite of biscuit, grimaced, threw it into the bin and tried another one.

'Anyway, apart from the obvious, how *was* the now-famous Larry?'

'Tall, good-looking, white teeth, smelled of chewing gum. Good kisser. And before you ask, no, we didn't.' In truth, Kath was starting to feel rather ashamed of her behaviour the previous evening. Larry might have been a good kisser, but there was no tenderness, no emotion. She still remembered that kiss with Vic, so sweet, so poignant, both of them knowing it might be the last time they would meet for many months, perhaps even years. 'Who did you dance with?'

'You expect me to remember all their names?'

They sat companionably on the floor, leaning back on the bunk, sipping in silence.

'Oh, I nearly forgot to say,' Marcia said. 'I saw your Indian prince there. I was rather surprised you weren't with him.'

Kath gaped at her. 'You must be wrong. Vic hates dances, and anyway he's posted miles away, near London. It was probably some other bloke with dark looks.'

'Well, it certainly looked like the same fellow you were snogging at the bus station in Lincoln.'

The breath seemed to stop in Kath's chest. Surely it couldn't have been him? Among so many hundreds of people it wouldn't have been surprising if they'd simply missed each other, but why hadn't he told her he was there? Come to think of it, she hadn't heard from him for a while.

Another appalling thought. 'Oh my goodness, what if it really *was* him? What if he saw me with Larry?'

'Not good, I'm afraid. You were all over that fellow like a rash. There was only one conclusion your prince could have come to.'

Kath rubbed her temple, where the headache had begun to throb once more. 'Was I that bad?'

''Fraid so. A few too many cocktails, maybe?' Marcia checked her watch, sighed and rose to her feet. 'Sorry, love. I've got to go. I'm on duty in thirty minutes.'

Back in her own bunk, waiting for exhaustion to overtake her, Kath replayed the previous evening in her head. She tried and tried to recall the faces in the bar, and the couples spinning around the dance floor, but they remained a blur. Surely she would have known at once, had she seen Vic? He'd have stood out a mile.

Why hadn't he written lately? It was unlike him. He was usually so attentive, so well organised. With a sudden sharp pang, she realised she'd been so busy that she hadn't even found out where the pigeonholes were. The more she thought about it, the more sleep evaded her. Eventually she gave up, got dressed again and went over to the clock tower. The post room was in a shed just across the way, they said.

She had four letters. One was from Mark – as usual he wrote only about generalities, food, parties and sporting escapades, with scarcely any reference to when or what he was flying, even though she knew he was risking his life every day – and no fewer than three from Vic, all forwarded from her parents' address. Back in her room, she began with the first, a long missive from a fortnight before, describing his travels to different airbases, saying how much he'd enjoyed their day in Lincoln and how much he'd missed her. The second was briefer.

Dear Kath,

You are back at the old place! What wonderful news, especially as it means you can be close to your family.

The even better news is that I shall shortly be posted really quite close to where you are. They haven't told us how long we'll be there for, but I hope we can make the most of this turn of good fortune. It would be perfectly possible for us to meet somewhere in between if you would like to, and if we can co-ordinate our leave. I'm sure you are settling in by now and starting to get to grips with the different systems, and hope you are enjoying yourself too.

I will write again just as soon as I have a proper address.

With love,

Vic

The third letter was shorter still, confirming in coded references that his new posting *was* at Martlesham. Kath groaned, holding her head in her hands. It *must* have been him Marcia had seen at the dance. There couldn't have been too many men like him at a USAF base.

She took out her writing case and ruined several sheets of good Basildon Bond trying to find the right words. In the end she decided just to ignore any reference to the dance, simply expressing delight at the prospect of seeing him once more, followed by a few observations about how her life was going back in 'the old place'. Although it was too soon in her posting to apply for leave, she said, her shifts allowed a thirty-six-hour break every ten days.

She told herself not to worry. So what if he'd seen her with Larry? Did he have any right to stop her having fun with other men? They weren't exactly dating, after all, had never called each other boyfriend or girlfriend, never before declared any feelings for each other apart from fondness and friendship. In all the time they'd known each other, they'd shared only a couple of chaste kisses.

On the other hand, how would she feel if the boot was on the other foot, and she'd spied him smooching with another girl? The realisation was shocking. *I'd hate it. I'd be jealous as hell.*

She read his letters again, trying to glean any further clues. It was only then she noticed that he'd changed his sign-off. *With love.* All of sudden she knew, with a clarity she'd never known before. To hell with all the Billys, the Donalds and Larrys, all those glamorous, handsome men, all those wonderful dancers with their wandering hands. Vic, with his shy, sweet ways, was more important to her than all the others put together. She couldn't bear to lose him.

Each day, morning and afternoon, she checked her pigeonhole, but each time there was no response. A week went by, then ten days. At first she was concerned for his safety. Or had he perhaps been posted back to his original base for some reason, and her letters hadn't reached him? Her greatest concern, a fear that rose its ugly head when she was most vulnerable, alone after an exhausting shift, or in the middle of the night when she was trying to get to sleep, was that he really had seen her at the dance snogging Larry, and was so appalled that he'd decided to cut her off.

When she went home that Sunday – Mark had leave, and Ma was cooking to celebrate his birthday – her remaining flicker of hope was extinguished.

'No post?'

'Expecting something from lover boy?' Mark teased.

After lunch, Pa had to go back to the station for an hour to sort out shifts for the coming week and Ma said she still had to decorate the cake for tea. 'Go off for a walk, you two. Make the most of this lovely weather.'

'Where would you like to go? To the sea?' Mark asked as they set off.

'No, it breaks my heart to see all those barricades on the beach,' Kath said. 'Let's walk in the marshes. At least there we can half pretend there's not a war on.'

Here, in the open spaces of salty wetland, they were able to speak more freely. He asked about her time at HQ, and about her new posting.

'What about you?' she asked.

He shrugged. 'Flying a bomber is like driving an elephant after those lovely little Spitfires, but you've got five or six others on board with you so there's a great team spirit. We keep each other going.'

'Do you ever worry about the people down below?'

'The ack-acks trying to kill us?'

'The civilians, I mean. Like the people who copped it from the Germans in London and Coventry.'

'Of course, but you try not to think about it too much. We don't have any choice, to be honest. We won't defeat the Germans unless we can destroy their industries, so that's got to be our priority. We try to avoid residential areas.'

A flock of ducks rose into the sky with a noisy chorus of alarm calls.

'There goes a good supper,' Mark said.

'We sometimes mistake them for aircraft,' she said.

'Friend or foe?'

'It soon becomes apparent when they start wheeling about.'

'You're right. We don't do a lot of wheeling these days.'

They laughed and walked on. Low sunlight streaked rays of gold across the marshes.

'It's so beautiful here,' she said. 'It's easy to forget, sometimes, what we're fighting for.'

He gave a small sigh and stopped walking. She turned. 'What is it, Mark?'

'I just wanted to say...' He took another breath. 'Has anyone ever told you how reassuring it is to know that you lot are tracking us, Kath? A few weeks ago some of our guys had to ditch into the sea and the rescue team was there in minutes. Said they'd been alerted by you lot.'

'What day was that?' He told her. 'Blimey, that was on my first ever shift! I saw them, Mark. I was so worried. Thank heavens they were okay.'

'You saved a few good men that night.'

'That's amazing. Makes it all worthwhile, knowing that.'

'They were heading for Sutton Heath. Just didn't quite make it.'

'Sutton Heath?'

He paused. 'Perhaps I've said too much. It's top secret, so you won't say anything, will you?'

'Of course not. Tell me.'

'Sutton Heath. Official name RAF Woodbridge. It's an emergency landing strip, what they call a crash 'drome, a ruddy great long runway – three of them, actually – with all the rescue equipment, fire engines, medical facilities and the rest, for any plane in distress, low on fuel, whatever. They're on standby twenty-four hours a day, seven days a week. They even burn fires to disperse fog on bad nights. Stanmore alerts them, based on your reports.'

'Heavens, is that why we see so many low-flying aircraft on our screens? I never saw any down in the West Country. Have you ever had to use it?'

'Not yet, thank the lucky stars. But it's very reassuring to know it's there, I can tell you, and that your lot are onto us, too. Who knows how many lives you've saved, between you all.'

'I'm so glad you told me.'

A chill wind had got up, stroking the fluffy reed-heads into waves. 'C'mon,' Kath said. 'Ma will be waiting for us to get back for tea and cake.'

He checked his watch. 'Crikey, yes. Mustn't miss the five o'clock bus, either. I've got to get to the base for a seven p.m. briefing.'

'Briefing on what?'

'Big mission on Tuesday,' he said. 'You'll probably see us on your screens.'

'Stay safe, Mark, won't you?'

'I'll do my best, sis. I've got a new friend, by the way. Someone to live for.'

She knew at once what he meant, and was glad for him.

CHAPTER 26

Vic buried himself in work. There was certainly plenty of it, and dealing with the Americans required great patience and diplomacy. Accustomed to operating in small teams on tight budgets but with relatively high levels of freedom and flexibility, he simply could not get used to what he saw as the profligate ways of his US counterparts.

'If there's a problem, throw money at it,' seemed to be the usual response. 'Or bring in more people. Just make it happen.'

Working in larger teams meant it took much longer to reach decisions, and American systems were so bureaucratic that it took forever to extract the permissions they needed to move forward. It was endlessly frustrating. The timetable Vic had planned for what they'd now been told would be just four weeks at Martlesham soon went out of the window. By the end of the first fortnight they had barely started.

Through working all hours and putting himself to sleep at night with a few tots of the sweet American whisky he'd acquired from the mess for an absurdly cheap sum, he successfully managed to banish all thoughts of Kath for several days in a row. It was only when he lowered his guard – if he found himself alone in the barracks, or if the whisky failed for some reason to work its usual magic – that he found himself yearning for her.

That halo of red curls glinting in the sunshine, the sweet gap-toothed smile, those pale cheeks that coloured at the slightest hint of pleasure, excitement or confusion, the freckles he'd once playfully tried to rub off her nose. The moments they'd shared on the Cliff Walk, watching the North Sea in all its moods and weathers. The ease of their conversation, walking through the grounds at Bawdsey, imagining the gardens in their heyday and laughing about the White Lady said to haunt the Italian Garden at night. The way Kath seemed oblivious to his difference, the way she stood up to the bullies. That terrible day of the crash, when she had sought him out and comforted him. Their kiss in the bus station at Lincoln.

One night he dreamed of her, of the feel of her arms around him, the touch of her lips on his, and woke in a flush of desire before remembering the sight of her snogging that US airman. That vision, seared into his brain, was just too painful. His head throbbed with the after-effects of the three strong whiskies he'd drunk the night before. Of course he recalled Lizzie's advice about perseverance, but that morning he realised that any hopes had been dashed and he had to conclude that she no longer cared for him. The only way of saving himself was to cut out the hurt, like a canker.

That morning he took the small packet of her letters and burned them on the ground behind the engineers' hut.

'Everything all right, sir?' The security guard regarded him suspiciously, fingering his holster.

'Fine, fine. It's just the smoke,' Vic said, wiping his eyes.

'May I ask for your ID, sir?'

Vic handed over the pass in its battered cardboard wallet. The man scrutinised it carefully and passed it back, frowning as though unconvinced.

'Thank you, sir. But may I remind you that any unauthorised disposal of documentation is taken very seriously here on the base? You are required to use our special facility for such purposes in the Admin Block.'

'I wasn't aware. Sorry, mate.' Being friendly didn't usually wash with these types, but it was worth a try.

'Next time, then, sir?'

Vic nodded, scattering the ashes with the toe of his boot.

'Good. Enjoy your day, sir.'

*

The teletext message from Stanmore, decoded and transcribed, arrived at breakfast a few days later in a sealed buff envelope. It had Vic's name on it and was stamped in red, top secret: for addressee only. He tore it open.

RDF TEAM REPORT RAF BAWDSEY IMMEDIATELY IFF TX FAULT CAR
WAITING 1600 HOURS TODAY TUESDAY STOP PADMORE

His heart sank. 'Oh, hell. Why us?'

Bawdsey: he'd loved the place once, but now it was the last place he wanted to go. What if he should bump into Kath? What could he say? Would she even acknowledge him?

He passed the note to Monty. 'Can't you go on my behalf? There's so much to do here.'

'It says "RDF team", Vic, and if there's one person in the world who can sort it out, it's you. You practically invented the system, after all.' Monty started to hum the tune of 'Oh, I Do Like to Be Beside the Seaside'. 'At least it gives us a break from the Yankees. Whatever's wrong with the place, anyway?'

Vic shrugged. He wasn't going to bare his heart to Monty. Anyway, there wasn't any choice; you didn't say no to Padmore. The new commander of RAF Bawdsey was notoriously tough.

The security at the gatehouse was tighter, with a smart new barrier and guards with guns who no longer recognised him. But as always the sight of the place worked its magic, lifting his heart. It was the first time that he'd ever arrived by car, let alone one with a smartly uniformed American driver.

'My, how we've risen in the world,' Monty gasped, as the car swooped around the courtyard, coming to a stop in front of the stone porch. 'And this was where you lived for a couple of years? Where you invented it all?'

Vic nodded. It reminded him of returning to school after an exeat: for twenty-four hours beforehand he'd have headaches and be too nervous to eat, but once he got there and saw his friends, it felt as though he'd never been away. To his relief, as they climbed out of the car and entered through the front porch, he saw no sign of Kath, nor any other WAAFs. They must all be at work or asleep in the new barracks they'd seen behind the clock house.

As they sat in the panelled hallway waiting for the station commander to arrive, he recalled that very first day, how overawed he'd been by Watson-Watt's palatial, leather-lined office, and how he'd tucked into leftover cake and biscuits as the big man described his astonishing vision.

'It's Mackensie and Montgomery, the two M's, I'll be bound. Come to the rescue, I hope.' The commander's voice boomed through the hall. 'Come in, come in, you are most welcome. Would you care for coffee?' He rang a bell, and a batwoman arrived to take their orders.

Vic found himself sitting in the very same spot, on the very same overstuffed leather sofa in front of the manorial fireplace. 'By golly, we're pleased to see you,' Padmore said, after the batwoman had left. 'We're in a bit of a fix with the IFF receiver. Stanmore's shouting blue murder and the girls are going spare.'

Vic glanced out of the window at the darkening sky. 'You want us to fix it *now*, sir?'

'There's a big push on tonight, and we'll need to count them back again tomorrow morning. Sooner you can fix it, the more likely you'll save me from getting court-martialled,' he added without the hint of a smile. 'Just wait a sec while we get your passes. They're a lot tighter on security than when you were here last, Mackensie. Get a bit jumpy around chaps in civvies. Oh, and you'll need a room key. Here you go; it's one of the guest rooms just above here.'

The key fob said Room Six. The same one Vic had shared with Johnnie. *Wish me luck with this one, old friend*, he murmured as he turned the key.

Of course he had no idea which of the radar systems Kath would be working on, or how the shift patterns worked, but as they made their way in darkness across the courtyard and past the clock house, he prayed that she would not be on duty tonight. He still hadn't worked out how to react, should they meet. And how would she respond, on seeing him? She would be startled, of course, and it would be no surprise if she blanked him completely. Perhaps that would be for the best.

He'd steeled himself for visiting the receiving room, dreading flashbacks to that overheated wooden shed with its new paint fumes on the terrible day when Johnnie died. But this enormous bunker, with its mingled smells of fresh concrete and cigarette smoke and the array of new pieces of kit that he'd helped to design, was astonishing – almost overwhelming.

To his relief, all the faces were strangers. 'We've come to look at the IFF system,' he said. 'How's it doing?'

'Bloody hopeless,' one of the girls replied. 'Hasn't been working for twenty-four hours now. Hope you're going to fix it?' It was a posh voice, confident and imperious, the sort he remembered from the older boys at boarding school. Her face registered a flash of recognition. 'Hold on a tick. Do I know you?'

'Vikram Mackensie,' he said. 'How do you do?'

Her eyes twinkled with an expression he could not quite discern. 'Marcia Bonham. I am most pleased to meet you.'

They quickly discovered that the problem lay not with the kit in the bunker but in the calibration of the receivers, although why on earth the RAF engineers on site could not have worked this out they didn't ask. At the workshop they found two engineers huddled over a blazing pot-bellied stove in a fug of cigarette smoke. Vic tried to explain the problem.

'You'll need to go up the mast to fix it,' he said.

The pair looked blank. Vic knew they would be reluctant to take orders from civilians – indeed, they had the right to refuse – but it was worth trying. 'The commander says it's vital, lads. It must be fixed tonight.'

'It can't wait till morning,' Monty added.

'We're not qualified,' one said, clasping his mug. 'Need to ask the boss.'

'Then where is he?' Vic snapped. 'Go and find him at once.'

The man shrugged and hauled himself up from the stool. 'On leave. *Sir.* Back tomorrow. *Sir.*' He gave an insolent half-salute.

Vic and Monty exchanged glances. They had two alternatives: disturb the commander and ask him to order the engineers up the mast – and even then, have to trust that they wouldn't make the problem worse – or…

'It'll have to be us, then,' Monty said.

'Ever done this before?' Monty asked, peering up into the blackness from the base of the mast. The moon was half full and still visible, but a cloud bank was fast approaching from the east. They'd borrowed overalls, torches and a small bag of tools, now slung from his waist.

'Just the once,' Vic said, starting to climb the ladder, its rungs slick with damp. *Go for it, old man*, Johnnie whispered in his ear. *One step at a time. No problem.* He shouted encouragement to Monty, following close behind: 'Nearly there, mate. Just a couple of dozen more steps.'

Just as they arrived at the top, the moon disappeared and Vic's torch died. He cursed, giving it several whacks on his palm, but it made no difference. Monty's was also fading fast.

'Authorised procedure for batteries, revival of,' Monty said, hugging the two torches in his armpits. It worked, and they revived just long enough for Vic to make the adjustments he hoped would bring the system back onto line.

It was as they were feeling their way back down the ladder that they first felt the reverberations in the air. An almost imperceptible growl at first, it grew into a deafening roar that vibrated in their chests as wave after wave of heavy aircraft passed overhead, wing and tail lights a vast twinkling sky of red and white stars.

'Go get 'em, boys,' Monty shouted. 'And come home safe.'

'Are they Brits or Yanks, do you think?' Vic asked.

'Hard to tell in the dark. But they're brave bastards either way.'

In the receiving room, the screens were a blur of blips.

'IFF working yet?' Vic asked.

'It's impossible to tell with this lot going over all bunched together,' Marcia said. 'Thanks for having a go, anyway.' She gave him that curious look again. 'Excuse me, but... I have a feeling you might know my friend Kath Motts?'

The sound of her name ran through his body like a jolt of electricity. He swallowed, trying to compose himself, to find the right response. 'Indeed, yes. Please give Miss Motts my regards, should you see her.'

'I'll certainly pass it on,' she said with a slight smile, before turning back to her screen.

'Now what do we do?' Monty asked.

'Wait here, till they get a chance to test it.'

'No point in us both staying up all night,' Monty said after a moment. 'I'll take first shift. You go and get some shut-eye.'

Vic checked his watch. It was already ten-thirty. Every bone in his body seemed to ache from the tension of the climb and trying to recalibrate the receiver in the darkness. 'Are you sure? That's a darned good offer.'

'Then accept it, you idiot.' Monty gave him a friendly shove. 'I'll come and get you if there's a problem. Otherwise I'll see you at breakfast.'

Snuggled down on his old bed in his old room, waiting for sleep, he heard Johnnie's whisper: *You did well tonight, old mate.*

CHAPTER 27

It was the one they all hated most, the 'graveyard shift': eleven till eight in the morning. Halfway through, around three o'clock, your mind would start to drift off, your eyes longing to close, your shoulders aching from tiredness and tension.

Kath usually went to her room after supper for a few hours' rest beforehand. It was the wrong time for sleeping, but she found it helped to close her eyes and try to relax. Tonight, she lay awake thinking of Mark. Just after ten o'clock, even before she heard them, she sensed the vibrations. She opened the window and peered out into the night listening to the deafening roar of hundreds of heavy aircraft flying low overhead in the direction of North Germany. The whole building seemed to shake and any further rest was impossible as wave after wave passed over, the noise undiminished for a full half hour until the rear markers passed over the coast and the land went silent again.

The moon was out at the moment, she noticed, but they were flying towards a bank of cloud in the east that would conceal them over enemy territory. The Met Office men had got it right for once. The crews would be more dependent on RDF to find their targets, but at least they would be less vulnerable to anti-aircraft fire from the ground.

She wished Mark hadn't told her about the mission, but now she knew he was up there she could think of nothing else. She would have to wait at least twenty-four hours before she knew whether or not he had returned safely. Fear lodged in the pit of her stomach, a constant ache as debilitating as any pain of her monthlies, but impervious to the two aspirin she'd taken. She went for supper just before the shift, but had no appetite. Every mouthful tasted like cardboard.

'Have you seen him yet?' Marcia whispered, at the shift changeover.

'Him? Who?'

'Your Indian prince?'

'What? Here? Stop teasing.'

'No, I'm serious. He was here to fix the IFF. His mate's over there.'

Monty was sitting in the corner, head rested back against the wall, eyes closed, his slightly gaping mouth emitting small, rhythmical snores.

'Fix the IFF? What's wrong with it?'

'Buggered. In a word.'

'A technical term?'

'Our engineers were perfectly clueless, so they called in the boffins. Him over there and your prince. The pair of them had to go up the mast in the dark, bless 'em.'

Vic, up a mast in the dark? That's pretty heroic. Is it working now?

'We haven't had any targets to test it on yet, but the bombers who went out earlier will be back in a few hours, no doubt. Did you hear them?'

'Hitler would have heard them in his bunker.'

'Let's hope they blast him to hell.'

Kath's head was in a spin. It was enough to worry about Mark without the embarrassment of bumping into Vic again. He still had not replied to any of her letters, and she assumed he'd taken umbrage after seeing her with the wretched Larry at Martlesham. The memory of those kisses still left a sour taste in her mouth. If only she'd taken more notice of Marcia's warning about the cocktails.

They bid goodnight to the previous shift and immediately settled into their stations. Kath took the first turn on the screen, and for the first hour everything was quiet except for the occasional ship passing by, so they had time to listen in to reports being sent to HQ at Stanmore from other stations. These were usually a staccato blur of acronyms, technical language and map readings that were almost impossible to follow. But every now and again a few terrifying phrases would emerge – 'taking fire over Bremen', 'two down', 'identified hostile' – that could grip you with panic if you listened too hard. It was easier when you were too busy to worry.

She'd taken her turn on the plotting tables and returned to the screen when it began to light up with faint blips. She took plots, range and height, and calculated that there must be thirty of them, perhaps more, still eighty miles out. *Probably our own*, she thought, *returning from the raid*. By now Vic's mate had ceased his snoring, introduced himself as Monty and was on full alert, peering at the screen over her shoulder.

As they came closer, friendly aircraft would transmit a signal that showed up on the screen as a small extra downward spike – but only if they weren't all bunched together, and only if the receiver was working properly. There was no other way of telling except, sometimes, by the tightness of the formations and the distance between the groups.

The tension, as they waited, was almost unbearable.

At last, they saw it. That extra little spike. 'Friend,' they shouted, simultaneously. Everyone in the bunker cheered, clapping Monty on the shoulder. The system was working again. These were RAF bombers returning to base in a group. She prayed Mark was among them. But that was only about thirty planes out of what they'd calculated to be three hundred who'd flown out.

Over the next hour or so they counted them back, reporting to Stanmore and keeping their own score on a blackboard. The numbers crept up but the formations were all over the place, twenty-plus here and thirty-plus there. It was no doubt they'd had a rough time. Aircraft returning from a raid would often arrive in ragged bunches of sometimes only twenty, or fewer. Even in ones or twos. You could read it from the screen, like a picture in the sky, as you worked your way along the length of the trace, plotting every blip, then back to the beginning again. Plot, range, height, plot, range, height. All of them friendly.

A lone aircraft appeared at forty miles out, very low and coming in very slowly. She tracked it carefully: twenty miles, fifteen miles, ten, then just five. The message went to Stanmore, and she imagined telephones ringing at Sutton Heath, calling code red for the fire and ambulance crews. She prayed that it managed to land safely.

They estimated that at least five planes were still missing. She tried to calm herself by calculating the odds: five out of three hundred had failed to return, less than 2 per cent. Or, put another way, there was a 98 per cent chance that Mark had come home safely. She moved from the screen to the plotting table, but there was nothing to plot, so she continued watching over the shoulders of her fellow WAAFs.

'Stragglers!' The shout made them all jump. 'One, perhaps two, coming in low.' Everyone ran to look. The blip for one of the planes came closer and closer before passing right overhead. One of them at least was probably safe. The other suddenly disappeared about ten miles out. The message went out: someone called air-sea rescue, giving map references of the last sighting. Ten minutes later a blip appeared, most likely the spotter plane. Kath prayed that the men had managed to get out safely before they crash-landed.

Now only three planes were still unaccounted for.

Then, suddenly, a single plane at sixty miles, then thirty, flying low. Another straggler? They tracked it minute by minute. But something was wrong. It began to act strangely, rising, then levelling off before dropping again. It turned and flew away from the coast, then steadied, as though it was moving along the coastline.

'What the hell's he playing at? Ruddy thing's wheeling round like a Catherine wheel,' the WAAF swore.

Wheeling. The words she'd said to Mark: *It soon becomes apparent when they start wheeling about.* 'Is it hostile?' she called. 'Strange time for reconnaissance.'

'Can't tell. The IFF signal seems to be playing up again. Sometimes I see it, then I don't.'

Monty groaned. 'I thought we'd fixed it? It was working okay before.'

The WAAF fiddled with the controls. 'Nope, can't see it. Not at all.'

Kath ran back to look over her shoulder. It was definitely a single blip. For a few seconds, she thought she saw the second spike on the screen that would indicate friendly craft, but it disappeared so fast she fancied she must have imagined it. There it was again. Now it had gone.

'D'you mind if I have a go?'

'Be my guest,' the WAAF said, relinquishing her seat.

Kath sat at the controls, her right hand on the goniometer wheel. Nudging it gently clockwise, then anti-clockwise, she took readings: height, range and trajectory. She peered at the screen so hard that her eyes burned. Definitely no double blip. She stood up again and the WAAF resumed her place.

'Nope, nothing.'

'Best inform Stanmore, anyway,' someone said.

Kath's head whirled. 'And have them send a fighter to shoot the poor bastard down?' she said. It would be her responsibility to make the call, but what if the plane was ours? What if it was Mark?

'That "poor bastard" might be coming to bomb us.'

'But are we really sure it's hostile?'

'We have to leave it to them to decide. They'll have tracks from other stations, after all. Make the call, Kath,' someone said.

She hesitated.

'*Do it*, Kath.' More urgently this time. 'Before they bloody well blow us to kingdom come.'

As the phone operator on rota, it was her duty. She dialled and spoke into the receiver, giving the identification code for the station, followed by the time. 'Craft acting suspiciously, possibly hostile,' she said, giving range, height and co-ordinates.

'Roger that, thank you.' As she replaced the receiver it felt as heavy as a stone.

Everyone was still gathered around the screen, watching as the plane continued to circle, up and down the coast. It was like nothing they'd observed before and hardly likely to be activity of an enemy aircraft, they all agreed. Kath became more and more convinced that the plane and its crew were in trouble, trying to find their route to the crash 'drome at Sutton Heath.

Ten minutes later they tracked a fighter, heading out towards their latest sighting.

'If they're German, they're toast,' someone said, and the others cheered.

But what if they're not? The question repeated itself over and over in Kath's head. *But what if they're not?*

Moments later, just as the other girls arrived to take over the shift, all trace of the mysterious plane disappeared. Even though she felt nauseous with anxiety and fatigue, she waited as they tracked the fighter home, and the screens cleared of all signals.

By the time they emerged from the bunker the sun was already rising and the remnants of dawn lingered to the east, sending darts of pink into the sky reflected in an almost flat sea. Birds were staking noisy claim to territory in the trees to the side of the Manor, and a roe deer slipped across the path in front of them.

'Going to be a fine day,' Monty observed cheerfully.

'Off to bed now?' someone asked.

'Nope, I'm going to get the boss. I reckon we're going up that mast again. Need to double-check the IFF receiver just to make sure. At least it'll be in daylight this time.'

The boss? Kath realised he must be referring to Vic. After all the stress of the shift and the worry about Mark, she'd almost forgotten. As Monty peeled off in the direction of the Manor, she realised that as civilian visitors he and Vic would be served breakfast in the officers' mess while she and her fellow WAAFs were heading for the grim fare of the cookhouse. Their paths were unlikely to cross, unless one of them…

On impulse, she called to Monty's disappearing back, 'Tell him Kath says hello.'

He swivelled round. 'You mean Vic?'

She nodded, conscious of the others' questioning looks.

'Will do, miss,' he said with smile and a mock salute.

CHAPTER 28

'You old fox,' Monty said, finding Vic at the breakfast table.

'I've been called some things in my time, but to what do I owe this compliment?' Vic said, tucking into fried bread and scrambled eggs. The bread had a faint but not unpleasant tang of kippers.

'I gather you are acquainted with a certain leading aircraft-woman Motts?'

Vic took a mouthful of food, then wished he hadn't. With some effort, he managed to chew and swallow without choking. 'Yes, I am. What of it?'

'She said to say hello.'

'You met her? What exactly did she say?'

'Just that, nothing more. Sorry to disappoint, old chap. She was on duty in the receiving room. We had quite a night of it, I can tell you.'

'What happened?'

Monty gave a brief summary.

'So we need to check that calibration again?'

''Fraid so. Hey ho. Up we go.'

As he climbed the ladder Vic wondered where Kath would be now. Asleep, probably. Hearing that she'd mentioned his name to Monty, his heart seemed to unfreeze a little. So what if she enjoyed the occasional fling with other men – especially Yanks, who could provide such delights as swing bands, ice cream and nylon stockings? He'd never laid any claim to her and had only hoped, but never presumed, that she might consider him a longer-term proposition.

Now, more than anything, he wanted just to see her, to straighten things up between them before he had to leave for Martlesham and then, in two weeks' time, go back to London.

'Phew,' Monty said, climbing onto the platform behind him. 'That was easier than last night.'

'It's a fine view in the daytime.' Vic shielded his eyes with his hand. 'You can see for miles. That's Harwich, down there. That's Landguard Fort, an old Napoleonic defence and now home of the Territorials. And up in that direction, except you can't quite see it from this level, is Orfordness, where Watson-Watt first started his experiments.'

'I prefer the Yorkshire hills myself,' Monty said. 'But Suffolk has a certain charm.'

From here you had an almost perfect aerial view of the different gardens, and for the first time Vic realised that the Round Garden was not perfectly circular but actually a slight oval, following the footprint of the old Martello tower that had once stood guard from its clifftop position.

The IFF calibrations seemed perfect but he tweaked them all the same, and they climbed down the ladder once more. 'Let's go back to the bunker to check this receiver's working properly,' he said. 'Then I expect we'll have to head back to Martlesham.'

In the receiver room, they waited until a few planes had flown overhead. The system was working perfectly. 'Your Miss Motts will be reassured,' Monty said. 'She was very anxious when they couldn't identify that plane acting oddly. It must have been a German doing a recce or something. Anyway, he's probably dust by now.'

'How did it go last night?' Padmore asked, smoothing his luxuriant moustache.

'There was a bit of a commotion early this morning, sir,' Vic said. 'They weren't entirely sure whether the IFF was working properly, so we've been up the mast again this morning. It's working perfectly now.'

'You went up the mast yourselves? In the dark? And again this morning?'

'Yes, sir. The engineers seemed reluctant without their manager's say-so.'

Padmore lifted the phone and barked into it. 'Find out which engineers were on shift last night and get them to my office. Pronto.'

He put down the phone and turned back to Vic and Monty. 'Hmm. This leaves me with a quandary.'

There was a knock at the door.

'Come.'

One of the engineers they'd met the previous evening entered, his face pale with terror.

'Take a seat outside, gentlemen, would you?' Padmore said to Vic and Monty. 'Just for a few moments.' Even through the heavy oak door they could hear his barks. They exchanged glances.

'Poor bastard,' Vic whispered.

'Deserves it,' Monty mouthed.

The engineer re-emerged shortly afterwards, now red-faced, and they were summoned back into the office.

'It's like this, chaps,' Padmore said. 'The only engineer who has any gumption is on leave and won't be back till tomorrow, and I'm reluctant to risk another event like yesterday. With your permission, I'm going to ask Martlesham whether they can spare you, or even just one of you, for one more day just to make sure it's all tickety-boo.'

Another day at Bawdsey Manor, with nothing to do except enjoy the comforts of Room Six and the officer's mess? And perhaps the chance to find Kath?

'Yes, sir, certainly, sir. It will be a pleasure,' Vic said.

Padmore picked up the receiver. 'Get me Martlesham.' He gestured to Vic and Monty to take a seat. They perched on the leather sofa as the call went through. But there seemed to be some kind of hitch. 'Yes… yes… hmm… I do understand. But you see my dilemma too…? Yes, of course… Look, hold the line and I'll ask. They're just here.'

He looked up, hand over the mouthpiece. 'Seems they're a bit reluctant to let me keep both of you. Apparently there's some kind of big pow-wow planned for this afternoon and they'd like one of you RDF fellows to attend. Would one of you agree to stay? Don't mind who, we can decide later, but do you agree to this, in principle?'

Vic glanced at Monty, and they both nodded. The CO finished his call.

'Thanks very much for this, lads. Now off you go. Just let me know which one of you is staying, if you don't mind. The car will be here for the other one at ten prompt.'

'Toss for it?' Vic said, back in their room. That would give him at least a fifty-fifty chance.

'No, *you* stay, Mac,' Monty said. 'Give you a chance to meet up with that sweetheart of yours. I can grab some sleep when I get back.'

'That's very generous. I'll owe you, my friend.'

'Hope it works out,' Monty said, with a conspiratorial wink.

On his way back to the receiving room he met Marcia going in the same direction.

'No sleep for the wicked,' she said with a weary sigh. 'Have you seen Kath yet?'

He felt his cheeks flush. 'No, afraid not. Any idea where she is?'

'She only came off shift at eight, so she's probably asleep. But if I see her, I'll tell her you're looking for her.'

It was all quiet in the skies, so Vic decided to take a walk to clear his head. After the bitter cold of recent weeks the clouds had cleared. He took a lungful of air, fresher and saltier here than anywhere else he'd ever lived. The North Sea looked beguilingly calm, almost benign, its tea-coloured waters concealing the terrible tragedies of war: burning planes, ditched crews, torpedoed convoys; a burial ground for hundreds of lives lost and bodies never recovered.

It was surprisingly warm, almost as though spring had arrived, although a nip in the shadows was a warning against complacency. He passed the laundry cottages, the dairy cottages and the mock Tudor frontage of the farmhouse with its curve of stables, all badly neglected these days, before retracing his steps going via the walled kitchen garden. The wooden structure of the lemonry seemed even more derelict than before, but he took a few moments to sit on the bench, resting his back on the whitewashed wall and warming himself in the weak sunshine. He took a deep breath and slowly exhaled, feeling his shoulders relaxing, perhaps for the first time in months. He did it again, and a feeling of wellbeing crept over him. It felt wrong, somehow, being here in this paradise while other men were risking their lives.

When he grew chilled he continued his walk, noticing with pleasure as he crossed the kitchen garden that the old vegetable beds were now pressed into full use: sprouts and kale being cropped, other areas tilled and ready for planting. Emerging from the gate at the southern end, he turned towards the entrance to the Cliff Path, only to discover that it had been blocked by an ugly concrete pillbox housing a heavy gun. He remembered now that Kath had written about this, but even so, the disappointment of being barred from his – their – special place came as a shock. He sighed and retraced his steps, heading back to the Manor through the tunnel that led to the Round Garden.

He was striding with purpose now, hoping to find coffee being served back at the Manor, but as he emerged into the dell his feet stopped in their tracks. The usually deserted garden was already occupied by a figure sitting on one of the benches: a WAAF with her back to him, capped head in her hands. He paused in the shadows, unwilling to disturb her.

Just as he turned away to retrace his steps the girl sat up and pulled off her cap, running her fingers through curls that caught a stray ray of sunshine with the unmistakable glow of red.

Kath.

Scarcely daring to breathe, he began to move slowly forward. At the crunch of his footstep on the gravel she turned, registering her recognition with a weak smile. Her eyes were dark smudges, her face grey with exhaustion.

'Oh, it's you,' she said flatly. 'I heard you were here.'

'Yes, it's me. May I join you?'

'Of course.'

He sat at the other end of the bench. The gap seemed as wide as an ocean. 'It's nice to see you.'

'It was certainly a surprise to learn you were here,' she said, a touch of acid in her voice. 'You never replied to any of my letters.'

'I'm sorry. I didn't think you'd want to hear from me, after...' he hesitated. Why poison this moment, now?

'Go on, say it, Vic. After what?'

'After I saw you at Martlesham with that American, I realised how stupid I'd been ever to imagine you'd be interested in me.'

'Oh, hell, Marcia was right,' she groaned, dropping her head into her hands once more. 'I didn't believe her. You hate dances. And anyway, I didn't even know you were posted there.' When she turned to face him her cheeks were wet with tears. 'It didn't mean anything, Vic. Nothing. Nothing at all,' she repeated more firmly. 'You have to believe me. Those cocktails had gone to my head and I had no idea what I was doing. I hated myself later for being such an idiot.'

He gave a bitter laugh. 'I was an idiot too, not writing back because of my silly wounded pride.' He moved closer, took her hand and squeezed it.

She squeezed back. 'Am I forgiven?'

'Of course, if you forgive me.'

'Well, we're here now, and that's all that matters.'

They sat in silence, hand in hand. Even though they were only yards from the sea, the walls of the dell seemed to insulate them from the sound. They could hear only the faintest of roars as the waves hit the beach, and the sigh that followed as the shingle shifted beneath the retreating waters.

'I heard about the problems last night,' he said, at last. 'Monty said it was a really difficult shift, counting back the stragglers after that raid.'

'He doesn't know the half of it,' she said quietly.

'Do you want to tell me the other half?'

She gave a great, weary sigh. 'My brother was on that raid. That's why I'm out here. Can't sleep for worrying about whether he got back safely.'

'Most of them made it home, Monty said.'

'But there was one – he probably told you – acting strangely, who we couldn't identify. Flying along the coast, then wheeling and coming back again. We couldn't see any "friendly" signal. I had to alert Stanmore, and they sent out the fighters.'

'Which was the right thing to do.'

'But what if it was *him*, Vic? What if it was *Mark*? And because of me he was shot down?' Her voice broke.

'You mustn't allow yourself to think that, Kath. The IFF was working fine – we checked it again this morning.' Even as he tried to reassure her, he heard the voice in his head: what if the receiver had failed, even after his adjustments? His mind flashed to that long-ago day in the old receiving room, the glow of pride when the test system worked, and the sickening moment when Scott uttered those terrible words, 'They're saying the plane is down, sir.' He could still smell the new paint, even now.

Her voice brought him back. 'I'm sure it was nothing to do with that. I heard about your heroic climb up the mast, Vic. I keep trying to tell myself that it was just circumstances. Maybe the plane's transmitter was damaged; or perhaps it really was an enemy plane.'

'You just reported what you saw. Stanmore would have verified everything before acting, and anyway the fighter crew would have checked the plane before firing at it. You did what you had to do in the circumstances. Whatever it was, it's very unlikely to have been your brother. He'll be safely cuddled up in his bunk, completely unaware that you've been worrying about him. It's all in a day's work for those guys,' he said.

'I hope you're right. I put in a call to his base, but they never give out information till they've made completely sure...' She shivered slightly. He put his arm around her shoulder and she snuggled up against him. In spite of her obvious distress, an unfamiliar feeling of contentment seemed to invade every pore of his body as he felt her warmth against his chest. He seemed to have been locked into a frozen state for weeks, but now something inside was melting, like frost on a lawn yielding as the sun chases the shadows away.

'C'mon, you're getting cold,' he said. 'Shall we go and get a cuppa? I could probably rustle up a biscuit too, although there's no carrot cake these days. Nor cake of any kind, for that matter.'

'Cake or no cake, that sounds nice.' She paused. 'But I'm not allowed in the officer's mess.'

'We can smuggle them up to my room, if you don't think that's too forward of me. It's rather grand, and it has a terrific view.'

When he returned from foraging for tea and biscuits, she was sitting in Johnnie's chair. For once it didn't make him sad; it felt right to see her there.

'You weren't exaggerating about the view, you lucky thing. I could look at it forever.' She stood and went to the window.

He put down the tea tray and went to her side. 'This is the room I shared with Johnnie, you know.'

'Oh Vic, I'm so sorry. Does it bring back sad memories?'

'Sad and glad. Glad to have known him. We had a lot of fun together, he and I. We seemed to read each other's thoughts, and made each other laugh. A lot. I've seen his widow and children a few times since, as well. They've become almost like family to me.'

'Did I ever tell you that it was a friend of Mark's piloting that seaplane?'

'Captain Burrows?'

'I was so worried that they'd find it was his fault.'

'And I was terrified they'd find it was caused by the kit we'd installed. But in the end, it was a problem with the plane's construction that no one could have predicted.'

'All those deaths. And the war hadn't even begun.'

'But somehow it feels better, having you here.' He put his arm around her. 'I was so afraid I'd lost you, too.'

She turned and took his face in her hands. 'You'll never lose me again, Vic.'

It was the most passionate kiss he'd ever known. The shabby room, the view and the sound of the waves beyond the window seemed to melt away, the whole world reduced to the focus of her lips, her tongue and the fire of his desire.

The tea went cold.

It was the first time for both of them, a muddled, embarrassed, fumbled affair that in the end, against all odds, felt like the most perfectly natural thing in the world. Delicious, in fact, utterly overwhelming, beyond anything he could ever have imagined. And it seemed to be the same for her. Afterwards, as he watched her sleeping beside him in the narrow bed, he believed himself the happiest man in the world.

CHAPTER 29

Dearest Kath,

I am now back at base and trying to sleep, but it is impossible. My heart still pounds when I think of the astonishing, wonderful things that happened between us yesterday, and I cannot put into words how much it meant. You are the most beautiful girl on the planet and it broke my heart to leave you. It feels so utterly and horribly cruel. We are meant to be together, not torn apart.

I have two more weeks here so will put in a request for leave at the end of our assignment and hope you might be free to meet me somewhere, for a couple of days. We could go to a hotel, if you like the idea.

I'm such a coward that I failed to say it this morning when we parted. But please believe me, Kathleen Motts, I am head over heels in love with you.

Write soon.

With all my love forever,

Vic

Dearest Vic,

Did it really happen? I feel so blessed and loved, but also miserable that you had to leave so soon.

Work continues here and there is no news from Mark, which I pray is good news. I will move heaven and earth to arrange leave so we can have a little more time together before you have to go back. Yes, yes, yes to a hotel. How risqué!

I miss you horribly already. If only this bloody war was over and we could be together.

With all my love,
Kath

Dearest Kath,

Hurray, I have leave! March 25th–27th.

Being a Suffolk gal, you probably already know the White Horse in your local town. Shall we meet there? My friend says it's quite comfortable in an old-fashioned way. Apparently Charles Dickens stayed there and wrote about it in The Pickwick Papers, *which I tried to read in school, though I have to confess most of it has been erased from my memory, as has so much of my school learning. I'll try to get hold of a copy so we can read it together.*

I do hope you will be able to make it. After that I will have to go back to London and it might take some time to get leave again.

With all my love forever,
Vic

Dearest Vic,

I have been given leave! Imagine, two whole days (and nights) together!? I cannot wait! What time shall we meet on Thursday?

Still no news from Mark. I'm trying not to worry but it's getting very hard. Seeing you will be a great distraction.

All my love,
Kath

*

Dearest Vic,

We have just heard that Mark is missing in action. I am devastated, and Ma and Pa are in pieces, so I have to be at home with them and cannot come to meet you.

I'm bitterly disappointed, but I'm sure you will understand. How can I be happy for us when this terrible thing has happened? So sorry, sorry, sorry.

All my love,
Kath

Dearest Kath,

I cannot imagine what you are going through and though of course I'm disappointed not to see you, I perfectly understand that you must be with your family. Have you any news how or where he went missing?

Please be reassured that I shall always be there for you, through thick and thin.

Tomorrow Monty and I must return to HQ and I will fit in a short visit to see my Pa and his ghastly new wife before heading back to London. The boss has written to say he wants to meet me ASAP as he has 'exciting news'. Heaven knows what that could mean. But please go on writing to me, when you can, c/o the old address.

I think of you every moment of every day, hoping you get better news.

With all my fondest love,
Vic

Dearest Vic,

Mark didn't return from the raid, along with the rest of his crew. His fellow pilots believe the plane was hit and disabled in some way. They saw him heading for home but after that, nothing.

I still cannot believe it and keep expecting him just to turn up at the door one day.

I am trying not to think about the straggler we couldn't identify that night. I have asked our CO to check with Stanmore whether they ever got a firm identification, but they are so busy and it would require someone to trawl back through the records of that night, so he isn't hopeful of a reply.

I am back at work now and just managing to get through each day as best I can, but I'm completely broken up inside. Ma and Pa are putting on the old stiff upper lip, of course. He works all hours on the trains and she continues to be queen of the WRVS but I know they are devastated, as am I.

Marcia and the others have rallied round and try to make sure I am never alone, although sometimes that's exactly what I want, time on my own to cry for my lovely brother.

I so wish you were here to put your arms around me.

Your loving

Kath

Dearest Kath,

I'm sure everyone's been trying to comfort you by telling you that 'missing' doesn't mean dead and that miracles do happen – and they can, of course. But I also know how hard it is to cling to any hope when you've had news like this. In the meantime you absolutely must not, for a single moment, believe that Mark was in that 'straggler' plane or that you had anything to do with it. Other planes failed to come home that night. It was not your fault.

Here is my new PO address.

With all my love forever,

Vic

*

Dearest Kath,

I think of you every moment of every day, and miss you so much. But I'm afraid this letter brings mixed news. The Yanks were apparently so impressed that they want me to join a research team over there into some really cutting-edge developments in our field. It's so confidential they're not even sharing many details until I get there, although the boss has given broad hints. Of course they have oodles of money to throw at these things so it's a pretty exciting opportunity.

But it means I shall, for at least a while, be even further away from you, my darling Kath, the love of my life, at a time when you most need comfort and support. I am so sorry, but there is no way of refusing this posting, I'm afraid.

Know that my heart will always be yours, however far away, and that we will be together again just as soon as this bloody war allows it.

I leave on Friday, and will send my address as soon as possible. Your letters are a lifeline.

I love you,
Vic

Dearest Vic,

I'm pleased for you, of course, but how I wish you weren't going to be so far away. Please travel safely and go on writing as often as you can. I miss you terribly.

There is still no news from Mark. And I've just heard that my best friend Joan's husband has been killed. He was a Quaker, and defied his parents to go and fight. What a bitter irony. Joan is devastated, of course, and has been given leave from her ambulance driving. I try my best to support her, but despite the lovely weather and encouraging progress across the Channel, everything here seems very bleak. Please write soon.

Your loving
Kath

Dearest Vic,

I haven't received any letters from you for two months now. I keep trying to persuade myself that this is perhaps because you are moving around so much, so I have also sent copies of my letters to HQ hoping they might forward them and find you that way.

There is good news, of a sort. We have heard at last from Mark. He is in a PoW camp somewhere, which is probably quite horrible, but at least he is safe. Apparently he managed to get out of his stricken plane that night and he and two surviving crewmates were rescued by a German gunboat after floating for forty-eight hours in an inflatable dinghy. All three of them were injured. I cannot imagine the agony of wondering whether you will ever be found, or will simply die of starvation and thirst in the middle of the North Sea.

I am so relieved that he wasn't in that 'straggler' plane. And you must now stop worrying about any part the IFF problems might have played that terrible night.

Please write. Please, please.

Your loving
Kath

Dearest Vic,

I hope you receive this. I'm getting desperate. I have not heard anything from you for four months. Please write and let me know your current address.

Your loving
Kath

Dearest Kath,

I've still not received any letters from you, and am utterly miserable. We have moved labs, twice, but I have left forwarding addresses each time and also checked with them by telephone, but they say there's been no mail for me.

Work is fascinating and challenging and we live in relative luxury here but I feel so guilty that you are all still living with the fear and stress of it, as well as rationing and other miseries. I pray (to anyone who might be listening, Christian and Hindu gods alike) that you and your family are safe. I miss you so much and it is purgatory not knowing what is going on in your life, or whether you have met someone else.

After the 'dance incident' I vowed never to be so pig-headed and proud again. So I beg you, even if your heart is elsewhere, please write and let me know at least that you are well and happy.

Fondest love,

Vic

EPILOGUE

Now, as the tea cools in his cup and the clock hand inches closer to six, the other customers of the tea room end their conversations, pull on their coats and gather up their Christmas shopping, wishing him 'Merry Christmas' as they walk out into the bitter night.

When the last of them has left, the absurdity of this whole ridiculous expedition hits him. Here he sits, alone in an empty cafe, waiting for someone he vaguely imagines could just possibly be a woman he once knew thirty years ago, based on the slimmest of evidence: the taste of a piece of carrot cake. In his head he calculates the odds: how many Kathleens per head of population, how many in Felixstowe, of the right kind of age? Surely one carrot cake recipe is much the same as any other.

What a poor deluded fool he is, clinging to an illusion, a pipe dream. And even if it is her, what would she want with this aged, faded fellow who has clearly given up on himself, who has no money, nowhere to stay and not a single clue what to do next? He wonders abstractedly whether, if he slept in the car tonight, he would freeze to death. Perhaps he ought to try it, throwing his life to the fates. If the weather turns cold enough to kill him, so much the better. At least he wouldn't have to make that decision.

Yes, that is what he will do. His mind is made up. He stands and gathers his coat, rummaging in the pockets for all the loose change he has, hoping it will be enough to pay for his tea and cake. But then, just as he moves towards the kitchen door to ask for the bill, it swings open and a woman asks, 'Can I help you?'

It is the voice that gives her away, for he does not immediately recognise the worry-worn face, the close-cropped grey hair and the middle-aged spread of her hips.

'Excuse me,' he says, and falters. He clears his throat and says instead, 'Kath? Is it you?'

Her eyes are wide with astonishment; still the same hazel flecked with green. 'Vic?' she whispers. 'No. Can't be. Oh my goodness, it really is.'

They gape at each other, wordless.

'Whatever are you doing here?' she says at last. There's an edge to her tone, not entirely friendly. 'It's been *thirty* years, Vic, for heaven's sake. You never wrote back to me, even when I pleaded. I thought you'd stayed in America and I'd never see you again.'

It is as though he's been smacked in the chest. 'No, *you* never wrote back to me,' he gasps, trying to absorb what she's just said. He's become so used to accepting that she'd simply found someone else. 'Oh my goodness… you mean…? No… I can't believe…'

Abruptly she turns away, through the door into the kitchen, and for a long, fearful moment he thinks she has left for good, unable to face him. A deep ache of desolation creeps through his weary bones. All his attempts to find her were in vain, and now this. She never received his letters, and he never received hers. A whole life spent apart, through the vagaries of the wartime postal system. Such a loss of what might have been.

Then she is back, dabbing her face with a handkerchief. 'I'm sorry,' she says, sniffing. 'It's just so unexpected. Seeing you again.'

He cannot think what to say.

'But really, what brings you here, after all this time?' she asks now.

'It's a long and ridiculous story.'

'I've got time to listen if you've got time to tell it,' she says. 'Let me get some more tea and make up the fire. There might even be a couple of slices of cake left.'

*

When they are seated and she has poured the tea, adding milk and half a teaspoon of sugar without even having to ask, he tells her about the newspaper obituary and his impulsive decision to make the pilgrimage from London to pay tribute to his old mentor, Robert Watson-Watt. And how, by the time he'd finally got here, the ferry had stopped running, and on his way back he'd seen the cafe and decided to come in just in case, and once he'd tasted the carrot cake he'd become convinced it was hers.

'Ridiculous, of course,' he says. 'Forgive me, I'm such an old fool, but I've always loved your carrot cake.' He lifts a slice from the plate and takes a bite, including the icing this time, munching with little murmurs of appreciation. Now at last she smiles, and he feels warmed by it. That little gap between her two front teeth, the one that first melted his heart, is still there.

'And what about you?' he asks. 'You're still baking wonderful cakes, at least.'

'That, and being a mother,' she says.

'You have a child? How wonderful. Son or a daughter?'

'A daughter,' she says. 'Vicky. She probably served you, earlier.'

'Ah yes, a lovely young woman,' he says. 'Your husband…?'

'It didn't last.'

'I'm so sorry,' he says.

'Did you marry, Vic?'

'Yes, to Ella. We met after I got back from America. She died last year.'

Even now, their conversation is stilted. Despite the joy of being here with her, the tea warming his throat and the blazing fire beside them, he feels uneasy and he senses that she does, too. Bitterness hangs like a veil between them.

'I thought you'd forgotten all about me,' she says at last.

'How could I ever forget you, Kath? I wrote again and again, honestly. You must believe me. I wrote to Bawdsey and your parents' address,' he says. 'I even went to WAAF HQ in London when I got back from the US, I was that desperate to trace you. They said if I wasn't a relative they couldn't divulge any information.'

It had been his final hope, and he could still remember the dreadful despondency weighing over him as he'd walked away that day. 'I came back here trying to find you, but your house had been bombed and though they reassured me no one had been killed, nobody seemed to know where you'd gone. Or perhaps they just weren't prepared to tell this odd-looking stranger.'

'Our house was destroyed by a doodlebug in 1944,' she says quietly, not looking up. 'We moved inland, to relatives in Stowmarket. But I went on writing to you, Vic, right up till the end of the war: to all of the American addresses, to HQ, to your lab in London. I even wrote to your father – I couldn't find a proper address, so I just wrote to "Mr Mackensie senior, Tunbridge Wells". I couldn't believe you had just disappeared. And then when the war ended and there was still no news, I assumed you must have met someone over there and didn't have the courage to tell me.'

'No. No. NO,' he almost shouts. 'It wasn't *like* that. Not like that at all.' How can he persuade her, get her to understand how much he suffered, that terrible heartache, that interminable agony of loss? He looks up into her shocked face. 'Oh, Kath. I missed you so much. But when you didn't reply, I thought…'

They gaze at each other, each trying to understand how random acts of fate have broken them apart, leaving each of them thinking so ill of the other. How different their lives could have been. She leans across the table and places her hand on his, and he feels ashamed at the state of his bony fingers, the nails that need a trim – and, now he looks more carefully, aren't even particularly clean.

Tears are now running unchecked down her cheeks. 'How did we manage to lose touch like that?' she says.

'I loved you, Kath. So very much.' His voice is thick, shaky.

'And I loved you. That day we met again in the Round Garden…' She grabs a napkin and wipes her eyes, takes a deep breath and straightens her shoulders. 'Oh, this is stupid. It's all so long ago.'

'And we're here now. Better late than never,' he says, with a wry laugh.

In the distance there is the sound of a church bell. He remembers it from his first years here, before they were silenced during the war. It chimes seven.

'Heavens, is that the time?' she says, glancing round the empty room. 'I'd better lock up. Where are you staying tonight, Vic?'

He hesitates, reluctant to admit that his absentmindedness has left him effectively destitute. 'Well, I planned to stay at the Manor, but when I found the ferry was closed I went to a bed and breakfast place. And then I discovered I've left my wallet at home, back in London. God, I'm such an idiot.'

'Then that's quite simple.' In her smile he sees the girl she was back then: the halo of flaming curls, the freckles on her nose. 'I have a spare room. We'll light the fire and open a bottle of wine, have some supper, if you're not too full of cake?'

'I can think of nothing I would like more,' he says.

An hour later he is full of scrambled eggs and they are sitting companionably either side of a roaring coal fire in her small terraced house, well into their second glasses of wine.

He asks after her brother and she tells him how Mark's plane had been so damaged he'd had to ditch, then was captured and spent the rest of the war in a PoW camp. 'I wrote to you about all of this,' she says.

He ignores the jibe. 'So he wasn't that straggler, after all? Or anything to do with the IFF?'

'No, thank heavens. All that guilt disappeared just as soon as we knew he was safe.'

'What a relief, Kath. Did he come back safely?'

'He's an aeronautics engineer in Southampton, happily living with his partner. He's always said he'd like to meet you and shake your hand some day, because radar saved his life more than once.'

'I'd be honoured. He and his fellow fliers saved our country.'

They watch the flames for a few moments, remembering those desperate, dangerous days, when everyone's future hung in the balance.

'What about you, Vic? I hope you've had a good life?'

He tells her about his time in America, his peacetime work for the Met Office on radar for weather forecasting and his most recent job developing microwave technology. 'I got caught by one of those new radar speed guns last year,' he laughs. 'And wished we'd never invented the ruddy thing.'

She asks about Ella, and he tells her they were happy for twenty years, and how he has found himself so lonely since she died. 'I'd rather given up on life, I'm afraid,' he says. 'But meeting you has been a real tonic. I'm going to pull myself together from now on.'

'Did you have children?'

'We hoped for it, but it never happened.' He shakes his head. 'By the time we got together we were both a bit over the hill, I suppose.'

She tells him about her marriage 'on the rebound' to an old flame, a charmer called Billy Bishop, and their move to Leeds, where he worked as an engineer. 'It was such a stupid thing to do – he persuaded me that he'd changed, and he was lovely with Vicky. It worked well at first, but I never felt at home in Leeds. It was hard to make friends; they could never make out my accent, and I couldn't understand theirs.'

They were short of money and she'd tried to go back to work, hoping for a job related to physics, or at least in science, as a laboratory technician or something similar. But all she was ever offered was mind-numbing menial work that barely covered the cost of a childminder. 'There weren't even enough jobs for all those men coming back from war,' she said. 'Women didn't really get a look in.'

'That's a shame. You were always such a clever lass,' he said.

She shrugs. 'Besides, my marriage was already on the rocks and by the time I'd caught him having affairs with three different women I'd had enough. So I brought my daughter back to Suffolk and got a part-time job in the teashop. When the owners decided to sell, Ma and I went into partnership to buy the place. It's made us a good living, over the years.' She laughs, that same laugh that warmed his heart all those years ago.

'What's funny?'

'I was just remembering something you said to me, that first day we met on the Cliff Path.'

'Heavens. I hope it wasn't too pompous?'

'Not at all. I thought it was rather profound. I'd never met anyone who talked like that before.'

'You're worrying me now. Whatever did I say?'

'I was wittering on about you being such a clever scientist developing important secret things and you said, "Yours is by far the most important work. The human race wouldn't exist without food".'

'I was right, of course,' he says. They laugh together now and it feels as though the years were never lost. They stare into the flames in comfortable silence, immersed in memories.

'Are you still in touch with him, your husband?' he asks after a while, not really knowing why. Seeking reassurance, perhaps.

'Well, my daughter still sees him from time to time.'

'That's nice. Well, nice for her father, anyway.'

'He wasn't actually her father,' she says suddenly, her cheeks colouring. 'It's complicated.' She sighs. 'Anyway, she's a married woman now, and they're expecting a baby in March. My first grandchild.'

'You must be thrilled,' he says, with more than a twinge of envy: the comfortable house, the daughter, the growing family around her. He recalls Ella's depression when no children arrived and pictures his empty flat, the cupboards still filled with her clothes that he hasn't had the heart to throw away, and the empty hours he spends, barely speaking to another soul, sometimes for days on end.

She fills his glass once more, then her own, pokes the fire and sits down. He thanks her and stares into the flames again, so distracted by his own thoughts that at first he doesn't hear her.

'Sorry? I'm getting a bit deaf these days,' he says.

'I said there's something else I need to tell you, Vic.'

'Go on.'

She is struggling for words, he can tell. 'Oh, never mind,' she says, getting up to tidy the plates. 'Water under the bridge.'

He waits until she returns from the kitchen and sits down again. 'You were going to tell me something,' he prompts, gently.

She shakes her head. 'No. It's all so long ago.'

'Try me,' he says.

'I don't know how.' There is another agonising pause before she bursts out: 'I named her after you, Vikram.' For a second he's confused, until she explains. 'My daughter. Victoria – Vicky for short.'

'Goodness, how wonderful. I'm very touched.'

'Don't you want to know why?'

He nods, his spine tingling with a powerful premonition that what she's about to tell him will change his life forever.

'Because she is *your* daughter, Vic.'

He is so astounded that he doesn't for a moment understand. '*My* daughter? What? How…? When…?' His face is numb, and his lips won't work properly.

'After you left for America I began to feel slightly unwell, but I assumed it was because of my grief over Mark, so I just buckled down and got on with it. And after a while the sickness passed. When my skirt wouldn't do up any more I put myself on a diet, but that didn't work either. I must have been five months gone when it dawned on me what had happened. I just couldn't believe it.'

He feels light-headed. He has not taken a breath all the time she has been speaking.

'Good God. But why didn't you tell me, Kath? I'd have been here like a shot.'

'*Tell* you? Of *course* I bloody told you. I wrote to you, again and again, but when I didn't hear anything, I just assumed you didn't want to know. I felt so ashamed and embarrassed, Vic. I was such an innocent. How could it have happened after... you know, just the once? Eventually I confided in Marcia, and she gave me the address of a clinic in London and lent me some money, but they said I was too far gone. If I didn't want the child, they said, I could have it adopted, and I was all set to do that, but as soon as she arrived I realised it was completely out of the question. So I kept her. Ma and Pa were brilliant. I'd never have got through it without them.'

'All that time, and I never knew,' he gasps.

'And all that time you never replied to my letters, Vic,' she retorts, sharply. 'Can you imagine how that felt, for *me*?'

He is almost in tears. As he puts down his glass he notices that his hand is shaking.

'Oh Kath, I'm so sorry you had to go through all that alone. For what I *put* you through. For what I've missed.'

He stands and goes to her, reaches to pull her up into his arms. She doesn't resist. It feels just as it once did, thirty years ago. She even smells the same. They hold each other for long minutes.

Her words are muffled into his chest. 'What a sorry mess we got ourselves into.'

He pulls away, hands on her shoulders, and looks into her face. 'If only I could turn back the clock to make amends, believe me, I would. But after what you've told me, how can I be unhappy? I've spent my life longing to have a child.'

A shadow crosses her face and he realises, too late, that in the joy of this extraordinary discovery, he's assumed too much. 'Will you tell her?'

'I'm not sure, Vic.' She sits down again, and he's left standing. 'Do you want me to?'

'My goodness, of course. There is nothing I would like more.'

'I'll ask her if she wants to know,' she says.

That night he sleeps in what was once his daughter's bedroom and his dreams are filled with what might have been: Vicky as a baby in his arms, as a small child being pushed on a swing, as a teenager who looks just like Kath when they first met. He wakes several times and listens to the silence of the house, this house in which this girl, his *daughter*, has grown up surrounded by her family, her mother and her grandparents, and he grieves for a life he has lived without them.

Finally he sleeps soundly and then, waking late, he goes downstairs. Breakfast is laid and there is a note: *Help yourself. Back in a few minutes.* He is about to tuck in when he hears voices, the front door opens and Kath enters with her daughter – *their* daughter – following behind.

They are both smiling.

A NOTE ON THE HISTORY THAT INSPIRED *OUR LAST LETTER*

Although *Our Last Letter* is entirely fictional, it was inspired by real-life events, people and places, especially Bawdsey Manor itself.

The history of Bawdsey Manor is well documented: William Cuthbert Quilter, a local landowner and MP, bought the land in 1873 to build a Victorian gothic 'seaside home'. Over the next twenty years he added towers and facades in Flemish, Tudor/ Jacobean, French chateau and Oriental styles to accommodate his growing family and lavish house parties. His wife, Lady Quilter, set about creating extensive formal gardens, a vast, walled kitchen garden and most notably the Cliff Path, using an artificial rock called Pulhamite.

In 1936 Bawdsey Manor was bought by the Air Ministry. Sir Robert Watson-Watt and his small team of brilliant scientists moved from nearby Orford Ness, working in utmost secrecy and under great pressure to develop new radio direction finding technology before the feared outbreak of war. Stables and outbuildings were converted into workshops and the first receiver and transmitter towers were built. Just eighteen months later RAF Bawdsey became the first fully operational radar station in the world.

In a frantic race before war broke out, dozens of similar stations with their distinctive towers were hastily constructed all along the south and east coasts of Britain. Watson-Watt – whose mother had been an early feminist – shocked everyone by declaring that they should recruit and train women as radar operators because they had better concentration, more patience and the delicate touch needed for the sensitive instruments.

After war was declared, thousands of young women joined the newly-created Women's Auxiliary Air Force (WAAF), and were put through rigorous aptitude tests. Because of the secrecy, those chosen to be radar operators had little idea of what this meant until they started the intensive period of highly technical training. Even then many failed to make the grade.

The work was hard and demanding; intense concentration and nerves of steel were required. Shifts operated day and night scanning the skies for signs of enemy aircraft and tracking our own during dog fights. Later, they provided a vital early-warning system against bombing raids. It was also dangerous; the stations were highly vulnerable in their coastal positions and easily identifiable by their tall masts. Several suffered disastrous bombing but the women never deserted their posts.

When America joined the war and the USAF began building dozens of new airfields in readiness for the arrival of thousands of planes and troops, radar research was given a huge boost of additional funds and expertise. After the war, radar developed into microwave technology which today has countless applications in our everyday lives such as speed cameras and air traffic control, as well as in space.

All around East Anglia are the remnants of wartime airfields, none more chilling than the top-secret RAF Woodbridge (the official name for Sutton Heath), just a few miles inland from Bawdsey. Known as a 'crash 'drome', its especially wide runways were designed for use only by aircraft in trouble and it was fully equipped with extra-bright lighting, emergency medical facilities and heavy-lifting equipment to remove the wrecks. More than four thousand RAF and USAF planes crash-landed on this airfield during the war, and many lives were saved.

Felixstowe, one of the most easterly towns in Britain, has always been on the front line of war. At its southern end, Landguard Fort – now overlooked by the giant cranes and gantries of one of the largest container ports in Europe – has its origins in the sixteenth century. The coast is ringed with Martello towers built to defend Britain against Napoleon.

During the First World War, a flying boat squadron at Felixstowe played a critical role in tracking German U-boats and later became the first Marine Aircraft Experimental Establishment for flying boats and seaplanes.

The work of the scientists who developed radar and the women who operated it remained an official secret for many decades. Now, the work of Watson-Watt and his team is widely credited with being a major factor in winning the Second World War, particularly in the Battle of Britain but also during the Blitz and in subsequent phases. Yet sadly their inventions and the dedication of thousands of radar operators are rarely celebrated, and are certainly far less widely recognised than the code-breakers of Bletchley Park.

Bawdsey Manor continued as an RAF base throughout the Cold War when Bloodhound missiles were sited on the cliffs but today it is in private hands (as an activity centre for young people) and not open to the public. However, Bawdsey Radar Trust has set up a small museum in a former transmitter block with exhibits explaining how radar began, how influential it was and still is today. A millennium-funded project has enabled the recording of fascinating oral histories from the women and men who worked there. The Museum recently won the Suffolk Small Museum award and is well worth visiting. Find out more at www.bawdseyradar.org.uk.

Here are just some of the books, exhibitions and websites that have helped in my research:

Gwen Arnold, *Radar Days: Wartime Memoir of a WAAF RDF Operator* (Woodfield Publishing, 2000)

Jim Brown, *Radar: How it All Began* (Janus Publishing, 1996)

Robert Buderi, *The Invention that Changed the World* (Touchstone, 1998)

Juliet Gardiner, *Wartime: Britain 1939–45* (Headline, 2004) Ian Goult, *Secret Location: A Witness to the Birth of Radar and its Postwar Influence* (The History Press, 2010)

Phil Hadwen, John Smith, Ray Twidale, Peter White and Neil Wylie, *Felixstowe from Old Photographs* (The Lavenham Press, 1990)

Phil Hadwen, John Smith, Peter White and Neil Wylie, *Felixstowe at War* (The Lavenham Press, 2001) Phil Hadwen, Ray Twidale, Peter White, Graham Henderson and John Smith, *The Hamlet of Felixstowe Ferry, Pictures from the Past* (The Lavenham Press, 1990)

Gordon Kinsey, *Bawdsey: Birth of the Beam* (Terence Dalton, 1983)

Colin Latham and Anne Stobbs, *Radar: A Wartime Miracle* (Sutton Publishing, 1997)

Virginia Nicholson, *Millions Like Us: Women's Lives in War and Peace 1939–1949* (Viking, 2011)

Robert Watson-Watt, *Three Steps to Victory* (Odhams Press, 1957)

RDF to Radar, a film made by the Telecommunications Research Establishment Film Unit in 1945/46. On DVD from Bawdsey Radar Trust.

Bawdsey Radar Trust runs the transmitter block museum: www. bawdseyradar.org.uk

Felixstowe Museum at Landguard Fort: www.felixstowemuseum.org

A LETTER FROM LIZ TRENOW

Hello, and thank you so much for choosing to read *Our Last Letter*.

If enjoy this book and want to keep up to date with all my latest releases, please sign up at:

www.bookouture.com/liz-trenow

Your email address will never be shared and you can unsubscribe at any time.

This is a very personal novel, based in a remarkable place that I have known nearly all my life, and which is very dear to me: Bawdsey Manor, on the easternmost coast of England.

My father was a keen dinghy sailor and as children we spent many anxious hours watching him from the shingle at Felixstowe Ferry in Suffolk. Across the river, we could see fairy-tale towers peeping enticingly above the pines, and when the tides were right we would pack buckets and spades and take the ferry over to the small sandy beach at Bawdsey Quay. But the Manor itself, at that time still in the hands of the Ministry of Defence, remained firmly out of bounds, with soldiers at the gatehouse and Keep Out signs posted all around the fences.

Several decades later, our friend Niels Toettcher was sailing on the River Deben when he spied a For Sale sign. The Ministry of Defence was selling Bawdsey Manor and all its grounds and cottages. He landed, visited the place and fell in love with it, and for the next twenty-five years he and his wife Ann lived and ran a successful English language school there.

Of course we visited often and fell in love with it, too. How could you not? The mansion is remarkable in itself, but with the addition of its extraordinary military role (see my Note on the History), its masts, since taken down, and curious outbuildings, it is irresistible. I so enjoyed 'living' there once more, in my imagination, as I wrote *Our Last Letter*.

I love hearing from readers, so do get in touch! If you want to find out more please go to www.liztrenow.com. You can also follow me on Facebook, on Twitter and on Goodreads. I'd also be very grateful if you could write a review. It makes such a difference helping new readers to discover my books for the first time.

Thanks,
Liz

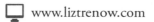 www.liztrenow.com

 liztrenow

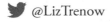 @LizTrenow

ACKNOWLEDGEMENTS

This book would never have happened had our friends Niels and Ann Toettcher not decided – in a brilliant, crazy moment – to buy Bawdsey Manor from the Ministry of Defence and set up an English language school there. We were among their first guests and fell instantly in love with the place. The memories of many happy times in that magical place live on in our hearts.

The wartime history of Bawdsey Manor and in particular the extraordinary story of Robert Watson-Watt's invention of radar is being wonderfully told through the work of the Bawdsey Radar Trust and the museum they have set up in a wartime transmitter block. Thanks to all who gave me their time and advice, particularly their former chair, Mary Wain.

Steph Merrett and her team at Felixstowe Library in Suffolk, England, are possibly the friendliest librarians in the world, and were very helpful in sourcing research materials about the town in wartime. Long live libraries!

I am, as always, eternally grateful to my tireless agent Caroline Hardman and to Maisie Lawrence and the team at Bookouture who have helped to ensure that this book reaches my wonderful readers in North America, for whom the development of radar and its vital role in winning WW2 is very much a shared history.

Last but not least, I could not do what I do without the love and support of family and friends – you know who you are.

Manufactured by Amazon.ca
Bolton, ON